# INCAPABILITY BROWN

## AN IZZY BROWN STORY

CRESSIDA BURTON

Welcome to Nether Ousebury!

Cressida Burton

10th anniversary second edition
Published by Magpie Cottage Books

First published in 2012 under the name Cressida Ellen Schofield.



Cover design by CJB Designs 2024.

*For my beautiful sister, Marisa,*
*the original Izzy,*
*who did indeed drop her mobile phone in a cup of tea.*

# CONTENTS

# THE ST. VALENTINE'S DAY MASSACRE

'Good luck, Izzy. You can do it!' read the email from Caro.

Izzy re-read the email, a masterclass in pep talks, with sceptical eyes. Her best friend might be full of confidence that she could do it, but Izzy herself didn't hold the same opinion. Not when she considered her track record, anyway.

No one knew better than Izzy that she wasn't An Achiever. She didn't have a glittering career, or hold a dazzling academic record, or have any history of sporting glory or any particular special attributes such as an unstinting devotion to charitable works. Instead she managed to lose boyfriends, jobs, most of her personal possessions, and quite often her dignity and self-respect too, with alarming regularity and was regarded by all who knew her as a bit of a walking catastrophe. Not only could she be, on unintentional occasion, clumsy, tactless and absent minded; she was also vague, ditzy and jittery. If she could break something, she did. If she could lose something, she would. Born on April Fools' Day, she was sometimes forced to question whether she was fate's own practical joke on the world.

Izzy knew it was fruitless to try and deny her shortcomings. She knew she wasn't organised, or tidy, or a fast typist, or graceful. She acknowledged readily that she couldn't cook, or sing, or dance with any competence, but she did try very hard to be thoughtful, even if her consideration was sometimes misguided, and she was loyal to her few friends. Generally useless at remembering dates, she somehow managed to never miss a birthday or anniversary and always took time to ask people about the well-being of their pets and children.

Izzy wasn't unintelligent, but she wasn't an intellectual either, which often proved to be a problem when she considered that her closest circle of friends consisted mostly of barristers, brokers and bankers. She wanted to be the kind of person who watched Sunday morning magazine shows on arts and culture and listened to Radio 4, read *The Independent* and had interesting and insightful things to say about politics and current affairs. The unfortunate thing was that she wasn't that person. She never used words like verisimilitude, grandiloquence or sesquipedalian. *Newsnight* was turned over in favour of *Friends* re-runs, and Saturday nights, when she wasn't out on the lash, consisted of game shows, *The X Factor* and *Strictly*. Encyclopaedic when it came to pop culture, she loved music television and could name every single winner of *Big Brother* and *I'm A Celebrity*, but couldn't have identified the Shadow Chancellor or the Minister for Education in a line-up. She related more to Take That than *La Traviata*, more to *TV Wow!* than *The Telegraph*. When asked, at one of Caro's dinner parties, who her favourite soprano was she had replied in all innocence that she didn't know as she had never watched the show. She did enjoy the occasional West End show but much preferred Lloyd Webber to Chekov, *Legally Blonde* to Ibsen. She tried to be cultured because she felt it was expected of her, and that in some way she would be viewed as less worthy if she didn't, but in truth culture bored her and when she got bored she was easily distracted. And it was when she was distracted that things inevitably went wrong. Her mother, who was as equally vague as her daughter, had once said that Izzy had a grasshopper mind, because it jumped from one thought to another with no pattern or plan. Alas, her mouth tended to voice these thoughts, however random, which often left those around her bewildered, grasping at conversational threads, unsure as to what they were discussing in the first place. Worse still, she was often misinterpreted, which only served to cause unintended offence and aggravation.

Nevertheless, at the age of twenty-eight, after a litany of personal and professional debacles, she mistakenly believed her life was perfect at last. She had an ongoing lease on a perfectly proportioned flat in North London — every room was small and square, you didn't get more perfectly proportioned than that — which she had just sublet to a young couple so that she could finally, after months of relentless badgering, move in with her boyfriend, Scott, a poster boy for Hackett with his sulky, square-jawed good looks, tousled black hair styled to casual perfection, disarming lopsided smile and snappy suits.

She'd managed to keep hold of her job as junior secretary to a junior solicitor in a top London law firm for almost a year now, a feat never before achieved, and was aware that Scott, himself an up-and-coming executive working for Citigroup, was keen for her to exercise some ambition. So, when the position of paralegal had been advertised in the firm's internal newsletter Izzy had been the first to apply. Between herself and her oldest and truest friend, Caro, they had written her letter of application and conjured up a spectacular but questionably perjurious reference. Caro, a successful barrister, had beefed up Izzy's CV and personal statement with absolute stacks of legal-esque bullshit guaranteed to impress and persuade, which had filled Izzy with confidence.

Alas, shame had rendered Izzy simply unable to confess to some of her more ignominious work experiences. Therefore Caro, having not been in possession of all the facts — insufficient evidence, as she would have said in court by way of mitigation — had been genuinely encouraging and upbeat about Izzy's chances. The end result was that Izzy's own confidence in her application was misplaced. Blissfully unaware, she'd arranged an informal chat with HR about her intended pitch for the job.

By curious coincidence or sheer bad management, Izzy had managed to arrange this meeting for nine-thirty on the fourteenth of February. Deliberately called early to unnerve her, Izzy had only been seated at her desk for ten minutes when she was summoned to one of the client interview rooms. Muttering about not having five minutes to get herself her first coffee of the day, Izzy gathered up her notebook and pen, so she could take efficient notes and remind herself of the sensible questions she thought she might ask about the position.

The head of the HR team, Mr Woodcock, called her in. Izzy sat down, quivering with excitement, her newly tweaked CV in her shaking hand.

'We wanted to talk to you before we issued the interview schedule,' said Woodcock. He was flanked on one side by a mute note-taking assistant, who spoke volumes with her eyes, and on the other by the head of the employment law department. 'Just to be fair.' Izzy gave a small smile. Surely this must be good news.

'Thank you so much. I know I can exceed your expectations in this role. I won't let you down.'

Woodcock looked pained and just a little uncomfortable.

'You misunderstand me, Isabel. I've called you in to tell you that you won't be invited to interview. We couldn't possibly consider you for such an important position.'

'But I know I can do this,' Izzy protested. She looked at

each of the staff members in turn, moving from face to face in rapid succession, trying to gauge their reactions. Three stern faces stared back at her, revealing nothing.

'Then you are the only one,' said Woodcock, all attempts at congeniality abandoned. He rustled some papers in front of him. 'Let me refresh your memory of some of your more recent accomplishments. When one of your colleagues, a friend of yours I understand, sent a global email advising of the sixtieth birthday of one of the partners you replied to her saying, and I quote: 'Sixty, my arse. The wizened old bugger looks about a hundred and four. Methuselah has fewer wrinkles.' Unfortunately you didn't hit reply, you hit reply all and this extremely offensive and upsetting email was sent to every inbox within the firm. That spans three continents, Isabel. We have offices in Europe, North America and Australia.'

'I know, and that's why I'm so keen to better myself within the firm. No one is more aware of the scope for opportunity—'

'You were very lucky not to be dismissed there and then! Isabel, you're simply calamitous. Last week you failed to use your mute button on your phone and the client, a very important one I might add, heard you call him a 'bad tempered old fart' as you transferred the call. Do you realise how much spadework it took to coax him round?' It was only to prevent sniggers from his colleagues that he refrained from mentioning he also knew it had been Izzy who had coined his nickname of Splinterballs, which had since become his nom de plume throughout the lesser rankings of the firm. As a direct result he disliked Izzy intensely and was more than delighted to put his beautifully cut but highly practical boot in. 'You're persistently late, your attendance record is abysmal, your work is scrappy. You've already had two written warnings for your timekeeping. Your excuses are beyond belief. Your bus didn't turn up, the Tube was delayed, you caught your heel in a manhole cover in Piccadilly Circus and had to wait three quarters of an hour until a firefighter could come and release you. Why didn't you simply step out of the shoe?'

'They were Blahniks,' Izzy explained, in all seriousness. 'That one shoe cost two hundred and fifty pounds. I couldn't just leave it there.'

For the briefest of moments Woodcock gaped at such extravagance, then ploughed on regardless.

'The irony is that if you hadn't applied for the promotion we probably wouldn't have scrutinised your work record so carefully. It's a cruel twist but we have had to ask ourselves the question not why should we promote you but why on Earth should we continue to employ you? I'm sorry, Isabel. The fact that you have had the temerity to submit this application, which has clearly been written by someone else and is riddled with fabrications, tells us that you're either deluded about your abilities as a secretary or you're simply mocking this firm. In either event, we aren't prepared to continue with your employment. You should consider your contract with this firm terminated with immediate effect.'

'On what grounds?' Izzy cried. 'I work really hard.'

'When you are here, yes. I'm sorry, Isabel. We're quite within our rights. Not only are you a proven liar—' the CV was jabbed at '—but you have shown yourself to be a liability and therefore a threat to this firm's reputation. As I've mentioned, you've already had two written warnings and, seeing as you haven't yet completed a full year of employment with us, we therefore have no legal obligation to you. To be honest, we consider ourselves to have been very generous in keeping you on this long. I'm afraid your journey with us has come to an end. You have the rest of the morning to clean out your desk. Any paperwork will be forwarded to your home address.'

After Izzy had left the room the other two attendees

turned to each other, glad it was over, blowing out their cheeks in relief. Sackings were never enjoyable, regardless of how unsuitable or inept the employee was and especially so in this case where the young lady in question was ridiculous rather than unpleasant. Only Woodcock, heartless to his core, tapped his sheaf of papers on the desk before standing up.

'Fortunately, ladies and gentlemen, in the singularly ridiculous case of Miss Isabel Brown, her loss is our gain.'

---

In a daze, Izzy packed up her desk. Her goods and chattels consisted mainly of novelty stationery, stuffed toys and several pictures of her and Scott in various drunken comedy poses. The more established secretaries took pains to study their computer monitors. 'Don't engage in eye contact' was the message they telepathically transmitted to each other, with their audio headphones in their ears so they could justifiably pretend not to hear her sniffles, even though every single set had been muted. After all, they had to make sure she did actually go. They viewed Izzy as a parasite. Invariably one of them was called in to make up her shortfall, or correct her mistakes, or cover her absences. No, she wouldn't be missed. Not by them.

But if the upper echelons didn't like her, Izzy was certainly popular with the office juniors, temps and receptionists. Not only did she frequent the coolest clubs and have the most amazing shoe collection in the secretarial pool, she was inherently kind-hearted and generous. She was the first to offer to water plants when colleagues were on holiday and was happy to dole out helpful items from her top drawer, which should have contained bits of generic stationery but instead was crammed with Alka-Seltzers, sachets of hot lemon, painkillers and tampons. Nor did it harm her popularity that her mistakes were often twinned with deeply entertaining consequences. Word having spread within the quarter hour, she was soon surrounded by half a dozen or so concerned colleagues.

'We heard. It's terrible.'

'What are you going to do? You'll keep in touch, won't you?'

'Splinterballs is a sour old bastard,' one sweet-faced secretary said crossly as she quickly mopped up the plastic cup of water Izzy had managed to knock over before it could seep into a pile of Charge Certificates. 'Cuts are being made everywhere because of the recession. I heard they're just looking for excuses to get rid of anyone they can, on the flimsiest of reasons. That dishy new graduate in Accounts was fired just for updating his Facebook status whilst he wasn't on his lunch break. It's so unfair!'

'She's right,' piped up another voice belonging to a young, less-tactful junior. 'I overheard a couple of the partners agreeing that it was a great opportunity to save some cash by weeding out some chaff. It could happen to any of us.'

'Oh great,' snapped Izzy sarkily, slinging hot pink Post-its and pencils with fluffy, feathery ends into a long-abandoned boot box she had unearthed from beneath her desk. 'I'm chaff.'

'I didn't mean it like that,' muttered the junior, blushing. Annoyance evaporating, Izzy looked at her with empathy. How many times had she herself ended up saying the wrong thing when all she'd been doing was trying to be nice?

'I know. It doesn't matter,' she said.

By some miracle managing to keep her tears in check, Izzy left to a chorus of goodbyes and good lucks. Once she was outside the swish glass frontage of the building, desperate for a shoulder to cry on, Izzy rang Scott. She got his voicemail. She then rang Caro to arrange an emergency summit in their favourite bar.

'Izzy, I'm due in court in ten minutes. Damned

prosecution have just presented a new witness who claims to have seen my client threatening the victim, for Christ's sake. Why they couldn't have disclosed this yesterday, I don't know. Oh no, it has to be after lunch on a Friday.' Caro always spoke quickly, as though her brain was two sentences ahead of what her mouth was saying. 'Listen, Iz, it's not the end of the world that you've lost your job. I know a top recruitment agent who owes me one for getting her son off a dope charge. She has a name like a Chicago private detective but don't let that put you off. Here's her number, have you got a pen? Okay, write this down.' Izzy scribbled frantically. 'Arrange to see her this afternoon. Mention my name. I'm sure she'll be able to find you something. Listen, I've got to go, the clerk is calling us. Meet me at Rah-Rah's at half seven. If I'm not out of court, and I bloody well hope I will be, I'll get my clerk to give you a bell. Let me know how you get on. And don't worry, these things always work themselves out in the end.'

Struggling to keep her box of possessions under her arm, Izzy made her way down Holborn onto Shaftesbury Avenue. At last she found sanctuary in a Starbucks just off Covent Garden. After ordering a coffee she settled down to telephone the recruitment agent. Three short questions confirmed her worst fears. There was nothing in law, there was nothing in admin and, worst of all, there was nothing in London.

'The thing is, Isabel, whilst I do sometimes make clerical placements, I specialise in residential positions. Nannies, residential helpers, au pairs, personal tutors, that sort of thing. I have a very nice position in Yorkshire at the moment, as a companion to a little girl. Absolutely no experience required. Would that be of any interest to you?'

'Not really. I have a flat here.'

Two flats really, Izzy thought. She had her own sublet flat in Uxbridge, and also Scott's plush Hampstead pad. Oh God, she had to go to Marks's to pick up the lobster she had on order for that night's Valentine's dinner. He'd go spare if she didn't remember. The problem with Scott, Izzy considered as she tried his mobile again, was he was so bloody organised. He had a memory like a professional quizzer and never forgot important dates, or numbers, or appointments. He never mislaid important telephone messages or left his mobile on the Tube. He never accidentally left the deep fat fryer on, nearly burning down the flat and kippering the neighbours with billowing clouds of fishy black smoke. Worse still, he was unsympathetically unforgiving when it came to other people's inadequacies. Izzy drove him to insanity and she was just a little bit concerned about what he would have to say when he heard that she'd been axed.

Finally she got through. She clicked him onto speakerphone so she could look at the photo of his handsome, clean-cut face on her mobile as she spoke.

'God, babe, I've had a totes awful morning,' Izzy began. Scott cut her short.

'Where are you? Covent Garden? Okay. Hang fire there. I'm in the City so I'll be with you in ten minutes or so. Oh, and can you get me a decaf latte to go whilst you're waiting?' Izzy closed her phone in ecstasy. He must truly love her to come racing to her side in her time of need. She'd had many doubts about Scott's feelings for her over the past eighteen months. He'd been loathe for them to live together so soon and it had only been Caro heaping pressure on, as only a barrister could, that had finally convinced him to give it a go after a particularly booze-heavy New Year's Eve. Now nearly six weeks had passed and nothing too drastic had happened. True, she'd dyed all his Hudson & Harvie shirts Easter-chick-yellow by washing them with a duster, and had put all his CDs back in the wrong cases so that putting them back in the correct order was equivalent to some fiendish psychometric test, but he seemed to have forgiven her.

As was the norm, he appeared a few minutes before he was due, looking immaculate in a Prince of Wales check three-piece suit and not even a little out of breath. He spotted Izzy sitting in a squashy chair. She beamed at him.

'I'm so glad you're here. The most awful thing has happened—' she began.

'I know. You lost your job,' Scott said, not quite sitting down on a wooden chair but rather perching his exquisitely pert bottom right on the very edge of the seat. 'Is this my latte?' He drew the paper cup over to his side of the table.

Izzy frowned, confused. 'How did you know?'

'I knew your interview was today so I rang your office about half an hour ago to see how you'd got on,' Scott said. Izzy studied his face. It was expressionless. Rather similar to the three people who had just fired her.

'Not to worry though,' she gabbled, keen to reassure him that she was in control. 'I've already been in contact with a recruitment agency and I should have a sparkly new job in no time. In the meantime, it frees me up to concentrate on making this weekend amazing. This afternoon I shall decide what I want to do with my career whilst at the same time dash round and pick up everything for tonight. I haven't forgotten about the lobster, by the way. I'll go and get it as soon as we're finished here.'

'There's no need to collect the lobster,' Scott said. His latte was untouched in front of him.

'Don't be silly. It makes sense for me to go and get it. After all, I don't have to be anywhere else.' Izzy gave a shrill little laugh which belied the utter shame she felt about having lost yet another job.

'I mean, there's no point in going to collect it. I rang and cancelled it,' said Scott.

'Why? It's the centrepiece of our celebration.' Izzy was genuinely confused. Scott took a mouthful of latte, and grimaced.

'Look Izzy, there's no point in me being cryptic about this. For one thing you wouldn't understand or you'd end up with the wrong end of the stick. Worse still, you'd set that death grip lawyer friend of yours on me. I can't continue with this pantomime. You're a disaster and now you're tainting my life with your misrule. I simply can't handle it anymore. I think we should take a break.'

'A break? Oh no, I don't want to. Why don't I cook us something really nice for dinner and we can discuss it over a couple of bottles of wine?' Izzy asked.

'You're not even listening to me. I don't want to discuss it over a bottle of wine, which no doubt you'd expect me to pay for only for you to spill it all over the rug. I've had enough. I want out. In actual fact, I want you out. You getting sacked has been the last straw for me. I feel like I'm carrying you constantly and it's wearing me out, not to mention bankrupting me.' He couldn't even meet her horrified stare. 'That's why I wanted to meet you here. I want you to move out... today.'

'You're kicking me out?' Izzy shrieked. Several heads turned to stare. 'Where am I supposed to go? I sublet my flat so I could move in with you, remember? There's eight months left to run.'

'Sorry though I am about your circumstances, Izzy, that's not my problem,' Scott said. 'Although it comes as no surprise that you expected me to bankroll you whilst you're jobless. You can go to your parents or to Caro for a change. Let her put up with you for a while.' Scott took another swig of latte. 'Is this unleaded?'

Izzy gave a guilty grin in the hope she looked endearing. 'I'm really sorry. I forgot. It's regular.'

'For Pete's sake. This is exactly what I'm talking about. You can't even follow a simple instruction. There's absolutely no hope,' Scott snapped.

'Are you sure you don't want to talk about this? Please, Scott.' Izzy could hear herself begging and she hated herself for it.

'I really am. I think it would be easier if you used this afternoon to clear your stuff out of the flat. That way we can have a clean break. You can post your key back through the letterbox once you're done.'

As Scott stood up Izzy was overwhelmed by panic. It rose in her stomach, through her chest and fought to escape through her throat and mouth.

'Please don't break up with me. Please! I love you. I love you so, so much.' In desperation she made a grab for his thigh. Scott shook her off as though she were a humping terrier. Unbalanced, Izzy knocked into the condiments stand, causing a newly-filled glass shaker of cinnamon to overbalance and fall onto the tiled floor below, where it promptly shattered. Around them everyone started sneezing as the vaporous red powder curled into their nostrils.

'Christ, Izzy, just bloody stop making an exhibition of yourself. People are staring. This is precisely another case in point,' Scott hissed, his face a mask of furious embarrassment. 'You're just a bloody disaster zone and I'm pig sick of being associated by default. Get off me!' Izzy had started to claw at his jacket in an attempt to prevent him from leaving. He plucked her fingers off him and strode away. 'Goodbye, Izzy.'

'Sco-o-o-ott!' she shrieked at his rigid, departing back. Scott was the only person within a ten-yard radius who didn't turn to stare at her. She collapsed into the squashy purple chair, sobbing hysterically. First her job, now Scott. How could this have happened? It was just too much to absorb in one day.

Izzy knew she should try to contain her emotions like Caro was always telling her to, but couldn't. Instead she wept for five full minutes in Starbucks until all the baristas and most of the customers were staring at her. Aware that she was inches away from being asked to leave, she grabbed her box of possessions and a handful of napkins with which to wipe her face and blow her nose, and fled. Then she had to go back in to pick up her handbag, which she'd left on the chair. After that she sobbed her way to the Tube station, stopping to sit on benches or stand in doorways like a tramp until she could bear the stares and sniggers no longer, and then along the Northern line to Hampstead. Even the drunks and nutters were staring at her and gave her a wide berth.

Once she arrived at the flat a fresh storm of tears broke out. She wished she had the nerve to break a few of Scott's belongings, but instead just collected her own things and, howling like a wolf on Hallowe'en, threw them into two black bin bags she found beneath the sink. The only thing she could be thankful for was that she hadn't moved all that much of her stuff from her own flat into Scott's place. At least the bulk of her possessions had been packed away in boxes and stored in her parents' loft.

Loathing herself and feeling twelve again, whilst at the same time proving to herself that she had a pair of Alberts, she used Scott's landline to ring her mother's mobile. The Browns senior, having lived and raised their family in North East London, were now enjoying their retirement in a compact three-bed, or rather a two-bed-and-one-unused-mini-gym, semi in a market town on the Wiltshire-Somerset border. Victor Brown, once a civil servant, had taken up golf, whilst Barbara whiled away the days attending the local WI and gardening. Izzy's only and elder sister lived in Australia, with her perfect husband and perfect children, where she never made an exhibition of herself or was clumsy or inane, and took after their father: tall, robust, astute and organised. Izzy, petite and doll-like, was the image of her mother.

The similarities between Izzy and her mother extended far beyond the physical alone and rendered the arguments both for and against 'nature or nurture' redundant as well as proven. Whether learned or inherited, Izzy was a carbon copy of her mother's blueprint. As incapable at the practicalities as her daughter, Barbara Brown had always relied heavily on her husband to ensure the household ran smoothly. She had never paid a bill in her life, or made arrangements with a workman or had even learned to drive. Her stock answer to most questions was: 'Oh, I don't know, dear. Your father deals with all that. He won't let me do anything in case I muck it up'.

Her mother picked up almost instantly and Izzy began her shameful confession. She hated letting her parents down, again, knowing they would be disappointed she'd been fired from yet another job, but she'd never had any reason to doubt their love for her. Her mother listened to her before dashing any last hopes she might have to the ground.

'I'm sorry, Isabel. We've just let the guest room to a Swedish lodger called Viggo. Lovely lad, he is, but he does drink a lot of spirits. He encourages your father to join him. Sometimes I feel like I'm the lodger, not him. You can always camp out on the sofa for a few nights but I imagine the commute into London would be a bit fierce. Darling, I'll have to dash. I've a pan of milk on and it's just started to boil over. I'll ring you back after six. Bye!'

Despondent, Izzy set down the receiver. What the bloody hell was she supposed to do now? She had no job, no home and no boyfriend. She could probably count on Caro to put her up for a couple of nights, but no more. Caro's fiancé, Jonty, wouldn't tolerate Izzy for longer than forty-eight hours. He had once stipulated this as a make-up condition during the aftermath of a massive argument between himself and Caro. Caro had persisted, arguing it was unfair to banish Izzy for fewer hours. What would they do if they all had to attend a wedding or other unavoidable event, she'd reasoned. None of it had made any difference. It was one of the few arguments Caro had lost.

Reluctant to leave but unable to stay, Izzy gathered her belongings and headed outside. As she posted her key back through the letterbox, trapping her hand in the bristle guard as she did so, she considered her position. Here she was, all her worldly belongings were by her feet in two bin bags and a tatty old hold-all, she had no home to go to, no job and her hand was stuck in a letterbox. It could only happen to her! She sat on the doorstep for a few minutes, with her hand suspended above her head and her mind a complete blank. Then, unbidden and unexpectedly, a thought entered her head.

---

FORTY-FIVE MINUTES later Izzy found herself in the offices of the Merle Miller Recruitment Agency. She'd tidied up her wrecked face in the loos of the spit-and-sawdust pub situated beneath the agency and coerced the young receptionist to look after her bin bags by bribing her with the BeneFit gift set she'd bought Scott as a Valentine gift and now would no longer need. Satisfied that she looked neither like a clown nor a bag lady, Izzy was ready to face the agent. New career, here we go!

Five minutes later her hopes were dashed. No one was hiring, Merle Miller explained, looking beleaguered. The recession had hit everyone, including herself, and therefore the only position Izzy was suitably qualified for was the one in Yorkshire.

And that wasn't all.

'I'd be a nanny?' Izzy asked, crestfallen. She'd never been around kids that much, and she certainly didn't know what to do with them.

'No, no, not a nanny. More of a… err… companion for the little girl who lives there whilst her father, a widower, is away on business,' Merle said. Izzy noticed that she fiddled with her files a lot. Not that Izzy was one to judge. She was shaking like Shakira in a salsa bar. Between the pair of them they were twitching more than a *Springwatch* roadshow.

'So, what's happened with Scott?' Caro asked, not unkindly. After listening to Izzy's mournful regalement of her newly-single status Caro was, as usual, reluctant to see the half empty.

'On the upside, Merle Miller rang me about a reference,' she said as she indicated to the bartender that she would like a glass of wine. 'In fact, better make it a bottle, please.' She turned back to Izzy. 'That's got to be good. Of course I gave you a glowing reference with barely any embellishments. But she said something about living in Yorkshire. Is this true? I need details,' she said in the strident tone that terrified innocent witnesses in court. Izzy stared at her with owlish eyes. Caro sighed. 'Look, have you considered that this might be a blessing in disguise? Clearly law isn't for you. It's a ball-acher of a profession to keep afloat in, especially as a woman. It's better to get out before the quicksand pulls you under. Also, all this has shown Scott up to be the complete shit that he is. I'm sure he only wanted you to get the promotion so he could boast that his girlfriend is a lawyer. This mother's helper thing might be just the change you need. You can get away from London, law and Scott for a few months to sort your head out. Then, once your flat has freed up, you can come back full of gusto and renewed vigour. Come on, let's see the spec on this job. What's the wage like?'

Izzy slid the job sheet over the table. It was already crumpled. It looked rather like an estate agents' house particulars with a close-up picture of The Paddocks on it which told the observer only that it was a vast modern house built in a mock Georgian style. There were no other pictures. Inside was set out like a tariff with a brief, stark blurb about what the job entailed followed by details of salary and holiday entitlement. Caro raked her eyes over the typeset, her lawyer's mind interpreting what was said, and, more pertinently, what wasn't.

'They don't go into much detail, do they?' she asked,

handing the leaflet back. She didn't feel inclined to comment further on the sparse information provided. Personally she wouldn't have touched the position with a barge pole but it seemed it was Izzy's last hope and she wasn't prepared to jeopardise that for her. 'The house looks lovely and big though, and quite modern. How far away from this Loxley place is it?'

'Just on the outskirts, Merle said.'

Caro thought nothing of the sort but Izzy was so miserable she didn't have the heart to tell her that 'just on the outskirts' probably meant about as close to the town centre as a budget airline's airport.

'Looks posh. I imagine it's on one of those marvellous gated estates where you need a remote control and your passport to get in. You know, where they frisk the paperboy and the pizza delivery man for drugs, flick knives and fake Burberry caps. The salary is pretty generous too.' Caro nodded her head in genuine approval. 'Especially seeing as all you'll be doing is reading bedtime stories and watching the angel child jump up and down on bouncy castles at her rich little friends' birthday parties.'

'She'd better not be sick,' Izzy said, gloomily swishing her wine round her glass like a master sommelier. 'You know how I can't do vomit. It makes me gip from twenty yards away.'

Caro looked horrified. Dedicated to her career and not a fan of children at the best of times, she was adamant that she was never going to board the Mother Ship. It was a constant source of friction between herself and Jonty, who had grandiose visions of Caro giving birth to a brood of well-behaved, publicly schooled geniuses and raising them in some *House and Gardens* Surrey mansion.

At that moment Izzy's phone rang from deep inside her handbag. She scrabbled to answer it, desperately hoping the caller was Scott. It wasn't. It was Merle Miller ringing to confirm her appointment. With conflicting emotions, Izzy closed her phone slowly and raised her eyes to Caro.

'So, I guess I'm going to Darkest Yorkshire. They want me to start tomorrow. She said if I keep my train ticket they'll reimburse me once I get there.' For a few moments Izzy's panicked eyes raked the interior of the bar, as though looking for a means of escape. 'Can I please stay with you tonight? I know Jonty will pass a stone at me being in the house but I've nowhere else to go,' she added gloomily, then flitted to another topic. 'Do you think they'll have animals too? Christ, I don't do animals any more than I do kids.'

Caro looked astonished. 'That's very fast. Did she mention anything about a DBS check?'

'She mentioned something about it. She said she would sort it out whilst I was in the position.' Izzy said. Caro looked disapproving. 'I'm not concerned, it's not like she's going to find anything,' Izzy added, defensively.

'Lucky for Merle Miller,' said Caro drily. 'Some of her practices leave something to be desired. I'll pretend not to know that she's breaking the law. Although knowing what I know about her offspring I suppose I shouldn't be surprised.'

Not that Caro had any doubts about what Merle Miller would, or rather wouldn't, find. No one knew better than Caro that Izzy was a good and honest soul, despite her many flaws, and that she'd never committed an illegal or ill-intended act in her life. As far as Caro knew, Izzy had never so much as sparked up an illicit cig, or nicked a lipstick from Superdrug, or had even, as a youngster, snooped to find her Christmas presents before the big day itself.

Caro and Izzy had been best friends since childhood. Not only had they attended all the same schools but their parents had been neighbours and Caro, being two years the elder, had been given the thankless and quite frankly impossible responsibility of keeping the younger girl out of trouble. Not thrilled at this prospect Caro had done her best to avoid this duty until one day, when she was eleven and Izzy nine, Izzy had had to be rescued from a pack of rough kids who were trying to pinch her new Nintendo GameBoy. On that day, as she waded in to assist, Caro's hitherto latent deep-rooted thirst for justice was awakened and Izzy learned that she had a friend, ally and protector. That had been just shy of twenty years ago.

Not that being Caro's best friend always reaped benefits. Izzy suffered from constant inferiority. Caro was often heralded as the perfect daughter, even paraded in front of her by her own parents during periods of Izzy's more idiotic exploits. 'Why can't you be more like Caro?' they had despaired repeatedly. From an early age Caro had displayed exceptional ability, drive and grace. Even their respective figures reflected their personalities. Caro was tall and elegant with marvellous knockers and chestnut hair that never, ever crimped in the rain but flowed in natural glossy waves to her shoulders. Izzy was just a peanut over five foot, skinny, and had no curves to speak of. In addition she had frizz-tastic fieldmouse-brown hair which needed constant visits to the hairdresser to keep its glossy caramel shine. Izzy couldn't help but feel inferior by comparison, not appreciating how captivating her nymph-like figure was or how wonderfully neotenic were her wide blue eyes, the colour of polished lapis lazuli, or that because she was so petite and soft featured, just like the actress who played *Buffy the Vampire Slayer* on the television, that men just wanted to put her in their pockets and look after her.

In Izzy's opinion, Caro was so capable it was painful. Her life ran like clockwork. She achieved exemplary exam results, from GCSEs through to a first in law from Oxford, then had sailed into a pupillage at the Inner Temple, where she developed a reputation as a formidable barrister at an aggressive speed. Now in her ninth year of practice she was hotly tipped to become one of the youngest women to ever earn the title of QC.

By way of contrast, Caro's other friends simply couldn't understand why she continued to carry Izzy. No one understood less than Jonty, Caro's equally successful fiancé. Himself a rising star at Citigroup, he refused to tolerate Izzy with her talent for chaos. It was one of the few things he and Caro fought about. Having been integral in introducing Scott, who was one of his departmental colleagues, to Caro and hence to Izzy at a dinner party at their flat, he'd never forgiven himself for this serious miscalculation of judgement. It had been Izzy's delicate, kitten-esque appeal that had captivated Scott at this dinner party. But alas, in much the same way that the naïve doesn't realise how destructive an adorable, huge-eyed kitten can be until they take it home and it starts sharpening its claws on their sofa, so it was the case with Izzy. Nor was Scott prepared for her constant need for attention or the ceaseless pawing she used to distract him from whatever he was doing. Scott recounted all Izzy's shortcomings to his closest work colleague, Jonty.

Therefore, having already been fully briefed by Scott about his and Izzy's split, Jonty knew that Caro, and therefore himself by default, would be implicated in the fallout. Upon returning home, after a gruelling day of wrangling, to the apartment he and Caro co-owned in Marylebone Village, he was irritated but not surprised to find a bedraggled and emotional Izzy in situ on the sofa. He took one look at her pale little face with its rat-red eyes and tear-stained cheeks, and the heap of bags and coats strewn across his lounge floor, and promptly grabbed his coat and wallet before u-turning towards the door.

Not entirely unprepared for this reaction, Caro pursued him. She caught up with him in the hallway.

'Where are you going?'

'Out. Don't wait up for me. I'll find somewhere to doss

down. From a conversation I had with Scott earlier today I understand there's plenty of room at his place now.'

'Oh, for God's sake, don't be so unfeeling. She's had a really rough day, not helped by your prat of a best friend, I might add, and it's only for one night. Can't you try and be civil for a mere twenty-four hours?'

Jonty's intolerance of Izzy was one of the very few flaws in Caro's and his relationship. Having met at university during their first year they had soon both identified their own ambitious, hardworking, unwavering streaks mirrored in the other. Equally intelligent, equally driven, they were a perfect match. Each wanted nothing more than to achieve the highest possible level of success in their chosen career path. They even admired the same qualities in other people: drive, acumen and determination. Izzy was the only exception.

Although, Jonty had to concede that Izzy wasn't brainless. Indeed she had been bright enough to get good grades in her GCSEs and A Levels and had even managed to scrape a BA in Contemporary Women's Literature from Roehampton University. Admittedly it had been with the barest of margins but that hadn't been due to her lack of aptitude but rather because she had forgotten her registration pass on the last day of finals and had wasted half her allocated exam time running back to her digs to retrieve it. Nor had it helped that she'd left her completed and bound dissertation on the District line Tube three days before submission and had had to throw a duplicate together at last minute. It was her choice of degree that Jonty had issues with, claiming, with arrogant derision, that it was basically a degree in chick lit and that spending three years reading books with glossy pink covers was hardly an academic stretch. The fact she'd done her dissertation on the comparative analysis between *Pride and Prejudice* and *Bridget Jones's Diary*'s respective Mr Darcys simply laid him out on the floor. Seeing himself as a bit of a raconteur, he loved to regale this as an amusing anecdote about Caro's 'eccentric friend' at the many networking dinner parties they attended.

As usual, it was down to Caro to defend her friend.

'It was actually an analysis of the glut of modern reworkings of Jane Austen's classic work.'

'I'm afraid you're never going to convince me that watching *Bride and Prejudice* is valid dissertation research. When we were in our third year you were memorising *Hansards* and I was reading the *Economist* and analysing the stock index. There's simply no comparison,' Jonty would crack back, revelling in the hoots of mirth from his peers.

If Izzy was blissfully unaware of her infamy amongst the great and good of London's business district, she was all too painfully aware of the argument taking place in the hallway. About her. Sitting on the sofa, she could hear every word. Jonty's dislike of her couldn't be more apparent. In turn, she was just a little bit afraid of Jonty. Even by his own admission he was 'very good at what I do' and spent all day yelling at people whilst disguising his core of steel by wearing an innocent, ingratiating smile and pastel pink shirts with jokey ties from Jermyn Street. Izzy hugged a cushion to her chest and wondered if it were humanly possible to feel less wanted than she did at that moment. Even Shuffle the cat was judging her, watching from his post on the windowsill with uncompromising, contemptuous amber eyes. Thank God for Caro. At least there was one person who didn't balk at the sight of her.

Out in the hallway Jonty was unmoving.

'I'll come back when she's gone. Although I wouldn't be surprised to come back to find that she's fused every light in the building, flooded the bathroom and that the cat is wearing a cone collar. Give me a ring when the calamity has left town.'

Exasperated by his lack of compassion, Caro let him go. Plastering a bright smile on her face, she re-entered the lounge.

'Jonty's decided to spend the night with the lads. Fine by me. We can have a girls' night in, have a couple of bottles of vino and get you all ready for your northern adventure.'

'You don't have to pretend, Caro. I know he can't bear me and that he's gone round to Scott's for a slag-off-Iz sesh,' Izzy said. 'I overheard everything.'

Caro didn't patronise Izzy by contradicting her. Instead she plonked herself down on the sofa next to her and patted her knee.

'I'm sorry Jonty doesn't like you better. I thought he'd have come round by now.'

'It's not like he's the only one,' Izzy said, her voice thick with hurt and bitterness. 'It seems to be the day for it.'

'I've tried reasoning with him, encouraging him to be a bit nicer but unfortunately Scott has his ear. He feeds back to him everything you do and say that displeases him.'

'Well, I suppose you feed back to me everything Jonty does and says that displeases you,' Izzy said. Caro gave a short laugh.

'Sometimes you're more insightful than you give yourself credit for. Listen, we'll have a better time without him. You decide on red or white whilst I get the takeaway menus.'

Later, after a Chinese takeout and a bottle of Shiraz apiece, Izzy lay sprawled on the lounge rug. She was wearing one of Caro's white towelling dressing gowns (now ink-blotted with more black bean sauce than she had managed to eat) and peering out from beneath a red Virgin Atlantic eye mask that she had found in a bathroom drawer. Caro was curled up in an armchair wearing flannel pyjamas and fluffy pink lounge socks. She'd stretched her legs out and was pointing her toes like Darcy Bussell. They were passing a litre carton of Ben and Jerry's between them. Soaps were being played on loop from the Sky+ planner.

'When was the last time we had one of our legendary girls' nights in?' Caro asked. 'Do you remember how many we used to have when we lived at home? How many pints of ice cream do you think we used to eat in a month?'

'I daren't even think of totting it up,' Izzy said. 'We went through cartons of the stuff. What was that retro brand we used to love? Gino Ginelli. Remember that?'

'I remember my mum buying some posh liqueur ice cream from Fortnum's for a dinner party baked Alaska, and we ate the lot in one sitting,' Caro said.

'Except we didn't eat the lot. We melted half of it so we could pretend it was shots of booze, but I spilt it on your new carpet. Your mum went ballistic and ratted on me to my mum and I was grounded for a week.' After a brief moment of nostalgia Izzy's face fell. 'Although, when wasn't I grounded? Always in trouble, always in a scrape.' She paused. 'I don't like being like this, you know.'

'Like what?'

'A loser. Always fucking things up. I compare myself to you with your amazing career, big fat sparkly rock on your third finger and this gorgeous flat and I just despair. I've got nothing. No job, no home, no boyfriend. I'll be thirty next year and I've achieved absolutely nothing. Nothing!'

'You wouldn't want Jonty—' Caro tried to keep the conversation lighthearted.

'No,' Izzy said with honesty. 'But I do want what you have, the relationship you share. He'd be all wrong for a disaster like me but he's perfect for you. Why can't I meet someone nice? Someone who doesn't want me to be something I just can't be? I'm fed up with being the butt of everyone's jokes. 'Did you hear what Izzy's done now?' I try so hard to be more like you, to be organised and conscientious and punctual but something always goes wrong and everyone thinks I don't care or that I'm lazy or a waster and I'm *not*. I try really hard and I'm as fed up with me as everyone else is. I'm sick and tired of being such a… a… stupid arse!'

Caro didn't know what to say. She couldn't deny what Izzy had said but didn't want to corroborate it either.

'But look at you,' Izzy changed the subject, embarrassed by her outburst. 'By this time next year you'll be a QC. That's so amazing. You'd just better make sure you do it before the Queen pops her clogs as at least that way you'd be a QC. If you wait until we've got Charles in charge you'll be a KC and subject to endless gags about the whereabouts of the Sunshine Band and other such inanities.'

'Might be better than all those cracks about dry sherry and monocles,' said Caro with wryness. 'If only I already were then I might have been given a crack at the Konstantine case.'

'What's that?'

'Oh, just a big case coming up. Multi-millionaire businessman accused of a contract beating. The victim's still critical. It'll be good and juicy.'

'Oh,' said Izzy, her mind wandering as it always did when Caro started talking about her work. On the telly court cases were always made to be so interesting and dramatic but in real life Izzy found them yawn-making.

Just after midnight Izzy crawled into Caro's spare bed in a state of great inebriation. Deprived of Caro's company and the distraction that it had provided she instantly began to obsess about Scott. An irresistible urge to ring him overtook her. Well aware that she should switch her mobile off and bury it deep in the pit of her chronically untidy handbag, Izzy ignored her conscience and began to tap the keypad until she found Scott's landline. It rang... and rang, and then was disconnected. Scott had pulled the wire from the wall. Now desperate, Izzy called his mobile.

*The mobile phone you have called has been switched off.* The voiceover woman's confident, well-spoken voice seemed to be mocking her. *And let's be honest, Izzy, can you really blame him? I wouldn't be so stupid as to lose my home, my job and my boyfriend in one day,* it may as well have added.

Frustration, overwrought and in emotional agony, Izzy sobbed herself to insomnia, streaking Caro's beautiful bedlinen with thick black stripes of eyeliner and mascara. Not until the very first shafts of light eked their way through Caro's Cath Kidston curtains did Izzy finally fall asleep, only for Caro to drag her back to consciousness two hours later.

Peeling her eyes open, Izzy could hear the strains of Radio 4 from the kitchen across the hall, and groaned. Even worse, Shuffle was laying at the foot of the bed, watching her.

'Degenerate beast!' Izzy said to him. She wasn't sure of cats. Shuffle's only response was to blink once, very slowly and calculatedly.

Both apprehensive and hungover, Izzy sat at the breakfast table which was littered with broadsheets and glossy magazines and which only served to make her feel inadequate, uncultured and stupid. As she wrestled with fatigue, she cradled the mug of strong black coffee which Caro had wafted under her nose. Not the ideal state to be in for starting a new job, she considered. She recalled her baleful rant of the previous night and acknowledged she hadn't exactly made the best start to her new attitude.

After a shower, hair wash and a forced breakfast Izzy felt at least able to face the coming minutes, but not the coming day. Terrified of staying with strangers in an unfamiliar place, she felt sick as she collected her belongings. Not even when Caro gave her two of her own splendid suitcases, complete with matching vanity, did she cheer up. Not that she wasn't grateful. Caro's cast-offs were still one hundred times smarter than her own tatty old stuff.

'There,' said Caro as she zipped up the second case. 'You look quite the seasoned traveller. We can't have them judging you on your appearance now, can we?'

No one was more aware of this than Izzy and hence she'd spent ages straightening her unruly hair and applying her make-up, including an extra layer of bronzer. Even more time had been squandered picking out the perfect 'first day at work' outfit: best and most expensive jeans, killer heels and a powder-blue button down shirt which she had bought from Selfridges in the sale and which she loved as it made her look as though she had decent boobs.

Caro was such a good and sweet friend that she even took the Tube with Izzy to King's Cross and waved her off from the platform instead of bundling her out of the door.

'I've never been to the countryside before,' Izzy said, struggling to keep her bottom lip still as she ascended the two thin steps into the East Coast Express. 'What if I hate it? What if they hate me?' She looked pitifully at Caro, who found she couldn't quite return her gaze.

'You'll be fine!' Caro cried jovially. The whistle blew. The doors closed. 'Good luck!' she added, her eyes moist. 'I'm only an email or a phone call away if you need me. Let me know how you get on.'

As Izzy slumped into an empty window seat the tears she'd kept in check all morning would be contained no more. As the train pulled away from the buffers they flowed so freely that Izzy wondered if they would ever stop.

# DARKEST YORKSHIRE

To hide her shame, Izzy wore dark glasses for the duration of the train journey to Loxley even though the sky was overcast. To avoid comment from her fellow travellers she gazed continually out of the window, head pressed up against the glass, not caring about the unidentifiable streaks and smudges on it or the headache it brought on. At least no one could see the tears sliding out of her eyes. Anyway, anything was better than leaning against the vast sweaty man that had sat next to her at Peterborough and who had insisted on hogging the arm rest with his ginormous arms. For once she didn't worry about falling asleep and missing her stop, which had happened before on more than one occasion, as not only was there the constant *tsss-tsss-tsss* of several sets of headphones and the intermittent nerve crunching beeps from mobile phones but there was also a fractious baby screaming for God-only-knew what reason. She had her own iPod in her bag but refused to listen to it. If the eyes were indeed the windows to the soul then Izzy believed the MP3 player provided an additional peephole. The tiny device in her handbag contained six gigabytes worth of memories, roughly equating to one thousand two hundred and fifty songs and each one a bleak or painful reminder of a life she no longer had. If it played, by cruel irony, *Rule The World* by Take That she'd collapse completely. It had been her and Scott's song, at least in her opinion. Scott had refused to acknowledge it and instead tried to force Usher and Taio Cruz on her. And another thing about the iPod was that the wretched thing itself was a horrific reminder of Scott. He'd bought it for her as a gift. Well, he'd actually been given a new one at work as a freebie and passed his old one on to her but she'd cherished it as though she'd been presented with a gold ingot nonetheless.

Any visions Izzy had of *Wuthering Heights* and wonderful wild moors rife with handsome men with mesmerising gypsy looks who would fall madly in love with her were quelled as soon as she set foot off the train. Nothing could have prepared her for the horror of Loxley Station in the rain. Bustling, cold, windy and dirty; it was hardly the quaint picturesque halt she had envisioned when she had read the job spec. Knocked from pillar to post by visiting shoppers as she dragged her luggage along the platform, Izzy desperately looked for directions to her connecting train. Totally misreading their northern energy and humour for commonness, Izzy felt like everyone was either staring at her or scoping her out for a mugging. Both too shy and unnerved in the face of such unfamiliarity to ask for help she struggled on alone. By this time completely flustered, not only did she manage to rip the tip off her stiletto heel in a broken tile but then she had to hobble her way through the slippery underpass to the farthest flung, uncovered, rain-soaked platform from where her connecting train departed. The train, of course, was late and when it deigned to turn up it was a filthy two carriage affair that looked like a bread bin on wheels and had slashed seats — hideous pattern — and no working toilet. Outside it was already dark but Izzy could still see that the windows were splattered with grey mud that even the ceaseless February rain couldn't remove. Izzy sat bolt upright, her nose wrinkled in distaste. It was worse than the Tube. Again, she had no fears of falling asleep as the train bone-shook her all the way to the market town of Greater Ousebury where she found herself alighting at what was nothing more than a halt. Gasping for a can of Coke or a bottle of water, she looked around for a vending machine. She looked in vain. Her eyes focused on a short man standing at the end of the tiny platform. He was holding a piece of A4 paper. On this was written a name. Izzy squinted.

*LIZZY BROWN*

That's me, she thought glumly. So rubbish, not only was she not named twice, she wasn't even correctly named once. Dragging Caro's lovely luggage behind her she limped along the platform towards the man. Her hair, which she'd spent hours straightening that morning, had drizzle-frizzle. With that and her limp she looked a bit wild and not at all sleek and sophisticated as she had wanted.

'Hi,' said the man, lowering the paper and looking her up and down. He seemed as genuinely taken aback by her as Izzy was by him. Close up, Izzy realised that he wasn't short at all, just stocky. Beefy was the word her mother would have used. He still had considerable height over her even with her heels on. He was wearing jeans and a navy-blue waxed jacket and had a craggy, weather-beaten, gritty, no-nonsense face.

'Here at last, eh? That bloody train's never on time. I'm Jared Walker. I've come to collect you. Hope you had a good journey.' He was definitely a Yorkshire native. 'Here, let me get those for you.' He reached for her cases. Surprised at such chivalrous behaviour — in her personal experience the London men she knew were too busy carrying their own man-bags to help with a woman's — Izzy forgot to say thank you. Jared raised an eyebrow but desisted from comment. He set off down the platform with Izzy teetering behind him, her four-inch heels skidding on the wet platform. From behind, she admired the muscular legs and buttocks clad in well-fitting jeans. Good jeans, Izzy noticed with surprise. Perhaps life in Darkest Yorkshire wouldn't be so bad after all. This Jared chap seemed rather nice. He turned round and took another good look at her.

'Bloody hell! How do you walk in those buggers? They've more straps than a show pony's bridle,' said Jared, staring at Izzy's heels. 'We'll have to get you togged out with a decent pair of wellies.' Izzy, not knowing how to reply to this, decided he wasn't nice at all. Bleedin' yokel. What was wrong with her shoes? And what would she want wellies for? She wasn't going to be hiking over the moors beseeching for Heathcliff. He could bleedin' well come and find her.

Jared led her over to a mud-caked Range Rover. Izzy was surprised to see it was a new plate, although she could barely distinguish one number from another, so thick was the mud. He opened it with a blipper. The interior was as filthy as the exterior and contained several bridles, a New Zealand rug (scrumpled, not neatly folded), two bulging Sainsbury's bags-for-life and a vast sack of dog kibble. Izzy, used to travelling in black cabs and little else, opened one of the back doors.

'It'll have to be up front with me,' said Jared, giving her a look of suspicion as he heaved her two cases into the boot. 'Steptoe won't move for you or your luggage.'

Steptoe? Who the hell was Steptoe? Izzy wondered as she was forced to scale up the side of the Range Rover into the passenger seat. She soon found out. She emitted a shriek of horror as the New Zealand rug moved. There was a murderer lurking in there, ready to attack them from behind with a garrotte as soon as they pulled away. It happened all the time on *Emmerdale*. Jared laughed — the heartless pig. He leaned into the car and flicked back the edge of the rug to reveal a little white face with black, turned down ears and observant, inky eyes.

'This is Steptoe, my Jack Russell, except he's actually a Parson Russell because he has long legs, but no one's ever heard of them.' Steptoe grinned at her insolently, as though proudly aware that he had frightened her. Jared ruffled the fur on his head and was rewarded with a brief lick. 'All right, soft lad?' The New Zealand rug jiggled up and down as Steptoe wagged his tail. 'He won't be moved from his comfy seat, not even for a lady.'

'Oh,' said Izzy. What was she supposed to say? She was sorely tempted to ask Jared where he kept his flat cap too, but couldn't be bothered. Instead she asked how far out of Loxley the house was as she fastened her seat belt.

'Not far,' said Jared. 'About forty-five minutes on a good day, mebbe an hour at rush hour. We're only seventeen miles out.'

'Seventeen?' Izzy nearly fainted. The moon was closer to civilisation.

After that they travelled in silence. Izzy stared out of the side window. Not that she could see much between the darkness and the rain. There was no moon or stars or even streetlights, for Christ's sake. How did this Jared know where the road was? As the Range Rover bounced along Izzy surreptitiously grabbed hold of the Jesus-handle above her door.

'The Paddocks is in Nether Ousebury, just a five-minute drive from the station,' Jared told her. As he turned to face her his eyes flicked up to her hand, which was by now holding the handle so tightly her knuckles were white. Again, he made no comment. 'Everyone's been looking forward to your arrival,' he added.

Everyone, thought Izzy. Who was 'everyone'?

Now they were passing through a village. This would be Nether Ousebury then. What did 'Nether' mean anyway? It was hardly a kicking place. There wasn't a soul in sight. Everyone must be tucked up in their houses. At least there was a pub. The only other lights were from the church, for God's sake. Izzy was so tired she couldn't even be bothered to laugh at her own pun. They pulled up to a pair of plain wrought iron gates. Jared stretched his arm down into the cavity in the driver's door and pulled out a remote control. This he aimed at the gates. They began to open smoothly.

'You'll be given a remote for the gates too. You can use almost all of the cars in the garage so make sure you keep the remote in your pocket. You can always call into the house and ask them to open the gates from the inside, but Mrs Firth is as deaf as and never hears the buzzer. Taryn's not much use either. She finds it highly amusing to deny entry and simply giggles down the intercom, the little horror. Carlotta's even worse. She'll keep you waiting out of sheer spite. You could be stuck out here for hours.'

Izzy wanted to ask who Carlotta was. She had been told about Taryn, the toddler, and that there was a housekeeper and a gardener, presumably this Jared geezer. Not once had there been any mention of another person.

The Paddocks proved to be a big house. As they approached Izzy could see that it was lit from within by every room light possible, with another couple of outside lights for good measure. As Jared turned his key in the lock a frenzy of barking could be heard. Roused from his lethargy at last, Steptoe joined in with gusto. Izzy winced at a couple of his more high-pitched woofs. The barking was getting louder. How many dogs were behind that door? A bloody wolf pack?

Jared abandoned her luggage in the vast, tiled hallway where she was immediately circled by a loop of sniffing dogs. There were at least seven, Izzy noticed in horror, plus little Steptoe had joined the mêlée. Some big, some little, some that looked as though they would have her by the throat if she so much as twitched. No need to worry about burglars then. No criminal in his right mind would attempt unlawful entry with that lot prowling round.

'I won't tell you the dogs' names now. You'll never remember them. I'll take your luggage up to your room in a minute. Come and meet Mrs Firth first. She'll consider it an unforgivable insult if I don't take you to her straight away.' He led her through the well-decorated hallway into a large, farmhouse kitchen dominated by a black and white chequered floor.

Are we playing draughts? thought Izzy irrationally. The kitchen smelled of freshly baked bread and bergamot.

It was a real cook's kitchen, fitted with the most expensive units Izzy had ever seen, including a Smeg fridge, a central island over which painfully shiny copper implements were hung and a cheerful red four door Aga upon which was stacked a pile of neatly folded laundry topped off by, OMG!, a curled up cat. Surely that couldn't be sanitary? To the left was a glass-fronted chiller crammed to the hilt with horizontal bottles of wine, champagne and designer beer. Jared followed her gaze.

'We have to lock that when Carlotta's home otherwise she'd have it emptied within the week,' he said, with some dryness. There was a mention of this Carlotta again, Izzy thought. Who was she? The absent owner's girlfriend? The gardener's wife? There was no more time for thought as a homely-looking woman with a rotund, red face that clashed with her lilac demi-wave advanced towards her. She was dressed in a ghastly patterned floral dress, wrinkled thick black tights and sturdy lace-up shoes. She must have been in her early seventies. Izzy had expected a gaunt-faced stick of a woman dressed in a severe black uniform with a white pinny. This round-faced, jolly woman completely threw her.

''Ello, love. 'Ere at last then. I'm Betty Firth, the 'ousekeeper 'ere. You let old Betty know if you need anythink. You sit yersen down. You must be exhausted after that long journey. Kettle's on.' A firm hand pressed her into one of the chairs surrounding a vast kitchen table. 'Milk? Sugar?' The woman had a voice like a gravel pit, rough and grating from years of smoking pack after pack of Park Drive cigs. 'Eee, you're lovely and brown. Have you been on holiday?'

'Err, no,' Izzy replied.

Jared dumped the two Sainsbury's bags on the table that was clearly the focal point of the room.

'Here are your groceries, Firthie,' he said. 'Everything all right whilst I was out?'

'It's been as quiet as. Thanks, love,' Mrs Firth rasped. 'Although Taryn's been lungeing the dogs on the back lawn again.' Her little pudgy hands began raking in one of the bags, drawing out packets of flour and caster sugar and stacking them on the kitchen table like multi-coloured bricks.

'Oh well, they needed some exercise anyway,' Jared said, disappearing, presumably to take Izzy's luggage upstairs. Steptoe trotted after him, his little paws tickety-ticketing on the black and white tiled floor. Mrs Firth watched him with fondness.

'He's a grand lad, our Jared. Do right by him and he'll do anything for you.' It was an innocuous enough statement but Mrs Firth managed to inject just enough steel into her tone to make it plain that she and Jared were great allies and no interference would be tolerated. Evidently the warm and fluffy exterior was somewhat misleading. A minute later a mug of strong, steaming tea was plonked in front of her. A milk jug, which Izzy waved aside, and a plate piled with biscuits and cakes soon followed.

'Battenberg?' Mrs Firth asked, pushing the plate towards Izzy.

Izzy shook her head.

'No thanks.' Didn't Mrs Firth realise how many calories a slice of the pink and yellow horror contained, not to mention

E numbers and colourings? 'I ate on the train.' This was a lie, but who was to know?

Mrs Firth shrugged. 'Suit yersen.' She didn't appear to have taken offence but was simply matter of fact about the refusal.

At that point Jared returned. Another steaming mug was handed to him, which he accepted with alacrity. Next he helped himself to a slice of cake and two biscuits. These disappeared within the minute. Izzy watched as though entranced as a second slice of battenberg was devoured. Where did he put it? He was stocky but he wasn't fat, or even anywhere near remotely overweight. Jared grinned at her, seemingly amused and unfazed by her scrutiny.

'Drink your tea, then we'll get you settled in,' Mrs Firth was saying. 'You'll like it here. Taryn can be a little monkey but she's very lovable, and this is a good village. You'll soon get to know your way round. There's a good pub and a nice little shop with its own Post Office, and a new café's just opened up too. And you wait until spring finally gets here when the cherry blossom trees along the avenue are all pink and white. It's like a postcard. Everyone's very friendly.' Izzy wasn't convinced. She was certain that if she dared venture into the pub her presence would put an instant stop to all conversation. The jukebox would be rendered silent too as all eyes turned to her — The Southerner. Oh yes, she'd heard all about rural life. You had to have lived in a village for at least twenty-five years before you were accepted as local.

Tired, on edge and weepy, Izzy felt that, kind as they appeared to be, these two people were scrutinising her, and consequently asked where the loo was in order to compose herself. She was shown to a downstairs cloakroom which was bigger than her entire bathroom in her flat and which was beautifully but ostentatiously decorated in cream and muted lime-green and kitted out with matching soft Egyptian cotton towels and L'Occitane toiletries. It was the epitome of decadence, as opposed to Izzy's appearance, which was the epitome of scruffy. Catching sight of herself in a vast gilded antique mirror Izzy noted with a groan how her carefully straightened hair had ballooned out to epic proportions. Her make-up was sliding down her face, giving her addict-esque black shadows beneath her eyes and an unattractive oily sheen on her blanched skin. Her carefully applied bronzer appeared to have gone back down south. To her own eyes she didn't look tanned at all. Her left side was half an inch lower than her right courtesy of her broken shoe and one sleeve of her jacket was covered in black dust from leaning against the window on the train.

Returning to the kitchen, having resigned herself to her appearance, she overheard the dregs of a conversation between Jared and the housekeeper.

'Bit jumpy, isn't she?' said Mrs Firth, just before she noticed Izzy hovering in the doorway. Disconcerted at being caught bitching so soon, Mrs Firth began to show a keen interest in a stack of newly laundered tea towels sitting on the work surface.

And snooty, thought Jared, watching carefully as Izzy slid, mutely, back into her chair. Her eyes seemed to be focusing on everything except the two people in the room. In an attempt to diffuse the atmosphere that was brewing Jared started talking shop.

'I expect Merle Miller briefed you thoroughly on the set up here but it's really not as daunting as it must have sounded. You'll already know that MK, as we all call him, is abroad on business and won't be back until after Christmas. Carlotta is away at school but should be back at Easter, God help us all. On the whole we have a pretty quiet existence here anyway so, for the first few weeks at least, all you'll need to do is ferry Taryn to and from prep school and to any kiddie parties she might be invited to. It's not too far, only in Loxley.'

Izzy's head snapped up. 'Prep school? But I thought Taryn was small. *Toddler* small.'

'I'm not small. I'm eight and a half,' said a high-pitched voice behind her. Izzy spun round on the stool to face an adorable-looking munchkin with a thoughtful, serious little face, with eyes the same deep brown as a shot of espresso, framed by a blue-black Louise Brooks bob. She was dressed in pink satin pyjamas, which looked incongruously adult on her tiny frame. Pink fluffy slippers completed the ensemble. Izzy wouldn't have been surprised to see her holding a G&T in one hand and a cigarette holder in the other. Instead the little girl carried a hot pink teddy bear which matched the pyjamas.

Shit! This kid wasn't pre-school. She was a miniature adult.

'What are you doing out of bed, young lady?' Mrs Firth asked.

Taryn pouted.

'Don't be cross, Firthie. I only wanted to meet Lizzy.' She gave Izzy a conspiratorial smile. 'You're pretty. You look just like Jenny Gordon from *Black Beauty*. I have them all on DVD if you want to watch them later.' All this was lost on Izzy who was still reeling from the prospect of having to look after this amazingly confident creature, who was now climbing onto the chair next to her. 'Can I have a glass of milk?'

'Please,' said Mrs Firth.

'Please,' repeated Taryn. She turned to Izzy. 'Can we go for a ride tomorrow? I can't wait to show you Jester. He's my own pony and he's best. Better than the other ponies. You can ride Jet. He belongs to Carlotta, but we won't tell her.'

'*Ponies?*' Izzy yelped. She had paled visibly. 'No one said anything about ponies.'

'But the agency said you were a competent rider. It was one of the requirements of the position,' Mrs Firth said, looking crestfallen. 'They were adamant.'

'Well, they were lying through their teeth,' Izzy said crossly. 'And not just about the ponies. That's quite clear.' She was beginning to feel panicky.

'Oh well, not to worry,' said Mrs Firth. Did nothing ever fluster this woman, thought Izzy. 'A couple of lessons with Jared and Gemma and you'll be riding like a Whitaker.'

'What's a Whitaker?' Now Izzy's eyes swivelled to Jared, who was still eating cake whilst scanning his eyes over a local newspaper. She couldn't imagine this man on a horse. And Jee-suz, how big was the horse that would carry him?

'Bed, young lady. It might be a weekend night but you still have a lot of chores to do tomorrow.' His eyes never left the headline story as he spoke.

'I hate chores. They're boring. Can I take Steptoe upstairs with me?'

Jared looked at her. 'If you must. But don't feed him anything. He's greedy enough as it is.'

Izzy watched in astonishment as the little dog trotted obediently after Taryn. She strongly suspected that Taryn wasn't going to be as malleable.

'Are you sure you don't want any supper?' Mrs Firth asked. Izzy shook her head. 'We have breakfast late on a Sunday. About nine o'clock. Someone will wake you. Come on, let's get you to your room. You look about to conk out.'

'Okay.' Izzy didn't have the energy to argue or even be horrified that these people considered nine o'clock to be a late start. Waves of fatigue, the tell-tale sign of depression, were crashing over her. All she wanted to do was sleep for a year and wake when all this had passed. She had no doubt that, once she was safely encaged in her room, her unsuitability would be discussed long into the evening but she was so tired that she didn't even care.

Scraping her chair back she asked one brief question which caused Jared and Mrs Firth to gape at her in disbelief.

'Who's Carlotta?'

---

IZZY WALKED into her bedroom like a zombie but even so she couldn't help be surprised by its size and luxury. Of considerable square-footage and extremely modern, it had a fully fitted en suite and a vast HD TV bracketed to the wall. A few nondescript ornaments and contemporary, unidentifiable abstract pictures had been dotted around. Her first impression was that it was blank, but then that was the vibe she got from the entire house. It reminded Izzy more of a hotel room than a bedroom. This suited her fine as she could never imagine herself considering this place home. The en suite was stocked full of various high-end toiletries to which, she was told, she could help herself. She would literally want for nothing.

Mrs Firth peered at Izzy's luggage. Nosy old bag, thought Izzy.

'You've not brought much, have you?' Izzy shook her head. She couldn't bring herself to say there hadn't been much point, seeing as she wouldn't be staying.

'You'll have to get yourself into Loxley or Leeds to do some shopping. Feel free to change things round if you want. Some of the other girls have put up their own pictures, brought their own bedlinen, that sort of thing. It's your room to do with what you like. MK wants you to feel right at home here. We all hope you'll settle in quickly.'

Izzy merely nodded. A wave of homesickness had engulfed her, rendering her unable to speak. She let herself mourn for her lovely Harvey Nichols bedlinen that she'd forgotten to take off Scott's king-size bed. God knew who he would soon be entertaining on them. He was far too charming and attractive and, quite frankly, randy, to be on his own for long. She was so caught up in her own misery that she didn't realise how rude she was appearing. Mrs Firth nodded and left the room. 'Sleep well.'

Alone, Izzy brushed her teeth, removed her make-up, dragged on her pyjama bottoms and a dirty tee shirt, which she'd raked out of Scott's laundry bin as a keepsake and which still smelled of him, and which provided some starkly painful comfort, and climbed into bed. Only when she had turned out the light did she finally give way to tears. She curled up, knees to chest like an assault victim trying to protect themself from further blows, and tried to silence dry, rasping sobs.

Then she heard a dreadful scraping at her bedroom door. Frozen into immobility, Izzy pulled the duvet over her face. It smelled so unfamiliar. The scraping continued. Then realisation dawned. It was one of those wretched animals badgering to be let in. Irritated rather than afraid, Izzy climbed out of bed and dragged herself over to the door. She'd tell the beast to clear off. As she yanked the door open Steptoe mooched in as though never in any doubt that access would be granted and, with a little grunt that clearly said 'about bloody time too', he sprang onto the bed, circled three times, grunted again, then curled up adjacent to where Izzy had been laid. Hand still on the door handle, Izzy stared in disbelief. With neither the energy nor the inclination to boot him off she closed the door and got back into bed. The warmth of the little dog's body reminded her so acutely that she was, for only the second time in almost two years, sleeping alone that the tears came again. A rough little tongue licked away at them. Izzy had no idea if Steptoe could sense her despair or simply had a salt craving, but she derived comfort from his company nonetheless.

---

STICKY EYED AND GROGGY, she was woken by a shrill voice in her ear.

'Breakfast time, Lizzy.' Izzy peeled open her eyes to see a

miniature showjumper stood beside her bed. Taryn looked like a child model in cream jodhpurs, white shirt and tweed riding jacket. Of course, the same fluffy pink slippers made the outfit look rather bizarre, like a toy tin can that spun round to show different outfits on the same person. 'Hurry up. We're allowed eggs and bacon on Sunday as a treat. If you're late Jared will eat it all, the greedy pig.' With that Taryn was gone.

So tired she felt as though she had been anaesthetised, Izzy dragged on a pair of jeans and a shirt (un-ironed) and ventured downstairs. She hadn't bothered to brush her teeth or her hair, which was now sticking out at right angles. What was the point? There was no one to impress here.

The kitchen's air was steeped with hot fat. It smelled like a greasy spoon. Everyone was active. Taryn was setting the table with placemats and cutlery. Mrs Firth was frying interlocked eggs with yolks as yellow as buttercups in an industrial-sized frying pan whilst Jared was shooing dogs and cats out of every doorway. He was fully dressed already and looked extremely lively for a Sunday morning.

'Mornin', sleepy head,' he said when he saw her. 'Jesus, you look rough. Did you sleep all right?'

'The lack of street lights made it so dark that my brain thought I was dead,' Izzy said, sliding into a seat. She had expected the country night to be dark but she hadn't been prepared for it being as black as hell itself. There hadn't even been a moon and any stars had been extinguished by a thick blanket of cloud. Worse still, some unearthly creature had been emitting a ghastly shrieking from across the fields, which had woken her up several times. Plus she had developed an unfamiliar scratchy sensation in her throat overnight that had prevented her from falling back asleep once wakened, enabling her to 'enjoy' a gleeful dawn chorus of cheeping, chirruping and whistling with a cackling magpie thrown in for good measure. The resident village pond ducks had also added a few sarcastic quacks. This she relayed to her audience with a completely straight face.

'I'll ask them to keep it down,' Jared said drily.

'Thanks,' said Izzy, in all seriousness. Jared could do nothing more than gape at her.

'Fried or scrambled?' Mrs Firth asked, brandishing the frying pan like a weapon. 'Lizzy?'

'I feel scrambled,' Izzy said. She surveyed the heaving table. There were sausages (three different types she was told), bacon, mushrooms, tomatoes of every variety known to man, beans, bread — buttered, toasted and fried. The food seemed to stretch for miles. The table wasn't the only thing heaving. Her stomach was doing a pretty good job too. 'No eggs for me, thanks,' she said. 'I don't eat much.'

'I can see that. You're naught but a bag o' bones,' Mrs Firth studied her carefully, taking in the puffy eyes and pale face but not commenting on them. 'Could you manage a slice of toast?' she asked kindly. 'We've some lovely jam made from last year's rasps.'

Toast and jam. That sounded okay. Izzy gave a small nod.

'There's fresh coffee and tea on the side. Help yourself.'

Coffee? Thank God! Izzy leaped up and poured herself a mugful from a hissing percolator.

'No milk for me, thanks. I drink it black,' she said when Mrs Firth offered her a jug of milk.

'Ah, just like Jared,' Mrs Firth said. 'He drinks both tea and coffee black too.' Izzy looked at Jared in surprise. She would have pegged him for a builder's sort of bloke. Jared raised a bucket-sized mug to Izzy in a mock salute.

'Ready for your first riding lesson?' Taryn squeaked between open mouthfuls of sausage. 'We can start straight after breakfast.'

Izzy looked horrified.

'Leave her alone, child. Let the woman get settled in. I can't imagine she's even unpacked.'

'I take it you don't have any riding gear in those posh suitcases you've carted with you?' Jared said. Izzy gave him a black look. For some reason Jared seemed to think mocking her was a great source of amusement.

'Correct,' Izzy said frostily.

'Not to worry,' Jared continued blithely. 'I'll whizz you along to Pets & Ponies this week and get you kitted out. In the meantime you can borrow some of Carlotta's gear. You look about her size.' Jared raked his eyes up and down Izzy's body. There was something so expert in his assessment of her that it made her blush.

'Carlotta hates anyone touching her stuff,' Taryn said darkly. Her eyes were as wide as ten pence pieces. 'She'll be angry if she finds out.'

'She'll get over it,' Jared said. 'She has to find out first and none of us are going to tell her, *are we*? So long as Lizzy doesn't fall off and damage something we'll all survive.'

'Better she damages herself than anything of Carlotta's,' Taryn said darkly.

Izzy paled further.

'I still think she should be allowed a day's grace before you start subjecting her to those great beasts.' Mrs Firth had decided to intervene. Izzy gave her a look of gratitude. 'Yesterday she didn't even know she'd have to ride at all. You don't want to go scaring her off.'

'She can at least have the grand tour of the house and the stables,' said Jared, between mouthfuls. Did he ever stop eating? 'The sooner she's familiar with her surroundings the sooner she'll settle. Plus it'll keep Taryn amused and let them get to know each other.'

Izzy wanted to shout that she was still there. And that her name was not 'she'.

Ever watchful, Jared had noticed that Izzy was continually rubbing her eyes. She was also subjected to frequent batches of sneezes.

'Do you have a cold?' he asked.

'Don't think so,' she replied. I just woke up with itchy eyes. Maybe I have conjunctivitis.'

'Allergies,' said Mrs Firth, nodding sagely. 'That's what that is.'

'I didn't know I had any allergies. Perhaps I have some dust up my nose.'

Mrs Firth took offence to this comment.

'What are you saying? That my cleaning isn't up to much?'

'What?' Izzy asked, startled. When had she said that?

'Mebbe it's the animals,' Jared said. 'Do you have pets at home?'

'What?' Izzy repeated, turning to face Jared.

'Pets,' Jared said, slowly and with emphasis. Was she gormless? 'You know, dogs, cats, creatures with fur—?'

'Oh! No, no pets.'

'What, not ever?' asked Taryn, her little face contorted with amazement.

'No, my mum's allergic—' Realisation began to dawn on Izzy's face. 'Oh!'

'Penny's dropped, has it?' Jared said wryly. Feeling stupid, Izzy studied her coffee mug. At least Mrs Firth's face had softened.

'Jared'll drive you into Greater Ousebury tomorrow. You can get some antihistamine from the pharmacy plus it'll do you good for you to get your bearings.'

Not even given chance to have a shower before Taryn dragged her off straight after breakfast for her tour of the house, Izzy was shown the lounges and dens. These were decorated in beautiful muted greens, ochres and blues, with imported Georgian fireplaces with real fires which burned wood and coal, not that anyone could get near a fire for the inevitable mass of dogs stretched out in front of them, and enormous HD TVs and home cinema systems. Next came the dining room with its polished mahogany table and eight chairs.

'We only ever eat in here at Christmas,' Taryn said dismissively.

The largest lounge was at the front of the property, an enormous room big enough to accommodate three squashy sofas and a fireplace that Izzy could stand inside without bumping her head.

The library contained not only more priceless books than its namesake at Alexandria but also enough CDs and DVDs to fill a branch of HMV. Izzy was astonished at such wealth. Each room was a curious amalgamation of the ancient and ultra-modern. Cutting edge technology sat beside priceless antiques, making Izzy think that the house was actually more like a museum than a hotel, as she had first thought. Each and every room was filled with expensive, irreplaceable ornaments that Izzy could knock over and smash into millions of tiny shards that no amount of superglue would fix. There were pictures of the absent Carlotta and Taryn receiving rosettes or jumping what seemed to Izzy to be vast fences all over the house. There was even a mini-gym.

'Jared practically lives in there,' Taryn said. Never having seen the appeal of strenuous activity, Izzy vowed silently never to set foot over the threshold.

Upstairs Izzy was made to gaze upon every inch of Taryn's bedroom. Twice the size of any bedroom Izzy had ever seen, Taryn's room was painted princess-pink with more toys than any little girl could possibly need or want. Dolls, books, games and clothes hid a spotless white carpet. Floor length sequinned voile drapes hung from the sash windows. It was like standing inside a stick of Blackpool rock. There was the requisite TV and Blu-ray DVD player, CD player and also one of each of the most recent games consoles and a karaoke machine complete with built in monitor. The pale pink pyjamas were strewn across the unmade bed. Izzy noticed that Taryn not only had a full sized walk-in wardrobe chock full of clothes and shoes but also that her dressing table was laden with the highest quality cosmetics and toiletries. Little wonder she looked like a mini adult and was confused to boot. The hot pink and silver en suite told the same tale. There was evidence of horses everywhere, from the riding clothes littering every chair in the room to the books and figurines on every surface. The room was light and airy with views over the front lawn from the three generous sash windows.

Carlotta's room was across the hallway. Her room was even bigger than Taryn's. Similar in layout, it had the same three windows but these looked out over the back of the house with views of the stables and the fields beyond. Originally Tiffany-turquoise, Carlotta had painted one wall coal black. No doubt to match her temper, thought Izzy, having by now been briefed in full about Taryn's elder sister and her dichotic mood swings.

There were other differences. Most evident was the absence of toys and games and the posters on Carlotta's walls were of angry bands like Green Day, Linkin Park and Paramore, and famous showjumpers rather than ponies and dogs. It had also been dusted and polished by Mrs Firth, who took the opportunity to gain entry to Carlotta's room whilst she was absent.

Izzy stepped into the room, heedless of Taryn's gasp at such fearlessness. Upon closer inspection she noticed the large framed photograph of an incredibly beautiful, and somewhat familiar, woman wearing sunglasses on the dresser. This must be the mother, Izzy thought. There were no cosmetics or toiletries on the dresser or in the perfect aquamarine and white en suite. There were even light bulbs round the mirror of her dresser. Half the clothes in the walk-in wardrobe were missing and yet it was still healthily full. All in all, the room had a half lived, half loved feel about it.

Rather like a room in a stately home that wasn't used by the family but opened up for public viewing.

If Carlotta's bedroom was stark and lifeless it was nothing compared to the clinical pallor of MK's rooms, a self-contained suite at the end of the corridor. Always locked and strictly out of bounds, Taryn had half-inched Jared's keys whilst he was in the shower and let Izzy peep in.

It was immaculately tidy. There was not one item out of place. It was a single man's domain through and through, decorated in earthy browns and beiges with ebony fixtures and fittings throughout the sitting room, bedroom and en suite. The decor was indubitably masculine with no frills or fancies. There was nothing personal about the room except for a photograph of the same beautiful woman, this time with her face half obscured by a wide-brimmed hat, with a young girl who looked like Taryn but was actually the six-year-old Carlotta. There was no picture of Taryn. The beautiful woman was heavily pregnant. The picture must have been taken just before Taryn was born, and therefore just before her mother had died. Izzy felt her eyes well with tears. She brushed them away impatiently. She was only emotional due to losing Scott and her career and all that had happened in the past two days, she told herself.

'What's in there?' Izzy pointed to a firmly closed door leading from the sitting room.

'Papa's office,' Taryn said. 'Only Jared is allowed in. Carlotta once pickpocketed the key and went in. Papa went mad and banned her from hunting for three whole months as a punishment.'

'Oh.' Didn't sound like much of a punishment to Izzy. Taryn suddenly tilted her head.

'Quick! The water's been switched off!' Taryn scurried off with the keys. When she came back she was breathless and giggling.

'Jared and Mrs Firth sleep up in the attics on the second floor,' Taryn said.

'Not in the same room, I should hope,' Izzy said under her breath. Taryn heard her and giggled.

'Eurgh, that's horrid, Lizzy.' Taryn gave Izzy a good, long look. 'You're silly.'

That's me, thought Izzy. So silly even an eight-year-old is highlighting my shortcomings. The fact it had taken a child less than a day to ascertain this fact did nothing to improve Izzy's mood.

'Let's go outside. I can't wait to show you the stables.'

In the early hours of the morning a harsh northeasterly had blown the rain clouds away towards the Pennines, leaving a legacy of clear skies and plummeting temperatures. Outside the air was still and white with frost, making the evergreens and grasses look like they had been put through a blue filter. Izzy could hear the local church bells ringing as family communion was kicked out. Envying Taryn her tweed jacket, Izzy hugged herself to keep warm. Her wrinkled shirt was simply inadequate. Moreover, Izzy couldn't remember the last time she'd been up before noon on a weekend. Hitherto she had only seen dawn on a Sunday morning from the other side of a night's clubbing. A sprightly blackbird warbled from on top of a fence. Planters filled to the brim with early spring bulbs — snowdrops, dwarf narcissus and crocus — lined the gravel pathway to a vast American-style Dutch barn.

Beyond this there was a full sized all-weather, floodlit manége. Behind this two lush green paddocks stretched out to the horizon. In the fields were a couple of grazing horses, well rugged up to protect them from the elements. All the other horses were stabled due to the cold February weather, explained Taryn, who was dancing from foot to foot with eagerness and pride to show Izzy inside.

And little wonder, thought Izzy. The stables were

amazing, with not a blade of straw out of place. Inside were half a dozen generously proportioned loose boxes, each fetlock deep in fresh straw that covered the polished Staffordshire red brick floor. Each stable had a painted green and white wooden partition and a matching holly-green door, complete with a shining brass nameplate stating the horse's name. Adjacent was a spotless feed store and a tack room, alarmed to the teeth, and filled with gleaming tack. Another door led to a well-stocked log store, which also contained a sharp vertical ladder up to the hayloft that ran the entire length of the building. Rosettes had been pinned up above the horses' loose boxes and all over any spare patch of wall space in the tack room and the food store, providing a wonderfully chaotic splash of reds, blues, yellows, greens, oranges, pinks, purples and whites to offset the obsessive-compulsive neatness.

Taryn led Izzy from stall to stall, giving a full life history of each horse.

'This is my pony, Jester,' she said as they stopped in front of a stable that contained a small brown and white pony. It gave Izzy a baleful look as she peered over the stable door.

'Why is he two coloured? Was his mother a brown horse and his father a white one?' Taryn giggled until she realised that Izzy wasn't joking.

'He's a skewbald. It's a perfectly natural colour for a horse,' she said huffily. 'Don't you know anything?'

'Not really, no. He reminds me of the traveller horses that are roped to the heath where I used to live,' Izzy said, unaware she'd said something inappropriate. Taryn gave her a cold stare. 'He's the best show pony in the area,' she said icily. Izzy coloured up. Taryn, still keen to show off the stables to a captive audience, forgave her. 'He used to be Carlotta's but she outgrew him. She's nearly outgrown Jet too but daren't say so in case Papa makes her have Vega.' She fed Jester a carrot that she'd filched from the chopping board whilst Mrs Firth wasn't looking. Aware that she would be told off if she were caught, she slid her eyes toward Izzy.

'It's okay. I won't tell,' Izzy said. Taryn grinned. They moved on to the next stall.

'This is Jet. He's eight and can jump four foot six practically from a standstill. Carlotta thinks she's going to win the Junior Showjumping at the Great Yorkshire Show on him in the summer but I think she can think again.' Izzy gazed at the pretty black pony in the stable. Jet had four white socks and a slightly concave face with a white streak on his face which, unbeknownst to Izzy, mirrored a devilish streak in his soul, and a long swaying mane and tail. He was munching hay from what looked like a vast suspended hairnet and looked serene and good-natured. 'He's part Arabian. This is who you'll learn on,' Taryn added. At the same moment Jet gave a deep whicker, stamped his hoof on the floor and, turning his enormous black arse towards Izzy, let out a long, airy fart. Taryn giggled again but Izzy couldn't help but imagine that this was Jet's way of letting her know who was going to be boss. Her heart sank. Perhaps not so good-natured after all. Most of the pinned up rosettes were above Jet's box, and the majority of these were pillar-box red. Carlotta was clearly a talent.

Taryn moved along the line. The next stable belonged to an enormous white horse called Ghost. Izzy gazed in horror. The white horse carved into the hillside across the Vale was smaller.

'This is Papa's horse but Jared rides him when he isn't here. He's very quiet but he can nap if he sees a hay wagon on the road. We think he may have been frightened as a foal.' Taryn could see Izzy assessing the big horse. 'He's a white horse but in equestrian terms he's called a grey.' Taryn gave him a pat. 'We've also got three more horses. The Tank, a chestnut hunter who's a right old gluepot, and who you would have learned on but he's out to grass at the mo as he's slightly lame. He only has two gears: walk and canter, and he can do either for miles and miles. That's what makes him so great across country. Mini Cheddar's out there with him. He's an ancient Shetland that we've had for years and we all learned to ride on as babies and no one rides anymore in case he drops dead from the exertion. And then there's Vega.' Taryn and Izzy stopped in front of the last stable in the block. Inside was a stunning golden horse that looked like a gilded statue. 'Vega's an Akhal-Teke, they're really rare and that's why she has that metallic sheen, but she's a bitch. She bites and rears and bucks. Papa bought her for Mama as an engagement present. She was the only one who could really control her and they won lots of cups and rosettes, although Carlotta doesn't do too badly with her—' Taryn sniggered. '—When she can stay on. No one else is permitted to ride her. Not even Jared.' Taryn giggled at the look of immense relief on Izzy's face. This turned to pure shock as Taryn added: 'she's worth a bloody fortune.'

Izzy had already ascertained that she wouldn't be expected to help out in the stables, or with tack cleaning and mucking out — that was Gemma the groom's job — but she would be expected to help Taryn with her seemingly endless hutches of rabbits and guinea pigs.

'Hulloooooo!' called a female voice from outside the barn. Taryn grinned.

'Gemma's here. Come on, you'll like her. She's fun.' Taryn dragged Izzy back to the doorway of the barn. Izzy had reservations. Usually when someone insisted she would like someone else, the actual opposite transpired and it ended up being hate at first sight. Not Gemma though. Izzy took an instant liking to the merry-faced girl who stood grinning at her even if she did remind Izzy somewhat of a Jaffa Cake with her rich, dark-ginger hair and hazel eyes that sparkled with life and mischief. Years of horse riding had toned her body to perfection and made her heavily freckled skin glow with health and vitality. It didn't escape Izzy's notice that she was far more attractive than herself. With bee-sting lips and a figure like Jessica Rabbit, Gemma exuded femininity and confidence. Noting how Gemma's curvy frame filled out her jodhpurs in all the right places, Izzy felt like an underdeveloped fourth former by way of comparison. Having looked Izzy up and down and satisfied herself that she was the prettier, Gemma extended the hand of friendship.

'Hi, welcome to the madhouse,' she said.

'Gemma takes care of the horses plus she comes nearly every day to teach me riding and stable management. She's got her BHS accreditation.'

'British Home Stores?'

'British Horse Society, silly,' Taryn said scornfully. 'You really don't know anything, do you?'

'We'll soon get you up to speed,' Gemma said with a merry laugh. 'I live in Greater Ousebury, so it's easy for me to get here.' She indicated towards Taryn. 'You'll find that one of these two monkeys is easier to deal with than both. Why don't you finish your tour and then we can go for a hack,' she added to Taryn. 'I'll tack Jester up for you, just this once.'

After the stables Izzy was dragged round to the right side of the house to view the extensive vegetable plot, complete with raised beds, several polytunnels, wigwams and a greenhouse so big it could easily have been relocated to Hyde Park and used as a replacement for The Crystal Palace. Beyond this lay a well-stocked orchard. A dozen or so chickens roamed free, pecking at the ground. That giant dog kennel must be their coop, Izzy thought, shuddering. Because hens gave her the creeps she turned her attention back to the vegetable garden, which was looking rather spartan to say the least. Only a couple of rows of sprouts and the last of the winter cabbages offered any colour. A parked-up wheelbarrow contained a sparse selection of carrots, parsnips and swedes. Steptoe was sniffing around in the hedgerow, looking for varmints. Jared, she noted, was hard at work, forking over a square of compost ready for a new season's sowings. For a few moments Izzy was mesmerised by the speed and skill with which he churned the earth. She found herself curiously attracted to the whole 'man working the land' scenario. It made him seem rather powerful and manly. As if aware of Izzy's scrutiny, Jared looked up as they approached, stabbing the fork into the well-turned-over ground and leaning on it. He seemed glad of the distraction.

'What do you think of our little world?' he asked, grinning. Izzy didn't know what to say. The house was a curious mix of wealth and wholesome, rural life. It was like nothing she had ever encountered. Uncertain as to what she was expected to say, she remained silent. 'MK likes us to be as self-sufficient as possible, hence my role here,' Jared continued. 'He's keen for the girls to enjoy a healthy lifestyle and so most of the food Mrs Firth cooks for us is home produced.'

'And where is the battenberg grown?' Izzy couldn't help but ask. She got the distinct feeling she was being mobbed up. Jared grinned even more widely.

'Touché!' he acknowledged. 'Although I said 'most of'. Anything else we might need is shipped in from Sainsbury's. A little bit of what you fancy does you good.' And then he roared. Izzy couldn't be sure whether he was being smutty or not.

'And will I have to pick up a trowel and muck in?' Izzy asked, a hint of sarcasm in her voice.

'Only if Taryn feels the need to tend to her vegetable corner—' Jared pointed to a two-square-metre patch of wilderness in the corner of the plot that clearly hadn't been touched in months. 'She was keen to grow some pony carrots, once, but then realised that Jester didn't care that they had been tended by her own loving hands and was equally happy with the ones from the fridge. Eh, Taryn?' Taryn scowled at

Jared, who simply laughed in her face. 'I think you're safe from the horrors of horticulture.' Carlotta, it transpired, had refused to have a vegetable plot in the first place. 'Are you nearly done, Taryn? Lizzy and I have a lot to go over after lunch.'

'Just about. Gemma wants to go for a hack before lunch.'

'Good, I'll walk back with you then.' Jared stabbed the fork into the ground. 'I want to speak to Gemma about feed deliveries.'

Jester was already tacked up and tied to the barn door when they arrived. Taryn disappeared into the tack room to retrieve her riding hat, crop and gloves. Whilst they waited for her to reappear Jared and Gemma discussed oats and chaff. They spoke in a very clipped, very professional, almost rehearsed manner, rather like an employer's training video. Feeling redundant, Izzy stood and fidgeted until the reappearance of Taryn brought their discussion to a close.

Taryn deftly mounted her pony. Even Izzy couldn't help but realise how good she was and how adorable she looked.

'You'll be doing that in a week,' Jared said to Izzy, laughing. Izzy scowled at him.

Gemma led out and mounted the enormous Ghost from the mounting block. She looked very sexy, thought Izzy, in a purple Puffa gilet and buff breeches and with her wonderfully vibrant red hair lifting slightly in the wind. Scott would be all over her like a cheap suit. Izzy felt a stab of anguish. What was he doing right now? Was he thinking of her? Had he even noticed she'd gone?

'Can you tighten my girth, Jared?' Gemma asked, rather flirtatiously, pushing her left leg forward so that Jared could lift the flap of the saddle. Wordlessly, he acquiesced. 'Ta.'

Jared checked his watch. 'Which route are you planning on taking?' he asked, his hand resting calmly on Ghost's big square arse. 'I don't want you going near the old abattoir when I'm not there.'

'Nowhere near there. Through the village and along the river to the toll bridge, then back through Prickett's Copse,' Gemma said, gathering up her reins. 'Shouldn't be longer than an hour and a half.'

'Got everything, Taryn?' Jared addressed the little girl directly. She nodded once. 'Good girl. You know the drill if you get into trouble.'

Izzy and Jared watched as they clattered out of the stable yard. Jester was swishing his two-tone tail like a pendulum.

'Let's get you inside. You look frozen.' Jared accompanied her back into the house via the left side. He led her under a laurel archway through a charmingly fragrant walled herb garden and into a clematis walkway which opened out to reveal a jewel-green lawn which was as flat and perfectly mown as a cricket crease. A two-seater swinging seat was hibernating under a transparent plastic tarpaulin until spring.

'The back of the house is west facing so we get the sun for almost all of the day,' Jared said. He pointed to the edge of the lawn where a bank of willows and dogwood, its winter bark felt tip red, formed an impenetrable border. 'All along that border is a little brook which attracts ducks and mallards, moorhens and coots. It runs all the way into the village. By rights the brook is winterbourne and should dry up for the three summer months, except it hasn't in recent years because of the crappy weather. The steep hill at the very edge of our land is the edge of the Vale of Loxley. Up on the top is the start of the North Yorkshire Moors. MK chose this village, and the positioning of this house, which was built to his own specification and design, because of the security that that incline provides. As you can see, it curls right round the property.' Izzy didn't share MK's vision. To her the hill seemed to loom above her, trapping her. She found it claustrophobic. Shuddering for a second time, she turned to face the house.

Adjoining the house was a sixty-foot length of decking

upon which stood a long glass-topped table, several matching chairs and loungers, all covered with the same tarpaulin as the swing seat, and a trio of freestanding gas heaters which, having been huddled together, resembled a large chrome mushroom fairy ring. At the far end of the decking was a custom-built brick barbecue the size of an inglenook fireplace. Halfway along there were double French windows which led into the larger of the lounges that Taryn had shown her earlier.

'To help you get your bearings,' Jared explained before u-turning.

He led her back into the walled herb garden and into the house through a sun-faded stable door, straight into a utility room. This led into the kitchen where Mrs Firth was busy planning the meals for the coming week and writing a shopping list longer than the Dead Sea Scrolls. A delicious waft of fresh bread was seeping out of the Aga. Having skimped on breakfast Izzy realised she was starving. Jared made a note to repaint the stable door on a pretty cottage-style chalkboard before returning to the garden.

They would have their discussion straight after lunch, he said before he left. Other than that she was free to do as she pleased until lunch was served.

As Mrs Firth was still engrossed with her groceries, Izzy was loath to disturb her. Engrosseried, thought Izzy. She desperately wanted to ask if there was a computer she could use to check her email but instead wandered into the body of the house. Catching sight of herself in the hall mirror, Izzy gave a shriek of horror and decided to take a shower. With hair like this she would terrify the ponies rather than them terrifying her. Half an hour later, after a scalding hot power shower (the shower head was as big as a dinner plate) and playing pick 'n' mix with the posh toiletries, she felt a little better. As she viewed her sleeker and rebronzed reflection in the anti-steam mirror she wondered again if Scott had missed her at all. Had Jonty told him where she was yet? Did Scott even care? If only she could get online and send him a message. Even though Taryn had kept her occupied for most of the morning her longing for Scott lingered at the back of her thoughts, always present, patiently waiting to catch her out and remind her of her misery. Perhaps she could access her email on her mobile via Wi-Fi? Filled with hope, Izzy shot across the room and grabbed her phone. Her optimism was short lived. Her mobile had no signal no matter how she tilted it or held it up to the window. Emergency only, said the facia.

'This *is* an emergency!' Izzy wailed. 'My heart is completely defunct.' Frustrated, she flung the phone down on the bed. Then she flung herself down after it. Devoid of resources, stunted by the unfamiliarity of her surroundings and lacking the confidence to ask for help, all Izzy could do was loiter in her bedroom until she heard the welcome clip-clop of hooves on the driveway. How pathetic that an eight-year-old was the only company she could hope for.

After a light lunch of home-made soup and sandwiches, of which Izzy managed to eat only a little despite her earlier hunger, Jared summoned her to the winter den for a couple of hours' discussion on the coming week and what would be expected of her.

The winter den had the same black and white floor as the kitchen but was saved from the wintriness insinuated by its name by a roaring coal fire. Two oxblood leather sofas and a huge Merlot-red rug, placed in front of the hearth, added warmth to the room. Charmingly low windowsills enabled Steptoe to rest his front paws on the sill and observe any outside activity like a canine sentinel. As was becoming an apparent theme in the house, everything was brand new but had been designed to give the impression of a period property. Situated at the back of the house the winter den provided an excellent view of the manége and the paddocks.

Glancing out, Izzy queried the dressage letters which were propped up against the perimeter fence of the school.

'Is Taryn learning her alphabet?' she asked, in all seriousness. Jared didn't look in the slightest bit amused. Also in the school were half a dozen Olympic standard showjumps. These terrified Izzy almost as much as the horses themselves.

Jared went through the lot: the cars in the garage, the route to Taryn's prep school, a brief run-down of Taryn's friends, what Taryn was allowed to do, what Taryn wasn't allowed to do... Izzy wished she could have taken notes. Mrs Firth had one weekend off a month and used this to visit her invalid sister in Leeds. On these occasions she would be expected to help absorb the housekeeping duties such as cooking, bed making, et cetera. She was also issued with a set of keys so big and cumbersome she felt like Ploppy the Jailor. These were for the house, garages, stables and other various outhouses and her own blipper for the electronic gates. She was also handed a state of the art smartphone.

'I have my own phone,' Izzy protested.

'Now you have two,' Jared said, rather sharply. Izzy passed the mobile between her hands, confused. It had four bars of signal. 'The girls already know this number off by heart which makes it easier for them,' he added in a softer tone. 'You're expected to have it on at all times, even through the night. It's pre-programmed with all our numbers. You're free to use it for personal calls. Don't worry about talk time or the cost of a call. The bill is paid direct from the housekeeping account.'

And on and on he went. Izzy would be given the rest of the day to settle in — Mrs Firth would ensure Taryn did her weekend chores and went to bed on time — but from the next day Taryn would be Izzy's (or rather Lizzy's) responsibility. Izzy would need to get Taryn ready for school, drop her off and collect her later in the day, make sure she did her homework and chores, oversee her bath and mealtimes, help prepare her for bed and generally accompany her in whatever means of recreation she decided upon, be it watching the television, playing a game or — horrors! — riding the ponies. Of course, Izzy wouldn't be expected to do the latter until she was a competent rider. Things would change slightly during the school holidays. Not only would Carlotta be home but there would be Pony Club rallies and local gymkhanas to attend, although Carlotta didn't bother so much as she was trying to crack the junior national circuit. This meant county qualifiers. All of which Izzy would be expected to attend and assist at. But that was weeks away yet and, until then, any time when Taryn was at school or in bed would be Izzy's own to do whatever she pleased, within reason. The only proviso was that she must be contactable at all times.

'Do you have any questions?' Jared asked, when the lecture was finally over.

'Yes,' said Izzy. 'Is there a computer I can use?'

---

Izzy would have been mortified if she'd overheard the conversation taking place in the kitchen.

'What do you reckon?' Mrs Firth asked. 'Do you think this one can hack it?'

'I think she's gormless,' said Jared, unforgivingly. 'She's barely on this planet. I give her a week, tops.'

'Well, I suppose she's got two choices.' Mrs Firth's sighed, giving her stock answer for most conundrums. 'I really hoped they'd send us someone decent this time.'

---

Izzy spent the rest of the day manhandling an iMac the size of a widescreen television, scouring her email, Facebook and

Twitter for word from Scott and was horrified to discover that he'd cut all ties with her. When she'd rung him from the new and therefore unidentifiable mobile Jared had given her, he hung up as soon as she said hello. Although she hated to admit it, part of Izzy wasn't surprised by this. The other part was devastated. He didn't even care enough to know whether or not she'd been lured to an abominable fate by northern nutters posing as employers. The fact that she hadn't was irrelevant. After sending Caro and her mother a brief email apiece to let them know she'd arrived safely and wasn't being held hostage by the aforesaid northern nutters, Izzy realised that she had no one else to email. Surely, she had plenty of Facebook 'friends' but in truth these were nothing more than acquaintances or ex-colleagues who collected friends only for show, rather than with a view to forging any real friendships. Aware that not one of them would in any way care that she was now living in Yorkshire and looking after a child, Izzy didn't see any point in updating her status but left it stating that she was looking forward with delicious fervour to a Valentine's Day to remember. (Oh, the irony! thought Izzy.) Unless she was bopping the night away in Rah-Rah's with a blue mojito in her hand and wearing bang-bang heels they wouldn't give a rat's ass, so let them continue to think what they wanted. With a sigh, Izzy switched off the computer. Bored, lonely and unhappy, she wandered to the only place where she could be guaranteed company. The kitchen. Sure enough, as soon as she appeared so did the requisite mug of tea and biscuit tin. Taryn was sitting at the kitchen table eating shortbread and learning a long list of words for a spelling test the next day.

'How do you spell desolate?' Taryn asked by way of cruel coincidence.

'Eye zed zed why,' muttered Izzy under her breath. Nevertheless, she slid into a chair and reached for the tin.

She'd better not start misery eating or she'd end up the size of a buffalo.

'Don't eat all those, Taryn, or you'll not eat your tea,' Mrs Firth cautioned, whipping away the biscuit tin.

'Where did the dog park his car?' Taryn asked, giggling. She didn't bother waiting for anyone to guess the answer. 'In the barking lot.'

This lot are barking, thought Izzy in horror, unthinkingly shovelling in two more biscuits.

'Go and wash your hands. You've got five minutes.' Grumbling, Taryn climbed down from the table. Mrs Firth turned her beady gaze to Izzy.

'Getting sorted?' she asked. Izzy gave a bleak smile.

Whilst Taryn was eating a light tea of lamb chops, mashed potato and more varieties of veg than an average eight-year-old should be able to identify, under Mrs Firth's careful supervision, Jared appeared.

'I thought I'd take Lizzy to The Half Moon for a bite to eat tonight,' he said to the housekeeper.

'Good idea, love,' Mrs Firth rasped. 'Show her the bright lights of the village, heh heh.'

Jared turned to Izzy, who was nursing yet another cup of tea at the table.

'You up for a couple of drinks and a pub supper?' he asked. Izzy, who was feeling more and more claustrophobic by the hour, jumped at the chance of a trip out, especially one that included a drink or two. Half an hour later she found herself walking down the brick driveway, in a pair of Carlotta's wellies, with Jared at her side and Steptoe trotting along between them. Jared had found her a waxed jacket that fit her in the downstairs cloakroom.

'You'll need this,' he said as he helped her into it. 'It's bitter out there.' Izzy put her hands in the pockets only to find them filled with pony nuts. Jared himself had dithered over his own choice of coat, eventually jettisoning his own worn waxed jacket in favour of a well-tailored leather coat the colour of burnt umber and which flattered his weather-beaten complexion and dark blonde hair.

A chalky full moon hung above the village rooftops, which had been frosted by the cold February night. Izzy had never known such quiet. At least the pub was warm and welcoming. Everyone greeted Jared, and Steptoe, by name as they entered.

'Usual, Jared?' called the landlord.

'Please, and—?' he turned to Izzy who gaped at the choice of drinks behind the bar. 'A bottle of beer?' Izzy looked horrified at the thought. 'What do you usually drink?'

'Blue mojito,' Izzy said sulkily. Jared looked impatient.

'This is a village pub, not Tom Cruise in *Cocktail.* Will wine do?'

'Yes please, rosé' Izzy said.

'A large glass of rosé for the lady and two menus, please.'

'Who's this then?' the landlord asked as he handed over the drinks and Jared's change.

'This is Lizzy. Our new girl,' Jared said. 'I thought I'd introduce her to your good self, Col.' The landlord gave Izzy a nod and a smile which was friendly, but not overtly so.

'I'll give you a couple of minutes then I'll send Rachel over for your order.'

Jared led them over to a round table next to a crackling open fire. Steptoe made himself comfy in front of the flames.

'This okay for you?' he asked. Izzy nodded. She took in her surroundings as she shrugged off the waxed jacket. The pub wasn't as she'd expected. Whilst the décor was decidedly rustic there wasn't a horse brass to be seen. Instead there were clear glass vases holding white fairy lights entwined with ting-ting, tea lights in hurricane lamps and farmhouse chalkboards advertising the day's specials. None of the furniture, crockery or cutlery matched, which only served to increase its individuality and quirkiness. An impressive array of Good Pub awards were displayed behind the bar. A couple of young lads were playing pool in the corner. Other than the glance of assessment they had given her, no one had stared at her when they'd walked in. There had been no silence or finger pointing. Even more surprisingly, the jukebox was playing all the latest chart hits and the menu boasted some very contemporary dishes. Izzy took a sip of her wine. That was decent too. Craning her head to face the bar she noticed that it had been poured straight from the bottle rather than through an optic and that the grape and vintage were from the new favourite Californian vineyard that all the Sunday supplements had been recommending. Her expression must have betrayed her surprise in its quality.

'You do realise that we're only two hundred *miles* from London, not two hundred light years,' Jared said, shrugging out of his jacket to reveal a navy tee shirt and well-muscled, brown forearms, one of which was very badly scarred. Realising she was staring, Izzy looked away quickly but it was too late. Jared had followed her horrified gaze.

'I'm afraid I got involved in a rather big fight,' he said, holding out his arm so that Izzy could clearly see the darkened skin, bobbled where it had healed from second degree burns and the scars from several lacerations. 'Don't worry. I'm quite safe. What do you fancy? The steaks are very good here. Col sources his beef from a local farmer.' He scanned his eyes over the menu. Eventually Izzy chose tuna seared with lime and coriander and a Caesar salad whilst Jared settled for a T-bone, blue to rare, and chips. Once the aforementioned Rachel had taken their orders and brought them their cutlery and condiments Jared gave Izzy a serious look.

'Thanks for agreeing to come out tonight,' Jared said, taking a long draught of his pint. 'I wanted to fill you in on the situation at the house. The Paddocks isn't a traditionally happy home. Taryn is a good kid — spoilt, yes — and at heart a kind girl. But she's lonely. She hasn't many friends in the village who she can invite over to play and all her other friends are from school in Loxley. She's desperately lacking any sensible female company in her life. Mrs Firth dotes on her but is inclined to be over indulgent. Taryn spends most of her time in the stables.'

'What about Gemma? She seems personable,' Izzy said. Jared grimaced.

'She's okay. The problem is that, other than when Taryn is actually sitting on a horse, Gemma also lets her do exactly as she pleases. You see, Taryn is quite agreeable to any instruction or request on the proviso that she wants to do it. As soon as she's required to do something that she doesn't want... that's when the shit hits the fan. Then there's Carlotta—'

'Ah yes. Carlotta. The mystery sister,' Izzy said, rather sarcastically, taking another swig of wine. 'Taryn tells me Carlotta is ungovernable and only MK continuing to pay the school double fees is stopping her from being expelled.'

'Taryn should curb that tongue of hers. I'm sorry you weren't told about Carlotta. That's rather an oversight on the agency's part,' Jared said, looking grim.

'One of a few oversights,' said Izzy. Her inner turmoil, misery and terror, buoyed up by half a glass of wine on an almost empty stomach, made her uncharacteristically feisty. 'I was told there was only one infant child and the house was on the outskirts of the city centre. There was no mention of teenagers or horses and certainly not of living in the middle of nowhere.'

'We're sorry about that too. We never asked them to find someone for us at all costs. We certainly never asked them to lie to candidates,' Jared said. 'Although, in fairness, we were told our fair share of lies too. They told us you could ride. Still, at least you do have some experience in home supervision. You were working for a barrister in London, yes?' He sat back as the pretty blonde waitress set their meals down in front of them. 'Thanks, sweetheart.' Jared smiled up at her.

Izzy gave a small, bitter smile. Whether it was because she wanted to get back at bleedin' Merle Miller for being such a lying jade or whether it was because she literally didn't have anywhere else to go, Izzy let her imagination run amok and found herself recounting her imaginary life as a nanny in London.

She'd been looking after two young children, she said. One eighteen months — little Jemima — and an adorable ruff-tuff boy of four called Roderick, Rory for short.

'I'm so much better with the younger ones. I've never had to deal with teenagers before.' At least that was true, she thought to herself. Mind, in TV spy dramas the hero always based his cover on real life facts. Encouraged by this, Izzy warmed to her theme. It had been a live-in post in Marylebone, working for the Oakeses, a wonderful married couple. He, Jonty, was a City banker whilst Caro was the barrister. 'I was with them since Rory was a newborn. Since then they've become like family to me. I'm fortunate enough to now call Caro my best friend. I'll miss them all so much. I've been so happy with the Oakeses,' she said, hoping to have injected the exact right amount of wistfulness into her voice.

'If you were so happy there why did you leave?' Jared asked, forking near raw cow into his mouth.

Why was he always so bloody straight to the point? Izzy thought crossly. She'd have to box clever out of this one.

'Oh, Caro was desperate to spend some quality time with the kids so she decided to take a couple of year's hiatus from the bar,' she said airily, relying on her knowledge of daytime soaps to provide her with a plotline.

'Not something I'm likely to do,' said Jared, draining his glass. 'Col, two more of the same, please!'

'I didn't want to step on her toes,' Izzy carried on, waving her fork in the air. 'I'll probably go back when Caro returns to work.'

'I see. You're not a long term prospect then,' Jared said wryly. 'Still, you're here now and you don't seem to be a lunatic or a criminal so I guess we can make do. We can get round the horse riding problem easily enough and Taryn seems to have taken a shine to you. That's more than she has with the others. One of the girls we were sent was so timid that Taryn locked her in the wine cellar for half a day, just to see what would happen. She had her bags packed and was waiting at the front door for me to drive her back to the train within three quarters of an hour of being released. The agency complained about our treatment of her. Turned out the poor girl was an arachnophobe and that cellar is riddled with spiders. I think you're the fourth girl they've sent us. We're really banking on you being able to hack it.'

'Isn't it a bit weird for a mere gardener to be so involved in the girls' welfare?' Izzy asked, not realising she was putting her size fours in it. Jared didn't drop his eyes from her gaze.

'MK has been away for nearly six months now and he won't be back until the end of the year. As I said, you're the fourth girl we've been sent. Those poor girls have no stability. Father absent; mother dead. Mrs Firth has been at the house since Carlotta was a baby and they've known me all their lives too. Between the two of us we're all the stability they have. That makes us pretty well qualified to care for them and look after their best interests, wouldn't you say?'

Izzy studied her plate, embarrassed and keenly aware she'd judged Jared in the same way that Scott had always judged Izzy — by the job they performed rather than the person they were. 'I didn't mean to criticise,' she said. 'All I meant was that it was unusual.'

'Yeah, well, it's an unusual household,' Jared snapped.

Then he relented. 'Look, we appreciate you weren't told the truth about our set up, but we weren't told the truth either, so that makes us even. I won't lie to you, you're not ideal but we're desperate for someone to be a bit more permanent. All we care about is the girls. With that in mind, we want you to know that you can count on all the help we can give if it means that you'll stick around for longer than a fortnight. In return all we ask is that you do your best with them. We're quite prepared to give this a go if you are. Whadya think?'

'Okay.' She didn't have much bleedin' choice.

'Now, as long as you show an interest in ponies you should be okay with Taryn. As for Carlotta, we'll jump over that triple bar when we get to it. She's not due home until Easter. We should have you fully up to speed by then. Now, if you'll excuse me, I just need to siphon the python.'

Izzy found herself mesmerised by the way Jared spoke, with a very slight but very West Yorkshire trill on his r's and decided she rather liked him. She then promptly changed her opinion as, when he returned to the table, he proceeded to grill her about her life in London, her family, her friends, her job history, her childhood.

'Ah, so you're an Essex girl. Now I understand.'

'What's that supposed to mean?' Izzy bristled, riddled with indignation.

'Nothing, nothing—' But Jared's shoulders shook silently as he lifted his pint to his lips. After that the interrogation continued.

'I suppose you want my shoe size too,' Izzy asked sarcastically, setting her knife and fork together.

'Yes please,' Jared replied, not missing a beat. Izzy gaped at him.

'Wot for?'

'You'll need a pair of your own riding boots and wellies.'

---

Next morning Izzy was tugged from sleep like a reluctant weed by an irritatingly bubbly Taryn. After shoehorning her into her school uniform and forcing the poor bugger to eat a bowl of Mrs Firth's home-made porridge, Izzy drove Taryn to school. The sat nav took care of the directions but still Izzy almost skidded off the toll bridge, which had frozen overnight and was icier than an Orange Mivvi, and got lost twice, before grinding to a halt in the school car park nose to tail with some other parent's Jag. Fortunately there was no damage and, better still, no witnesses. Confident in the popularity that the irresistible combination of wealth and beauty brings, Taryn skipped happily into school. Upon her return to The Paddocks Izzy would have liked to have gone back to bed for a kip but Jared insisted she accompany him into the village to run some errands.

'Lip up, fatty,' he said, quoting the title of a favourite song. 'The fresh air'll put some colour in your cheeks.'

'Fatty? I'm not fat,' Izzy squeaked.

'He's being sarky with you, love. You don't eat, so how could anyone think you're fat? There's nowt on you. You're made of twigs,' Mrs Firth said, clearly disappointed by Izzy's lack of appetite.

Feet dragging, Izzy hauled on her adopted waxed jacket once more. Nor were any of her shoes suitable for a stroll round the village. She tugged on Carlotta's wellies for a second time.

Outside the air was thick and damp with freezing white mist and smelled of farmyards. Izzy turned her nose up in distaste and buried her chin in her jacket. It must be at least two degrees colder than London.

'What's the matter now?' Jared asked, impatiently.

'It smells of pigs,' Izzy said.

'Course it does. This is a farming community. What did you think it would smell like, the perfume counter in Harrods? Come on, look lively.'

It was Izzy's first proper look at the front of The Paddocks in the daylight. A long, snaky, slate-blue brick driveway led down to the electronic gates. Thick, high leylandii hedges bordered the entire plot, offering both privacy and security. To one side stood a quadruple garage, to the other a vast stone fountain topped by a life-sized sculpture of a rearing horse, its front hooves boxing the air. In the swirling mist it looked like a wraith's horse emerging from the fogs in *The Lord of the Rings*.

The house itself, despite its antiquated interior, was new build. Very modern and symmetrical, with no olde worlde charme whatsoever, its exterior was purely functional. The only flamboyance was the two ghastly Corinthian columns standing guard on either side of the enormous black front door. They looked incongruous in comparison to the dull brickwork and plain black and white masonry.

'Are we fans of the Parthenon?' Izzy asked, casting a judgemental eye over them.

'MK spent his childhood in Athens. His father was Greek.'

'Oh.'

As it was too cold to remain stationary, Jared set off down the driveway at a brisk pace. All of the dogs, obedient and off lead, none of whom Izzy could have named except little Steptoe who had dashed to the front of the pack in his capacity as leader, followed Jared. How ironic, thought Izzy as she struggled to catch up with Jared's straight, broad back, that such a tiny creature should be the undisputed boss of so many bigger animals. She hoped it wasn't indicative of Taryn's power over her. Thinking it might be a good idea to appear interested she pointed to a scruffy looking dog.

'What brand is that one?'

'Brand? It's a dog, not a box of cornflakes. Don't you mean breed?'

'Okay then, what *breed* is it?'

'She's a Border Terrier, called Hobbit. The two golden Labs

are Dude and Sprite, the two black Labs Breeze and Nugget, the Border Collie's Tig, and the Heinz 57 is called Pongy, who is aptly named because he does exactly what it says on the tin,' Jared explained. 'You'll probably pick up all the cats' names as you go along. We have about six, including a couple of ferals that don't come into the house.'

Izzy wished she hadn't bothered asking. She'd never been allowed a pet of her own and found all these animals disconcerting. She was frightened of dogs, suspicious of cats, would rather chew her own foot off than pick up a hamster and positively quaked at the thought of sitting on a horse. It was a bleedin' live animal with a mind of its own, for Pete's sake.

Izzy's first venture into the village in daylight elicited surprised amazement at its quaintness and beauty. She gasped over the triangular village green with its currently ribbonless Maypole, the duck pond and the cherry trees. She admired the thirteenth century church with its well-kept graveyard and kissing-arch gateway. She pressed her nose against the pristine window of Philippa's Kitchen, the new café, and looked longingly at the cakes and pastries laid out in the glass cabinet.

'Is that a thatched roof?' she shrieked, catching sight of an exquisite whitewashed cottage covered with dormant damask roses and clematis in the window's reflection.

'Haven't you ever seen one before?' asked Jared, amused.

'Only at Alton Towers.'

The pub, locked and shuttered until opening time, its beer garden bleak and forsaken with its all-in-one picnic-style tables huddled into a corner like a herd of pasture cows, sold more than a pint and a pie. Locally sourced fruit and veg, free range eggs, milk and meats could all be bought from a hatch at the back of the bar. The newly opened café brought even more business into the village and did a roaring trade selling bread, cakes and croissants to take away and seasonal jams, honeys and chutneys. Every so often a delicious waft of fresh bread was belched out of the kitchen's vents. Jared and Izzy both sniffed like the Bisto Kids.

Outside the café was a tall, thick wooden post.

'What's this? A sacrificial totem?' Izzy asked, circumnavigating it in fascination.

'It's a tethering pole for the horses. They can be hitched to this for a few minutes whilst the rider nips off to collect something.'

'Huh, I wondered if it was where the local witches were burned by the village mob.'

'What a mediaeval remark,' said Jared, scathingly. He then grinned. 'This is a posh village; the witches get burned in a chimenea.' He turned up a driveway to a formidable red bricked house. 'This is us. I need to talk to a chap about getting my blades sharpened.' Izzy looked at him as though he was about to whip a knife out from beneath his waxed jacket like Crocodile Dundee. Jared grinned again. 'For my garden shears.'

Jared's business didn't take long. As he and the blade sharpener talked on the doorstep, Izzy stood to one side wondering what on Earth she had got herself into. She could barely believe that forty-eight hours had already passed since she had left London. It was as though she was living another person's life.

As they stepped back onto the pavement it started to rain: icy, vicious lashings that stung the skin and made the eyes water. A surly wind rattled the bare branches of the cherry trees that lined the avenue. Jared gave the thickening sky a cursory glance.

'We'd better head back. Taryn's going to be very disappointed; there's no way we can get the ponies out in this.'

# ONE BRAKE HORSE POWER

The elements continued to conspire against Taryn as the cold front, which blew in from Scandinavia bringing with it icy rains and bitter winds, lingered for several days like an unwelcome houseguest and put paid to her plans to have Izzy atop a horse before dinner each day. It wasn't until Thursday afternoon that the manége had dried out sufficiently for Izzy's first lesson.

'Go and find some suitable clobber in Carlotta's room,' Jared instructed her over breakfast. 'I'm afraid the day of reckoning is here.'

Izzy groaned aloud.

Fully decked out in Carlotta's two-tone hot-pink and lavender jodhpurs, which served only to slim further her already skinny chicken legs, riding boots, crash cap and a body protector that made her feel as though she was about to engage in warfare, Izzy trudged her way down to the stable, muttering all the way. What did she have to learn to ride for? Waste of bleedin' time. She was only going to be here for a few months anyway. It was barely worth it.

Taryn was waiting at the front door of the stable block. As

usual she looked immaculate, rather like a cover girl for *Pony* magazine. At least Jared was nowhere to be seen. Izzy stomped along, unused to the restrictiveness of the riding boots. Her knees, knocking from sheer terror, were an added hindrance.

'I feel such a fool,' she grumbled.

'You look fine,' said Jared, appearing from inside the barn. Steptoe was following at his heels, a rawhide chewstick hanging from his jaw like an unlit cigarillo.

Damn! She hadn't seen him there.

'Are you ready to face the enemy?' The enemy, in this case, was Jet. Tacked up, he looked even more like a show pony than ever. Moreover, he seemed to know this. He pranced towards Izzy, who shrank back and accidentally stood on Steptoe's paw causing him to yelp. Startled, Jet jerked his head. The reins tore through Jared's hand, who swore at the pain, then swore at Jet. 'Give over, ye daft bugger.' He turned to Izzy. 'He can sense your fear. You'll have to learn to be less afraid if you want to become a rider.'

'Who sez I want that?' Izzy said under her breath. She gave the saddle a mutinous look. 'Will riding horses give me a big bum?'

'Enormous,' lied Jared cheerfully. 'If you ride every day your arse will grow to a size disproportionate to the rest of your body. It's nature's way of providing you with a nice, big cushiony part to land on when you fall off.'

Izzy felt green. It was therein that the real problem lay. The 'F' word. She had seen showjumping and three day eventing on the telly during Olympic fortnight. Those riders were the very best their country had to offer and they still fell off, and spectacularly too! What chance did she have? Whether he had done so deliberately or not, Jared had indicated this to be an inevitable truth. *When* she fell off; not if. Knowing this, Izzy really did *not* want to learn how to ride but she was determined to not admit defeat before she'd even begun. Outwardly, she raised her chin and, feigning courage, walked towards Jet.

'How do I get on it?'

'You don't yet. First I want to show you how to walk up to and around the pony, then we'll put Jet on a lunge rein and you can mount from the block.'

Izzy thought he might as well be speaking a different language. What the hell was a block? Five minutes later she found out. Five minutes and thirty seconds later she was sitting astride Jet, rigid with terror, as Jared led them towards the manége. Taryn followed on foot, eating crisps. Each time her hand delved into the packet Jet napped at the rustling noise.

It was unfortunate but unavoidable, thought Jared as he adjusted Izzy's stirrups and showed her how to hold the reins correctly, that The Tank, who was inordinately gentle despite his aggressive moniker, was lame, and that she was forced to have her very first lesson on Jet, who should have been at school with Carlotta, but had been shipped home in ignominy as a punishment for her serially bad behaviour. He was fresh as a result of overeating and not enough exercise. Gemma was a little too big to ride him plus she didn't have the time. She also had to attend to The Tank, exercise Ghost and lunge Vega. Taryn, into whose hands Jet would eventually pass, chose not to ride him not only because she preferred riding her own pony but more pertinently because she didn't want to rouse her sister's inherent possessiveness.

Jared was unfurling the lunge rein until there were three metres between them. Not for the first time since her arrival at The Paddocks, Izzy felt isolated and vulnerable.

'Now, I want you to stay in that position but relax. Relax, I said. I'm going to make Jet walk in a circle. Taryn, pass me that schooling whip, please.'

To Izzy's horror Taryn bent down and retrieved from beside the manége fence a long whip the likes of which she had only ever seen before in an *Indiana Jones* film. Jared swished it so that it writhed behind Jet like an angry snake. Next minute Izzy was hanging from Jet's tossing head.

'We call that the monkey swing,' Taryn piped up, now on her second packet of Monster Munch.

'Sit up! Sit up!' bellowed Jared. Within seconds he had grabbed Jet's reins and the horse was still once more. Taryn, sitting on the post and rail fence, giggled. Izzy glared at her as Jared heaved her back into the saddle.

Jared was talking to her again. 'You did nothing wrong there. Jet is just being naughty because he can sense your fear.'

'He's a nutter,' Izzy snapped as Jet jerked his head a few times, yanking the reins from her hands. 'He wants to put me on the ground. I'll end up brown bread.'

'So long as you do as I tell you, you won't fall off,' Jared said. 'You need to sit up nice and straight and let the reins be a bit looser. All your tension is being transmitted down the reins to his mouth. If you let the reins go slack he can't feel your tension.'

'If I let go he'll run off.' Izzy felt close to tears but was damned if she was going to let Jared or Taryn see it.

'He won't. I have hold of his head and he is more wary of me than you are of him. All you need to worry about is sitting in the saddle. I'll control his brakes and steering. We'll try a nice steady walk first. Do you have any idea what to do to make the pony move?'

'I dunno. Giddy-up?' Izzy ventured.

'Hardly,' Jared said. The schooling whip whooshed again. Jet started to move forward. Izzy sat rigid on his back. 'That's very good. Try to relax a bit more. I won't let him hurt you. And push your heels down. Further than that. That's better.'

'It feels weird. Why do I have to push my heels down?' Izzy asked.

'It stops your foot from getting caught in the stirrup when you fall off. That's how you get dragged,' Taryn piped up from her perch on the fence. 'It happened to the sister of one of my friends from Pony Club. She broke her arm and had to have two stitches.'

Izzy felt as though she was going to be sick and paled visibly. Nor was Jared amused.

'Shut up, Taryn,' he snapped. 'Ignore her. She's just trying to wind you up. Firstly, you aren't going to fall off. Secondly, even if you did, which you won't, your foot can't get caught in these stirrups as they have elastic safety bands on them. Thirdly, that girl was riding a horse far too big for her far too fast over cross-country fences far too advanced for her ability. It's nowhere near the same.'

Taryn continued to chatter whilst Izzy went round and round on the lungeing rein. As Izzy circled him, Jared couldn't help but notice that she held her lower leg naturally in the correct position and that her hands were nice and light despite her inclination to hold the reins between her fingers like a ninja death grip.

'Shall we try a little trot?' he asked after fifteen minutes of circling. He didn't give Izzy chance to reply. 'Prepare to trot, trot on!' Jet promptly lifted his tail, arched his neck and proceeded to treat Izzy to his showiest, most bouncy two-step.

'Oh! Oh! Oh!' cried Izzy as she tried to keep time. 'Make it stop.'

But Jared didn't. He made Izzy persevere until she could rise to the trot for a handful of strides. Round and round they went, alternating between walk and trot, first clockwise and then anti until Izzy was quite dizzy. She'd never been so exhausted. Only when he was satisfied that sufficient progress had been made did Jared reel in the lungeing rein.

'Thank Christ!' said Izzy, starting to slide out of the saddle. To her astonishment Jared placed his big gardener's hands on her back and pushed her back up. 'Hey!'

'You'll learn to dismount properly.' And another ten minutes were spent on the merits of a neat dismount. After that Izzy was lectured on untacking.

'I hope you know that none of that has sunk in,' she told Jared crossly as she hobbled back to the house.

'In that case we'll go over it tomorrow, and the day after tomorrow and the day after that until it has.' Jared noted how gingerly Izzy was walking and laughed. 'You'd better take a hot bath. Riding uses muscles that no other sport does. If you don't take action you'll ache like a bastard in the morning, worse still the morning after that. Remind me to buy you a couple of tubes of Jockey's Joy from the saddlers. There's nothing better for aches and pains.'

Having never ridden anything regularly other than the Tube, Izzy couldn't believe how sore her legs were the next morning. It wasn't so much saddle sore as entire lower body sore. Each muscle in her leaden limbs creaked as she moved but, even though she continued to feel gradually more achy throughout the course of the day, no one offered any sympathy, only tea. It was only when she started to sneeze and complain of a runny nose that Mrs Firth placed a pudgy hand on her forehead and pronounced the arrival of a cold.

And so for the second time in a week fate intervened in Izzy's favour. Unused to bracing northern fresh air and days full of activities other than cleaning out the shops in the West End twinned with drunken table dancing in Rah-Rah's, Izzy's body took the opportunity to recuperate. Whether it was a direct response to her change of lifestyle or plain and simple retribution for having abused her body for so long with booze and late nights, Izzy would never know. All she did know was that within a week of her being at The Paddocks she was besieged by a vicious cold which rendered her days miserable and uncomfortable but wasn't severe enough to justify her taking to her bed, which was something she would have indubitably done if she'd still been in London. Even with her nose blocked up, a back-bending cough and a throat that felt as though she had been swigging battery acid, she was expected to dose herself up with hot lemon and painkillers and keep going. She was, however, excused from further riding lessons until she felt better. This alone, in Izzy's opinion, made the cold a worthwhile evil even though she fell into bed each night literally sick and tired.

Jared offered no sympathy whatsoever. It was only a cold, was his opinion, and any whinging or moaning was met with a severe case of piss-taking. After Izzy made a meal of a coughing fit one evening she was surprised to feel a magnanimous pat on her back.

'Cough it up, love. It might be a gold coin,' Jared said, laughing. Izzy was left seething. Not only did she have a vile taste in her mouth and nose like she had swallowed a quart of swimming pool water, and what felt like a cat's furball in her throat, but her skin also chose its moment to break out in a remarkable constellation of spots which left her cringing with embarrassment each time she caught a glimpse of herself in a mirror.

Nor was she the only member of the household to fall sick that week. Taryn, she learned, wasn't quite as bonny and blithe as she appeared but was prone to hyperventilation attacks when distressed or frightened. Having defied Jared, who'd told her to go straight to sleep, Taryn watched in secret an eighteen-rated film in her room late one night. The film had turned out to be a slasher movie about hot nubile schoolgirls in a boarding school being hacked into bite-sized portions by a maniac with a machete masquerading as a pious RE teacher. Fearful both for herself and for her sister who was at boarding school, Taryn had then been subjected to terrible nightmares and refused to go back to sleep. For

Izzy, who had been roused from her drug-induced sleep by the dreadful screams of terror, it was the first time she encountered fully Taryn's obstinacy and bolshiness. In direct contradiction of her usual merry nature, Taryn became petulant and needy, demanding Izzy stay with her all night. Already worn out from the effects of her depression, her illness and the unforgiving early mornings, Izzy had a hard time keeping her eyes open and ended up curled up in Taryn's bed with the little girl sleeping fitfully beside her.

Next morning Taryn bounded out of bed as though nothing had happened with the intrinsic resilience of childhood. In comparison, Izzy was left groggy headed and reeling from fatigue, wondering what the hell had happened to her youth. Over a week had passed since her arrival at The Paddocks and nothing had got easier. She was simply floundering. She missed Scott and London with a physical ache. There was not one hour of one day that she didn't question her decision to remain so far away from everything that was important to her. The desire to go home was overwhelming and if it had been at all a possibility she would certainly have had her bags packed within the half hour.

She also struggled to relate to Taryn despite their initially promising connection. Never having had any contact with children before she was easily duped and Taryn soon learned that she could manipulate Izzy to her own ends. On other occasions Izzy mistook Taryn's behaviour as deliberate naughtiness when in truth she was only behaving like an eight-year-old.

'I need a glass of water,' Taryn said. Already tired, Izzy headed towards the en suite. 'Where are you going?' Taryn asked imperiously. She was sitting up in bed, rather like a demanding patient.

'To the tap,' Izzy replied wearily.

'I don't want that water. I only drink downstairs water,' Taryn said, her face resolute. And so Izzy stomped downstairs, her teeth gritted, to fill Taryn's glass with water from the kitchen sink. She was even crosser to discover, the following morning, that the glass was untouched.

Nor did Izzy appreciate that when an eight-year-old says she needs to wee, she means immediately and not in fifteen minutes. Battling to understand Taryn's maths prep, Izzy kept her waiting by which time, unable to hold it any longer, Taryn wet her knickers. Embarrassed and angry, Taryn refused to speak to Izzy for the remainder of the day.

A further hurdle was the language barrier.

'You talk funny,' giggled Taryn one morning at breakfast. Taryn wasn't allowed to watch *EastEnders* or reality TV and thus didn't understand the concept of cockney rhyming slang nor had ever encountered the words 'reem' or 'ennit'. Mrs Firth gave a loud rasping laugh. Izzy shot her a look of hatred. She need talk. The day before she had said something like 'put t'wood int'oil' which apparently could be translated loosely as 'please close the door'.

Nor did Izzy become easily accustomed to country life. She was freaked out by the night-time shrieks of the foxes and owls and the lack of street lamps sent her plummeting to the depths of despair. Worse still was the prevalence of bats that swooped down like vultures as soon as dusk came. It didn't matter how many times Jared assured her they wouldn't get caught in her hair as per urban legend, she still ran for shelter, yelping, upon every sighting.

She was also horrified by the sheer volume of creatures that resided at The Paddocks. Dogs, cats, horses, rabbits, guinea pigs, chickens; the list was endless. It would be enough to make Longleat proud.

'I don't know why you don't advertise and charge admission at the gate,' Izzy grumbled at feeding time, gazing in disbelief at the array of coloured bowls lined up on the utility room counter into which Jared was doling out scoops of kibble like Mr Bumble. Steptoe, front and centre as per usual, was the Oliver Twist of the scenario because he always wanted more, be this food, walks or attention, and was standing on his back legs, begging like a performing bear. 'You could drive little kiddies round the paddocks on your sit-on lawnmower like a budget safari.' It was inevitable that once the dogs had been fed they would race upstairs and wipe their dirty faces on whichever duvets they could gain access to. It was a week before Izzy learned to close her bedroom door firmly behind her. Pongy, the little salt and pepper mongrel, had taken a shine to Izzy and actively sought out her clean clothes and bedlinen as facecloths.

Steptoe had also developed a fondness for Izzy. A canine bed whore, he crept between bedrooms during the night. He always started in Izzy's room though, as though sensing that she found his presence comforting and that she needed him most and couldn't get off to sleep alone. Every morning she woke to find him gone.

It took longer for Izzy to remember that, if she was first down on a morning or if little Steptoe wanted to go out for a pee in the middle of the night, she had to disarm the burglar alarm before venturing downstairs. After she had set the bleeder off for the third consecutive night Jared bollocked her. Only sheer bloody-mindedness kept the tears at bay. No way was she going to cry in front of the big bully. If she'd had somewhere to go she would have walked out there and then.

Nor did Izzy reconcile herself to village life with ease. Used to a racketeering London lifestyle, Izzy's world had consisted of high heels, hip bars, flashy suits with bulging wallets and sugar-frosted cocktails. In London you only ever associated with your own circle of friends and colleagues and you never, ever came into contact with strangers more than once unless you were really unlucky or they had decided to stalk you. She'd always viewed the metropolis as consisting of lots of individual, insular little pockets all grouped together to form one big, unfriendly mass. Not so in the village. Rusticating herself from the majority of Nether Ousebury's population during her first fortnight, she had bitched about having to wait for an age behind some other grumbling, dawdling customer in the village shop to the assistant, not realising she'd been referring to the assistant's cousin. Unfortunately for Izzy, most of the village was connected to each other by friendship, blood or marriage. Thus she made herself extremely unpopular in a very short space of time as the word spread. Her other nemesis was the labyrinthine single track roads that spread out around the village like a spider's web and which were inevitably dominated at peak time by creeping tractors spewing out clumps of straw-ridden dirt or horse riders who expected her to slow down to ten miles per hour as she passed them. She lost count of the times she'd got herself lost and had been forced to ring Jared for directions.

Any spare time she had she spent online, checking for word from London. Each time she was disappointed.

'Hotmail? Coldmail more like!' she raged as her inbox remained stubbornly empty.

---

IZZY'S second riding lesson was with Gemma, and which Izzy found to be far less stressful. Infinitely more patient than Jared, Gemma was also less pushy as a teacher and succeeded in making Izzy much more relaxed.

'If you feel Jet is starting to get fractious just sit back and yawn. It'll calm the pony down. It seems that yawning relaxes the entire body and this is transmitted through the saddle.'

'Oh! I thought you meant that if I yawned the horse would yawn too and be more tired. You know, just the same as if someone yawns it sets everyone else off.'

Gemma gave a tight smile.

'I think not.'

It didn't harm that the lesson took place whilst Taryn was at school and thus couldn't watch and comment on her every mistake. By the end of the lesson Izzy had mastered rising to the trot and had even walked Jet round the perimeter of the manége without the aid of the lungeing rein. There had only been one dicey moment when The Tank, still recuperating in the paddock, had whinnied at Jet. In turn Jet, thrilled to be summoned by his friend for a gallop, had tossed his head in delight and pranced towards the gate. Izzy had shrieked and shrieked until Gemma snapped at her to shut up and stop terrifying the pony.

Afterwards, Gemma made Izzy a cup of coffee in the tack room. Biscuits were produced from a tin and shared with generosity. Gemma seemed intent on sharing more than just biscuits too. It wasn't long before the topic of conversation turned from ponies to Jared.

'He's gorgeous,' Gemma said, with a conspiratorial wink. 'It took me ages to hook him.'

'You and Jared? I had no idea,' Izzy lied. She wasn't surprised. Although there'd been no sideways glances, no hidden touches, no indication of private jokes or intimacy, there had been that curiously clinical interchange between them on her first day. In her experience people who saw and worked with each other every day fell into a comfortable pattern. They didn't address each other like polite strangers.

Gemma grinned.

'That's a good thing. MK doesn't want the girls to know and so we have to keep it secret. You mustn't ever tell.'

'Blimey,' said Izzy. She was a little lost for words. And curiously, a little disappointed to have it confirmed so soon that Jared wasn't available. Not that she was interested in him, or even found him attractive, but it was always nice to have someone who might become an admirer.

'Once, we made love in the back of MK's roller. We both knew he'd go bonkers if he caught us but that just made it all the more erotic.' Gemma gave a cat-like stretch as she cast her mind back. 'I've never known anything like it. I can remember everything about it; the smell of the leather and the way the vehicle moved beneath us.'

Izzy didn't really know what to say.

'It must have been... err... cramped?' was the best she could come up with.

'Certainly was.' Another lascivious smile. 'That's a lot of man to fit into a small space.' The innuendo was blatant. 'I had to straddle him like The Tank on the back seat. I kept banging my head against the roof of the car. Best ride of my life, and that includes Hickstead.'

Izzy's discomfort was put to an abrupt end by the sound of footsteps on the gravel.

'There you are!' Jared looked cross. 'I've been searching everywhere for you. Taryn's had a hyperventilation attack at school and her teacher has asked that she be brought home. Can you set off straight away?'

Never before was Izzy so glad to be dragged away from a gossip session to do a chore. 'Sure.'

'I'll wash these.' Gemma whipped the mug out of Izzy's hand. 'That way you can get off sooner.' She turned to Jared. 'I've noticed some heat in Vega's off hind. Can you come and take a look at it?' She gave Izzy another wink as she followed him out of the tack room.

It was only when Izzy was well en route to Taryn's school that she realised that Gemma's revelation about her and Jared's Titanic-esque sex romp in the Rolls Royce had been more than mere gossip. It had been a distinct warning. And it said Keep Off.

Later, Izzy did a bit of fishing.

'How was Vega?' she asked Jared, all innocence as they sat down for dinner.

'Vega?' Jared looked genuinely baffled.

'The heat in her leg. Is it serious?'

'Oh that. Nah, it was nowt.' The dismissive tone in his voice was undeniable and confirmed Izzy's suspicions that there never had been a problem with Vega's leg. It had just been a ruse for them to have a roll in the hayloft.

---

WHEN SATURDAY CAME Izzy was dragged to Pets & Ponies, which was situated on the outskirts of Greater Ousebury, to get her 'togged out'. Unenthusiastic from the outset, Izzy trailed round the outdoor pursuits store with a face as flat and expressionless as a pan lid. Only when she realised that she wouldn't be expected to pay for anything did she perk up and begin to show an interest. Everything was so unfamiliar, she thought, as she traipsed down aisles filled with shelf upon shelf of equestrian kit. Who would have thought that jodhpurs came in so many colours, or that there were so many different types of riding boot? Her jaw dropped even lower as they wandered through the saddlery department and she saw the rows and rows of leather straps and fastenings.

'Holy Christ! It's like a fetishist's dream come true.'

Jared was grabbing items off the shelves and chucking them into the trolley. Two pairs of jodhpurs, riding boots, some rather snazzy hot pink Hunter wellies, a crash cap, two fleeces, a body protector, a gilet, whip, gloves, the list was endless. Izzy couldn't believe the total spent as everything was rung up on the till. At the last minute Jared slung in an outer of chewsticks for the dogs as well as a copy of *Pony* magazine 'to shut Taryn up'.

---

Another week passed with no cause for celebration or hope but Izzy did at least start to form some sort of a routine. Not that she found it easy.

Early morning had never been a close friend of hers but now she was expected to rise at the crack of dawn and get Taryn ready for school. Nor was there any opportunity to skive. Previously, when Izzy had wanted to sack off work, all she'd had to do was say the Tube was cancelled, or full, or late, or that she had a family crisis, or unbearable women's troubles. Now she had no excuse. Here there were no lies in, no days off, no escape. Every day Taryn needed to be organised and taken to school and so every day Izzy was dragged out of her pit at six thirty, regardless of whether she was well or not. For the first couple of weeks Mrs Firth took pity on her and charmed her out of bed with a coffee. After that she merely sent in the dogs, who bounced all over Izzy's bed until she got up. Most mornings Izzy opened her eyes to find Steptoe staring at her, his muzzle inches from her face, his hot tripey breath warming her cheeks.

'Jesus!'

Gradually she learned to adapt but couldn't really say that she settled. Still moping internally about Scott, she'd never mentioned him to any of the residents at The Paddocks. The only exception was little Steptoe, who'd taken quite the shine to Izzy and kept her company throughout the long nights and listened to her sobbing soliloquies about how much she missed Scott, his little furry face tilted to one side like a therapist.

There were some high points. Gemma looked like a promising mate and they'd even gone for one or two brief shopping jaunts in Leeds and Loxley whilst Taryn was in school. Here Izzy took the opportunity to buy some bits and pieces to give her bedroom a bit of personality. Mrs Firth had been right on the ball, as the first thing she bought was a new comforter for her bed and a couple of new chart CDs, which

Taryn promptly nicked, a decent pair of trainers and a new pair of Ugg boots to replace the ones she had ruined beyond redemption by stepping in a dollop of horse muck. There wasn't really anything else she had to buy. Five star board and lodgings were included in the package, rather like a Sandals resort, Izzy thought wryly, and anything remotely connected to equestrianism was paid for by MK.

Trips to The Half Moon were also frequent, sometimes with Jared, which felt like work, or more often with Gemma, but never with both. The latter tended to be jolly occasions with copious amounts of wine drunk and scurrilous gossip traded. Even Col the Landlord, who turned out to be the stepbrother-in-law of the cousin of the shop assistant that Izzy had slagged off, thawed out sufficiently to ask how she was settling in and offered her a bowl of complimentary peanuts. But no matter how much Pinot Izzy drank or what indiscreet confidences Gemma shared, not once did she reveal the truth about why she'd landed at The Paddocks.

However, for every one high point there were low points to the power of ten. Izzy's salary was generous, to say the least, but she was expected to earn it. As her horse riding and stable management improved so her smorgasbord of duties increased. She found herself continuously being asked to carry out unsavoury tasks such as picking up dog poop from the gardens — 'I have never done this before in my life!' — and helping Taryn muck out the ponies when Gemma had had a doctor's appointment. She was most put out by the horses' lack of good manners, declaring to Jared that it was most rude of them to wait until after their stables had been mucked out before depositing a hot steaming crap on the fresh straw.

Nor was Izzy reticent about her displeasure. Her complaints and grumbles were becoming the stuff of legend, so voluble and protracted were they. Jared, who thought she was too silly for words, took to calling her Moanie Mouse, which only served to wind her up even more.

Deep down Izzy knew she only had herself to blame for their mockery and impatience. She made it clear that she didn't want to be there. She dragged herself around, sighing heavily whenever she was asked to do something. Nor did she make any effort to hide the fact that she despised Jared for his coarseness. About five foot eleven, he had astute grey eyes in a well-weathered face and unruly hair, which she'd noticed had a broad stripe of silvery-white on the left hand side just above his ear, rather like the Mallen Streak, which he never styled but just rubbed with a towel until it was dry. Nor did he have any interest in clothes but lived in jeans and tee shirts. He couldn't have been more unlike Scott if he had tried. He took great delight in finding things to tease her about and ever since Izzy had made the mistake of confessing to her enormous celebrity crush on Gary Barlow, and had consequently been ribbed mercilessly for it, she learned to keep her mouth shut for fear of providing him with more ammo.

Worst of all was that Izzy never had a minute to herself. She lost track of what was happening in all her favourite soaps — *Corrie, 'Enders, Emmerdale, Neighbours* and *Hollyoaks* — and grumbled incessantly about this.

'What are you chelping about now?' Jared asked. Which annoyed Izzy even further.

Strangely enough, it was a chance incident involving Taryn that gave Izzy a reason to focus. Early one school morning, slumped at the table, feeling teary because she was exhausted from yet another bad night's sleep and missing Scott and London, Izzy couldn't be bothered to listen to Taryn's complaints about breakfast. She didn't want porridge, she didn't want cereal, she didn't want toast and jam. Why couldn't she have a boiled egg? She went on and on, disobeying everyone's instructions to be quiet and eat what she'd been given, until Izzy was so exasperated that she reached behind herself, grabbed a banana from the fruit bowl and lobbed it across the table towards Taryn, who responded by screaming like a murder victim.

'What did you do that for?' Jared yelled, snatching the banana away and hiding it under a placemat.

'To shock her into silence. What's the big deal? It never touched her. I only wanted to snap her out of her snit.'

'Taryn has a fruit phobia,' Jared snapped. 'She's terrified of fruit, including bananas. You probably just nearly gave her a heart attack.'

Izzy refused to repent.

'A fruit phobia? Are you kidding me? She can gallop like a lunatic across country jumping solid wood fences and yet she's scared of a bunch of grapes?' she asked, astonished. At the mention of grapes, Taryn shuddered.

But, because fear, and the restrictions it placed on your life, was something Izzy understood, she made it her mission to try and cure Taryn of her fruit phobia. It shamed her that she'd never noticed that she'd never seen Taryn hold or eat a piece of fruit, not even to give her pony a slice of apple, recalling how on her first day Taryn had fed Jester a carrot.

Determined to do some good for once, she first did some internet research and discovered that Taryn suffered from a form of cibophobia, this being the fear of food, and that it was likely that her fear was a conditioned phobia rather than biologically predisposed. With the first seeds of understanding sown she then spent all her free time reading about deconditioning until her eyes turned to spirals. Start small, all the advice said, and gradually work up until the individual is desensitised and completely cured. It also recommended trying to find a reason for the individual to want to face their fear, such as a benefit or a reward. A plan formed in Izzy's mind. She would begin by encouraging Taryn to look at pictures of fruit, and then touch those pictures without feeling fear. At the same time she sought to make fruit a normal part of Taryn's surroundings by buying her strawberry shaped and flavoured soap and fruit shaped jelly sweets. She then tried to understand why eating, touching or even looking at fruit was such anathema to the little girl.

'It's slimy and gross,' Taryn said, looking nauseous. 'It makes me barf.' Apples were the worst, she said. After a bit of digging it turned out that Taryn had been very sick as a child, after pinching and eating cooking apples, aided and abetted by Carlotta of course, and her phobia hadn't been dealt with because everyone was still grieving about the death of the girls' mother. Instead it had been left to stew for several years.

Izzy's next approach was to make fruit appear useful to Taryn.

'Think how happy your ponies will be when you can give them an apple as a treat. Do you think you could hold a tiny piece out for Jester to take? He loves apples, so how can they be so bad? They never make him sick.' Seeing how much her pony pricked his ears when Izzy approached his stable with a big, juicy apple held in her palm piqued Taryn's interest to such an extent that she agreed to try, something she'd never done before. It was a tiny but satisfying victory.

Progress was slow. Taryn still refused to touch or even be in close proximity to apples and oranges. Nor was she easily conned by fruit that was disguised, such as smoothies, toffee apples or fruit pies drenched in custard. In time Taryn was able to prod small fruits such as cherries and grapes with her finger, shuddering all the while, but was nowhere near able to either hold fruit in her hand or nibble a tiny segment.

Izzy tweaked her tactics, concentrating on creating happy memories of fruit for Taryn. First she showed a cowering Taryn eight Granny Smith segments. Then she gobbled them down before Taryn had time to run away, her cheeks puffed out like a hamster's.

'Are you still scared of the apple? It's inside me now.' Can you put your hand on my tummy?' Reluctantly, Taryn did this. Izzy giggled, pretending that Taryn was tickling her which caused the little girl to giggle also. 'See how close you are to the apple. That's *very* brave. I think that deserves a chocolate biscuit, don't you?' And Izzy left it there, happy with the progress they were making.

On more than one occasion she was aware of Jared's scrutiny during these sessions. Sometimes it was hard; there were tears (on both sides), retributions and consequences, mainly in the form of vomit or hyperventilation attacks. She would have been very surprised to learn how impressed he was with the sweet-natured patience she displayed. Mrs Firth was also in encouragement of Izzy's efforts.

'You couldn't try these methods on her aversion to eating her greens as well, could you?'

'I didn't know she was frightened of veg too,' Izzy said, aghast.

'She isn't. She just doesn't like them.'

And so Izzy expanded her to vegetables too, chattering to Taryn as she helped Mrs Firth prepare Sunday lunch.

'Just imagine sprouts are mini cabbages. Very expensive, exclusive gourmet miniature cabbages. Very popular in Hollywood.' Taryn looked at her with suspicion, but did agree to try one.

Of course, there were times when Izzy was in total agreement with Taryn. Mrs Firth had prepared an enormous stew, filled with root vegetables and light, fluffy dumplings the size of tennis balls. Jared and Izzy, whose appetite had returned with gusto once her body accepted how hard it now had to work, fell on it like starved tigers, ladling great portions onto their plates. Taryn's was the only dissenting voice. She'd noted the presence of leeks in the dish and, raising a forkful so that they hung down, dripping with gravy, declared that they looked like worms and refused to eat them. She pushed the plate away and folded her arms. Only too aware that this was the third consecutive night Taryn had found reason not to eat her dinner, and that she was being closely observed by both Jared and Mrs Firth, Izzy felt panicked.

'It's not worms though, is it, Taryn? It's just lovely, delicious leeks. See?' To prove her point Izzy shovelled in a great mouthful. Unfortunately, she had been able to see Taryn's point. The leeks had indeed taken on the invertebrate, segmented looks of earthworms and, unable to force this image from her mind, Izzy found herself gipping as she chewed.

'Please, Taryn. Eat your dinner like a good girl,' Izzy pleaded. Taryn refused to budge. 'I'll watch *International Velvet* with you tonight,' Izzy bargained, inwardly groaning at the thought of watching the ancient film for the fifteenth time.

'And *Hannah Montana* too?' Taryn said, gimlet-eyed. Oh God, that was even worse! Dejected, Izzy agreed, knowing that she'd been outmanoeuvred yet again. Also aware of this, Jared grinned evilly at her from across the table.

It didn't help that the relationship between Izzy and Taryn wasn't equally weighted. Not having any experience in childcare, Izzy far too often let Taryn have her own way just to avoid having to deal with a tantrum. It had taken Taryn less than a week to realise this and proceeded to run rings round Izzy. On the few occasions that Izzy stood her ground, Taryn would run to Mrs Firth, or worse, Jared, regaling tales of exaggerated woe with the sole intention of having Izzy's decision overruled. It was only due to both long-standing members of the household being wise to Taryn's manipulations and backing Izzy up that Taryn didn't control her completely. An added complication was that, having been brought up in a world where she wanted for nothing, Taryn was difficult to coerce or impress. Having grown up in a household that existed on a budget, Izzy found she couldn't relate easily to Taryn's spoiled nature. On one particularly shaming occasion Izzy offered to loan Taryn her battered iPod for a school trip and was scoffed at for her efforts.

'Yours is crap. Mine's much better than that,' Taryn said bluntly and proceeded to produce a top of the range iPhone complete with apps of every variety. Determined not to be fazed Izzy started to tell Taryn about her childhood Walkman and how it had once been state of the art.

'It would play one tape at a time. If you were lucky you might get maybe ten songs on each side of a cassette if you recorded them off the radio. You had to be quick though otherwise you got the DJ talking as well. You could also buy what they called a pre-record and these had only about five songs on each side. I had a box like a mini suitcase which I carried all my tapes around in it and I was always swapping from one tape to another to listen to my favourite songs.'

'Sounds rubbish. I've got ten thousand songs all in one place,' Taryn said.

'It ran off batteries which never lasted very long because if you wanted to listen to a song more than once you had to fast forward and rewind until you found the right place. Isn't that funny?' Izzy continued, determinedly undeterred.

'Not really. I saw one once… in a museum,' Taryn said, not interested. Izzy felt ancient.

Successful she may have been in helping Taryn face her fruit demons, Izzy had not lost her ability to wreak havoc. Not a day passed that she wasn't yelled at for some misdemeanour or another. Hopelessly forgetful, she was constantly misplacing things but the final straw came when she'd been instructed to turn out Jester and Jet one pleasantly warm mid-March afternoon so they could stretch their legs in the paddock with the other horses. Never having had the responsibility for this before Izzy carefully led them across the yard and into the paddock, ensuring to turn them away from the gate as she removed their headcollars so they couldn't barge back through and raid the oat barrel in the foodstore, as she'd been duly instructed. Alas, she forgot to clip the safety latch on the gate. Jester, who lived up to his name in spades, was a tricky little customer with a Houdini complex and, with his brown and white lip curled, was able to open the gate unless the latch was on. Thrilled at such an unexpected opportunity, he promptly opened the gate and, with a gleeful whinny, cordially invited his equine chums to join him in a jaunt up the village's main street to Philippa's Kitchen where he had often been brought a piece of carrot cake, to which he was especially partial, by the charmingly pretty eponymous proprietress. Quite by unfortunate coincidence, the front gates were also open to allow the coal man to make his monthly delivery. Mouth agape, he had no choice but to back his chubby little body into the gate like a boiled egg in a slicer as, hooves clattering like coconuts on the driveway, all six horses cantered past him, causing his flat cap to be whisked off his sooty globular head by the slipstream.

Bedlam ensued. Within minutes all the phones in The Paddocks rang like a charity hotline as disgruntled gardeners found their lawns covered in hoof marks and their budding blooms and shrubs gnawed away. Worse still, The Tank being in part of heavy horse lineage and therefore having an inbuilt penchant for a bucket of best, had shoved his whiskery ginger face in through the open window of The Half Moon's kitchens and frightened the brassy-haired landlady to screaming conniption. Jared, roaring like a brown bear, tracked Izzy down quite happily reading *Heat* magazine in the kitchen and, instructing her to bring six headcollars and enough pony nuts to fill the village green water trough, tore after them. Sprinting down the drive like a running back he nearly took out the poor coal man, who had just regained his composure. He found Jester and Mini Cheddar frolicking like wood nymphs in the vicarage garden. The Tank had been incarcerated in the pub's barrel store by Col the Landlord, having been tempted in by a packet of pork scratchings, and now could be heard braying indignantly for his freedom from deep within. Ghost, being of inordinately good manners, was merely cropping grass on the village spinster's lawn. Such a gentleman, he'd even thoughtfully relieved himself of a massive shit on her prize roses instead of her lawn. Worst of all were Jet and Vega who, both of uncertain temperament, were working out their ya-yas by terrorising the local duck and coot community round the village pond. Between the flapping of wings and Jared's swearing no one heard Izzy's gulps of laughter.

'Ger'ere, ye brute!' Jared shouted as Jet's face loomed malevolently round the side of a bunch of reeds at a squawking mallard. 'And you can stop laughing,' he yelled at Izzy, who was now holding her sides to ease a stitch.

It took Jared the best part of the afternoon to round them all up by which time Izzy had calmed down sufficiently to be apprehensive about Jared's retribution. Preoccupied, she barely listened to Taryn's continual chatter on the school run and only answered her in monosyllables. Her intention had been to offer profuse apologies as soon as she saw Jared but never got the opportunity. Before she'd even had chance to cross the threshold Jared despatched an agog Taryn to her room before proceeding to tear a landing strip off Izzy.

'The horses could have been lamed, or worse, killed. As it is I'll have to ring for the vet to check them all over. How could you have been so fucking stupid? Anyone'd think you'd been born without a brain like the bloody scarecrow from the Wizard of Oz,' Jared had roared.

'Well, if I'm the scarecrow you're the heartless tin man,' Izzy had screamed back, never one to relinquish the last word. 'How was I supposed to know that Jester was a bleedin' escapologist? Not having been born and raised around horses I wasn't aware that they had the ability to pick locks with their hooves. Maybe that's why they're called bleedin' hoofpicks.'

'Don't be fatuous,' snapped Jared, launching into another tirade, this time colder, his rage unnervingly controlled. 'You're a bloody liability. One more cock up like this and you'll find yourself back on the East Coast Express faster than you can say Gor Blimey!'

# NORTHERN DISCOMFORT

Izzy couldn't believe it! Within a week she was in bother again.

Mrs Firth had trawled all the bedrooms for dirty laundry and had scooped up, together with all the other clothes Izzy had strewn across the shagpile, Scott's smelly tee shirt. After her riding lesson that day, when Izzy dragged herself back to her room bruised and cross after being decanted by Jet several times, she found all her clothes beautifully laundered (creepily, even her pants were ironed) in a neat stack on her bed. With a moan of horror she noticed the distinctive Paul Smith tee shirt in the stack and yanked it out. Her worst fear was confirmed as she held it to her nose and inhaled deeply. She had treasured it for nearly a month but now there was no trace of Scott's scent or the sexy, spicy aftershave he always wore. It had all been eradicated by a 40 degree wash.

Fury fuelled by grief, Izzy stormed downstairs and into the kitchen. The tee shirt was still clutched in her hand.

'How dare you go through my stuff, you interfering old busybody. If I wanted my washing doing I'd bleedin' say so.' Mrs Firth's head snapped round in surprise but, used to

Carlotta's venomous outbursts, wasn't fazed. Uncurtailed, waving the tee shirt like an SOS flag, Izzy continued to rant for several minutes before screaming back out of the kitchen. Jared never stopped eating his lunch but merely observed the outburst in silence.

Gibbering with rage, Izzy logged on to the computer in the study. First she checked her Facebook, then email, scouring the screen for a message from Scott. She scrolled through many, many junk emails interspersed with the occasional email from her sister with myriad attachments of her nauseatingly overachieving nieces and nephews winning trophies and certificates galore. There were no emails from any friends with the exception of a few chain emails sent to her from people who she wasn't really in contact with anymore but they sent her them as a way of making up the numbers so that they wouldn't be besieged with eons' worth of bad luck. Izzy pushed the stark evidence that she didn't really have any friends to the back of her mind, something for her to deal with another time, and instead continued to look with hope for an email from Scott. As usual, there was nothing.

Why hadn't he been in touch? Had the eighteen months they had been together meant so little to him that he had forgotten her already? Miserable, disappointed and still bloody cross about the tee shirt, she began to email Caro, guilty in the knowledge she'd woefully neglected her one friend since her arrival at The Paddocks. Of course, it wasn't like she'd had a lot of spare time. Jared saw to that. Typing like a demon, Izzy found herself pouring out vast paragraphs of pent up misery and spleen about the previous month.

> *Caro-babes! Just a quick email to fill you in on life in Darkest Yorkshire. It's okay, I guess. The gaff is massive and beyond luxurious. Jonty would be well jel! The only problem is I don't have a spare minute to enjoy it. The kid I have to look after, Taryn, is all*

*right I suppose, except she's eight, not a toddler and has more attitude than an X Factor reject. She's quite a good kid — so long as she's doing something she wants to do otherwise she can't half strop. The worst thing is that the thing she always wants to do is ride bloody horses. Honestly, they're all horse mad here. And guess what? I'm expected to ride them too! I know — can you believe it? OMG! Me, on a horse?! I nearly died. In fact, I have nearly died several times over both from fright and from falling off the damn things. I have to have a lesson every... single... day. Jesus! I've never known such pain from aching muscles and I've got a patchwork of bruises all over my body. Nasty, smelly creatures. I don't see the appeal myself.*

*I have my lessons with either the stable girl — Gemma, you'd love her, she's a top laugh and really pretty and the one bit of sanity in the house — or with the gardener (yes, you read it right — the farcking gardener of all things) who is called Jared but I call him bleedin' Hitler. For a gardener he has a pretty big opinion of himself and jackboots around like he owns the place. I don't know how the owner (mysteriously known as MK — get that!) will take it when he comes back. He's still away on business. Not that anyone bothers to tell me where. They all clam up whenever he's mentioned. Of course, everyone else thinks he's the best thing since Creme Eggs but I can't stick him — Jared, that is, not MK. The housekeeper-cook-woman is called Mrs Firth and she idolises him. She's nice enough and a fantastic cook but she's as common as muck with a voice like a metal rasp. Even Gemma thinks he's marvellous. Mind you, she would seeing as she's knocking him off in secret. No one is supposed to know that! He doesn't know that I know either. I bet he'd have a fit if he did. Serve him right too. Conceited pig. He thinks he's God's gift. Believe me, I'd make sure I kept my receipt and exchanged him within 28 days. He's not even that good looking. He has a face more leathery than a fake Gucci handbag and which is in dire need of a facial and is so 'male' it's sickening. He delights in burping and farting and swears like God knows what. So uncouth.*

*Country life is something to behold. It's so quiet, especially at night — and DARK. I can't bear it. I really miss London. Not that anyone here cares. They just expect me to be like the pack of dogs that follow Jared around all the time like the bleedin' Pied Piper. There must be at least half a dozen of them. The house is armed to the teeth but no burglar would be stupid enough to break in for fear of being savaged alive. Either that or Mrs Firth would talk 'em to death or clobber 'em with her rolling pin. Honestly, it's so primitive. Then there's an endless army of cats that like to sleep on clean laundry, leaving hairs everywhere. I found one in my belly button last week — so disgusting. A hair that is, not a cat! LOL! :-) I've spent most of my wages on antihistamines.*

*There's also another kid — Carlotta — who I haven't yet met as she is incarcerated in boarding school. From what I can gather she's as wild as a polecat and is a likely candidate for a custodial sentence. I'm sure boarding school is just a training camp before she gets carted off to one of Her Majesty's hotels. She's another top stunner — and by the sounds of it she doesn't 'alf know it. I'll get to meet her at Easter. Aren't I lucky? (sarcasm).*

*It's not all mediaeval though. Last week Gemma and I had a day off and took one of the cars (there are four: a Golf, a Chelsea tractor, a Beemer and a bleedin' Roller as well as a bloomin' great horsebox the size of a juggernaut) into Leeds. Did you know there's a Harvey Nicks up here? It's not a patch on ours in London but it was better than nothing and I did manage to pick up a GORGEOUS pair of Louboutins. They have some quite decent shops but unfortunately they're all full of Yorkshire people — which does take the shine off somewhat. Anyway, the one good thing is that I don't have any outgoings living here. Grub and lodgings are included in my salary plus I never get to go anywhere to spend any money unless you count the village shop and the local pub. I've never been so well-heeled. Not that I get the chance to wear any heels here. The nearest I've got to footwear glamour is a pair of pink gumboots.*

*Well, I suppose I'd better get back to the grindstone before My Lord and Master finds me something to do. Last week I was expected to muck out a stable. It stank. I've never been so nauseous in my life. I can't wait to come home. Have you seen anything of Scott? I've tried emailing him but I just keep getting an 'undelivered mail' message. Probably the stupid ancient servers they have up here. I've tried to text him as well but I can never get a signal — or a reply. Anyway, email me back with all your news. I'm so bored and lonely up here you wouldn't believe it. :-(*

*Take care of you, Iz xxx*

Just as she was signing off her email and about to press send, Jared appeared in the doorway. Purged by her three page screed to Caro, Izzy was feeling much calmer and turned to face him with an expression of peace. It was wasted on Jared.

'How dare you shout at Mrs Firth,' was his opening line. He then proceeded to bawl her out in no uncertain terms, firstly about her verbal assault on the housekeeper before progressing onto dredging up all her previous misdemeanours and highlighting her many shortcomings in equal measure. As he yelled his eyes kept darting to the screen, picking out the most offensive, insulting sentences of the email until Izzy realised what he was doing and minimised the screen.

'And if you're gonna slag us off it might be an idea to do it a little less ostentatiously,' was his parting shot, slamming the study door behind him.

---

THE FOLLOWING Saturday did not start well for Izzy. She woke to find that her monthly friend had set up shop two days early, catching her on the hop. Since her split from Scott she'd been so ill-tempered and emotional that she hadn't even noticed her PMT. It had simply merged into all her other trauma like a ghost in the mist. With a groan she pulled back the duvet and saw the blood seeping into the fitted bedsheet. Bleedin' hell! She would have to wash and dry it herself. After her little temper tantrum earlier in the week she could hardly ask Mrs Firth for a laundry favour. She dragged off the sheet and chucked it in the base of the shower together with her pyjamas before leaping in herself. The water ran red, like she was purging herself of some heinous bloody murder. Luckily the duvet had escaped unscathed. Aware that she was late for breakfast she dragged the duvet back over the mattress and ran downstairs.

Jared and Mrs Firth were already tucking into poached eggs on toast. Feeling pissy, Izzy slid into her chair and reached for the muesli before Mrs Firth got the chance to ask her if she would like her new favourite breakfast, croque-monsieur, preparing for her. How come the bleedin' woman never bore a grudge?

Taryn was already chattering like a monkey, bombarding Izzy with instructions and requests. Would Izzy help her clean Jester's tack? Could they watch *Harry Potter* that afternoon? Could they go to Pets & Ponies so she, Taryn, could buy some new horse gear? In an attempt to shut out the noise Izzy pulled the cereal box in front of her nose. Taryn's questions continued incessantly. Communicating only through the medium of grunts and snorts, having come to the unhappy realisation she was stuck here, in horse central, for God knew how long, in addition to her abdominal pains and hormonal malfunction, Izzy wasn't prepared to be chipper. She picked at her muesli with a distinct lack of enthusiasm.

Frustrated at Izzy's unresponsiveness Taryn trotted off, a

pack of dogs trailing her for security, to collect the post from the little locked box by the front gate. She returned with a fistful of letters in her hand and a baffled look on her face.

'There's one here for a Miss Isabel Brown,' she said, her forehead furrowed. 'Must have the wrong address.'

'That's me,' said Izzy, her head snapping up. She stretched out her hand to take the letter but Taryn snatched it away.

'You're called Lizzy,' she said, her eight-year-old brain not catching up. Jared, having cottoned on to what had happened, was shaking his head in disbelief.

'I'm called *Izzy*. Please can I have my letter?' Izzy noticed the envelope hadn't been handwritten but was typed and the postage frank was that of Scott's employer. She'd emailed him with her new address in the hope that he would contact her and at last he'd got in touch. Was it too much to hope that he'd missed her horribly and was desperate for her to move back to London and back in with him? If that were the case she would be on the first train to King's Cross before lunchtime. There'd be no more kids, no more dogs and, best of all, no more horses.

'Why did you tell us that your name was Lizzy then?' said Taryn. Izzy was starting to get impatient. God, the child was like a dog with a bone.

'I didn't. You presumed and got it wrong. When Jared met me at the station he was holding up a card that said Lizzy and as I didn't think I'd be here longer than a week I didn't see the point in correcting him. You've all called me Lizzy ever since. Can I *please* have my letter?'

'Nice,' said Jared with considerable sarcasm. 'I'm glad you took this position so seriously.' Even Mrs Firth looked disapproving. She emitted a couple of tuts but refrained from comment. Her silence spoke volumes however. It infuriated Izzy.

'Don't give me that. Not one of you bothered to ask if you had my name right. Taryn, the letter!' So desperate to read it was she, Izzy considered launching herself across the breakfast table.

But Taryn was showing signs of distress. Her breathing was ragged, her individual breaths short and inefficient. Jared set down his spoon, concerned.

'Taryn, are you okay?' he asked. Taryn nodded. She handed over the letter and sat in her chair, bravely trying to use the techniques she'd been taught to regulate her breathing. Izzy accepted the letter without a word of thanks.

'I don't understand why you wouldn't give us your real name,' Taryn muttered. 'I thought we were friends.'

'Oh, for God's sake—' Izzy found herself saying. She knew she was being a bitch but the hormones racing around inside her plus the misery she'd been cooping up were overriding her conscience. Distracted, she ripped open the envelope and scanned the letter. Yes, it was from Scott. Her eyes devoured the contents.

It was typewritten, double spaced and in a large font. Clearly he didn't want to be misunderstood and as she digested the contents Izzy began to understand why. He asked that she please stop trying to contact him. It was over. He advised that he'd changed his mobile number and email account. He had caller ID on his landline and wouldn't answer any call from her. Any voicemails would be deleted without so much as a cursory listen. He wanted a clean break. Well, he'd bleedin' well got one, Izzy acknowledged bitterly. Her heart had cracked cleanly down the middle, with half left behind in London and the other half here in Yorkshire. Also enclosed was Izzy's P45, forwarded from her ex-employers at the law firm and a couple of photocopied bills, both in Scott's name but with a half share calculation scribbled on in red ink. A post-it note asked if she, Izzy, could please pay her share of last quarter's bills? Via cruel postscript he also requested his iPod back.

Jared, Mrs Firth and Taryn were all watching. They saw

Izzy's expression evolve from hope to disbelief before settling on something in between sheer unhappiness and faked nonchalance. She continued to eat her muesli, pretending as though nothing had happened, but couldn't prevent one lone tear from zig-zagging down her cheek and plopping into her cereal. Mortified at such a display of emotion, she propped the Alpen packet up in front of her nose and pretended to read it. Still no one else spoke. And then it was too late. All Izzy's heartbreak and misery decided that now was the time it would purge itself. Huge gulping sobs rose in her throat, aching and painful, until they could be contained no more. In a last ditch attempt to save her dignity she flung the letter and the muesli box across the table and fled.

Jared reached over the table calmly and retrieved the letter from a blanket of oats and raisins before Taryn could get her sticky jam fingers on it. He read it carefully.

*Izzy,* it read. Not Dear Izzy or even Hi Izzy. Just cruel, solitary, impersonal Izzy. Jared raked his eyes over the bills and the P45, which revealed Izzy's tower of lies in one fell swoop. The letter did a pretty good job of being a relationship P45 at the same time. Jared had never read anything so devoid of compassion in his life. Whilst Mrs Firth was busily escorting Taryn to her room for a calming lie down, Jared scooped up all the pieces of paper and exited the kitchen.

---

HAVING flung herself on her bed and sobbed like a madwoman for twenty minutes, Izzy was filled with mortification as she recalled her sharpness with Taryn.

It hadn't been the little girl's fault. Shameful, Izzy went to find Taryn to apologise. She found her lying on her bed reading a battered old copy of *Jill's Gymkhana*. She was quite calm.

'Can I come in?' Izzy asked, tapping lightly on the open

door. Taryn looked at her warily but granted access. 'I want to apologise.'

It was here that Jared found Izzy. She was sitting next to Taryn on the bed, an array of pony books spread out in front of them. Clearly Taryn had forgiven Izzy for her earlier outburst. As Izzy looked up he noticed that her eyes were red raw. Izzy noticed he had Scott's letter in his hand.

'I think we need to have a little talk,' he said, jerking his head towards the door. His face was devoid of expression.

As Izzy clambered off the bed she was overwhelmed by a feeling of impending doom. Was she going to lose this job too? Okay, so it wouldn't have been her first choice for a change of career but the house was more than luxurious and at least it was a decent place to lick her wounds.

Jared led her down to the winter den, closing the door behind him firmly to prevent outside interference or inquisitive ears from eavesdropping. As Izzy eased herself onto one of the squashy sofas Jared spread the letter, the bills and the P45 onto the occasional table. As soon as Izzy clapped eyes on this little array of truth she realised the ramifications of its contents. Her cover story had been blown to smithereens.

'I don't really know where to begin,' said Jared, skimming his eyes from one document to another. 'Clearly there've been a lot of things going on here that we don't know about.'

Izzy retreated into the back of the sofa. She wished she could climb into one of the enormous cushions and zip herself in, away from penetrating eyes and questions, until she'd figured out what she was going to say by way of mitigation.

'Do you want to tell me what's been going on—?' Jared made a show of consulting the letter. '—*Isabel*?' He stared at her, looking her straight in the eye. It made Izzy feel uncomfortable, like she was a criminal. Not knowing what she could possibly say to make the situation better, she remained mute.

'The evidence against you is pretty damning,' Jared continued, interpreting her silence as belligerence. He dealt out all the individual pieces of paper like a deck of cards, slapping them down on the table. Each slap made Izzy jump. 'A P45 from a law firm, *not* a recruitment agency, no mention of the incomparable Oakes family, bills for a flat in Hampstead *not* Marylebone Village and, to top it off, a rather extraordinary letter from someone who has plainly been an important part of your life. You wanna come clean? Who are you and why are you here? Has someone sent you?'

Izzy's eyes slid from left to right. Her heart rate was beating double time, her palms becoming moist. She was eclipsed by an overwhelming urge to run for the door. Over and over again her eyes flickered towards the door handle. Following her erratic gaze, Jared clocked this.

'It's locked. You're not going anywhere until I get some answers. Now, who the fucking hell are you?' More silence. '*Lizzy*! Who… sent… you?'

Izzy burst into sobs. Words began to pour out of her mouth, and then she found she couldn't stop them.

'No one sent me. Well, I suppose Merle Miller did actually. And I'm not Lizzy, I'm Izzy. Isabel Brown. I was a legal secretary in London but I got fired on Valentine's Day after going for a promotion and then I rang my boyfriend and he fired me too because I hadn't got the promotion and booted me out of his flat and I couldn't go back to my own flat because I'd sublet that to someone else when I'd moved in with Scott so I had nowhere to live and I couldn't stay with my parents because they'd just taken in a lodger called Viggo — I think he's Swedish — so I stayed the night at my friend Caro's, but I couldn't stay there for longer than one night because her fiancé hates me and has imposed this stupid rule that I'm not allowed to stay with them for longer than forty-eight hours on pain of death otherwise he'll call off their wedding, and I couldn't find another job anywhere so Caro put me in contact with Merle Miller who she knew because she got her son off a dope charge and, oh my farcking Christ, I shouldn't have told you that. Merle Miller said this was the only job she had going and that I'd be perfect for it but she never mentioned horses or Carlotta not that I think it'd have put me off because I didn't have a home to go to and would have had to sleep under Waterloo Bridge with all the other scratters. I was absolutely desperate. And I didn't lie. You just never bothered to ask me the truth.' Her sobs, temporarily paused by her ramblings, started up again.

Now it was Jared's turn to stare in silence, mouth agape. Eventually he found his voice.

'Do you ever draw for breath? What a dog's breakfast you've cooked for yourself. Jesus, woman, stop that dreadful din. You'll set the dogs off.' Raking in a bureau drawer he found a packet of travel tissues with ponies' heads on them and handed them to Izzy. 'I only got about half of that so, seeing as I really need to get to the bottom of this, I'll ask the questions and you can answer me as lucidly and as *succinctly* as you can. Okay?' Izzy peered at him from over the edge of a tissue. He was still terrifying, the Yorkshire Inquisition, but his tone had softened and his body language was less aggressive. Whereas before he had been perched on the edge of his seat, poised to grab her if she so much as twitched, he was now sat back in the chair, his long legs stretched out in front of him.

'I take it you don't actually have any experience of working with children?'

'Not unless you count the toddler that every man is reputed to keep in his underpants,' Izzy muttered.

'Well, that figures,' said Jared, refusing to be shocked. 'I think we'd best start from the top—'

Jared then proceeded to grill her about her previous jobs,

her family, her childhood, Caro and finally her relationship with Scott. How long had they been together? Why had it ended? Izzy found herself recounting the whole sordid tale, the cancelled Valentine's plans, her ignominious dumping in Jimmy Tarbuck's.

'And yet he still let you pay for his coffee?' Jared asked. Izzy nodded. 'What a tool. Sounds like you're well shut of him.'

'He could be very nice,' Izzy protested, although at that precise moment in time she was having some problems recalling any evidence of that.

'Sure, sure, none of us choose to live with monsters, liars and lunatics from the outset. Those revelations come later, when it's too late. So, your relationship went tits up and you lost your home to boot. That's tough to deal with. A relationship I was in broke down just over eighteen months ago so I can appreciate how hard it can be.' He didn't elucidate further. 'And what's this about an iPod?'

'Scott won an iPhone at a corporate event. He kept that one but gave me his old Nano because I'd broken mine.'

'Dare I ask how?'

'I dropped it in a mug of tea,' Izzy said, cringing.

'How…? Never mind. Knew it was a mistake to ask—' Jared said. 'Had he loaned you the iPod or given you it?'

'He said I could keep it. He said it was no use to him as it needed a new battery and had a cracked screen. He said he could've sold it on eBay but he'd only have got peanuts because it was so battered, so he gave it to me.'

'And now he's asking for it back? What a prince,' Jared said. His quick grin was judgemental rather than mirthsome. 'So, Izzy Brown, what are we going to do with you?'

'I can be gone by the end of the day. Please don't call the police. I never meant to deceive anyone.'

'What are you babbling about now?'

'Well, aren't you going to send me back?' Izzy was flabbergasted.

'Good Lord, no. We've only just got used to your little foibles. At least I now know what all the pissing and moaning was about. No wonder you've had such a miserable little face, lugging that around with you all the time. Plus, I can't think of any good reason to replace you with some other crackpot, especially as we've just spent two weeks getting you cantering on the right leg. Besides, Taryn likes you and, despite your quite astonishing capacity for disaster, you're not bad at your job. We'll consider it a new project: how to turn Izzy into a normal, functioning adult.'

Izzy simply gaped. This wasn't what she'd expected. She'd thought she was in for a bollocking and instead Jared had been understanding and surprisingly empathic.

'I will have to make some enquiries about your identity, you understand? Any objections if I contact this Caro? I presume she is an actual barrister and that was the one piece of truth in the entire fairytale?'

'You can contact her through the Inner Temple,' Izzy muttered.

'Go on with you then. You might be heartbroken but you're not getting out of your riding lesson this morning. Jodhpur up, Izzy Brown. It's pony time.'

Izzy groaned out loud then stopped when she saw Jared scooping up all the pieces of paper Scott had sent.

'What are you doing with my letter? Give it to me.'

'What? And have you brooding over it all week. No chance. It's going somewhere where you can't pore all over it, reading in between the lines for things that aren't there. Trust me, it's for your own good.'

'But what about the bills?'

'I'll deal with them.'

Izzy bristled. 'I can pay for my own bills myself.'

'Who said anything about paying them?' Jared said,

looking up in surprise. 'He wanted to live by himself therefore he can pay for these his bloody self. Nowt to do with you, your name's not on them.'

'What about his iPod?'

'He can whistle for that, an' all. Cheeky sod.'

'He won't like that.'

Jared shrugged.

'If he wants it back that badly he can come and ask me for it.'

---

AFTER A MODERATELY SUCCESSFUL RIDING LESSON, mainly because Jared was still feeling fluffy about Izzy's circumstances, Izzy was instructed to have a hot bath and a night off from entertaining Taryn. He would take Taryn and Mrs Firth to the cinema on this one occasion providing Izzy would be happy staying in the house on her own. The dogs would be there so she should be safe enough. Izzy welcomed the alone time, settling into bed to watch telly and eat warmed-up lasagne followed by far too many chocolate bars for one day's consumption.

Just before eleven Mrs Firth tapped on the door of Izzy's room and poked her head round to find Izzy in her pyjamas watching one of Carlotta's chick flick DVDs, surrounded by tissues and chocolates. Mrs Firth was brandishing the best cure for misery she knew: a cup of hot tea.

'We're back, love. Taryn's asleep in bed already. Bless her, she conked out no sooner than we'd left the cinema car park. Jared filled me in on your situation on the way home. At least it's all out in the open, love. You can settle in proper now. We look after each other in this house. We've had to. You'll be one of us in no time.'

Izzy accepted the tea with a small smile. 'Thanks.'

'Things'll get better from now on. You'll see.'

And they did.

Once her double life had been revealed Izzy found it much easier to settle at The Paddocks. If nothing else, Jared and Mrs Firth understood why she had wobbly moments and were more prepared to be sympathetic. They also no longer had to wonder about her introspective moments or whether or not she was unhappy at The Paddocks because of something they'd done. Not that Izzy chose to talk about Scott. Deeply ashamed of the debacle she'd made of her life, for the first time in her memory she kept her unhappiness to herself. Certainly, there were periods of sadness but she never spoke of their cause, simply referring to her split with Scott as 'stuff'. Jared and Mrs Firth respected this and, despite mocking and taunting her for all her inanities and mistakes, Jared never tormented her about her broken relationship. After the initial upset between Izzy and Taryn their friendship returned to normal with the exception that Taryn continued to call Izzy Lizzy, much to Izzy's irritation. Worse still, Taryn began to correct herself and began to call her Lizzy Izzy, which then prompted Jared to call her Dizzy Izzy, Bizzy Lizzy and various other alternatives which drove Izzy to despair.

''Cause I've never heard any of those before.'

---

JARED DID INDEED TRACK down Caro and enjoyed a twenty-minute conversation with her on the intricacies of Izzy's personality. Unbeknownst to Izzy, Caro had given her bloody good press, telling Jared how she was very kind-hearted at her core, despite her capacity for chaos, and stressing, in no uncertain terms, how she was better off far away from 'that arsehole Scott'. Jared was uncharacteristically chipper when he reported back to Izzy, who in turn was astonished to find herself watching Jared as he spoke, noticing that he had a beautiful mouth. Upon first impression it had appeared to be in a grim, straight line, almost morose, but it actually curled up at the sides as if slightly sardonic.

'I've spoken to your buddy and it's all sorted. I found a picture of her on the internet. She's a handsome lass, isn't she? Lovely red hair. Seems nice.'

'Everyone thinks so,' Izzy said, noncommittally. She didn't want to think about her perfect friend notching up yet another admirer. At least Caro had smoothed over the great walloping mess she'd made.

'How on Earth a madwoman like you has managed to keep such an intelligent person as a friend all these years is a mystery to me,' Jared added, unflatteringly.

Coming clean about Scott also seemed to improve her relationship with Gemma, who displayed a degree of relief that Izzy was pining for her ex and not setting her crash cap at Jared on the rebound.

Gemma was a likeable character. Very down to earth, her style was plain, boot-cut jeans, funky, colourful trainers and fitted shirts in pretty floral prints and simple cowgirl plaid. She very rarely wore a great deal of make-up, often only putting on a flick of mascara and a dash of clear lipgloss. Izzy, even with all her designer clothes, high heels and cosmetics, felt that she simply couldn't compare and envied Gemma her seemingly effortless flair. She was the epitome of the girl next door.

Gemma's daily routine was to arrive at The Paddocks early Wednesday through Sunday in order to muck out, groom and clean tack. After that she would exercise the larger horses and perhaps lunge Vega. Izzy would be subjected to her riding lesson, instructed either by Gemma or Jared, during the afternoon. Once Taryn returned from school she would have her riding lesson. Weekends meant hacks in the daylight, but not yet for Izzy. Gemma had Mondays and Tuesdays off as her 'weekend' and on these days Izzy was expected to help Jared with the stable chores. Gemma often invited Izzy to join her on her days off. They went for afternoon drives out to market towns or over to the coast. Izzy snatched at these invitations as it meant reprieve from a riding lesson or from chores.

As Gemma wasn't insured for the cars at The Paddocks, it mostly fell on Izzy to swing by her house in Greater Ousebury and pick her up. The first time she did so, Izzy was surprised to see Gemma's terraced property was in a state of disrepair. The front garden had waist high grasses and was accessorised by four bulging bin bags dumped next to the weed-ridden pathway. The front gate was hanging off its hinges. The pale blue paint on the door was chipped and peeling, as was the paintwork on the window ledges. The windows themselves were filthy. It didn't seem to suit Gemma's pernickety nature somehow, Izzy thought, mentally picturing how neat and tidy the groom insisted on the stable yard being kept.

The upstairs curtains, faded and unironed, were still drawn. Taking this as an indication that Gemma had slept in, Izzy was just about to toot her horn when Gemma came flying out of the house.

'I'd invite you in but my brother is staying with me for a few weeks. He's still asleep.'

'A brother? Is he as pretty as you?'

'No!' said Gemma, somewhat abruptly. Izzy didn't know how to respond. She'd only asked out of politeness, and maybe a little bit because there was such a dearth of available attractive young men kicking about the village. 'What I mean is, he is but he doesn't have much time for relationships because he's always moving around so much. He mainly does shift work. He mostly works down south but sometimes the work brings him up here,' Gemma backtracked hastily, realising how rude she had sounded.

'Sounds a bit like me,' Izzy said, laughing.

Every time after that all Izzy had to do was pull up to the kerbside and Gemma raced out of the house, leaving Izzy wondering if her brother was the bossy type. She never spoke about him and Izzy learned not to pursue the topic.

Taryn adored Gemma but Jared didn't seem thrilled by the newfound friendship between Izzy and Gemma, and mobbed Izzy about it on every possible occasion.

'Who else am I supposed to socialise with?' Izzy stormed. 'I can't exactly compare sex tips with Taryn or Mrs Firth, perish the thought.' Jared looked horrified at the prospect and never mentioned it again. Not that sex was an issue, Izzy thought sourly as she watched Jared depart.

---

THREE WEEKS LATER, on the first of April, more post arrived for Izzy in the form of birthday cards from her parents, her sister and Caro. Watched by three inquisitive pairs of eyes, Izzy felt obliged to open them at the breakfast table. The fact that she was now twenty-nine and only three hundred and sixty-four days away from the big three-o plunged her into depression. It no longer came as any surprise to Izzy that there was no sign of a birthday card from Scott.

'Why didn't you tell us?' Mrs Firth asked, her dismay apparent. Later that day, once the dinner plates had been loaded into the dishwasher, she proudly presented Izzy with a sponge cake filled with whipped cream. It was topped with candles.

'Please don't sing,' Izzy said, embarrassed.

'No bloody intention of,' said Jared, looking horrified at the mere suggestion.

'Make a wish,' instructed Taryn. Jared and Izzy's eyes met across the cake. His gaze was unwavering as she blew them out. He knows, thought Izzy in panic, he knows that I'm wishing to get out of here. To add to her confusion was the sneaking suspicion she might still be asked to leave on the basis of her idiocy. Only the previous day she had been subjected to a telling off having dropped dog kibble all over the kitchen floor.

'Oh, well done, Chas 'n' Dave,' Jared had said scornfully, reverting to one of his many nicknames for Izzy.

The tiny pieces of biscuit had scattered in all directions like a panicked crowd in a bombscare. Individual pieces sought refuge under tables, chairs and electrical appliances. The dogs were demented as they tried to retrieve them with flexed paws. Steptoe's face was alight with joy. This was the best game *ever*! Afterwards, several pools of textured dog vomit appeared dotted round the house

As punishment, Izzy was given the chore of bathing the dogs.

'Don't forget to brush their teeth and empty their anal glands,' Jared added as he walked out of the door. Izzy was sure she heard him snigger.

It became apparent that Jared had a mental scale on which he graded Izzy's inanities. The higher her mark, the more exacting he was during her riding lessons. As a consequence her progress was remarkable, but she paid with aching muscles.

Cold, tired and sore after a particularly gruelling session on the merits of trotting twenty metre circles — 'not ovals, it's not Easter yet' — Izzy stomped into the kitchen still in her boots and coat, which was forbidden, for some half time refreshment.

'Bleedin' slavedriver,' she muttered to no one in particular as she yanked a can of Coke out of the fridge. Mrs Firth, busily ironing in the utility room, stuck her head round the door.

''Ello, love. Nice riding lesson?'

Izzy grimaced.

'I feel violated. I'm sure Jared was a sergeant-major in a former life.'

'Don't know about that, love, but he was a captain in this one,' Mrs Firth said. 'Pass us that tin of starch will you? Thanks.'

'*What*!?'

'Oh, hasn't he told you? Jared used to be in the military before he became a gardener? Mind you, he doesn't like talking about it so I'm not surprised he didn't tell you.' With no intention of elucidating further, Mrs Firth disappeared back into the utility leaving Izzy standing by the open fridge with her mouth agape.

Izzy digested this information. It should have been obvious really. The straight-backed march, the imperious orders and the fact he thought he was the boss of everyone.

Mrs Firth reappeared with her arms full of empty coat hangers. Izzy had plonked herself down at the table, still in her waxed jacket.

'You still 'ere? Well, don't be sitting inside with yer coat on or you won't feel t'benefit,' Mrs Firth instructed her. Izzy stared at her as though she'd spoken in tongues. 'And were you born in a barn? Shut fridge doo-er behind ye when ye've been in it!'

All of which left Izzy deliberating not only over Jared's newly revealed military career but also whether Mrs Firth had been deployed as his second in command.

---

IT WAS ONLY a matter of time before Izzy began to appreciate the perks of living at The Paddocks. Mrs Firth was as reliable as daybreak. The house ran like clockwork. Delicious meals appeared on the dinner table at the end of each busy day as if by magic. Bedding and towels were changed with weekly regularity and dirty clothes were scooped up off the floor only to be returned, laundered and ironed, the next day. Izzy would return to her bedroom after a long day of chores to find her clean clothes left on the bed, like hotel freebies, with edges that looked like they had been measured with a set square. It was only when she ventured outside and saw her own cotton knickers, the same mucky-white as chewed gum and with great gaping holes where the elastic had torn from the fabric, blowing merrily in the breeze on the whirligig, that she was forced to consider that there were also downsides to such an efficient service.

'Extraordinary pants,' said Jared, circumnavigating them in fascination. 'They remind me of the old rags my granny used to clean her back step. The only way she could get them clean was to soak them overnight in a bucket of bleach in the back yard. She might have had a problem with these though.' Feeling humiliated and victimised, Izzy stropped off in a huff. If she'd always had matching bras and knickers would it have prevented Scott from going off her? He had once bought her some saucy underwear and then had been furious because she'd only worn them once. They had looked pretty enough in the tissue paper but in actuality had been hell to wear. Uncomfortable to the point of distraction, they'd been cut to cover only half the cheek and had constantly ridden up Izzy's arse. She preferred simple cotton knickers that stayed put and kept your bum warm when you were wearing hold ups. Nevertheless, she did make a mental note to buy herself some new pants on her next shopping spree with Gemma.

As more time passed, Izzy began to feel more at home. Her daily riding lessons were bearing fruit, she could now rise to the trot on the correct diagonal and canter one lap of the manége quite happily. She was even starting to bond with Jet, who pricked his velveteen black ears when she approached and no longer tried to bite her bottom as she clambered up into the saddle. She was making great progress and in a couple of weeks she could start jumping, Jared took great glee in informing her. She was a natural, he told her. Having never been a natural at anything, except perhaps being a natural fool, Izzy found this hard to accept.

There were still difficulties. Izzy had problems remembering all the terminology associated with equitation.

'This is a surcingle,' Jared explained as he taught Izzy how to put on a New Zealand rug.

'A what? A sur-sinkel?'

'Sur-*single*. As in single bed. It goes round the horse's belly to keep the rug secure.'

'I don't know why they can't just call 'em straps.'

Nor did it help that Jet was a naughty pony at his core and soon learned that Izzy's seat was still insufficiently secure to keep her in the saddle and thus developed the habit of putting his head between his own knees like a fainting victim. The inevitable consequence was that Izzy would somersault over his head. After this had happened several times Gemma decided that more work needed to be done on keeping Izzy aboard.

'You must sit back, and sit deep. If you feel his head dropping, give him a boot in the sides. That makes him pay attention to you instead of concentrating on mischief.'

There was so much to take in. Izzy learned how to find her way around the village on foot, gradually becoming familiar with the street names. The main thoroughfare was Cherry Tree Avenue, a broad, straight road which formed the backbone of the village, and which, once it had passed the gates to The Paddocks, funnelled off to a single carriage lane that snaked deep into the Vale of Loxley, past a couple of hamlets that were nothing more than mere gatherings of houses, remote and isolated. Back at the other end of the village, and at right angles to Cherry Tree Avenue, was Loxley Road or 'top road', as it was colloquially known, and which led to Greater Ousebury to the left and into Loxley to the right. From Cherry Tree Avenue one could turn off to the right, down School Lane, a slim and quiet road lined with pretty cottages. Further along was Back Lane, which ran alongside The Half Moon. On the opposite side of Cherry Tree Avenue, Church Lane led off to the left between the church and Philippa's Kitchen and led down to the recently renovated Rookery, a stunning, turreted Victorian Gothic manor encircled by a high, red brick wall. Once considered to be the requisite haunted house of the village courtesy of its dilapidated state and overrun grounds, it had been bought by Philippa herself together with her husband, Drew, and had been completely overhauled.

'It's stunning inside. God knows how they paid for it. Rumour has it they won the lottery,' Jared told Izzy one afternoon as they walked the dogs past it. 'The husband is the village celebrity too. He has his own magic and hypnotism show on one of the lesser known Sky channels. Decent bloke. Always stumps up for a round or two whenever he's in The Half Moon. Wife's bloody good looking too. Lovely red hair.'

Izzy was beginning to think Jared had a thing for redheads. It was the second time he'd used that phrase in the past two weeks. And then there was his entanglement with Gemma. They walked on, all the dogs gambolling ahead of them. They were all off lead, Jared being so confident that he could call them to heel with a single whistle if necessary.

Church Lane ambled alongside the river Lox which ran all the way across the county, into Loxley. Church Lane eventually rejoined Loxley Road halfway between the two Ouseburys.

Izzy's favourite part of the village was The Green. A scalene triangle of lush green grass enclosing a disc of reed-edged pond, like some fiendish trigonometry equation, it was edged along its hypotenuse by a terrace of half a dozen alms cottages. Two storey and each one painted a different pastel colour, they reminded Izzy of model village cottages. She loved their little cottage gardens and the way that ivy and wild roses crept up their multi-coloured front elevations, their long, leafy fingers seeming to cling possessively to the beauty they contained.

The surrounding villages were just as stunning and rural in equal measures. A car was essential. However, not used to driving in London because she always took the Tube, Izzy was appalled to find herself having to navigate single track country roads, horses and tractors and, on one occasion, even a flock of sheep. Jared encouraged her to take the Golf, which was the smallest car in the garage. Izzy, being a somewhat rubber-burning driver at the best of times, barrelled round the country lanes like a shiny silver pinball, often bouncing off hedgerows and verges along the way.

Taryn thought Izzy's driving was marvellous and whooped her on with gusto until the day a low flying pheasant rolled up the bonnet and the windscreen, leaving feathers sticking in the wipers like a fancy dress costume then scraping the paintwork off the car's roof with its tridactylous claws before bouncing off to the rear with an outraged 'craw'. This startled Izzy to such an extent that she physically ducked, taking her hands off the steering wheel in order to clamp them over her eyes.

'Farck-ing hell!'

The car promptly tobogganed into a hedge and both Taryn and Izzy were winded by the airbags deploying.

Jared hit the roof. Izzy had never seen him so furious. He raged on and on about how she could have killed Taryn and how was he supposed to explain that to MK?

'Don't mind about me,' Izzy finally snapped. 'I got bashed up too. It was hardly my intention to prang the car.' Jared merely stared at her in astonishment before muttering something about her first priority being the girls before stalking off. Izzy retreated to her bedroom, gibbering with rage.

After that Jared insisted on accompanying Izzy on a

couple of school runs. He was astonished to discover Izzy drove like a rally driver, windows down, radio blaring and quite prepared to tell anyone else on the roads what she thought of their driving.

'Those yellow blinky-blinky things on the side of your car are called indicators because they *indicate* to other drivers where you're going. You might want to try using them from time to time, you farcking stupid old fart!'

Worse still…

'Get out of the bleedin' way, you old bastards!' she screeched as a car full of cauliflower tops (who later turned out to be the vicar's wife and sisters out on a pensioners' treat) held her up on the top road out of Nether Ousebury. Even Jared, who having once been a trooper could indeed swear like one, was shocked.

To add insult to potential injury, she left the Golf in a shocking state with Rolos and Flakes melted into the fabric interior and sticky Coke stains on the foot mats from not-quite-empty cans as they rolled from side to side as she flung the little car round country lanes. Wrappers piled up like landfill on the back seat.

'It's hardly a good example to show Taryn, is it?' Jared asked bleakly before ordering Izzy to clean it up. Muttering, Izzy found herself equipped with a Henry Hoover and a can of cockpit shine.

If Jared was banking on Taryn paying much attention to Izzy's actions he was sadly mistaken. The little girl had worries of her own. Two weeks before the end of term it occurred to her that Carlotta was due home soon. This seemed to unnerve her to a disturbing extent. A series of minor strops and tantrums culminated in Taryn throwing a mega wobbler one Sunday afternoon.

She huddled into the corner of Jester's stable and refused to come inside for her bath. Nothing Izzy said would convince her otherwise. Eventually she lost her rag, yelling at

Taryn that she would drag her inside by the scruff of her neck if she didn't start being more obedient.

'Don't touch me, or I'll ring Childline and tell them you're abusing me.'

Izzy may have been prepared to put up with such nonsense but Jared wasn't. He marched round the corner and, without so much as a pause, scooped up a kicking and yelling Taryn under his arm and carried her into the house.

'You go ahead and report me,' Jared said in response to Taryn's continued threats and warnings. 'Then Social Services will come and take you away and put you in a children's home where there are no dogs and cats, or larders filled with delicious food, and definitely no ponies.' It took only seconds for Taryn to digest this, and shut up.

As it turned out Taryn's worries had been misplaced.

Later that same day, Izzy helped Mrs Firth bring in the washing as dark, pewter clouds threatened immediate heavy rain. High above them starlings were performing an intricate aerial ballet. They were much prettier in flight than they were on the ground.

'It's a mucky day,' said Mrs Firth, glancing up at the sky. 'Best get these in now.'

As they walked back into the house three magpies shot out of the perimeter hedge. Taryn always called them mag-a-pies, Izzy was astonished to find herself thinking.

'Three for a girl,' Mrs Firth said, counting them. 'Not as good as two but better than one.'

Back in the kitchen they found Taryn dancing from foot to foot, the cordless phone in her hand. She looked half thrilled, half terrified.

'Carlotta's coming home a week early. Queen Vicky's have left a message saying they've suspendered her because she fell out with another girl. She can't go back until after Easter and can someone go and pick her up?'

# CARLOTTA

Carlotta, it transpired, had done a great deal more than 'fall out' with one of her fellow schoolmates. Jared spent forty-five minutes discussing Carlotta's misdemeanours with her headmistress on the telephone before setting off in the Range Rover to collect her.

Having ensured Taryn was safely seconded in front of *Finding Nemo* in the TV room, so her little ears wouldn't hear things they shouldn't, Jared briefed Mrs Firth and Izzy on the chain of events that had led to the suspension before he left.

Carlotta had taken offence to a comment made by a fellow student called Ceridwen Jones, who she classed as her greatest enemy, during a riding lesson and had pulled her off her pony. A catfight had ensued. Jared didn't expound on what the comment had been but went on to explain that the fracas had flared up again in the dorm that night and the end result was that Carlotta had seized a pair of art scissors and hacked off the other girl's bum-length blonde plait at shoulder length whilst pinning her down in a wrestling move. Bedlam had ensued with the newly-scalped girl running screaming to the headmistress and parents being telephoned. Threats of legal action and demands of expulsion were made. Only because MK was considerably better off than the injured girl's parents and the fact that Carlotta had pleaded provocation had the sentence been reduced to suspension until the start of the summer term plus daily detention for the remainder of the academic year upon her return.

Jared returned three hours later with a petulant, unrepentant Carlotta and a car full of luggage, bin bags of dirty laundry and holiday homework she had no intention of doing. The first thing she did upon returning home was raid the fridge. The second thing was to ask how soon they could see their father as she urgently needed to speak to him.

'What about?' asked Jared, suspicious. Carlotta was suddenly animated.

'Nicola Ward at school — she's head girl — is being forced to sell her showjumper because her parents are getting divorced. They've got to sell their house and buy two smaller ones, neither of which have stables, so all their horses are going. She's absolutely gutted. Isn't it marvellous?'

'Well, not for Nicola Ward, I should imagine,' Jared said with considerable wryness.

Carlotta waived his comment aside.

'So, I want to buy him. He's a six-year-old grey called Polo, 16.1 and not a black hair on his body, absolutely pure white. Jumps like a grasshopper and never refuses. He's just been selected for the Equine Pathway 'cause he won the National Six Year Old Championship, so he's a bit pricey. But, given the right rider, i.e. me, he could be the next Milton and I could be the most famous girl showjumper in Britain,' Carlotta said, in between bites of a tuna sandwich. Whereas Taryn still had the slightest hint of a Yorkshire accent, Carlotta's had been thrashed out of her from years of prep and boarding school. Now she spoke with a sharp, clipped tone that held more than a hint of sarcasm and disdain. She turned to Mrs Firth who was tutting as she cleared away Carlotta's mess. 'Any crisps?' It was at this point that she noticed Izzy, who was sitting quietly at the kitchen table.

'Well, well, well. What's this? The new supernanny?' Carlotta drawled, circling Izzy like a hungry coyote. Izzy, who was used to being harassed by drunks and lunatics on the Tube, stared back, unfazed. This surprised Carlotta, who was more than adept at unnerving and intimidating people much older and wiser than herself, so much that she was stunned into temporary silence. This gave Izzy a few moments to study her new charge.

Having only seen Carlotta in a couple of framed photos, Izzy was amazed anew by her beauty. She was already taller than Izzy and, whereas Izzy was skinny and always gave the impression of being rather frayed at the edges, Carlotta even at fifteen had the same sleek, well groomed, well-fed air as the little show ponies Taryn drooled over in *Horse and Hound*. Because she was on the cusp of childhood and adulthood, Carlotta's skin was blighted by the odd well-concealed blemish but nevertheless it was evident to all that she was going to be graced with smooth, clear, luminous olive skin once she matured fully. Her hair was the same midnight-blue-black as Taryn's but was styled in long, flowing layers that ebbed and flowed down to the waist. Izzy idly wondered how Carlotta would feel if someone lopped her gorgeous locks off in a fit of temper. Furious black eyes darted round the kitchen, looking for something to criticise, terrorise or claim. Full, Jolie-esque lips alternated between a pout and a snarl.

'I'm going for a ride,' she snapped and stalked from the kitchen.

On the following day Jared whisked Carlotta and Taryn away to meet up with their father who, unusually but by happy coincidence, he explained, was staying within travelling distance. Both girls looked unrecognisable in dresses and smart shoes. Mrs Firth was subdued as she waved them off.

'A father should be at home with his children,' she said as she manoeuvred an enormous shoulder of lamb into the Aga. 'He shouldn't be—' she stopped herself, '—away so much.'

Izzy enjoyed a rare afternoon of peace. She treated herself to an uninterrupted bath and pamper and then settled to watch a DVD from the vast selection available. What a luxury to watch a film that wasn't rated U. Best of all, there was no riding lesson.

Taryn and Carlotta were brought back home in the early evening. Both were subdued. Taryn was tearful. Carlotta expressed her misery through the medium of pure rage. She stormed round the house in a blind fury, breaking things (other people's, never her own), complaining and generally making a nuisance of herself until Jared banished her to her bedroom. Only the threat of her entry form for the Great Yorkshire Show being shredded prevented absolute disobedience.

Taryn, being more sensitive than her sister, seemed more badly affected by the excursion. Exhausted from several hyperventilation attacks, she was despatched immediately to her bedroom for supper on a tray and an early night.

Devoid of appetite, Taryn diluted her chicken soup with tears.

'I just want Papa to come home and live with us again. I miss him so much.'

Sniffing, retching on any spoonful that managed to reach her mouth, she pushed her spoon round the bowl, her face portraying such abject misery that Izzy, sitting beside her on top of the bedclothes, could hardly bear it.

'You don't have to eat that if you don't want to,' she said softly. Childhood memories of having being forced to eat food she didn't want were still all too clear.

'Firthie said I had to,' Taryn stammered between stifled

sobs, still stirring. 'Every last bit and that it would do me good.'

'What Mrs Firth doesn't know she can't punish us for,' Izzy said, sliding the tray away from Taryn's lap. 'Do you want your chocolate bar or not?' After some thought, Taryn took the bar and placed it on her bedside cabinet. Izzy looked around, her gaze falling on the doorway to the en suite. Down the sink would be the simplest method of disposal but then, as she heard a scraping at the door, why should the soup go to waste?

Taryn even managed a small grin as they watched Steptoe lapping up the last of the soup straight from the bowl. He even wolfed down the brown bread roll, ingesting it in great gulping swallows. Then, smacking his chops, he proceeded to wipe his face on Taryn's comforter and belched before disappearing out of the door.

'No one need ever know,' Izzy whispered conspiratorially as Taryn wriggled down under the bedclothes.

'Will you stay with me for a while?' Taryn asked.

'Of course. Do you want to read?' Taryn didn't. Within ten minutes she was asleep.

Empty tray in hand, sneaking out by the dim pink light of Taryn's *Little Mermaid* nightlight, Izzy encountered Jared on the landing. Angry, thumping dance music emanated from behind Carlotta's bedroom door across the hall, together with a few random bangs and clatters.

'MK wasn't keen to buy the showjumper?' Izzy asked. Jared gave a slow nod.

'She didn't take it well. Let's leave it at that. Pub?'

A muffled sob could be heard from inside Taryn's bedroom. Izzy shook her head.

'I'd rather stay,' she said. 'The meeting with her father has upset her terribly. I'd be very surprised if she slept through.' Jared gave her an unfathomable, searching look. He took the tray from her. Sometimes he could be so gentlemanly.

'Bottle of wine, then—'

As they made their way downstairs they were met by Mrs Firth. She was the picture of indignation. In her hand was a bucket of detergent and a jay cloth.

'That bloody dog of yours has sicked up chicken soup all over the hall rug. How the devil he got hold of it I'll never know,' she fumed. Jared handed the tray back to Izzy, eyebrows raised slightly to indicate that he knew precisely how Steptoe had obtained the soup.

'You're on your own, sweetheart.'

And then, of course, Izzy reflected crossly as she faced a very irate Mrs Firth, sometimes he could be an absolute git.

---

CARLOTTA'S ARRIVAL completely altered the dynamic of the house. Suddenly there was tension, mainly caused by her incessant tantrums. Whereas Taryn only stropped when she wasn't getting her own way, Carlotta went out of her way to aggravate and annoy. She raged like an inferno about anything and everything. Taryn became introverted, torn between sheer terror of her elder sister and a grudging admiration, and clung to Izzy like a limpet. Izzy, used to being the protected rather than the protector, wrestled with unfamiliar feelings.

Both Jared and Mrs Firth, as Carlotta's official guardians in her father's absence, were twitchier, because they knew of what trouble she was capable.

Needing constant entertainment, Carlotta had a nasty habit of sloping off whenever she chose and this drove them to distraction.

'Where's Carlotta?' became Jared's new catchphrase. 'Honestly, she's harder to keep track of than the Scarlet fucking Pimpernel.'

'She's a teenager,' Izzy said in exasperation. 'She's just

doing what teenage girls do. Besides, what harm can she come to stuck out here in the back of beyond anyway? Worried she'll be mobbed by a herd of particularly aggressive sheep? Leave her to her own devices and she'll be fine. What's it to you, anyway? You're not her keeper.'

Jared merely glowered at her.

If Carlotta was aware that Izzy had stuck up for her, she certainly didn't show it. Instead she treated Izzy like a servant, barking out orders and being disrespectful in general.

Nor was it until Carlotta came home that Izzy fully appreciated how neurotic Taryn was. Quite a happy child when left to her own devices, Taryn was clearly unhinged by Carlotta's presence, becoming more demanding and whinging. Nor did Carlotta do anything to help. She seemed to derive great pleasure in tormenting her younger sister, revealing a cold, cruel streak which Izzy found unsettling. She booby trapped Taryn's bed with satsumas and even went to the trouble of making an intricate mobile out of grapes and kiwi fruit to hang in Taryn's room despite claiming to not have any time to do her chores. On other occasions she simply rolled blood oranges across the kitchen floor to where Taryn was seated. Taryn responded by screaming as though it were a hand grenade rather than a citrus fruit. Each time the end result was that Taryn had to be dispatched to her room for a calming lie down. One morning Izzy, aware all the good work she had done in getting Taryn less afraid of fruit had been reversed, finally lost her rag and yelled at Carlotta to stop but this just egged her on.

'You can't tell me what to do. You're just the help,' she said, juggling two Braeburns and a peach as she spoke as if to highlight how much she didn't pay attention to anything Izzy said.

'I can ring your father and tell him how you're tormenting your sister,' Izzy replied.

'Do,' said Carlotta rudely. 'He only shares a phone with sixty other people. Good luck getting through.'

Izzy looked confused. Jared intervened and Carlotta stropped off.

'That child is vile,' Izzy complained furiously, expecting Jared to sympathise with her. He didn't.

'That child is one of the reasons you have a job. If it weren't for her you wouldn't have a roof over your head and would be sleeping rough under Waterloo Bridge eating bakery leftovers and drinking cheap booze out of a brown paper bag. Yes, she can be trying, but she's a confused teenager with an absent father and no mother. She's bound to have some issues and it wouldn't hurt you to remember that and show a little understanding. So let's have less from you.'

He stalked away leaving Izzy spitting with fury.

Heading upstairs with the intention of rounding up any dirty laundry Izzy discovered that Carlotta had wreaked more havoc. Arms full of reeking jodhpurs, Izzy found Taryn in her en suite holding two halves of a soap bar in her hands.

'Carlotta broke it in half. I hate her. She knew it was my favourite,' Taryn said. Izzy took the pieces from Taryn and set them in the dish. They looked rather forlorn.

'Well, now you have two bars,' Izzy said, trying hard to find the half full. Taryn, after a few minutes' consideration, seemed to accept this. She carefully stored one half away in her cabinet and left the other out. Later, when she told Carlotta with a certain degree of glee that she now had two bars of her favourite soap, Carlotta responded as though she'd done Taryn a great favour. Taryn did get the last laugh, however. Later that week she 'accidentally' snapped Carlotta's favourite crop only to present her with the same argument. Carlotta was furious but, knowing she'd been outmanoeuvred, had to remain silent.

Conversely, although Carlotta bullied Taryn mercilessly, she would quite happily kick the arse of any village kid who tried to do likewise. On one occasion she marched into the kitchen, clothes and hair askew and with a grim expression of triumph on her face having dragged a local lout across the village green and pushed him into the water trough because she had witnessed him throwing apples at Jester's brown and white bum. Once Carlotta was home the phone rang ceaselessly, either with angry parents and neighbours complaining about something or other that she'd done, or with boys desperate to ask her out. She also had a habit of reverting to a curious language that Taryn referred to as Itali-Greek. This was a hybrid language spliced together from the Italian Carlotta had learned from her mother and her father's native tongue.

'Speak English!' Izzy found herself repeating over and over again. Even little Taryn could gabble away in Greek. If their needs meshed, which wasn't very often, Carlotta and Taryn ganged up on Izzy, conspiring in Greek until she was driven to despair. Mrs Firth simply ignored them, although even she knew some basic Greek.

If chattering in Greek was encouraged, arguing was strictly forbidden, which meant of course that Carlotta went out of her way to do this.

'You're not supposed to do that,' Taryn said, eyes brimmed with tears after she had received a particularly vicious lambasting from her sister.

Izzy soon learned not to look to Mrs Firth for back up.

'Don't look at me, love. I have no idea what she said. Please and thank you is my limit.'

Jared, to Izzy's astonishment, could speak Greek fluently and often either intervened or translated.

'Maybe we should get you up to speed on the basics,' he told a slack-jawed Izzy. As if she didn't have enough information to retain already! 'The girls can teach you a few words, if you like. It'll give 'em summat constructive to do with their time.'

Izzy didn't like. It was bloody mind-boggling. Carlotta and Taryn sat her down in the winter den with a book on Greek vocabulary and some notepaper. She could build up her own little dictionary, Carlotta said so amiably that Izzy was instantly suspicious.

She learned to say yes and no. *Oxhi* meant no, and *nai* meant yes. The latter was confusingly similar to the Yorkshire word *nay*, which was pronounced the same except it meant no. Upon learning this Izzy made a mental note to always clarify which language Carlotta was indeed speaking in the future, aware that she could easily be tricked otherwise.

'*Yassou* means hello, but only if you're speaking to one person,' Taryn told Izzy patiently. 'If you're speaking to lots of people it's *yassas*. Please is *perakolo,* and thank you is—'

'*Archimalakas,*' Carlotta added, smiling at her younger sister.

'That's right,' Taryn added, smiling back.

---

One of Izzy's less enjoyable duties was accompanying Carlotta and Taryn to the church graveyard so they could lay flowers on their mother's grave. It upset everyone including Izzy herself who was such a soft touch that a charity advert on the telly could make her cry.

There were some successes, however. Carlotta was most impressed that Izzy had lived and partied in London and was in awe of some of Izzy's more expensive outfits.

'Ooh, Jimmy Choos,' Carlotta breathed, turning a shoe over and over in her hands. 'Can I borrow them?' Because she didn't want to provoke another tantrum and because Carlotta could actually be quite good company when she was being agreeable, Izzy said she could. Nor did Izzy want to ruin the illusion Carlotta had created of her as a stylish and independent young woman by telling her most of her best things had either been bought and paid for by Scott or by Mr Visa. Both Taryn and Carlotta also approved of Izzy's make-up box. Taryn constantly wanted make-up lessons. Carlotta was worse and simply helped herself to whatever she wanted.

Only Gemma remained unaffected by Carlotta's premature arrival but this wasn't surprising as, like with Taryn, horses were the only thing Carlotta cared about.

Izzy was, in fact, nothing short of gobsmacked when she first saw the skill with which Carlotta rode. It was akin to a balletic grace.

Taryn was an extremely accomplished horsewoman, as was Gemma, but neither could compare with Carlotta. With Carlotta in the saddle Jet was almost unrecognisable from the naughty, belligerent pony Izzy rode. He was balanced, obedient and responsive. They were a perfect marriage of horse and rider. Izzy could do no more than stand and gape as she sat in on one of Carlotta's lessons with Gemma.

'It'll do you good to see how it's done,' said Gemma. She had Carlotta executing perfect gait transitions and intricate dressage moves before allowing her to finish off with a couple of rounds of four-foot jumps. Jet flew over everything with style, flicking his hooves out behind him as though showing off.

'To say you've not ridden him for a few weeks you're certainly in good form. It bodes well for the Easter shows,' Gemma said, patting Jet's glossy neck as Carlotta dismounted and loosened his girths.

'I can't wait,' Carlotta said, looking enthusiastic for once. Easter and summer holidays meant county shows, and county shows equated to area viewing trials. The most important of all of these would be the Great Yorkshire Show in July, when squad selectors would be present. Results would be collated and analysed and team places awarded. Carlotta was desperate to bag herself a place on the under 18s squad, if not the under 21s, although that might be a little optimistic as she was still only fifteen. Either way, she would form part of the junior Nation's Cup team and travel round Europe proudly displaying a GB rug and saddle pad. Therefore it went without saying that she needed to have a great season.

She raked in her pockets for Polos and pony nuts which she fed to an equally enthusiastic-looking Jet. All the while she showered her pony with hugs and kisses.

'Hurry up and untack Jet. Now that you're all warmed up it's time to see how you handle Vega.' As Carlotta wrestled with Jet's girth Gemma turned to a gaping Izzy. 'What did you think to our young star?' Carlotta stopped what she was doing and looked at Izzy expectantly.

'I thought she was incredible,' said Izzy truthfully, more than aware that Carlotta was already bigheaded enough without being given more compliments. If she had expected Carlotta to show some gratitude in response to her kind words she was mistaken. Instead she merely stalked into the tack room with Jet's saddle slung across her arm.

Five minutes later Carlotta was riding a thoroughly unmanageable Vega. Quite happy to crab sideways in either direction or hit reverse at will, the big golden mare refused to travel forwards in a straight line. Nor was the horse prepared to either walk or trot but bounced along in a gait somewhere between the two. After two laps of the manége Carlotta was puce in the face from the exertion of it all.

'Make her walk in a straight line,' Gemma barked. 'More leg on.'

'I'm trying,' Carlotta said through gritted teeth as Vega took the bit between her jaws and yanked on the reins. Carlotta was pulled forward as though attached to a bungee.

'Not hard enough.' Gemma was relentless with Carlotta in a way she never was with either Izzy or Taryn. 'I want to see more collection in her.'

'She's pulling my arms out of my bloody sockets,' grumbled Carlotta. Vega responded to her tugging through the medium of an enormous buck. 'Bitch of a mare.'

'You chose to ride her in a snaffle against my advice. You know how long it is since she's been ridden. Either start to obtain some control or change her bit.'

Izzy watched from the gate. She would have found it extremely difficult to express in words how very grateful she was that she'd never have to ride this crazed beast. Vega gave the impression that she was an angry brute, all flashing teeth and hooves. Izzy understood she'd had several weeks at grass with no exercise save for a few lungeing sessions with Gemma each week. Despite this she seemed to be remarkably fit and was so fresh that Carlotta was having great trouble keeping her under control. The language was nothing short of educational. So engrossed in the lesson was she, Izzy only noticed Taryn had joined her when the little girl spoke.

'I bet you a bag of Yorkshire Mixture that Carlotta hits the deck within five minutes,' Taryn said. There was a certain element of glee in her tone. To Izzy's untrained eye it looked as though the horse was submitting to Carlotta's skills. It was all she needed to make her decision.

'Done!' Izzy and Taryn exchanged a surreptitious high five. They continued to watch. Carlotta wrestled with Vega's head as the mare started to stargaze.

'If you don't get her moving forward she'll go up on her hind legs. Move her forward, move her forward! You're not using your legs enough,' Gemma yelled.

'I am, I am!' Carlotta yelled back. In Izzy's novice opinion it did indeed look like Carlotta was using her legs. She was flapping them against Vega's sides like bellows. 'She's not listening. I know how to get her attention.' In her frustration Carlotta gave Vega a wild swipe with her whip. The next minute she was sitting on the floor and Vega was panting like an overheated dog at the opposite end of the manége. Gemma strode off to retrieve the discarded pelham bit she had recommended Carlotta use. Carlotta, who'd been offloaded by a series of gymnastic rodeo bucks, simply sat and swore, hitting the ground with her whip. If the pairing of Carlotta and Jet had been a marriage of horse and rider then the pairing of Carlotta and Vega was a spectacular and painful divorce.

Taryn and Izzy turned to walk back to the house. They'd seen enough for one day.

'I'll go to the village shop for your sweets this afternoon,' Izzy told a triumphant Taryn.

---

THE WORST THING of all was that Carlotta insisted on not only spectating at but also commentating throughout Izzy's riding lessons.

'She's on the wrong diagonal. Jet was unbalanced round that corner. Tell her not to look at the ground. Her heels are up. Stop pulling on *my* pony's mouth like that, he's an expensive showjumping pony not a seaside donkey. You'll ruin his mouth. You're teaching him bad habits. His worth is decreasing with every second you're on his back.' She continued to rant until Jared yelled at her to shut up or get lost.

Unnerved by Carlotta's critique, which was unfortunately as accurate as it was cruel, Izzy's riding was the worst it had been in weeks and, after Jet had buckarooed Izzy for the seventh time, Jared admitted defeat. As though to express its absolute disgust at the standard of her riding a raven belched in the hedgerow.

After that Carlotta insisted Jet should only be ridden by herself in view of the advent of show season and Izzy found herself demoted to The Tank, who was less temperamental but harder work because he was such a fat slug, for her lessons. Izzy much preferred it when Gemma wanted to ride too because, with Jet resting either before or after a show, Jared on Ghost and Gemma on The Tank, there was no horse left for Izzy to ride.

'If Papa would buy me Polo there would be enough horses,' said Carlotta. She had no interest in Izzy and certainly no compulsion to be helpful. She was merely using every opportunity to further her own cause and needs. Not that Izzy minded staying at home instead of riding. In her opinion it was a Brucie Bonus which granted her free afternoons to do with as she pleased. Sometimes she whiled these away by lazing in her bedroom or watching DVDs in the winter den with a mountain of Mrs Firth's finest confections beside her, but mostly she spent them scouring the situations vacant for a splendid new job in London that would impress Scott and hopefully help her win him back.

It was also an unfortunate coincidence that Carlotta's unscheduled return from school collided with Izzy's first hack out. Worse still, Gemma had been called away on urgent family business so it was Jared who tacked up and mounted Ghost and accompanied them.

Carlotta was in a strop as Jared had allocated Jet to Izzy and bumped her onto Vega.

'I may as well book my own ambulance now. Bloody bitch!' Carlotta could be heard grumbling as she mounted. Izzy couldn't be sure whether Carlotta was referring to Vega or herself. She herself was terrified at the prospect of riding away from the safe confines of the manége. Twitchier than usual, she jumped every time Jet stamped a hoof or shook his head. Only Taryn, adorable on the perfectly groomed and interminably sweet Jester, showed any enthusiasm about the excursion.

Despite all this, it was a beautiful April day. The sky was a patchwork of blue and white. On the village green clusters of daffodils, as brightly green and yellow as Lego flowers, looked like they'd been plugged into the ground at strict intervals of twelve inches. The last of the blossom, as pink and white as toasting marshmallows, had dropped, leaving the entire village looking like a church's steps after a wedding. Primroses were like little yellow rosettes, as though giving spring third place.

It was so quiet in the village that they were able to walk four abreast down Cherry Tree Avenue, or rather three abreast with Carlotta foxtrotting ahead of them on Vega, who was thoroughly overexcited about being ridden out for the first time in months. She shied at everything: a suspicious looking carrier bag in the hedgerow, a malignant bird on a gatepost, a cat, spying on them from beneath a parked car.

Once they'd left the village Carlotta turned onto a cinder track that had once been a railway line but had long since had the tracks removed. It stretched ahead of them, broad, long and straight.

'Do you want to try a canter?' Jared asked Izzy. Most reluctant, but aware of Carlotta's scornful gaze, Izzy nodded her head. Vega was to go in front, just in case she went nuclear and Carlotta couldn't stop her, Jared said. Izzy should keep Jet alongside Ghost, who was as gentle as he was steady. Taryn, acting as mopper-upper, would bring up the rear. But alas... as soon as Carlotta gave Vega her head the mare exploded out of a colossal buck into a fast gallop. Jet, by now thoroughly wound up, gave a rodeo snort and belted after her. Izzy, caught off guard, gave a shriek of shock.

'Just sit it out,' Jared bellowed from behind her, kicking Ghost into a gallop in an attempt to catch up. 'Forward seat, heels down!' Little Taryn could be heard giving view halloas of joy as she trundled along behind them. On they galloped for almost a mile before Vega started to get bored and slowed down. Izzy, mortified that Jared would have had a superb view of her bobbing bony bottom as she bounced along, couldn't pull Jet up quickly enough. When they eventually ground to a ragged halt Carlotta turned to face them with shining eyes.

'That was fucking awesome!' she cried, patting Vega's shiny, metallic neck over and over again.

'It was fucking irresponsible,' Jared stormed, reining in beside her. 'Izzy could have easily been thrown and you know Jester can't gallop that fast. Well sat,' he added to Izzy, nodding in her direction. Blowing out her cheeks from both relief and the exertion, Izzy refrained from comment.

The one benefit from their wild gallop was it got out all the horses' kinks and from then on they became much calmer. Unfortunately, Carlotta seemed to be most disappointed Izzy hadn't been thrown and continually rode Vega close to Jet in an attempt to upset him. Neither Jared's orders nor Taryn's disapproval deterred her. Carlotta soon got her comeuppance though. Once they had ridden a good way along the single track road that led back to the village an enormous green John Deere tractor appeared in front of them.

'Shit!' said Jared. 'Into that gateway, quick!' This was something only Taryn managed to accomplish. Still fresh despite the gallop, Vega jibbed and began circling on the spot. Jet, also unnerved, was on his toes. Up and down, back and forth went Jet until Izzy felt quite seasick. It was like riding a rocking horse, she thought as Jet yanked on the reins for the hundredth time. By force of sheer leg power Jared rammed Ghost parallel to Jet, forcing him onto the verge where he had no room to misbehave. Vega, by virtue of Carlotta's superior horsemanship, was moving closer to the gateway with every spin. The tractor driver, used to such rural dramas, merely sat and read his paper until the four riders were organised. It was the Law of Sod that decreed that at the very same moment that all four horses were safely in the gateway, and the tractor started to inch forward, that a car approached from behind them. The driver, instead of backing up in order to allow the tractor to proceed, insisted on trying to squeeze past, mounting the grass verge as he slid the big saloon deep into the gateway. Vega, incensed by such an invasion of her personal space, promptly ceased to spin and plonked her gleaming gold arse on the bonnet. The metal creaked worryingly. The driver of the car tooted his horn and yelled. Jet was so frightened that he would have bolted if Jared hadn't grabbed the reins. Izzy thought her last hour had come. With a lot of frantic kicking, swearing and arm flapping Carlotta managed to get Vega off the car and into the adjacent field. Taryn, who for good reason was the best Handy Hunter competitor in the county, had used her initiative and opened the gate, allowing them to flood into a field of baby crops.

'Better some smelly cabbages get mashed than any of us,' was her reasoning. Jared had to concede it was a fair and logical argument. Vega had by this time had enough.

'See you back ho-o-o-me!' Carlotta cried as Vega carted her back towards The Paddocks at top speed. Fortunately Jet couldn't be bothered to do likewise.

Satisfied Izzy and Taryn were safe and under control in the field, Jared rode up to the car and, leaning down, peered in through the window. The expression of sheer fury on his face was enough to silence the angry driver, who was now beetroot in the face from ranting about the rump-shaped dent in his bonnet.

'No use shouting, mate. You've no one but yourself to blame and mebbe you'll think about having a bit of patience in future. You want to be thankful the horse only sat on your car and didn't kick it to shit. It'd have been no good suing either. You should have had more sense. It wasn't the horse's fault. You were far too close. And a good mechanic will be able to tap that dent out, so stop bleating.'

The rest of the ride passed without incident and after what seemed like an age, they clattered into the stable yard. Carlotta was waiting for them. She was hand walking a sweating Vega round the yard in an attempt to cool her down.

'Are we all happy hackers?' Jared couldn't resist asking as he dismounted.

'Not really,' Izzy said, white faced, as she slid to the ground, relieved to have managed to stay in the saddle for the duration of the ride. Carlotta seconded this opinion by way of a grunt. Only Taryn thought the ride had been a success.

---

THE BEGINNING of the Easter school holidays meant both girls were at home all day, every day. On the one hand, this was preferable as Izzy didn't have to schlep into Loxley twice a day on the school run. On the other, the end of term time heralded three weeks of country shows and equestrian fixtures. It was a heavy schedule and one Izzy was expected to accommodate alongside all her other usual chores. She found herself woken before sunrise and carted off to shows every other day by Jared, who loaded the ponies, tack and a packed lunch, prepared by Mrs Firth and big enough to feed a biblical gathering, into the horsebox and ferried them round the North of England.

There was occasional relief from such excursions if Taryn stayed at home. It was dependent on the type of show as to whether Taryn rode. If it were a country fair with several suitable showing classes and gymkhana events, Taryn would enter Jester. If it were a serious showjumping meet at an equestrian centre or a county show, Taryn often declined, knowing, if she went along just to watch, Carlotta would treat her like a dogsbody all day. Although she both adored and feared her sister, Taryn was no fool and often opted to stay at The Paddocks for a full day's peace and quiet or a day out to the cinema or bowling with Izzy, who savoured these instances greatly as they were few and far between. Literally more often than not, Izzy and Taryn were involved with show days.

As the horsebox could only seat three along its one front seat Izzy and Taryn were demoted without exception to the Golf and were forced to follow in convoy. These were often jolly journeys during which Izzy and Taryn played Take That and McFly CDs far too loudly and pigged out on Twixes and Dairy Milk. Jared, Gemma and Carlotta had their own exclusive little club of three and never took turns in the Golf. Carlotta and Gemma were as thick as horse thieves, had been for many years and refused to be parted. Jared wouldn't allow anyone else to drive the horsebox, especially not Izzy, and sat at the wheel, sleeves rolled up, knees at ten to two, like an articulated trucker.

'All he needs is a can of Irn Bru, a packet of McCoys and a Ginsters pasty and no one would know the difference,' said Izzy sourly. Gemma never missed the opportunity to travel in the horsebox as this meant she could snuggle up to Jared on the front seat.

Taryn showed relief at not having to ride in the same vehicle as Carlotta, who insisted on her own choice of angry rock music and temperature and who was especially scathing if Taryn needed to stop for a wee.

Show days were long days. Up at an ungodly hour, with long drives and lots of hanging around between classes. Izzy preferred the country fairs, rather than the serious competitions, as there were trade stands and other displays to amuse. Also, it came as something of a surprise to Izzy that she had become so invested in Taryn's riding. She found herself ringside, gripping the barrier, both pony and rider immaculate as they executed flying changes and half passes. Jester, of inordinately good nature, loved competitions and was a showman and such a jolly little pony that he always caught the judges' eye. Taryn was rarely out of the prizes. She cherished each rosette, be it red, blue, yellow or green, and bore them all home to be hammered above Jester's stable door by Jared.

Carlotta's fortunes were less predictable. If she were riding Jet she invariably cleaned up, raking in first prizes, show after show. Not that she was gracious in victory. She saw nothing wrong with whooping like a cowboy on her lap of honour and even flicking vees at her competitors if they'd said something to her beforehand that she hadn't appreciated. It was worse still if she didn't get the result she wanted, as was often the case if she'd entered Vega, who wore a red ribbon in her tail to warn other riders she was a kicker.

'Problem is, you have to go near her back end to tie the bloody thing on,' Gemma grumbled, clutching her arm, now bruised, where Vega had lashed out.

There were always repercussions. On a good day Vega was unstoppable in the ring. On a bad day she was simply unstoppable and often tore round the course, demolishing fences and scattering onlookers as she went. On one particularly cringeworthy occasion she'd taken umbrage with a display of pink and purple gladioli and bolted from the ring, jumping the barrier in her haste to escape the floral terror, almost landing on a pack of screaming Brownies who had been lining up for a parade round the showground with their flags and banners unfurled. Terrified further by these evil flapping enemies, Vega had galloped as the crow flies across the showground with a for once ashen Carlotta clinging on for dear life, jumping picnic chairs, an ice cream cart and even the bonnet of a Ford Focus as she went. Any person in the way could do no more than duck and pray.

'That mare can certainly jump,' said a wag in the crowd to a yell of nervous laughter.

'Enter it for the National,' yelled another as Vega's thundering rump grew ever diminished.

Exchanging looks of mortification and horror, Jared and Gemma had thrown Jester's reins at Izzy and pegged it after them in the Golf. They caught up with them in the village two miles away, both horse and rider blowing like a brass section.

'She never even slowed down,' Carlotta had panted as she slid off.

---

AT EASTER EVERYTHING started to come back to life, including Izzy. Outside the countryside was warming up. In the hedgerows ground elder began its annual invasion and the roadside verges were swamped with dandelions and daisies. Daffodils, white, yellow and orange, were fading. It only took one warm afternoon to fill the fields with rapeseed. In the woods and copses bluebells were starting to bloom. Out in the fields the ponies kicked up their heels in joy at being turned out without their New Zealand rugs. Mini Cheddar, the little Shetland, could be seen rolling, pedalling his stumpy bay legs in the air like women doing the 'bicycle' in a fitness class. The bigger horses all galloped round, tails kinked high and taking playful nips out of each other's rumps.

Easter was celebrated with gusto at The Paddocks. Both Taryn and Carlotta received enormous Fortnum & Mason Easter eggs from their father and smaller, more generic varieties each from Jared, Mrs Firth and Izzy. These weren't allowed to be eaten until Easter Sunday and had been displayed on the Welsh dresser in the kitchen. Izzy was amazed to discover she'd received two eggs of her own: the biggest KitKat egg she had ever seen from the girls and a smaller, prettier, but no less impressive egg from Betty's of Harrogate from Jared. Mrs Firth received the same.

'Nothing but the best for my two special ladies,' Jared had said, giving each of them a peck on the cheek before scuttling off in embarrassment. As Izzy added her eggs to the collection she felt an unfamiliar glow of belonging.

On Easter Day everyone went to the churchyard to lay a hand-picked bouquet of spring blooms from the garden on the girls' mother's grave. After that, to lighten the mood of the day, Jared and Gemma accompanied Carlotta out on a five-hour picnic hack. As this was too long for either Taryn or Izzy to be in the saddle they stayed at home and spent the afternoon helping Mrs Firth make chocolate Easter nests from cornflakes and Mini Eggs and baking an Easter fudge cake the size of a car hubcap for tea.

Under Mrs Firth's patient tutelage Izzy had also managed to make a batch of cheese scones which each were as big as a side plate. The three riders came home ravenous and everyone fell upon them like vultures. Jared, having sliced his scone in half and plastered it in butter, inhaled it in two bites.

'I spent ages slaving over those and you didn't even take the time to appreciate it,' Izzy complained.

'I did. I savoured every mouthful. Both of them,' Jared replied. Carlotta and Taryn giggled.

'You'll ruin your dinner,' Mrs Firth added, her mouth a thin line of disapproval.

Her gripings were without foundation. Everyone, including Gemma who didn't normally dine at The Paddocks, sat in the usually forsaken formal dining room and ate an Easter dinner of roast chicken, roast potatoes and Yorkshire puddings. Izzy was somewhat put off her dinner upon learning that the bird she had been happily tucking into had in fact been one of the chickens from the coop. It had been culled by Jared before being plucked by Mrs Firth, she was told, amidst smutty sniggers from the girls.

'Don't feel bad, Izzy,' said Taryn, as she gnawed unsympathetically on a leg bone. 'It was only Simon Cowell. She wasn't very nice and picked on all the other hens.'

During the meal lots of white wine was drunk by everyone except Taryn, who ingested far too much sugar in the liquid form of dandelion and burdock, and everyone got very giggly. Izzy decided this was the perfect opportunity to try out her newly acquired Greek and proudly said *archimalakas* to Jared after he had topped up her wine glass yet again by way of conveying her thanks.

'I beg your bloody pardon?' Jared spluttered. At the same time Carlotta and Taryn exploded into hysterics.

'*Archimalakas*,' Izzy repeated hesitantly, unnerved and disappointed by his reaction. 'Did I pronounce it incorrectly?'

Carlotta and Taryn erupted for a second time. Even Gemma was grinning at her from across the table. Mrs Firth paid no attention whatsoever and was instead concentrating on dividing the Easter fudge cake into six equal slices.

Taking in Izzy's bemused expression and the girls' uncontrollable giggling, Jared twigged.

'Oh, I see.' He turned to Carlotta and Taryn. 'Very well played, you two.' He turned back to Izzy. 'Did you mean to say thank you, because if you did you should have said *efharisto*. I wouldn't advise going round Greece saying *archimalakas* to anyone unless you want to get slapped. You just called me chief of assholes.'

This set Carlotta and Taryn off again. Izzy mock snarled at them.

'Oh, har har. You little horrors. I'm glad I'm such a source of amusement for you. I don't think I want to learn any more Greek, *efharisto*!' Then she grinned, and everyone had a good laugh about it. After this they attacked the fudge cake like starved tigers.

During Easter week Jared drove Carlotta, Taryn, Izzy and Gemma to Birmingham to see the British Open Showjumping Championships. As soon as they'd bought programmes and found their seats, Carlotta and Gemma immediately clamoured to go to the trade stands to see what was new to buy. Sometime later they flopped into their seats just before the first class was due to start, laden with carrier bags and in high spirits. Carlotta's good mood was soon quelled by the sight of her old bête noire, Ceridwen Jones, competing in the Pony Club team jumping competition, although it soon returned when Ceridwen clocked up twenty-four faults and had her score dropped from the team total as hers was the worst performance.

'Should've picked meeee,' Carlotta sing-songed loudly, causing the old biddy next to her to tut in disapproval at such an unsportsmanlike attitude.

After a short break the international classes started. For Izzy, watching the professional showjumpers was a revelation. She watched in awe as, over and over again, horse and rider flew over fences that were surely so big she'd be able to walk underneath them without bumping her head. She found herself buying into the whole atmosphere, groaning in unison with the audience whenever a pole fell and cheering and shouting like groupies for the British riders when it was their turn to jump. The puissance was the most exciting class of all. Izzy could barely watch as the wall grew higher and higher and yet still the brave horses heaved themselves over it. Eventually it was won by William Whitaker, a popular rider who was not only British but Yorkshire born and bred, Jared told her with pride. The crowd went berserk and Izzy couldn't help but be carried on by the audience's enthusiasm and delight and was on her feet like all the rest, clapping and whooping.

After the show had finished they headed home, tired but happy. Even Carlotta was in a good mood, having bought some new jodhpurs at mark-down price and having been recognised by two of the junior squad selectors.

The following day was not so enjoyable. Izzy knew it was going to be a testing day from the moment she opened her eyes and instead of clobbering her alarm clock, knocked a glass of water all over her bedside cabinet. From then on it went downhill. She spilled her shampoo all over her bathroom floor. Then, wandering round her bedroom with her toothbrush and paste in her hand as she decided what to wear, she dropped her tube of Aquafresh, and trod on it. Red, white and blue goop squirted all over the bedroom carpet.

'Shitbags!' she shouted. She was already late for breakfast but daren't leave such a mess untidied. She'd already been lectured twice that week by Jared for treating Mrs Firth like a slave.

'You're no better than the girls,' he had snapped. Izzy had felt very small.

Downstairs, she found the kitchen deserted. Judging from the stack of unwashed pots in the sink, Izzy ascertained that Carlotta and Taryn had eaten already and were no doubt in the stables. In the utility, an open washing machine indicated that Mrs Firth was hanging out a basket of laundry in the cool April air. Jared would be gardening somewhere, as usual. Only one of the cats was present and even that was minding its own business, sleeping, stretched across a rhombus of sunlight on the kitchen rug.

Still sleepy, Izzy poured herself juice and cereal. As she ate her flakes with a distinct lack of enthusiasm, her mind kept reverting to the Easter eggs, now stacked neatly in the pantry where they'd be safe from thieving paws.

'Don't let Steptoe, or any of the dogs, eat chocolate no matter how much they beg. It's poisonous to them,' had been some of Jared's first words to Izzy when she'd arrived at The Paddocks. Izzy had been careful to obey this simple rule and, although she gave the dogs toast crusts and left over potatoes, she never fed them sweets. They'd be wasted on dogs anyway, she thought to herself every time she ate the last piece of a chocolate bar in front of a slavering canine audience. Now the thought of a large sliver of thin chocolate egg tormented her. The girls were strictly forbidden to eat chocolate for breakfast therefore Izzy, who was expected to lead by example, was also discouraged from doing the same. However, Izzy convinced herself, as the girls weren't there to witness such indulgence, they'd never know and, more pertinently, not be able to blackmail her with it at a later date. The thought of chocolate was driving her crazy. She must be premenstrual, she thought, making a mental note to check her diary. That would explain her increased clumsiness, at least.

Temptation won. Balancing cereal boxes on her arm, Izzy reached for one of her eggs, broke off a chunk and rammed it into her mouth. She shoved the cereal boxes back onto their shelf and kicked the pantry door shut. Alas, the latch didn't click and as soon as Izzy exited the kitchen the pantry door creaked open. Steptoe, being both inordinately greedy and an accomplished opportunistic thief, crept in and out of this grotto within seconds, having pilfered not only a meat pie intended for that evening's dinner but also a half-eaten Toblerone egg, and wolfed it down, complete with chocolate innards. Twenty minutes later Jared, seeking a glass of something cold, walked into the kitchen to find Steptoe trying desperately to chuck up a length of foil wrapper that had got stuck in his throat. Several puddles of telltale dog vomit together with the damning evidence of the wide open pantry door told Jared all he needed to know and he whisked Steptoe off to the vet for x-rays and an emergency enema. Demented with worry for his beloved dog, he refused to leave Steptoe's side until he was given a clean bill of health and didn't return home until late afternoon. Nor was he the only one who was livid. Carlotta had to cancel a party invitation for that afternoon as there was no one to drive her. Izzy had been due to chauffeur her to and fro but had had to take over from Jared in taking Taryn to the dentist as neither Mrs Firth, who couldn't drive, nor Gemma, could be called upon to stand in. Carlotta, having been subjected to an afternoon of forced solitude, brooded, plotted and vowed to be avenged.

The following afternoon Izzy's craving for chocolate returned. She raided the pantry but there was none to be found. All the Easter eggs had gone, as had the biscuit tin that was usually full to the brim with Breakaways and Blue Ribands.

'Weird,' she said, remembering the full shelf from the previous day. Behind her Carlotta was reading *Horse & Rider* magazine at the kitchen table. Hearing Izzy muttering about sweets, she looked up.

'What's up?' she asked, a little too amiably but Izzy was so obsessed with her desire for chocolate she failed to notice it.

'The chocolate has all gone,' Izzy said crossly. Carlotta pulled a face.

'Yeah, I know. Stinks, doesn't it? Jared was really freaked out by what happened yesterday so he decided to throw it all out just to be on the safe side. He said if you had a problem with that you'd have to speak to him about it.'

Izzy sat down at the table glumly. It had been her fault the pantry door had been left open. She had no grounds to argue with Jared. Then she noticed that Carlotta was dibbing into a little bowl of chocolate buttons as she flicked the pages of the magazine. She couldn't tear her eyes away. Carlotta followed her gaze and pushed the bowl towards Izzy.

'Help yourself,' she said. 'They're yummy.'

Izzy accepted the bowl but, suspecting some trickery, gave the chocolates a good sniff first. The bittersweet aroma of cocoa hit her nostrils.

'Wow! They smell just like Cadbury's Caramel,' she said. She could see no reason to suspect Carlotta, after all, she'd been eating them just before she came in.

'They're some sort of limited edition,' Carlotta said airily, not paying any particular attention. Izzy threw half a dozen into her mouth in one go, waiting for the chocolate sugar rush to hit her. It didn't. Instead she ran over to the sink and spat them out.

'Oh my God, they've gone off. They taste like ash,' she cried, still spitting. 'Ugh, that's disgusting.' By this time

Carlotta was gulping with laughter. 'What did you do to them? Where's the packet?' Izzy demanded.

'In the dogs' box in the utility room. They were Good Boy choc drops,' Carlotta giggled. Izzy promptly threw up in the sink. Jared chose this moment to walk into the kitchen. He looked at them both with suspicion. Carlotta was now bent double, gasping for breath. Izzy was wiping her green face on a tea towel. The kitchen stank of sick.

'What the bloody hell is going on?'

'I hid all the chocolate and tricked Izzy into eating the dogs' choc drops. Honestly, Jarhead, she's so desperate and predictable. She thought I was eating them but I was hiding them under the magazine.' Carlotta flicked the magazine over to reveal half a dozen tiny brown discs. They made her spew,' she hiccupped.

'Like we haven't had enough chocolate-vomit incidents this week,' Jared snapped. He looked furious. 'You're both as bad as each other. Get out of my sight, the pair of you.'

Much later and in private, Izzy had to give Carlotta credit for such inventiveness. The prank had been so typical of her. The problem was Carlotta's wicked wit and fearless insouciance was hysterical provided one wasn't on the receiving end of it. Izzy pondered over Carlotta's ability to say what she thought, envying the fact that she wasn't hindered by appropriateness, bosses or the threat of being sacked.

Carlotta also kept them all in fits with her vivid yet scandalous accounts about her life at school. According to Carlotta, Queen Victoria's Boarding School For Girls was a St. Trinian-esque hotbed of sleaze, iniquity and debauchery. The sixth formers had their own hotline to the local doctors' surgery to enable them to get their morning after pills. The upper school had weekly locker checks for black market booze, cigs and ganja. The lower school were exploited by the upper school as go-fers and alibis. Not even the school teachers were exempt from gossip. Only just before Carlotta had been suspended had there been rumours of a lesbian romp on a fifth form field trip to the Lowry between the art mistress and the young, comely teaching assistant that had been drafted in to help her.

'And we've got a gym instructor called Mr Titman,' Carlotta had continued. Jared grinned. 'Aptly named too. He's a dreadful old perve. He's always trying to peer into the changing rooms after hockey class.' She hadn't bothered, however, to add that she had got detention for a week and had been barred from extra-curricular activities (although this hadn't stopped her from sneaking out for a sly ride on an evening) for a month for graffiti-ing 'Titman by name – Tit man by nature' on the common room craft table.

'I'm sure your father would be thrilled to hear that the extortionate school fees he is asked to pay for your top-ranking education is money well spent,' Jared said drily.

During the third week of the Easter holidays Carlotta snuck off to London for a few days, with the intention of whooping it up in the West End with one of her school friends, leaving nothing but a scrawled note to say where she'd gone before cadging a lift to Greater Ousebury on the milkman's electric float. Jared had exploded like a hand grenade and bolted to the halt in the next village intending to drag her back but he'd been too late. By the time he got there Carlotta was already winging her way to Loxley and the East Coast Express. Still furious, Jared spent the full morning tracking her down to ensure she was being supervised. It transpired that she was indeed staying with a school friend and would be well looked after. She'd be taken to see a show in the West End and out for a day at Thorpe Park, amongst other things.

'Don't worry about her,' Izzy overheard Mrs Firth say to Jared. 'If *you* don't know her whereabouts there's precious little chance anyone else does.'

'She's still gonna get a bollocking when she gets home,' Jared had said. 'London is far too dangerous a place for her to be. Anything could happen to her down there. It's a city of nutters.'

Still eavesdropping, Izzy felt a stab of pain for her home city. She missed Saturday morning hangover-brunch with Caro in Covent Garden, she missed missing the red buses and watching them turn the corner as she hobbled after them in her high heels, and she missed the grime and heat and bustle of the underground. The only things that went underground in Yorkshire were the bloody moles and rabbits. She loved spring in the city with its warmer days that hinted coyly at a long, hot summer but never delivered, when the royal parks burst into life and cafés and restaurants started to set chairs and tables outside on the pavements in a desperate attempt to appear more continental. She still missed Scott, and his flat, and going with him to Rah-Rah's for over-priced, short-measured drinks whilst all his snooty friends looked down their upwardly-mobile noses at her lack of achievement.

It'd been almost two months since she'd left London. It felt like an age had passed.

Four days later Carlotta swanned back home, ringing imperiously from Greater Ousebury halt for someone to come and pick her up ('needs putting down, more like' Izzy had grumbled to herself) and, when she finally got home, premiering a pierced nose and an aquamarine tattoo of a seahorse on her ankle. Mrs Firth wasn't impressed, either with these new additions or with the holdall full of laundry that had been dropped insolently at her slippered feet.

'You look a bloody fright,' she said, scooping up the clothes nevertheless. 'Your father will be very angry when he sees you.'

'I'll tell him Izzy said it was okay,' Carlotta said blithely, still holding out her ankle so all could see and admire. She wasn't quite so breezy when Jared got hold of her and subjected her to a forty-five minute dressing down in the winter den. Izzy and Taryn lurked outside for a few minutes, both relishing the thought of Carlotta being brought down a peg or two, but soon scattered when Jared, suspecting eavesdroppers, stuck his head round the door and bellowed at them to 'bugger off and find summat constructive to do'. Through the gap in the doorway Izzy caught a brief glance of a much deflated and, even more rare, tearful Carlotta.

The problem, Izzy thought as she wandered into the kitchen to help Mrs Firth with dinner prep, was neither Taryn nor Carlotta were accustomed to hearing the word no. Taryn responded with sobs and sulks; Carlotta with blind rages. Both were keenly aware that not Izzy, Mrs Firth or even Jared had the authority of a parent. Furthermore, both of them had a nasty habit of threatening Izzy with their father whenever she didn't do exactly as they wanted.

'My father will deal with you. He's a very powerful man —' Carlotta liked to threaten whenever Izzy disciplined her.

'That's enough, Carlotta!' Jared said, each time she wheeled this intimidation out. To Izzy's surprise Jared, and also Mrs Firth, often intervened. Carlotta's reaction was always the same. She glowered, but remained silent.

As the end of the Easter holidays loomed Carlotta's mood blackened further. Such was the force of her personality that this affected the entire household. Taryn cowed beneath the sheer force of her sister's rages. Izzy's patience was stretched to capacity and her body reacted by indulging in a cluster of agonising migraine headaches that banished her to her darkened bedroom for hours on end. Even Mrs Firth was uncharacteristically tense. Only Jared remained unaffected and continued to bark instructions to one and all, indiscriminate of human or animal form.

On the last Friday before Carlotta was due back at school she was nigh on unbearable and had taken to prowling round the house, being generally disagreeable and finding fault with everything, reporting back to whoever was in the kitchen like a shop floor foreman. Just after lunch she reappeared, saturated with spleen which she had every intention of venting.

'My clothes aren't washed and ironed, Jet's tack's filthy, the dogs have dug up my duvet and rolled on my clean sheets. What are you going to do about it?' she raged at Jared, Taryn and Izzy, who was struggling with the onset of yet another migraine.

'Nothing,' said Jared, unaffected. 'If you're so desperate for clean clothes you know where the washing machine is. If *your* pony's tack is so dirty, you know what to do about it. As for the dogs, I have no control over them and if you don't want them in your room don't forget to close the door.'

'It was your damned dog that did it.' Carlotta refused to listen.

'Do you have evidence of this accusation?' Jared asked, still not looking up from his newspaper.

'No.'

'Then it may have been one of your father's dogs. I suggest you take it up with him.'

'It was Pongy, and he doesn't belong to Papa. He belongs to *Taryn*!'

'He does *not*. You're a rotten liar, Carlotta!' Taryn cried. This led to a bout of furious, and voluble, bickering. Izzy, who was starting to feel nauseous, both from the pain and from having forced down a round of egg sandwiches in order not to offend Mrs Firth, was at the end of her rope.

'For Christ's sake, shut up!' she yelled, head in hands.

'Don't you speak to us like that,' Carlotta began, suddenly full of righteous sisterly solidarity.

'I'll do as I see fit,' Izzy said, cutting her off. Jared raised his head from his paper but said nothing. 'Taryn, don't your rabbits need cleaning out, or feeding, or stroking, or anything? And Carlotta, surely you know some poor teenage boy who you can torment over the internet?'

'I don't have to do what you say. I'm gonna tell—' Clearly, Carlotta wasn't giving up without a scrap.

'I don't care who you tell so long as you do it *quietly,*' Izzy said. She eyeballed both girls with a look of death. 'Just go,' she added, through gritted teeth. Taken aback both by Izzy's fierce expression and her stern tone, Taryn and Carlotta exited the room, whispering between themselves. Izzy waited until they had gone before she plonked her head back in her hands.

'There's a little pixie just behind my right eye chipping away at my skull. No brain left to work at so he's gotta go for the bone. Christ, I need some very, very strong painkillers,' she grumbled to no one in particular. When she raised her head she saw that Jared was grinning at her. 'Wot?' she snapped disagreeably, expecting him to berate her for shouting at the girls.

'Well done,' he said, nodding his head with genuine admiration. 'It takes some balls to shut just one of those two up, never mind both of 'em. Very well done indeed.' He rose from the table and returned a few minutes later with two cocodamol and a glass of water. 'There's plenty more in the first aid drawer in the utility. Help yourself.'

Ten minutes later Carlotta was back, re-energised and ready for another go.

'I want to take Jet back to school with me. Bloody Ceridwen Jones has got both her ponies at school and she gets to be ferried round to shows at the weekends by the staff. Do you know how many shows… how many *qualifiers…* I miss because I'm cooped up at school without a pony? Ceridwen Jones has won all across the North of England this year alone. I'll never get picked for the under 21s or the junior squad if I don't *qualify*! Ceridwen Jones—' She was like a broken record.

'You know the score. Your father made it perfectly clear that until you stopped getting into fights and your schoolwork improved—' Jared found himself repeating over and over again.

'Oh, I fucking know!'

'So, haven't you got some maths course work that needs completing so you can hand it in on the first day of term?' Jared asked calmly.

'Fucking maths. What use is it anyway? When am I gonna use Pythagoras Theorem in real life? And all this crap about if one train is travelling northbound at fifty miles an hour and another train is travelling southbound at seventy-five miles an hour. How about this? If the train is travelling at fifty miles an hour towards the level crossing, and Vega is bolting towards the same level crossing at twenty-seven miles per hour, the only thing I'm calculating in my head is how to make her fucking STOP!' Carlotta shouted, storming out.

'I am literally counting down the hours until she is back at school,' Jared said crossly.

'I'm going for a lie down,' Izzy said weakly.

---

Carlotta's last weekend at home passed quickly. Mrs Firth cooked a going-back-to-school dinner for her on the Saturday evening and Izzy helped her pack up her belongings. Gemma cheered her up slightly by giving her a new book on advanced dressage to read whilst she was at school.

First thing Sunday morning Jared loaded her trunk, riding gear, tuck box and tennis racquets into the Range Rover. Everyone was waiting to wave her off but Carlotta had disappeared. At first Izzy thought she was simply being bloody-minded as usual but then realised Carlotta was doing nothing more than procrastinating in order to delay her departure. After searching the stables and the house, Izzy finally tracked Carlotta down in her bedroom. She was sitting on her bed, looking younger than usual and ridiculously kempt, and therefore almost unrecognisable, in her school uniform of grey and black plaid skirt, white shirt, grey V-neck, tie, black knee socks and sensible shoes. Her hair was tied back in a neat French plait and her face devoid of make-up. She was the very picture of misery. Izzy sat down beside her. Her maternal instinct wanted to put her arm round the unhappy girl but this was counterbalanced by her survival instinct advising against it in case she got thwacked. Instead she nudged her gently with her elbow.

'Summer term is always the shortest. You'll be back home for your hols in no time and there'll be lots of hacks out and shows for you to win at. And in the meantime there'll be the Great Yorkshire Show in July to look forward to. And you never know, your father might even manage to come home for a visit.'

Carlotta turned towards her, her face a malevolent mask of scorn.

'God, Izzy, you can be so *dense*. Don't you understand? Papa isn't coming home.'

Just at that point Jared bellowed up the stairs for Carlotta to get a move on.

'Coming!' Carlotta shouted angrily, standing up, before turning back to Izzy. Her expression had reverted to sadness. 'Make sure you look after Taryn. See ya.' And she was gone.

It took Izzy a few moments to digest not only Carlotta's cryptic words but also her uncharacteristically mature attitude towards Taryn's welfare. It left Izzy with the uncomfortable impression that Carlotta was carrying the weight of the world. Thoughts gathered, Izzy raced after her.

'What do you mean—?' But she was too slow. By the time she caught up Carlotta was already climbing into the Range Rover.

'I don't see why you can't take me in the Roller instead of this filthy POS,' she could be heard grumbling as the door slammed shut. 'It's so shaming. Get over, dog. I don't want to arrive at school covered in hairs.' She didn't turn and wave as the vehicle pulled away.

To her astonishment Izzy could feel a lump in her throat as she waved them off. Beside her Taryn was openly crying, her bottom lip quivering, forcing Izzy to realise that, although Carlotta was simply beastly to Taryn, they were still sisters and still the only blood family they had. Izzy put her arm round the little girl, who clung to her like a monkey.

'Come on, let's have a cup of tea,' said Mrs Firth, her rasping voice gruffer than ever as she tried to conceal her own unhappiness at Carlotta's departure.

'Can we have cake?' Izzy found herself asking.

Mrs Firth gave her the smallest of smiles. 'That goes without saying, love.'

# DAZE IN THE COUNTRY

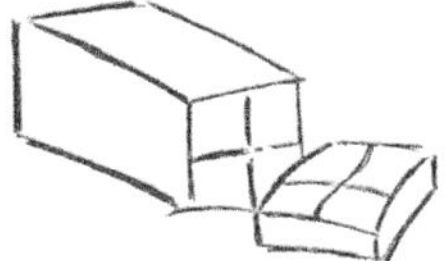

Carlotta's return to school left The Paddocks subdued and quiet. Everyone noticed it but none more so than Taryn, who clearly missed her sister terribly but hid it, not very well, behind a mask of serenity. Nor had it escaped Izzy's notice that Taryn was affected by any change to her immediate environment and, just as had occurred when Carlotta had come home, Taryn's hyperventilation attacks increased upon her departure too. Life was certainly duller without Carlotta's histrionics therefore it was with some reluctance that everyone slid back into their old routine.

Inevitably, as is the case with all employment, as Izzy's competence and skill-set grew so did her workload. She was now able, and despite what she'd been initially told, called on to assist Mrs Firth with the cooking and housekeeping.

It was a busy time for Jared in the garden too. There were early crops to be planted as well as the setting out of tomatoes, peppers, cucumbers and courgettes in slug-like growbags in the greenhouse. Izzy was thankful she wasn't expected to help here too. As a result Jared had less time to supervise Izzy and so she found herself left to her own devices a great deal more. Not that she had much in the way of free time. As soon as the summer term started the daily grind of ferrying Taryn to school and back, overseeing her homework, meals, pony chores and personal routine gobbled up most of Izzy's day. She was kept so busy she had little time to miss Scott and her London life and certainly didn't have time to job hunt. It would soon be three months since she'd left London.

In many respects it felt to Izzy as though she were living someone else's life whilst her own was being kept on hold. On other occasions it felt like she'd been split in two, creating separate but identical personas, rather like Taryn's Barbies who adopted a new lifestyle with every costume change. There was City Izzy, who wore designer clothes, teetered around in heels, worked in the private sector and rode the Tube, and there was Country Izzy, who wore wellies and a waxed jacket and rode horses. Like parallel lines, the two never overlapped but maintained their own identities, which only served to leave Izzy feeling confused, alienated from both and belonging to neither.

As April slid into May the earth warmed up. Verges, village greens and front lawns were plagued with dandelions. Lily of the valley, hyacinths and tulips faded away only to be replaced with masses of geraniums. Wanton scarlet, acid orange, salmon pink and white; they dominated the flowerbeds and terracotta planters and never failed to make Izzy think of hot summer holidays on the continent.

'That's why Papa loves them. He always says they remind him of home,' Taryn said one day, her tone wistful. Izzy, remembering Carlotta's bitter claim that MK wasn't going to return, hadn't known what to say. She also felt a pang of regret that just two weeks before Scott booted her out he'd been talking of the two of them travelling somewhere hot for their summer holiday. He'd been dropping big hints that it would be something special for her impending thirtieth birthday. Izzy felt another stab of grievous anger towards

Scott on account that he could have been so glib about something so important to her whilst all the time he was planning to offload her. Self-directed anger that she had been so gullible and naïve gnawed away at her once more. She didn't even grant herself the mitigation that she'd had no reason to suspect. She'd simply not seen it coming.

Inside the house the changing of the season was just as evident. Mrs Firth spring cleaned with all the energy and ferocity of a whirlwind. The dogs moulted in unbelievable proportions. Little Steptoe lost his thick winter coat in handfuls, leaving most of it on Izzy's bedspread, revealing smooth, silky, white fur. Even smelly Pongy began to look less unkempt. Alas, such was his singular skill at finding unspeakable substances to roll in that he reeked constantly no matter how neat his fur was. It was only now that Izzy realised that she hadn't needed to take her antihistamines for weeks. Her body had somehow become accustomed to the animal hair and just righted itself.

It also became apparent that the more daylight hours there were in the day, the more chores there were to fill them. Back in February, when darkness fell before afternoon had chance to turn into evening, everyone had downed tools at teatime and sought sanctuary in front of one of the many open fires throughout the house. As the evenings grew longer there was no such excuse. Jobs that had been postponed, such as laundering all the horses' rugs and dogs' bedding, could now be attended to. At first Izzy believed Jared was finding unsavoury jobs for her to do on purpose, to wind her up, but then she realised it was simply what happened every spring. Each of the dogs was subjected to a bath. The horses were also lathered and rinsed down with the hosepipe one freakishly warm Saturday before being let out into the paddocks, where they promptly rolled to a chorus of collective groans from the hard workers. In the yard itself the stables were swept and hosed and the tack room and feed store gutted, whitewashed and the paintwork freshened. Everyone was expected to muck in and everyone from Mrs Firth to Gemma dressed themselves in frightful rags in order to protect their clothes. Titillated by such sights, Taryn took several unflattering pictures on her phone and proceeded to post them on her Facebook page for all to enjoy. With a pang Izzy recalled the last bit of decorating she'd done. She'd misguidedly undertaken to paint the kitchen in Scott's flat whilst he had been out playing football one Saturday morning. Alas, a surprise was had by more than one. Izzy was mortified to discover that the paint, depicted on the tin as being a soothing pale spring primrose, once dried turned out to be the mucky harshness of the Yellow Pages. Scott had hit the roof and made Izzy swear never to pick up a paintbrush again.

Therefore, no one was more surprised than Izzy to discover that she had hidden talents. When she and Taryn settled down, dressed like tramps once more, to clean and repaint the rabbit and guinea pig hutches, Jared was keen to interfere. Desperate to stick in his twopenn'orth, he loomed over Izzy whilst she carefully edged the hutch door in a rather snazzy red paint, tongue clamped between her teeth as she concentrated. Irritated by such scrutiny, she looked up and scowled.

'Do you mind?' she asked.

'That'll need masking,' Jared said, taking a vast bite out of a king-size Mars Bar. For a moment Izzy was mesmerised by his chewing jaw. Did the man ever stop eating?

'Won't,' she snapped. 'I have a steady hand.' She continued to paint the thin strip of wood without a single flaw. Jared had no option but to look on in astonishment. Once she'd finished, and dropped the paintbrush into the jam jar of turps for cleaning, she turned to Jared and flicked her hand at him, like a rapper, in triumph.

'When you regularly paint an area on your body no bigger

than a square centimetre with coloured varnish you learn a thing or two about accuracy,' she said, not even attempting to control her smugness. Jared was forced to accept that, on this occasion, he was wrong. What surprised Izzy the most was that not only was he gracious in his apology but he seemed to derive genuine pleasure from her success and, basking in the glow of Jared's approval, Izzy said a mental ya-boo-sucks to Scott.

---

WITH JARED so busy it was mainly left to Gemma to teach Izzy but, whilst Izzy found Gemma's teaching less confrontational, there was something about Jared's presence that made her feel so safe. As a result of their duel tutelage and a great deal of patience, Izzy could now canter from walk, rein back and jump a figure-of-eight course of small cross poles. She could catch a pony, muck out, groom and even clean tack, albeit the latter still quite badly. She continued to have problems reassembling a bridle once she'd taken it apart for cleaning. Not only that, Izzy somehow managed to drench the tack room floor with soapy water every time she cleaned a saddle. Jared walked in to find her mopping frantically and couldn't resist taking the piss.

'Need a hand, Neptune?' he asked, inventing yet another nickname for her.

Lessons were interspersed with hacks whenever the weather was clement. Ever since the clocks had gone forward at the end of March, evening hacks with Taryn and Jared had become very much the norm and, without Carlotta's Pan-like interference, these outings were much less eventful and even Izzy began to enjoy a good canter across a nice flat field. Gemma would sometimes join them, dependent both on whether she was free, as strictly speaking she wasn't required to work evenings, and whether The Tank was sound enough to ride.

It was whilst out on one of these hacks one sun-drenched Thursday evening in mid-May, the country air fresh and sweet with the green-apple tang of freshly cut grass, that Izzy's mind was cast back to the summers of her own school days and the cruel first weeks of the summer term. She did *not* remember with fondness how the playing fields were mown during the Easter holidays and how the athletics track was marked out in crumbly white paint, which Izzy always ended up getting on her gym skirt. Izzy had been chronic at PE, always picked last. Naturally, Caro had been a superb sportswoman, able to turn her hand to any discipline. Not only had she repeatedly been elected Sports Captain, she'd led the hockey and tennis teams to victory on several occasions as well as being a county standard middle distance runner. Tall, Amazonian and graceful, to see her striding round a four hundred metre track had been quite a sight. She'd thrived on competitive sport, putting her in good standing for a career at the bar.

And yet here she was, Izzy thought as she, Taryn, Jared and Gemma hacked along Cherry Tree Avenue. She, Izzy Brown, the most un-sporty girl in her year at school, was riding a beautiful Arabian pony through the prettiest of sunlit villages. High above them a candy striped hot air balloon was suspended in the pink evening sky. At intermittent periods they could just hear the distant roar of its flames. Once this would have made Izzy edgy, but now she had enough confidence to transmit her ease through her seat and the reins to Jet, who understood that if Izzy wasn't afraid, he had no need to be. Yes, she'd certainly come a long way.

Maybe she was just a late bloomer, she thought. For once she didn't feel like an utterly hopeless case. Alas, her newfound self-esteem was not destined to last. She returned home to find an email from Caro awaiting her.

*Hi babe, how's life on Emmerdale Farm?*

Izzy bristled slightly, although she'd been the first to refer to The Paddocks as this. She felt it was acceptable for her to take the mickey out of Jared and the girls, but not for anyone else. Brushing her disapproval of Caro's mockery aside she scrolled down. Both she and Jonty were well, it read. Careers were both solid and they were finally getting round to naming a date for their wedding. This depressed Izzy slightly but not so much as the last paragraph of the email.

*I hate to be the one to tell you this, but I'd rather you heard it from me than from anyone else—*

Who else? thought Izzy crossly. No one else had bothered to keep in touch with her and she was now so certain that Scott would never contact her, she pledged to cartwheel up Church Lane in the nip if she were proved wrong.

*—but, in answer to your question about Scott in your last email, I'm afraid he's moved on and is seeing someone else.*

Caro didn't tell Izzy the truth, which was that Scott hadn't so much as moved on as was moving around and had been man-whoring his way all the way from Hampstead Heath unto the City.

*I know you're still hankering after him but my advice to you is to not waste any more time on him. He's clearly not worth it and has made it clear that it's over ad infinitum.*

Once a lawyer, always a lawyer, thought Izzy, half sourly, half fondly. She sat at the computer, staring at the typeset. She wasn't as upset as she thought she would be. With some reluctance she admitted to herself that she had always known it was over. It had been over the moment Scott had walked out of Starbucks all those weeks ago. She was more upset by the thought that she'd believed him for so many months. Never doubting, never questioning. She'd been such a *fool*. Now she felt rudderless. The Paddocks wasn't her home, and yet there was nothing for her in London either. Once more she considered Caro, who'd achieved so much in her short, flawless life what with her impending wedding and superb career. Feeling inferior wasn't alien to Izzy, but experiencing a deep and desperate need to do something about it was. But what? Brain racking and divine inspiration would have to wait, she realised as Taryn appeared in the doorway brandishing a DVD.

'We're watching *High School Musical* tonight,' Taryn said happily. Having already been forced to endure this particular film several times over, Izzy wanted to say no but realised, with a thud, that this was exactly what she was getting paid for. Instead of complaining she smiled at the little girl.

'Only after you've had your bath and done your chores,' Izzy bargained, almost automatically. 'If you do everything properly, you can eat your supper on a tray whilst we watch it.'

'Thanks, Izzy!' Taryn cried and scuttled off.

Taryn, Izzy reflected as she closed down the computer, was a lot easier to please than most other people she encountered. She seemed to be amused by Izzy's clumsiness and scatterbrained tendencies and positively encouraged her to say silly things. Nor was she judgemental when Izzy ballsed something up.

---

'Gardening is a bit of a dark art,' said Gemma. Whacked hollow after a long session on jumping, she and Izzy were in the kitchen enjoying a late afternoon cup of tea and a slice of cake before Gemma left for home. They'd been discussing their favourite foods and the topic of conversation had inevitably worked its way round to Jared and his veg plot. Gemma spoke of him in glowing terms whilst Izzy merely grumbled about him. Mrs Firth, disapproving of both their points of view, chose not to participate and instead worked round them in silence.

'So is cooking,' said Izzy, watching Mrs Firth ease a tray of majestic, golden Yorkshire puddings out of the Aga. Taryn would be thrilled when she found out that was what they were having for dinner. She loved to eat cold Yorkshires drizzled with tablespoons of golden syrup. Izzy thought this combination was repulsive but kept this opinion to herself. Taryn was fussy enough without Izzy giving her more reasons to complain about her food.

'Where is the Ace of Spades anyway?' Izzy asked, looking over her shoulder. Usually Jared could hear the distinctive rustle of a packet of bourbons being opened from one hundred yards.

'Where else? In the garden,' Mrs Firth answered. 'He's too busy to be idling away the hours chit-chatting.' It was a pointed hint.

Jared was certainly dedicated. As a result of his meticulous care the gardens remained immaculate no matter how many fresh weeds popped up overnight. Early cropping vegetables began to feature at the dinner table and in the greenhouse the tomatoes and courgettes began to flower. In a couple of months they'd be overrun with produce, Mrs Firth had said, not displeased. She loved nothing more than creating soups, casseroles, curries and pies in enormous quantities before stocking up the freezer. It was her misguided belief that her home-made frozen ready meals were eaten during her monthly absences. She had no idea that Jared, who had neither the ability nor inclination for cookery, gleefully filled the girls up with

McDonalds and Chinese takeaways instead. No one spragged, knowing that if Mrs Firth found out what went on in her absence she would insist on proper dinners being prepared in advance and the illicit fun of takeaways would come to an end.

During the Easter holidays, back when Carlotta had still been at home, Jared had driven Mrs Firth to the halt at Greater Ousebury and had been back in the house for no more than three minutes when he announced that as a special treat they could have fish and chips. This had been met with hollers of delight. They were purchased from the mobile chippy, which was nothing more than a big white van containing a fully functional fish shop that drove round the villages on a Friday night. As it entered each village it sounded its horn, which sounded like the Queen Elizabeth II coming into dock. It also sold cans of fizzy pop and penny sweets. It did a roaring trade, with families hanging over their front gates as they waited for it.

Izzy was sent down to the front gates to get one of each four times, plus a large curry sauce for Jared.

'Do you want scraps, love?' rasped the hairnetted woman behind the counter as she snatched the twenty pound note out of Izzy's proffered hand. Izzy was aghast.

'No, just the food, thanks,' she cried, panicked. Why were these northerners so aggressive? She almost ran back to the house.

'I'm never going to that van again. She asked me if I wanted to have a fight,' she panted. Jared looked genuinely concerned.

'What did she say?' he asked.

'If I wanted to have a scrap.'

To her astonishment, Jared threw back his head and roared.

'Oh, I'm so pleased that me being threatened is so amusing,' Izzy said, hurt. 'And you two can shut up!' she added to Carlotta and Taryn, who had been tittering at the table.

'She was asking if you wanted *scraps,* not a scrap.'

'Scraps? What the bleedin' hell are scraps?'

'Little pieces of deep fried batter. Don't tell me you've never heard of them. Anyone would think you were from another bloody planet sometimes. Don't you get scraps in London?'

'Only on a Friday night in Islington,' Izzy replied.

---

DAYS PASSED AS QUICKLY as hours. Weeks passed in a daze. Izzy fell into bed knackered every night.

Carlotta was due back for a full week for half term at Whitsuntide. As her arrival date grew closer the atmosphere in the house changed again. This time Izzy added her own apprehension to the collective tension. At the core, everyone was thinking the same thing.

What mood would she be in?

As it transpired, Carlotta was more amiable than usual. No one knew the reason why and no one dared to ask. Jared mentioned to Izzy in passing that it may be due to Carlotta's near-professional focus on her summer show schedule. Her sights were firmly set on winning the junior showjumping at the Great Yorkshire Show in July and she spent all of her spare time training Jet under Gemma's skillful eye. Not that the weather was helpful. In fateful alignment with Carlotta's return, the warm sunshine disappeared behind a dark cloud, and stayed there. For all of half term it rained, and rained… and rained. Not that any hacks or lessons were postponed. That's what macs were for, Jared told Izzy unsympathetically. Everyone was expected to ride as per usual.

Carlotta had opted to jump Jet rather than Vega at almost all of the summer shows she had entered. Her reasoning was twofold; firstly, it was likely that this was her last opportunity to compete on Jet before she outgrew him and, secondly and more simply, on Jet she would win. As a result she demanded that Izzy be barred from riding her pony and so Izzy found herself bumped onto The Tank once more. It hadn't helped that the last time Izzy had ridden Jet out in Carlotta's presence he began to limp and had to be led home, hobbling. Believing she had broken Carlotta's pony, Izzy had been terrified of her reaction, and her fears had not been without foundation. Carlotta had gone berserk until Jared pointed out that Jet had merely cast a shoe and rang the farrier.

Bridle paths spread out like filigree around the Ousebury area, providing rides suitable for all abilities and of every length. Taryn's favourite snaked alongside the river bank and through Prickett's Copse, a pretty little bluebell wood, before heading back along Church Lane which had marvellous wide grass verges. Carlotta preferred a route that took them across the toll bridge as this led to a long stretch of grassland that was always good for a nice long gallop. The route they used the least was a bridle path that skirted the edge of Greater Ousebury and bypassed a disused agricultural building that had once housed an abattoir. It was a pretty route that skirted the foot of the Howardian Hills and as a result commanded glorious views over the Vale of Loxley but nevertheless they always gave it a wide berth as the horses, freaked out by the faintest scent of blood, would jib and dance if they went anywhere near the old slaughterhouse. It was due to this that Jared had forbidden everyone to take this route unless he was present.

Of course, this didn't mean he was obeyed.

It was not just one, but a collection of reasons that resulted in them riding out towards the abattoir. Afterwards, Carlotta and Gemma argued it had been so wet that a hack which was predominantly road walking had been essential but the reality was they had exhausted all the other routes and

Carlotta, who bored easily, fancied a change. Jared, who most certainly would have forbidden them to hack out in such adverse weather conditions, never mind towards the abattoir, was away at a meeting with MK, who was yet again in the area, and was as a consequence ignorant of Carlotta's intentions.

They rode out under a damp, grey sky. After so much rain the ground was waterlogged. Everyone wore long waxed jackets with the collars turned up. Izzy hadn't been keen to ride at all but was ganged up on by Carlotta and Gemma, and even Taryn, until she agreed. Worse still, with Jet embargoed on Carlotta's command, Izzy was promoted to the enormous Ghost, who she'd never ridden before. Gemma insisted on riding The Tank, who she wanted to check was sound, and Carlotta braved Vega. Taryn, as usual, rode Jester.

Izzy couldn't relax as they clopped out of the village and along the top road towards Greater Ousebury. She seemed so far away from the ground. Ghost didn't help matters either. He shook like a wet dog whilst Izzy was in the saddle, causing her to yelp in terror. The others all seemed to think this was highly amusing. Nor did they seem bothered by the bitter wind that whipped their faces or the slick, wet surface of the tarmac beneath the horses' hooves. Every so often Ghost would skid slightly, his metal shoe rasping against the road, jarring Izzy as he righted himself. Up top, Izzy sat ramrod straight, petrified, which only served to unsettle Ghost further.

A hay wagon trundled towards them. Ghost lived up to his name and spooked, clattering sideways towards the middle of the road and into the path of an oncoming car. The expression of horror on the driver's face mirrored Izzy's own as she fought to regain control.

'For God's sake, Izzy, get a grip,' snapped Carlotta. It was all right for her, Izzy thought savagely. Vega was for once behaving and standing like a beautiful golden statue on the slender grass verge.

Thankfully, the turning for the bridle path was just ahead. As they passed the abattoir all the horses started to act up to such an extent that Gemma then decided they should return via a series of fields rather than retrace their steps back past the old building. But this meant they would have to jump a small ditch. Barely two feet wide, it was filled with leaves and reeds. For the second time that day, Izzy voiced her concerns but again the others goaded her until she agreed to try. Worried about the take off being muddy, Izzy forgot to worry about how slippery her saddle was from all the rain. Confused by his rider's mixed signals, Ghost hesitated on jump off then, giving an almighty bound, cleared the ditch with feet to spare. Alas, it was all too much for Izzy's still insecure seat. She slid off to the side, landed smack in the middle of the ditch with a comedy splosh before emerging from the muddy gloop covered from head to toe in mud and grasses and with her wet hair plastered to the sides of her face like a helmet.

'Oh Izzy, the absolute state of you. You look like a bog troll.' Carlotta was bent double with laughter. Even Taryn grinned. Having had a good laugh at Izzy's expense, Gemma finally regained her common sense and suggested they call it a day. The rain had begun to come down in stair rods but even so it was with some reluctance that Carlotta and Taryn agreed to turn their horses for home.

Mrs Firth was waiting for them. Indignant, she followed them round the side of the house and into the barn, berating them with every step.

'Oh, do stop fussing, Firthie,' Carlotta said in exasperated tones as she dragged a towel over Vega's dampest areas. 'We only got a bit wet and even Izzy had the good sense to fall off in something soft.'

'Stop fussing?! I've been worried sick. Fancy going out

riding in this weather. And look at the condition of you. Everyone is having a nice hot bath, especially you, young lady,' Mrs Firth said, pointing at Izzy who was shivering violently, unable to even consider removing Ghost's tack. She looked her up and down, and tutted. 'You other girls can sort out Izzy's horse for her. She needs to get warm straight away otherwise she'll catch her death.'

Teeth chattering, Izzy followed Mrs Firth back to the house and squelched her way into the utility room where she was instructed to strip.

'You're not walking all that filth through the house.'

Jared was already home and was drinking tea and reading the local paper in the kitchen, stockinged feet up on the table. He took one look at Izzy, still mud-ridden but now shivering in her bra and pants, and almost choked on his cup of tea.

'What the hell happened to you? Talk about Izzy *Brown*.' Izzy merely glowered at him.

When she got out, the bathwater resembled something a charity fundraiser might submerge themselves in, and she *still* wasn't clean and had to have a shower as well. Next time anyone suggested a hack that went anywhere near the old abattoir, she was pulling a sickie!

When Jared found out what had actually happened he went berserk. Carlotta was bollocked and even Gemma was hauled into the winter den for a ticking off.

'It was bloody irresponsible,' Jared raged. Not only should Izzy never have been told to ride a strange horse without his permission but any one of them could have been hurt or worse. If Izzy had lost control the knock on effect would have been terrible. Horses were herd animals. If Ghost had bolted, the whole lot would have gone, and Gemma would have been responsible. And what the frigging hell had she been thinking, letting them ride past the old abattoir?

Only Taryn, courtesy of her youth was exempt. Even Izzy was told, with considerable exasperation, that she should have stood her ground and refused to ride. She had felt cherished until that point.

Later, and as had become the norm, Izzy collapsed into bed absolutely banjaxed and was asleep within minutes. Outside it was still blowing a hooley. Rain was lashing against the windowpanes and rattling the guttering. It seemed as though only minutes had passed when the burglar alarm screamed through the night. Izzy was yanked out of sleep in the most unpleasant of ways.

'What the bleedin' hell—?' she muttered as she reluctantly pushed back the comforter. This couldn't possibly be good. It had been months since she had set it off by accident. She couldn't possibly be blamed for this one. It was probably Carlotta sneaking out for an illicit ciggie.

Out on the landing it was bedlam. Taryn and Carlotta, instantly exonerated by virtue of her presence, were already out of their bedrooms, tugging on dressing gowns as they went. Taryn was already showing the early signs of a hyperventilation attack whereas Carlotta looked thoroughly overexcited at the prospect of some mid-night drama. Mrs Firth was bustling downstairs, round as a barrel in her own flowery robe.

'Kitchen everyone, you know what to do!' Jared barked, overtaking Mrs Firth on the stairs. His sharp eyes had not missed the fact that everyone was present. Izzy was just a little bit freaked out. Was there actually an intruder? Jared was definitely taking it seriously. This was not a drill. As she ushered a panicked Taryn along the landing, Izzy tried to avert her eyes away from Jared's bare, ripped torso, complete with a tattoo of what looked like some sort of military insignia on the small of his back and deeply tanned from gardening without a shirt as he jogged the last few steps.

'And slippers please!' Mrs Firth added.

'Godssake,' Carlotta could be heard saying as she quickly snatched her slippers from her bedroom.

'Sod the slippers. Downstairs, now!' Jared said. 'Move it.'

Izzy allowed herself to be herded into the kitchen. Jared led the way, flicking lights on as he went until the entire house was lit up like a monument. Mrs Firth headed straight for the kettle whilst Jared began checking entrances and exits like a prison warden. The dogs, all frenzied and unsettled by the disturbance, were doing the Wall of Death round the room.

Once Jared was satisfied they were safe in the kitchen he instructed them to stay put whilst he checked the remainder of the house.

'I'm going to check all the animals are secured. No one leaves this room until I say so,' Jared said as he left, pointing first at Carlotta and then Izzy. 'That includes you two. Firthie, you're in charge.'

Jared was gone for at least half an hour which gave Mrs Firth plenty of time to ply the girls with mugs of hot chocolate.

'Can I have cake?' Taryn asked. 'I want cake.'

'No cake in the middle of the night,' Izzy said automatically. She wasn't even sure where the words had come from. Taryn pouted.

'Crisps then,' she bargained.

'Nope,' said Izzy, idly flicking through a supermarket magazine that had been lying on the kitchen table. 'You'll get indigestion.'

'What's that?' Taryn asked. Her eyes had taken on a steely hue which Izzy knew to be a portent of trouble.

'Stomach ache,' interjected Carlotta, helping herself to an apple from the bowl. 'Then terrible farts.'

'You're so full of poo, Carlotta.' Taryn turned to Izzy, her face belligerent. 'Why does she get to have a snack?' Izzy looked at Carlotta in exasperation. She swore she only did it to be difficult.

'You can have fruit if you like,' Carlotta said, selecting a banana and lobbing it at Taryn. 'Here, catch!'

Taryn screamed as the banana grazed her shoulder. Izzy turned on Carlotta.

'Do you always have to be such a bitch?' she yelled at her. 'Now we'll have to give her cake to shut her up.' Furious, Izzy snatched a chocolate cupcake from the cake tin and lobbed it to a gloating Taryn. Carlotta continued to hurl abuse at Izzy.

'Don't call me a bitch, bloody hired help. Don't forget that you're only *staff* and staff can be *fired*.'

Of course, Jared picked this moment to re-enter the room.

'Everything's nice and quiet out there which is more than I can say for in here. What the bloody hell is going on? Why has Taryn got cake at this time of the night?'

'Carlotta threw a banana at me,' Taryn said, mouth open as she triumphantly chomped on her cupcake. She'd managed to smear chocolate frosting all round her mouth. 'I got cake to settle me.'

'As if anything could settle you after all the sugar and upheaval,' said Mrs Firth with more than a degree of cynicism.

'Izzy, take the girls back to their rooms. I need to have a quick chat with Mrs Firth,' Jared said, turning his back on the three of them. Izzy had no choice but to shepherd the girls out of the kitchen but not before she heard Jared mention something about a breach at the back of the house. Craning her head in an attempt to hear what was being said she noticed a bulge in the back of Jared's jeans. Something solid, and metallic, and out of place. It looked like…

Suddenly aware he was being watched, Jared jerked his leg and kicked the kitchen door. Acknowledging how tired and disorientated she was, Izzy figured that she must have imagined it. It was the only logical explanation.

The following morning Jared offered his own explanation for what had happened.

'Must've been the bad weather that set it off,' he said dismissively at the breakfast table.

In the first instance Izzy believed him but then the situation was further exacerbated by the discovery of the mutilated bird the next day. Izzy had opened the back door, found it lying dead on the utility room doorstep with all its innards spilling out, and shrieked and shrieked. Jared, wondering what the hell had happened, dashed through wearing nothing but his boxers amidst a chorus of titters and catcalls from the girls and was singularly unamused to be disturbed over something so trivial.

'Probably one of the cats,' he reasoned. It would have left it there for its own convenience and would be back to retrieve it at supper time. This seemed to reassure Taryn, who never handled death well, but didn't stop Carlotta creeping up on her and regaling hideous tales of death and mutilation in lugubrious tones which scared the bejeezus out of her. Izzy, who had quite old fashioned ideas when it came to discipline, no doubt borne from years of being on the receiving end of it herself, believed deprivation was an effective method of punishment and promptly confiscated Carlotta's iPhone and banned her from using the internet until she apologised to her sister.

'Trust you to take her side,' Carlotta foamed.

Matters were worsened by the appearance of a second dead animal. This time it was a mangy rat that, upon first impression, seemed to have just conked out on the decking but closer inspection revealed it had sustained a broken neck. Jared passed it off as being a natural death by being dropped from a great height by a bird of prey, but Izzy could see he was rattled. It could be a coincidence, or it could be a prank. Carlotta overheard Izzy talking about the possibility of her being the culprit and this caused a row of simply colossal proportions and which ended in Izzy calling Carlotta a venomous little brat. Carlotta retaliated by calling Izzy a nasty, orange-faced, big-haired, thick southern bitch.

'Say what you see,' said Jared drily, before frogmarching Carlotta away for a time out.

None of which made for a happy household.

Tensions continued for the remainder of half term. Carlotta refused to talk to Izzy at all and only thawed out on the last night before she was due back at school because she'd seen Izzy and Taryn eating ice cream straight out of the tub and wanted to join them. To try and lighten the mood Izzy reconstituted the game she and Caro had played as teenagers and as a result each girl was trying to fit more ice cream on their spoon than the last, amid much spillage and giggling. Jared entered the room just in time to witness Taryn shoving an obscene amount of toffee fudge swirl into her tiny mouth. When she grinned at him, she looked rabid.

'Nice!' he said sarkily, about turning and stalking off. Secretly, he was relieved the rift appeared to have been healed.

The next day Carlotta returned to school and the household was plunged into sobriety once more. Izzy continued to grow to understand the girls. Taryn suffered less than Carlotta as she didn't remember her mother. Carlotta had six years' worth of memories. When she was feeling spiteful she would torment Taryn with these and, even worse, about the picture of Carlotta and her mother in MK's room.

'You're not even in that picture because Papa loves me best,' Izzy had overheard Carlotta say. Appalled, she confided in Mrs Firth, who confirmed over afternoon tea that Taryn felt inferior to her dazzling sister.

'But Taryn is just as special as Carlotta,' Izzy said, confused. Granted, Taryn's face wasn't as perfect as Carlotta's but was more expressive and as a consequence less haughty. She was also more academic than Carlotta and Izzy could see her excelling in science or literature when she was older. She had no reason to feel inferior.

'You and I know that, love, but Taryn doesn't. The problem with this house is that everyone is hankering after summat,' Mrs Firth said. 'Carlotta grieves for the mother she remembers, Taryn grieves for her absence of memories, Jared still isn't over his marriage and I worry for the lot of you.'

'I'm not grieving,' said Izzy, startled.

'Give over. You've got double rations. I just can't figure out what you miss most, that chap you're moping over or that London life you left behind,' Mrs Firth said, matter of factly.

Izzy was left staring after her. Jared had mentioned his broken relationship but never that he'd been married. It certainly gave her plenty to think about.

---

IZZY WOULD HAVE BEEN SURPRISED to learn that Jared couldn't find much to complain about in her work. Despite her natural aptitude for disaster she was a hard worker and picked things up quickly. Taryn was very taken with her, and she got along with the other members of the household too. She'd even begun to grumble less about the horse riding. Graced with an empathic nature that she hadn't been able to flex hitherto, she was very patient and understanding when Taryn was ill and was very gentle with all the animals.

A great triumph was the day Izzy and Taryn shared a makeshift chocolate fondue, dipping quartered strawberries and sliced banana into melted Dairy Milk. Taryn would only eat tiny bites of fruit and even then they had to be completely camouflaged by the chocolate, but it was still a great success. Both Jared and Mrs Firth were impressed.

'You did good, lass.'

---

Unable to banish the mental picture she had of Jared in the kitchen with what looked like a handgun in his jeans, Izzy found herself speculating on him. She remembered Mrs Firth mentioning that he'd been in the armed forces and wondered if he had problems letting go of his combative past. She began to ask Mrs Firth casual questions. How old was Jared? How had he come to be a gardener? What had brought him to The Paddocks?

Mrs Firth was always happy to gossip and filled Izzy in over several pots of tea and an entire packet of mint Viscounts.

Jared was about thirty-eight, mebbe closer to forty, she thought, and he came to work at The Paddocks when he left the military with an honourable discharge.

'He was injured on his last tour in Iraq. The truck he was riding in was behind another one, and which had driven over one of those IUDs.' Given her own propensity for malapropisms, Izzy felt it would be an impertinence to correct her. 'Anyway, the first truck had blown up straight away but had also set afire the truck Jared was in. He risked his own life mekkin' sure everyone got out alive. He was only just out himself when it exploded. He must have been born under a lucky star 'cause he walked away with nothing worse than an arm full of lead and a few nasty burns despite being flung over fifteen yards from the blast.'

'He told me his arm was scarred because he got into a big fight. He never gave any indication as to quite how big the fight was, as in an international one.'

'Aye, well he always has been modest. He doesn't see himself as being a hero, but we all know he is.' Izzy felt some discomfort as she remembered how she'd mocked him mercilessly for swanning round the house like he was some sort of crude, know-it-all superhero. Yorkshire Man, she'd called him.

'He received the Military Cross for his bravery, went to

Buckingham Palace for his invigoration and met 'Er Majesty and everything. He's got Operational Service Medals for Sierra Leone and Afghanistan, and the Iraq Medal too.'

'Sierra Leone? I didn't know it was a place. I thought she'd won *X Factor*,' Izzy confessed.

Mrs Firth gave a happy smile. 'He does look handsome when he's wearing all his decorations.' The smile faded. 'As soon as he was discharged his wife sent word that she was leaving him. That was two years ago, more or less, and he came to live with us. MK was away from home more and more and he was keen to have a strong man he could trust around the place. Jared and MK have been friends for many a year. It weren't even a case of one friend doing t'other a favour, it was just an agreement that suited 'em both at the right time. Jared was in a bit of a state when he first came here to live, suffering from a bit of that post stress disorder and still reeling from the break up of his marriage. He lost his mum not long after too. He was very raw for a long time. He's been here ever since and to be honest, it's the best place for him because this house is a great healer.'

Izzy was appalled with herself. How had she never known about any of this? She'd had no idea Jared had suffered so much. She'd simply presumed he was a brash, happy-go-lucky type who didn't care overly much for other people's feelings. Had she really been so self-absorbed that she hadn't picked up on the clues? And what else was there that she didn't know? She was reminded afresh about how little she knew about her new life. Well, she might as well start finding out straight away.

'He never mentions his ex-wife. When did they divorce?' she asked.

'They didn't. He's still married. They stayed wed for two reasons, I think. Jared absolutely adored her and didn't want to hurt her further by cutting off her income source. She'd lose out on his military pension, ye see. Plus I think he always thought they might get back together.'

Izzy simply gaped.

'But why did it break down? It sounds like he really wanted to make a go of it.'

Mrs Firth grimaced in disapproval.

'They rowed about many things but in the end it was the oldest reason in the world. He wanted a family, she didn't.'

This touched a nerve with Izzy. Growing up she'd always presumed that at some time, far in the future, she'd meet a nice guy, get married, buy a house and have children. Except that the future was fast becoming the present and she was no closer to a successful relationship than she'd been at age sixteen. She would be thirty next year. Most of the girls from her year at school had long since been married and could be seen pushing prams and buggies round the suburbs of Greater London. It had seemed to come so easily to them. Why hadn't it for her? What if she never met someone who was prepared to marry her, or at least not until it was too late for her to have babies? Was that something she was just going to have to accept?

An unfamiliar pain tore through Izzy, cutting her to her emotional core. Her body clock had kicked in. Not that she could understand why it was called a body clock. It seemed to her to be more of a body bomb, relentlessly ticking down the years until it reached its inevitable end, not exploding but merely fizzling out, destroying everything in its wake nevertheless.

'None of us were surprised. She used to come with him when he came up to visit MK but you could tell it was under duress. She was a stuck up little madam. All heels and handbags but no manners. She didn't like the countryside, she didn't like kids, she didn't like animals and she didn't like horses. All she was interested in was spending Jared's money and being taken posh places.'

Sounds rather like me, Izzy thought glumly. Mrs Firth seemed to read her thoughts.

'Don't you think on,' Mrs Firth said, accurately interpreting Izzy's expression. 'She were nowt like you. She had no heart, not a caring bone in her body. The pair of you couldn't be more different.'

'What did she look like?'

'Huh, pretty enough, I s'pose, but she had a hard little face. Lovely red hair, though.'

Figures, thought Izzy.

---

A WEEK after Carlotta had returned to school there was yet another nasty occurrence. It was one that put paid to any hopes that coincidence was at play, and also made Izzy feel very small that she'd suspected Carlotta, who on this occasion had an irrefutable alibi.

Jared had gone to unlock the barn door only to find a squirrel hanging from it. No damage had been done and nothing had been taken. Someone was infiltrating The Paddocks with the sole purpose of spooking everyone. Jared, having scoured the perimeter hedges and fences for signs of intrusion but found none, was extremely concerned and spent a couple of afternoons increasing security by patching up any weak spots in the boundaries and installing a couple more security lights.

'If someone really wanted to get in, they could,' he said. 'But hopefully they'll be deterred by these measures.' Everyone was to be extra vigilant, he instructed Izzy, Mrs Firth and Gemma, who had all exchanged horrified glances.

Taryn, thankfully, remained blissfully unaware of all of this.

'Let's keep it that way, too,' Jared said grimly.

# THE GREAT YORKSHIRE SHOW-OFF

Carlotta broke up from school at the beginning of July. She arrived home full of focus and enthusiasm for her summer schedule and in particular for her participation in the junior showjumping at the Great Yorkshire Show, which was to take place in a fortnight's time. Taryn was equally fixated on her own showing class and for two weeks Izzy was submerged in a bubble-like existence of equestrianism. The upside was that as both Gemma and Jared were fully occupied with the girls' preparation, Izzy was excused from riding until after the event. Not that this meant a lessening of her workload. Instead of riding she was expected to be at the girls' beck and call, almost like a groom. It went without saying that Carlotta abused this agreement but Izzy was surprised to learn that Taryn could be equally and as uncompromisingly demanding.

The night before the show was sheer bedlam. It had been a long day of unrelenting hard work and preparation. Not even Mrs Firth had been exempt and had spent the afternoon pressing jodhpurs, shirts and jackets, and which were now hanging in cellophane wrap as though from a dry cleaners, as well as preparing dinner and packed lunches. Despite being hungry, both girls were too nervous to eat their dinner and instead prodded their chicken and pasta round their plates.

Essential items disappeared without reason. Taryn screamed round the house searching for her riding helmet, which had mysteriously gone missing. Izzy suspected devilry on Carlotta's part but kept this opinion to herself, having learned that further antagonising an already moody Carlotta served no purpose whatsoever.

'Where's my crash cap?' Taryn demanded of Mrs Firth, who stared at her with incredulity.

'Cheeky imp. How am I supposed to know?'

Taryn then proceeded to open every cupboard and drawer in the kitchen and utility. She even opened the top oven of the Aga, much to Mrs Firth's annoyance.

'It's not in there, you little monkey. Get out of it. You'll be making my Madeira cake sink.'

Carlotta wandered into the kitchen and helped herself to a crisp sandwich.

'God, I'm starving!'

'Perhaps you should have eaten your dinner then,' Izzy said snippily. Carlotta grimaced behind her back.

'Have you seen my crash cap?' Taryn asked her sister, hands on hips. All eyes turned to Carlotta, who instantly adopted an expression of indignation.

'No, I bloody haven't. I have more important things to be worrying about than Taryn's stupid hat. It's probably beneath her bed along with all the other crap she shoves under there instead of siding it away properly.'

Prophetic words indeed! The crash cap was discovered under the bed and borne off to join the other tonnage of equipment that would be packed into the horsebox. Izzy looked on balefully as Jared stacked the horses' tack into the already bulging grooms' compartment.

'Don't forget to leave room for Jet and Jester,' she said bleakly. Jared grinned at her over his shoulder.

'I thought I'd pop them in the Golf with you and Taryn,' he said.

'Har har!' said Izzy, trying hard not to focus her eyes on Jared's denimed arse as he bent back over. Jesus, he had good glutes. Thoughts such as these confused Izzy. She knew she didn't fancy Jared, he was too coarse and craggy to suit her usual tastes, but on occasion she did find him curiously attractive. The first time she'd seen him on a horse had been one such time. There had been something so inherently masculine about the way he'd sat astride Ghost, with his muscles all taught and moulded, that had sparked something in her. It was for this very reason she tended not to watch him working in the garden either, what with all that forking and hoeing. Not that she was worried about it when it did happen, which wasn't very often. Experience had taught her that all it usually took to quell any lustful thoughts on her part was for Jared to open his mouth and speak. A well-timed insult from him was normally more than sufficient for reason to be restored. Only that morning he'd reverted to one of his favourite nicknames for her, Skeletor, on the grounds that she was so skinny and curveless. He never called Gemma names, she noted sourly as the pretty redhead appeared in the stable yard carrying a pile of lightweight rugs.

'Where do you want these, J?' she asked.

Which brought to the fore another complication, Izzy mused. Gemma. Even if she did fancy her chances with Jared, which she *didn't*, he was already spoken for.

In view of how early everyone would be required to rise, it had been arranged that Gemma would stay the night in one of the guest bedrooms. To her own utter surprise, Izzy realised she felt prickly about this. It didn't matter that Gemma had been employed at The Paddocks for as many years as Izzy had been there months. If Gemma's domain was the stable yard, then the house was Izzy's, and she was feeling distinctly territorial. It wasn't just that the girls viewed

Gemma with an idolatry level of worship, or that the three of them had their own little gang, or that because of this she had the ability to diminish almost any instruction Izzy had given. It wasn't even that Izzy disliked Gemma. She didn't. She thought the groom was pleasant and lots of fun, and she was the closest thing to a friend Izzy had at The Paddocks. It was something else, something deep-rooted in Izzy most likely linked to her lack of confidence, but for some reason Gemma being present in the house made her feel undermined, usurped even.

No one wanted to go to bed. They were too excited, too nervous, too awake.

'It's only just gone nine,' Carlotta complained, cross because she wanted to watch *Flicka* on Sky Cinema.

'I don't care if it's half past nine or high noon in the Arizona desert. Get yourself to bed,' Jared commanded. 'Everyone is having an early night. Tomorrow will be a long, hard day.'

Half an hour later Izzy trudged up to bed. Hearing scuffling and whispers from Carlotta's bedroom she pressed her ear against the door.

'Are you asleep?' she hissed.

'Yes,' came the high-pitched reply, followed by giggles.

'Fool!' That was Carlotta's voice. Izzy opened the door to discover both girls in Carlotta's king-size bed, duvet flush to their chins, expressions of innocence on their faces. Steptoe, comfy and cosy between them, yawned widely and blinked his eyes as light from the landing filtered in. The three of them looked so adorable that Izzy didn't have the heart to yell at them.

'Sleep tight,' she said, smiling as she closed the door. If they drew strength from each other's company it was worth letting them break the rules for once.

Gemma poked her head out of the guest room door having heard the exchange. She gave Izzy a wicked wink as

Jared passed on his way to the narrow spiral staircase that led to the second floor and his attic room. Izzy's heart sank as she realised what this meant. As soon as everyone was in the safety of their own bedrooms, Gemma would no doubt creep up to join him, sliding under the covers, all buxom and alluring. Early night indeed! Jared was clearly intent on having a long, hard night before his long, hard day. Disgruntled, Izzy climbed into her own bed, and tried to make sense of her feelings. What was she so pissed off about? It wasn't as though she didn't know what was going on between them. It just rankled sometimes that Jared, who was so priggish about the truth, could be so blatant in his own duplicity. Plus, and this was the most baffling thing of all, Izzy wasn't sure whether her pride was dented because Jared had chosen Gemma, or *hadn't* chosen her.

The big day finally dawned. Izzy, truculent and groggy, was not impressed to be watching said dawn arrive as she stood, hot mug of extremely strong leaded coffee in her perishing hands, at the threshold of the barn as she waited for the horses to be brought in. Dragged out of bed at four o'clock sharp, she wasn't in the mood to be romantic and whimsical about the rising sun, chirruping birds and pink and dapple-grey skies of daybreak.

There was stacks to be done. Mrs Firth had the best end of the deal, Izzy thought sourly as she watched the ponies be led through the paddock gate. She was inside, where it was warm, happily preparing both a cooked breakfast of unspeakable proportions and a packed lunch of equally comparable size.

Considering the importance of her competition, Carlotta had demanded both Jared and Gemma assist her in her preparations, which had left Taryn with a very reluctant Izzy. Thankfully, all the tack and other paraphernalia had been cleaned to painstaking lengths and packed the previous day, but the ponies had to be dealt with on the day itself. As soon as they'd been settled in their stables they had to be fed, washed and groomed. Manes and tails would be plaited once they were at the show.

Taryn had instructed Izzy to bathe Jester's white bits with a special blue shampoo which would make his white bits 'Daz' white. When Taryn was called in for breakfast, and went with considerable reluctance, she left Izzy with strict instructions to stay behind to rinse the potion off after five minutes before coming in herself. Grumbling, disgruntled at being treated like a minion, and with her stomach rumbling at the thought of bacon and eggs, Izzy, plonked herself on a hay bale, buried her nose in a celebrity gossip magazine and completely lost track of time. She was still sitting on the same hay bale when Taryn returned half an hour later.

Taryn's shriek of horror made Izzy drop the magazine. Taryn was frantically rubbing at Jester's coat with a sopping sponge but it was no use. Jester's white patches were decidedly palest blue and showed no signs of fading despite Taryn's energetic efforts. The racket caused Jared, Gemma and Carlotta to appear. Carlotta took one look at Jester and roared with laughter.

'Ha ha ha, he's no longer a skewbald but a bluebald,' she hooted. Jared told her to shut up but Izzy could see from his twitching lip that he too found it amusing. Gemma was the only one who took Taryn's reaction seriously.

'We'll wash him again. I'm sure it will come off,' she said. This seemed to appease Taryn. Only after it became evident that the blue wash wasn't going to fade by man-made means did Gemma's optimism abate. Taryn then proceeded to throw a hissy fit of gargantuan proportions. Her blame was very much directed at Izzy who she called every name she could think of, causing Jared to make a mental note to question her about the extent of her vocabulary. Jester's coat wasn't the only thing blue.

'I'll be laughed out of the ring,' Taryn stormed, stamping her tiny foot.

'No, you won't,' said Gemma, still trying to act as peacekeeper.

'Oh yes she will,' Carlotta said, still laughing.

'Shut up, Carlotta,' Jared snapped. 'You're not helping.'

At this point the excitement proved too much for Taryn, who collapsed in Gemma's arms in floods of tears.

'I don't stand a chance of being placed now. It's all Izzy's fault. She's hopeless,' she wailed. 'I'm going to scratch. I can't possibly ride him looking like that. I'm not going. *I'm not going*!' Her voice rose to a shrill, rasping screech and she threw the wet sponge at Carlotta, who cursed at her. It was at this point that Jared intervened.

'Gemma, could you please take Taryn to her room for a lie down before she hyperventilates? Carlotta, haven't you got your own pony to prepare? Scoot!' The three girls dispersed leaving Jared alone with Izzy, who was still seated on the hay bale but was staring at the floor and gnawing at the skin round her fingernails.

'Stop biting,' Jared said, not unkindly. 'It's not the end of the world. Taryn'll calm down before the morning is through.'

'But I've ruined her chances,' Izzy said, her eyes still focused on the ground.

'Nonsense! She's too much of a beastly little pothunter to scratch from the competition. Once she gets her grubby hands on the winner's trophy she won't care if Jester's blue, or pink and green with purple polka dots. In fact, the little oick will probably claim it was done on purpose and belittle the other miniature riders for bringing boringly coloured ponies.' He held his hand out for Izzy to take. 'Come on, you haven't had any breakfast yet and the last thing you want is Firthie after you because you're not eating properly.' That raised a small smile. Izzy accepted his hand and allowed herself to be despatched to the house.

Feeling better after a good feed, Izzy returned to the stables to find Taryn still sulking but back on schedule to appear at the show just as Jared had predicted. Both ponies were immaculately groomed and already wearing their travel rugs and leg bandages. Jet's were red. Jester's, thank God, were navy and matched his blue rinse perfectly. Gemma was throwing dandy brushes, stable rubbers, spools of thread, packets of needles and tins of hoof oil into a tack tray whilst Jared lugged bales of straw, oats and pony nuts to the horsebox. It was a mammoth operation. After that there was a flurry of activity in the house as everyone disappeared into their en suites for a shower. As Izzy dried her hair she idly wondered if Gemma and Jared would share a shower to top off their night of passion and couldn't help but imagine how beautiful they would look, all hot and lathered, their limbs entwined. They were remarkably discreet, she had to acknowledge. If Gemma hadn't let it slip about their fling she would never have guessed there was anything between them. Finally everyone was ready. Izzy and Gemma both looked efficient and just a little bit glamorous in jeans, tee shirts and gilets. Taryn and Carlotta were wearing sweat pants and would change into breeches and jackets just before their events.

Carlotta looked mournful as the ponies were loaded into the horsebox.

'I wish Papa were here,' she said. Izzy gave her a quick pat on the shoulder (she still daren't hug the tempestuous teenager) in an attempt to comfort her.

'We're going to take so much video and so many photos he'll almost think he was here.'

Carlotta looked at her scornfully.

'What's that got to do with anything? If Papa were here we could have used our usual rugs instead of these tatty old things,' she said. She might as well have been speaking to an infant.

'Carlotta!' Jared growled, having overheard this exchange, at which point Carlotta stropped off.

Show clothes were hung in the groom's compartment in the horsebox together with boots, so well-polished Jared's old lieutenant-colonel would have approved, and tack stowed beneath. The Golf was loaded with the packed lunch, fold-up chairs, picnic rugs and the camcorder and camera. Izzy and Taryn would travel in their usual convoy.

Mrs Firth, sad she couldn't attend, but someone had to stay at home to dog sit, waved them off, flapping a tea towel in the air like a pennant.

'I want to hear everything about it when you get home. Good luck! Take care! Don't fall off!' she cried as they finally pulled away. As no dogs were allowed in the showground a mournful Steptoe also had to stay behind and howled like a werewolf as they drove through the big wrought iron gates. Only the fact that he had been put on a lead prevented him from hurtling after his master.

The journey passed uneventfully. As they approached the Great Yorkshire Showground at Harrogate, Taryn began to fidget in her seat.

'All right, Taryn?' Izzy asked as they crept along the road that led to the competitors' entrance. Minions in fluorescent tabards were checking entrance requirements. Izzy went cold for a minute, having no recollection of putting Taryn's exhibitor's permit in the car, but realised that Jared, thorough as ever, had already stuck it to the dashboard. She blew out her breath in relief. Taryn would have *murdered* her if they'd had to turn round and go back.

'I've got the needle,' Taryn said. Izzy noticed the little girl had turned pale. In front of them Jared was manoeuvring the horsebox into a vacant space opposite the stabling area. Izzy followed suit and parked up next to them.

'You'll be okay, honey. Just imagine you're practising at home. Jester will do the rest.'

Carlotta was already out of the horsebox and banging a tantivy on the roof of the Golf as Izzy turned off the engine.

'Come on, hurry up dawdlers! We've got great stables right on the end of the block, and I've just seen Nick Skelton and Ben Maher,' she said, naming a couple of famous international showjumpers. She looked elated. Jared was unlocking the horsebox; Gemma was already inside having entered through the hatch in the groom's compartment.

'Ponies are both fine!' called her disembodied voice from within. 'Let's get the straw into the stables and then we'll unload them.'

Despite the early hour the exhibitors' area was already buzzing. Izzy could do no more than gape at the mass of horses and ponies, sheep, cattle and pigs that were being led to their pens and stables. An exhibitor dressed from head to foot in tweed strode past, half a dozen terriers surging ahead of him, all saying their piece. They reminded Izzy of Steptoe. The showground was vast and already heaving with tradesmen and businesses setting up their stands. Above them banners and pennants were blowing in the breeze against a porcelain-blue sky dotted with plump opaline clouds. The tannoy kept them updated. The first class of the morning, best mare and foal, was called into the White Rose Ring, causing an extra surge of activities as handlers and grooms scurried round to ensure their charges were immaculate. Izzy had accompanied Jared and the girls to many, many shows and competitions but never had she experienced anything on this scale. No wonder Taryn was nervous!

'Wake up,' said Jared's voice, interrupting her thoughts. He'd already lugged a bale of straw into each loose box. 'There's work to be done. Taryn's in the ring at ten-thirty. We've got just under two hours to get both ponies settled, have a cuppa and get both her and Jester ready to rock.'

'I feel sick,' said a little voice by Izzy's side. Looking down, she saw Taryn was no longer pale, but green.

'Let's get Jester in his stable and start to groom him again. A bit of work will calm you down,' said Gemma. She led the little skewbald into his allocated stall and whipped off his rug. Izzy's prayers had been ignored. He was still blue. Taryn's bottom lip quivered.

'Oh my God. Look at the colour of that pony's white patches,' said an unfamiliar voice. Two girl grooms had appeared at the stall door. 'How on Earth did you get him that colour?' Taryn shot an evil look at Izzy, who quailed. 'He looks awesome!' continued the girl. 'No one else is gonna stand a chance.' And they were gone. This seemed to galvanise Taryn who, after a bottle of lemonade and a KitKat to give her an energy boost, regained some colour in her cheeks. From then on the minutes flew. Gemma and Jared brushed, polished and plaited for all they were worth whilst Taryn changed her clothes in the horsebox. Izzy's fingers were all thumbs as she tied Taryn's number onto her coat. It seemed that no time at all had passed before Taryn was mounted and waiting to enter the collecting ring. To her surprise, Izzy felt quite choked up as Taryn, looking adorable in beige breeches, jodhpur boots and matching brown tweed jacket and tie that complemented Jester's beautiful brown patches, rode away.

'Just do your best,' she cried after her, echoing what her own mother had always said to her as a child, but her voice was drowned out by the tannoy.

'12.2hh and under riding show ponies, class six, is commencing in the White Rose Ring. Will all competitors please progress to the collecting ring,' it blared.

Gemma, being much more experienced than Izzy, had been chosen as Taryn's groom, leaving Izzy to watch, biting her lack of nails, at the ringside. Jared, complete with camcorder and camera, and Carlotta came to join her having reassured themselves that Jet was happy and secure in his loose box. Noticing Izzy was now paler than Taryn had ever been, Jared slipped a comforting arm round her shoulders. Izzy, still slightly tearful, couldn't meet his gaze but gave him a half glance and was relieved when Jared squeezed her arm ever so slightly, indicating that he understood her nervousness for Taryn. On her other side, Carlotta breathed the word 'gross' in response to this exchange, but Izzy noticed even she was tense and had her eyes fixed on her little sister. No one could ignore how tiny Taryn looked compared to the ten, eleven and thirteen-year-olds she was competing against. Surely she didn't stand a chance?

But Taryn was a crafty girl and managed to position herself directly behind a wild-looking bay with a long back and a tendency to overbend as they entered the ring, knowing this would make Jester appear even better behaved than he was.

The competitors were instructed to walk on the right rein in a clockwise circle around the judge and a steward.

Jester was walking nicely, on the bit. The steward signalled for the competitors to trot on.

Canter followed. Izzy realised the standard was much higher than many of the other country shows she'd attended. Here there were no bucking broncos or ponies crabbing sideways. The diagonal was changed and the same routine was performed on the left rein. Even so, other competitors let nerves get the better of them. One rider realised she was trotting on the wrong diagonal and almost yanked her pony's teeth out in her panic to correct him. Another was so despondent at being placed tenth that she let her pony rest his hind leg instead of keeping him alert and square.

Izzy gripped the barrier when she saw Taryn had been pulled in on the first row, admittedly in ninth placing, but would still get the opportunity to perform the little show she'd been practising for weeks. Unlike her neighbour, she was clearly taking great care to ensure Jester was alert and refused to let him flop into an untidy halt. The second row onwards was dismissed leaving only the one row of ten.

'They'll place to six,' Jared whispered to Izzy. Izzy noticed some of the older riders had prepared much more complex shows with leg yields and pirouettes and was suddenly worried for Taryn. Her worries were unfounded. When Taryn's turn arrived she simply showed how well she could walk, trot and canter on the bit in a figure of eight, executing a perfect flying change each time she changed the diagonal. Better still, Jester's pastel patches were diluted by the early morning summer sun, which bounced off his blueness giving the impression he was dazzling white. He whisked his beautifully pulled tail with a cheeky grace every time he passed the judge. Taryn finished her show with a perfect rein back and neat, square halt. From the applause that followed from the audience Izzy realised that on this occasion less had most certainly been more.

It was at this point that Gemma hurried over to Taryn and whipped Jester's show saddle off (carefully cut to show off his pretty shoulders) and gave him a brisk rub down with a stable rubber to remove any saddle marks, swiftly brushed his tail and polished his bit. Taryn was directed to walk out, turn and walk back, and then repeat the exercise in trot. Jester behaved like a true gent. Izzy noticed how Taryn remembered to push Jester round rather than pulling him, like a couple of the other competitors had.

Saddled once more, Taryn mounted deftly and followed the steward's instructions to walk round one final time. Gemma and all the other grooms melted away as if by magic. The judge deliberated for what seemed to be an age. He then swapped the top six round like a game of musical chairs until he was satisfied with the order. Tenth place hadn't changed, no doubt due to the earlier sloppy halt, but Taryn had been promoted to seventh, just out of the rosettes. With a groan

Izzy realised the judge was relaying his final positioning to the steward. Considering her age and size, seventh was a remarkable achievement but it would have been lovely for Taryn to win a prize. She had worked so hard and been so brave about her father being absent. Beside her Jared continued to film. On her other side Carlotta, who fancied herself as an amateur photographer, was taking picture after picture.

Then, just as the steward was writing the competitors' numbers next to their placings, the judge turned, stared at the line up once more and then gesticulated for the steward to make a change. Izzy gripped Jared's arm as the steward motioned to Taryn.

'Please, please,' she breathed. Was he moving Taryn up, or down? She could barely look. She covered her eyes with her hands, not even caring that Jared swung the camcorder onto her anguished face for a few seconds for nothing other than his own amusement.

'Yes!' yelped Carlotta in a stage whisper. The camcorder swung back to face the show ring. Taryn had been bumped into sixth place and this time the placings stuck. Izzy couldn't help but feel a little bit sorry for the young girl who'd been deposed by Taryn but not enough that she would have traded back.

After that it was over in seconds. The judge shook Taryn's hand and awarded her a certificate and her sixth place purple rosette. Then followed the lap of honour. Taryn cantered round at the back, her rosette clenched firmly between her teeth so she could keep both hands on the reins. At the start of the second lap the bottom five placings exited the show ring leaving just the winner to gallop round. Izzy, Jared, Carlotta and Gemma all crowded round a near delirious Taryn.

'Look! Look what I won! We showed 'em!' Taryn shrieked, to everyone's utter shame. She stood up in her stirrups and waved the rosette and certificate above her head like a cowboy's lasso. They all patted a smug looking Jester over and over again. More video footage and photos were taken before Gemma insisted Taryn dismount and Jester be returned to his stall for a well-deserved drink of water and a scoop full of oats as a reward. As they passed the poor seventh place rider, now in tears of disappointment, Taryn called out to her.

'Bad luck. Your pony's lovely and I'm sorry you weren't placed.'

Impressed by such good manners from a girl who could be such a little sod, Izzy forgave her for her earlier display of egotism.

As soon as Jester had been settled with a bucket of water and a hay net everyone fell on the sandwiches and snacks Mrs Firth had packed up for their lunch like a pack of starved hyenas in order to energise them before they all set to work on Carlotta and Jet.

'Do you realise it's almost six hours since breakfast?' Gemma asked as she ripped open a packet of crisps with her teeth. 'I'm famished.' Taryn helped herself to three Breakaways and ate them one after the other. Only Carlotta refused to eat. Instead she sat, elevated, on a hay bale and picked unenthusiastically at a piece of cake, flicking most of it towards a murmuration of brave starlings hovering around in the hope of a few stray oats. Considering Carlotta had such an important competition coming up, and Taryn had done so well in her class also, Izzy decided to turn a blind eye to both on this one occasion. The day contained further triumphs too. Taryn dithered for a few moments then grabbed an apple from the coolbox and headed over to give it to Jester, who looked like a greetings card as he looked over the stable door with his ears pricked. Granted, she had held it at arm's length as though it was a bomb, but it was a big step forward nonetheless.

It was at that moment that a horsebox of almost, but not

quite, the same size as the Stantons' pulled into the solitary space next to the Golf. Everyone looked in interest as a clean cut, good-looking man with a Johnny Bravo quiff and slightly flushed cheeks jumped out and started unloading two almost identical palominos. He was dressed in chinos, brogues and a green-and-white striped blazer. The whole effect was that of a posh packet of Pacer mints. Izzy heard Carlotta release a low hiss as a slender, blonde girl jumped down from the passenger seat.

'Look what the cat yacked up. Frigging Ceridwen Jones. Look at her with her matching Barbie ponies,' she snarled. 'Silly bitch.' Izzy craned her neck over the top of Taryn's head to take a good look at Carlotta's great rival from school.

Ceridwen Jones was of a comparable build to Carlotta and although she was attractive enough in an angelic sort of way, compared to Carlotta's strong, striking, Mediterranean beauty she looked as delicate and insubstantial as whipped cream. She smiled constantly and looked like she had never misbehaved in her life, which made Izzy instantly suspicious. She was charmingly pretty with pale skin, gently flushed cheeks (clearly inherited from her father) and innocent wide blue eyes, rather like a fifteen-year-old Katherine Jenkins. Her hair was the pale gold of summer wheat and had been restyled, since Carlotta had Vidal Sassooned her, into a mass of bubble curls that looked most becoming under her riding hat.

As if aware of Izzy's scrutiny, Ceridwen looked up and, clapping eyes on Carlotta, contorted her expression of angelic serenity into a scowl of sheer demonic fury. Taken aback that someone so pretty could make herself look so ugly, Izzy recoiled.

'I fucking hate her,' Carlotta said, still sitting on the hay bale. She spoke in a low voice so Ceridwen, or more pertinently, her father, wouldn't hear her.

'That's not very nice.' Izzy didn't know what else to say.

'Well, she's not very nice. She looks like butter wouldn't melt but she's a vindictive cow. She torments the lower school kids mercilessly. 'Do this, do that'. I just thank God she'll have left by the time Taryn gets there. And she's a dirty bitch. She's had most of the boys in the local village and there's a fourth form rumour that she once got herself off with her brother's—'

'With her brothers?!' Izzy was scandalised. 'That's terrible.'

'No! With her brother's Nintendo Wii remote control.'

'That doesn't sound much better,' said Izzy. Beside her, she heard Jared stifle a snigger which made Izzy instantly suspicious. Was she being wound up? Taryn was silent, taking everything in, her eyes wide.

'I understand they have quite an impressive vibrate when you wave them about. Her mother's furious, apparently,' Carlotta continued airily, thoroughly enjoying the scandal she was causing.

'Who on Earth told her mother about it?'

'No one, silly. She's furious because she spent a fortune on games and accessories for her brother's Wii to compensate for the divorce and now he won't touch it, and won't explain why.'

'What's getting off?' asked Taryn, all innocence.

'That's enough, Carlotta,' said Jared. Now was the time to intervene.

'I'm just saying—' said Carlotta.

'Well don't. You have a class to win. Why not concentrate on that?'

'I agree,' said Gemma, brushing herself down. 'Break's over. We've got a lot to do. Taryn, you groom one side. Izzy, if you can take the other? I'll concentrate on plaiting Jet's mane and tail. Carlotta, you might as well get dressed and wait for the course to be built. I want you to be one of the first to walk it.'

'And keep well away from Ceridwen Jones,' Jared ordered. 'I don't want to have to tell your father you were disqualified for fighting.'

Carlotta pulled a face, but stood up nonetheless.

'And don't forget your number—!' Gemma added as an afterthought.

They worked as a team for a good hour and by the time they'd finished Jet's black coat shone as brightly as the gemstone he had been named after. His tack gleamed and his plaits and leg bandages were perfect. Gemma even went to the trouble of using a bizarre device called a quarter marker that worked like a stencil and resulted in a chessboard effect on Jet's rump. Izzy couldn't even bring herself to yell at Carlotta when she realised she'd nicked her best hairspray and instructed Gemma to use it to keep the pattern in place.

The only thing more stunning than Jet was Carlotta. Looking like a poster girl for teenage equestrianism, she was immaculately turned out with her long hair French-braided and tucked into a hairnet. She looked over at Ceridwen with her bubble curls once more and curled her lip in contempt. Unlike all the other girl riders, who all wore navy-blue jackets, Carlotta wore a cherry-red coat, almost hot pink, in emulation of her idol, Ellen Whitaker, and which looked nothing short of amazing with her white jodhpurs and blue-black hair.

Riders were invited to walk the course. Gemma would accompany Carlotta whilst Jared kept watch over Jet. To occupy Taryn and to get both her and Izzy out from under everyone's feet, Jared sent them for a quick scoot round the trade stands.

'There's not much else to do here. You might as well stretch your legs,' he said. He handed Izzy a wad of folded up tenners. 'I'm trusting you not to let her buy any useless crap,' he said. Izzy looked at him owlishly. She didn't fancy her chances of success at his request.

When they returned, laden down with several carrier bags full of useless crap, Carlotta had mounted and was waiting to enter the collecting ring. Gemma was checking Jet's girth and martingale were tightened sufficiently whilst Jared gave the pony a quick flick with a stable rubber. Carlotta, contrary to her usual insouciance, had a face like granite.

All she wanted from life was to be a showjumper. Her ambition, once she'd successfully earned a place on the junior squad, was to be taken under the wing of an international showjumper in a professional yard and make a name for herself on the world circuit. But first she had a class to win. She was aware that not only was the selection committee present but also the junior squad *chef d'equipe*. Today's class was a golden opportunity not to be squandered.

She wasn't thrilled, therefore, to have been given a relatively early draw as this meant she was not only under great pressure to go clear but, should she get through to the jump off, she would have to ride like a maniac in order to lodge an unbeatable time. The course, she told Izzy through chattering teeth, was an absolute ball acher. As the ponies and riders started warming up over the practice fence the tannoy played *Saddle Up and Ride Your Pony*. The audience clapped in time to the beat.

'It's time,' Gemma said. She handed Carlotta her crop, then took Jet by the bridle and led him over to the entrance of the collecting ring. As they walked she gave Carlotta a pep talk.

'We'll be watching all the time, me from the collecting ring and the others from ringside. Jet knows what he's doing, so do you but, most importantly, no one in this field will have better big match temperament than you do. Concentrate on your distances and remember to get straight for that tricky stile. Just go and do what you do best and I guarantee you'll be in the rosettes,' she said, giving Jet a gentle slap on his chequered rump as Carlotta gathered up her reins. Izzy watched her ride away. She had an uncomfortable feeling in her stomach. She and Taryn had seen only the last few stragglers walk the course and the fences had looked enormous then, but only when the first pony entered the ring, cantered a circle and waited for the bell, did Izzy fully appreciate how big they were. At least four foot in height with spreads of up to four-foot-six and with a narrow brush stile and a vast red brick wall, the course was bigger than anything Izzy had seen Carlotta jump at any other show. There were also some very precise related distances between the fences, u-bend turns and a water jump. For the first time, Izzy was afraid for Carlotta. Surely sweet little Jet wouldn't possibly be able to jump such monstrosities?

Ceridwen Jones, Carlotta's arch-rival, had been drawn early for Jinx, and last out for Jonah, which enabled her to enter both ponies comfortably. Carlotta's draw was bang in the middle of them, thus giving her both an advantage and a disadvantage over her rival. Everyone watched Ceridwen's first round with interest with the intention that any useful insights would be reported instantly back to Gemma and Carlotta in the collecting ring. Never was Team Stanton so unified as when they were at a show.

'That pony can jump but it's big-bummed,' Taryn said about Jinx as she watched the round commence.

'Big-bummed? Is that a technical term?' Izzy didn't tear her eyes away from the palomino as she replied.

Taryn looked up at Izzy as though she were stupid.

'It's got a fat arse,' she said, scathingly.

'Oh!' was all Izzy could think to say. She was dismayed that, despite her rather fluffy style, Ceridwen Jones could certainly ride. Her pony, Jinx, was as fresh and fit as an Olympic heptathlete and fair bounded round the course to provide the first clear round of the day. It had a very big jump. Clearly its massive bum gave it a great deal of launch, thought Izzy.

'Bugger!' said Taryn. Which seemed to sum it up, really.

Worse still, Ceridwen appeared to set a trend. To the course builder's dismay there was a run of four successive clear rounds, including an absolutely dazzling display of horsemanship from one of the younger members of the Whitaker dynasty. By the time Carlotta's number was called there were already six riders through to the jump off.

'Miss Carlotta Stanton on Whitby Jet,' announced the tannoy. As Carlotta trotted into the ring Izzy covered her face with her hands, then peeped out from between her fingers. Beside her she heard Jared chuckle.

Izzy's fears were unfounded. Jet, a serial show off and attention junkie, loved nothing more than an enormous crowd and proceeded to show his quality fence after fence. Only once did he look like he wouldn't go clear. He did a double take on the approach to a simply enormous oxer, having been spooked by the four-foot cones, each with a fluorescent plastic scoop of pink ice cream atop, that had been placed on either wing in deference to the ice cream manufacturer sponsoring the event, jibbed, and looked like he might do the unthinkable and run out. Such was Carlotta's ability as a rider that she gathered the pony up, righted his approach and, with frantically kicking legs, got him over the fence.

'Jesus!' said Jared, blowing out sharply. Around them a few people gave a smattering of applause.

If Ceridwen had sparked a run of clear rounds, the pony that followed Carlotta put an end to it. Izzy felt sorry for the rider as her little bay ground to a halt at the very first jump, shattering any hope of a clear round, and then knocked down almost every fence. It could only have possibly been made worse by a toss, which is exactly what happened at the water jump. Drenched, defeated and disappointed, the rider led her pony out of the ring on foot. Remembering some of her own more spectacular falls, Izzy empathised. At least she had never hit the deck in front of an audience, and especially not one as large as this. It was the worst round of the competition. After that several ponies jumped reasonably well but the red brick wall did prove to be something of a bogey fence. Round after round, the bricks fell. The course builder breathed a sigh of relief. There was nothing worse for his reputation than every rider going clear.

The last rider was Ceridwen Jones on her second palomino, Jonah. Jonah was of a slighter build than Jinx, and had a star whereas Jinx had a broad, straight blaze. Predominantly a speed horse, he covered the ground much faster than Jinx but as a consequence wasn't as scopey or as careful a jumper. Several times he almost scraped the paint off the poles and clouted the bogey wall so hard that the top brick only remained by a millimetre.

'That pony goes like shit off a stick,' Carlotta observed, having left Jet with Gemma and joined the others ringside. 'Of course it *would* be her second ride. It's almost unbeatable in a jump off.'

'Shit off a stick? Why would shit be on a stick? And who has measured how swiftly it would come off? And for what reason?' Taryn asked. Izzy couldn't answer such questions. Instead she watched as Ceridwen notched up her second clear of the competition and cantered out of the ring with a wide grin on her face. Amidst murmurings and a tangible air of excitement from the audience, Izzy and Taryn found themselves despatched to the collecting ring to help look after Jet, thus freeing up time for Gemma and Carlotta to study the jump off course.

Back in the collecting ring, Ceridwen had covered each of her ponies with a lightweight rug. Carlotta didn't care for their pastel pink colour but was envious of the fact that each had their name embroidered in silver thread on the side. As Ceridwen was sponsored by her father's internet-based company, Grapevine Wines, these read Grapevine Jinx and Grapevine Jonah.

'I wish Papa would sponsor me,' Carlotta grumbled.

'He already does. He just isn't ostentatious about it,' said Izzy absent-mindedly, thinking of the amount of cash MK must pump into Carlotta's riding. Jared gave her a quick look of approval.

Out in the show ring, a fleet of cadets shortened and altered the course with terrifying speed and efficiency. Izzy was relieved to see the vile oxer that had spooked Jet had been omitted. Just before the jump off Jared returned to the horsebox for a hoof pick, leaving Carlotta with Izzy, Taryn and Gemma.

Ceridwen, already mounted, barged past them on Jinx, using his large arse to bump Jet, who shied sideways and trod on the foot of an old boy in a cravat who was spectating ringside.

'Mind where you're going. Clumsy oaf!' Carlotta spat at Ceridwen.

Sorry!' said Ceridwen, giving a sarky smile that implied she was anything but. 'I didn't see you there. How on Earth did you get over here so quickly? I'm sure I just saw you entered for the Pig of the Year competition.'

Carlotta's eyes narrowed to slits.

'Hadn't you better hurry up or you'll be late for the *cattle parade*?' she countered. She then shut up as Pacer-mint man bounded over. He had by now donned a straw trilby and was so blond and smiley that he reminded Izzy of Sprite, the Stantons' golden retriever. She wouldn't have been surprised if he'd dropped a tennis ball at their feet. He spoke with just a hint of a Welsh accent.

'Hello Carlotta. It is you! I wasn't certain until I saw you jump. I saw your pony's name in the programme but it said he was being ridden by someone called Stanton and that threw me. Been doing any more impromptu hairdressing recently?'

'Hello, Mr Jones,' Carlotta said, both wary and polite. Not even she dared cheek the father of the girl she had assaulted.

Ceridwen's father leaned in and offered his hand to Izzy.

'Hi there! I'm Marc Jones, Ceri's father. Great rivals, eh, our two charges? I gather you've been drafted in to help look after these two little horrors until Mika is out of the clink.'

'They're not horrors—' Izzy was quick to defend her two girls but Marc truncated her. In her indignation his words hadn't registered properly.

'I'm only kidding.' He then saw that Carlotta, who was standing directly behind Izzy, was gesticulating like a madwoman. He was smart enough to get the message. 'Oh!' He looked most relieved when Jared appeared, hoof pick in hand. 'Hello, Walker.'

'Jones,' replied Jared.

'Well, I'd better get back to my duties as pony boy. Ceri's always telling me that ponies don't groom and feed themselves. Shame really, as it'd save me a fortune. Good luck, Carlotta.' Carlotta nodded mutely. 'And I certainly hope to see you again,' Marc said to Izzy, giving her a charming smile and touching the brim of his trilby.

Jared watched stony-faced as the Joneses departed.

'That man is a gormless arsehole,' was his only critique.

'*Archimalakas*,' Carlotta and Taryn chorused instantaneously.

'I rather liked him,' Izzy said. It wasn't a lie. Even taking into account Carlotta's rudeness and the fact she'd Samson-ed his daughter's hair, he'd been flatteringly friendly. She watched Marc coach his daughter over the practice fence. Izzy noticed that Ceridwen was an aggressive rider, using a lot of spur and whip to encourage her pony to do what she wanted. She certainly got results but Izzy felt Ceridwen lacked the empathic connection Carlotta and her horses enjoyed.

Jinx, being the slower of Ceridwen's ponies, had not put in the fastest time but went clear again.

'Not a good enough time,' Taryn said, with all the opinionated wisdom and experience of a sports pundit.

The young Whitaker lived up to his famous name and delivered another stunning round that launched him into first place. As there were no other clears, Ceridwen was currently second with her faster ride still to come. Carlotta was next in the ring.

'She'll either go for a steady clear or hell for leather and hope she leaves everything up. You have to give that Jones girl credit; she's covered all bases with those twin blondes of hers,' Jared said as they waited for Carlotta to appear.

Carlotta cantered into the ring. Her face was set and determined but expressionless. Taryn took one look and knew instinctively what her sister would do.

'She's gonna go fast,' she said, her voice low.

'I daren't watch,' Izzy said.

Carlotta had a naturally good eye for related distances and it was this that made her so quick against the clock. Far brighter than any of her school teachers gave her credit for, she could calculate angles in her head with lightning speed. Face set, grimly determined, she did a crafty practice turn of the tightest turn on the course, letting Jet get a good look at what she would be asking him to do. As soon as the bell sounded she slammed on the accelerator. Jet shot off as though he had been in starting gates and made some hairpin turns that made Izzy want to cover her eyes. Jet had unconditional trust in his rider. It was all this combined that made her a cut above most other riders. The round was clear and her time was fast. Fast enough for second place with only bloody Ceridwen Jones still to come on her palomino rocket ship, Jonah. As they exited the ring Jet gave a collection of joyous bucks whilst Carlotta gave him great pats.

'Beat that, yabitch!' Carlotta yelled to Ceridwen as they

passed in the gateway. It'd all been going so well, too, Izzy thought, dropping her head into her hands with a groan of shame.

Everyone watched. Ceridwen was the last rider. Carlotta was currently in second place but Jonah was exceptionally fast, faster even than Jet. If he left everything up Ceridwen would indubitably take Carlotta's blue rosette, if not the red. It was evident no one was more aware of this than Ceridwen herself. Her face set, she booted Jonah towards the first fence with merciless spurs.

'That's mean,' said Taryn, frowning with disapproval. Even to Izzy's inexperienced eye, Ceridwen's brutal riding style was apparent. She yanked on the reins, forcing Jonah to swivel like an ice dancer.

'Do you think she's more desperate to win, or just to beat Carlotta?' Izzy asked Jared, who merely raised an eyebrow in indication that he was in complete agreement with her thinking. They continued to watch as horse and rider bucketed round the ring, slicing hundredths of seconds off Carlotta's time with every stride. All eyes were on the clock.

'She's quicker,' Jared said in anguish. Izzy glanced over to the collecting ring where she could just make out Carlotta's pale face peeping over the railings. She was guaranteed a third place, but she would dearly have loved to have been second.

Back in the ring it seemed as though time had stood still. Ceridwen was now whipping Jonah down to the last line of fences like a Grand National winner. The plucky palomino's ears were laid back in anger against his head as he galloped towards the last spread fence. If he left it up, Ceridwen would be second, and Carlotta third. Izzy closed her eyes and wished. A roar of approval rose into the sky, then faded away into a collective, sympathetic groan from the audience. With no allegiance to any particular rider, they merely wanted to see a good competition and a last-minute steal was always thrilling. Taryn's shriek of delight was lost amidst it all. Izzy opened her eyes to see the last rail of the final fence lying on the ground. Ceridwen's time may have been scorching, but without a clear round in accompaniment it was worthless. Furious to have been beaten, Ceridwen didn't even pat her pony as she exited the ring.

Izzy, Taryn and Jared ran into the collecting ring where Carlotta was still mounted, patting Jet over and over again, an expression of dazed delirium on her face as she exchanged anecdotes with the Whitaker boy who'd won the class.

'Well done, well done!' everyone cried as they converged on her. Carlotta looked absolutely stunning with her flushed cheeks and broad, genuine smile. Happiness was a look that suited her well, Izzy thought with a pinprick of sadness. It was just such a shame that she more often looked sulky and petulant. Taryn produced a packet of Polos from her pocket and began shovelling mints into Jet's eager mouth.

'Do you think the selectors saw?' Carlotta asked Jared and Izzy, her eyes shining.

'I'm sure they did, sweetheart,' Jared said, reaching up to give her a bear hug.

'You were absolutely brilliant,' Izzy added, patting Jet ,who'd decided to nudge his erstwhile friend in the gut in all the excitement. She couldn't quite believe she was able to competently ride this amazing pony.

The tannoy crackled again and the winners were announced into the ether. The announcer was accompanied in the background by the sounds of clanking cutlery and glasses and the distinctive 'haw-haw-haw' of toffs having a jolly good time in the hospitality tent. Stewards indicated to Carlotta, and away she went for the presentation and her lap of honour. Putting his hand-to-hand combat training to use, Jared barged through a wall of fond parents to get a good enough view to be able to record the event. Izzy, Taryn and Gemma also threaded their way through the masses and stood ringside, clapping their hands as the brass band launched into *On Ilkley Moor Bah'Tat* as the lap of honour commenced.

It was all over far too quickly. It seemed that only minutes had passed before Carlotta was untacking Jet and leading him into his stall. In the show ring, a swarm of cadets were building the track for the main showjumping event of the day, the *Cock o' the North*. The band was still playing merrily and was now thrilling the audience with a rousing rendition of *The British Grenadiers*.

'Do you think they'll play any Take That?' asked Izzy hopefully.

'If they do, we're leaving,' Jared threatened, knowing full well there was no way he would be able to drag Carlotta, Taryn or Gemma away from two hours of top international showjumping.

Nerves purged by her win, Carlotta was now cramming sandwiches and slabs of cake into her mouth.

Above them a tiny aeroplane crossed the showground. Billowing out behind it, plain for all to see against the clear blue sky, was a banner that read: 'Yorkshire's Great'.

'Where'd they get that?' Jared said. 'Statetheobvious.com? Come on, let's get these ponies settled quickly so we can bag a decent seat for the jumping.'

Just as they were finishing up, a plain youth sidled up and tried to present Carlotta with a ragtag posy of hand-picked wild flowers.

'I fink you shoulda won, bofe you and yer 'orse are gorgeous,' he mumbled. Uncharacteristically charmed, Carlotta held her hand out as though to accept them until Jared, who suspected mischief, told him to bugger off and take his weeds with him. If Carlotta hadn't still been so delirious about her second place she would most certainly have stropped. Instead she allowed herself to be dragged away to the seating area by Izzy.

Almost two hours later, and after a superb display of horsemanship, the competition was over and it was time to go home. Now came the uninspiring task of loading up ponies, tack and people into the two vehicles. Eventually, and after what seemed to Izzy to be an age, the horsebox was ready to load Jet and Jester. She could barely wait to get back home and collapse in bed, knackered.

Carlotta loaded Jet first then, as Taryn led Jester out of his stable, the judge that had placed her walked past. He looked at her as though he recognised her, then his eyes swivelled to Jester. In the early evening shade of the stable block he looked as blue as Wedgwood.

'Hello,' piped up Taryn. 'Thank you for my rosette.'

The judge's eyes widened in recognition, he then spluttered and strode off. The only thing anyone heard him say was: 'But that pony is *blue*.'

# CROOKS AND NANNIES

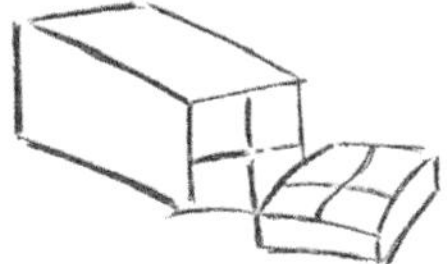

By the time Izzy turned the Golf out of the showground Taryn was already asleep, clutching her precious rosette in her hand. In her indignation Marc Jones's comment about MK being in the clink had been temporarily bypassed by Izzy but now, on the journey home, with Taryn sparko-ed and therefore unable to interrupt her thoughts, Izzy had plenty of time to dwell on it. MK wasn't in prison, she thought scornfully. He was away on business and wouldn't be back until the autumn. At least, that's what she had been told. Then she recalled Carlotta's bitter comment at the end of the Easter holidays.

*'God, Izzy, you can be so dense. Don't you understand? Papa isn't coming home.'*

MK wasn't in prison, or was he?

Izzy carried Taryn upstairs and placed her on her bed for a quick nap before dinner. She didn't wake even when Izzy tugged her boots off and covered her with her comforter. Only Taryn would be exempt from helping to unpack the horsebox and turning out the ponies. Once this was done Jared kicked off his boots in the utility and reached into the chiller for three ice cold beers. He handed one each to Izzy and Gemma.

'It's been a good day. Bloody tired now though,' he said, flexing his neck and stretching.

Mrs Firth had prepared a celebratory dinner of elaborate salads and jacket potatoes followed by summer fruit crumble made with home-grown rasps and rhubarb. There would be ice cream for Taryn who, although better with the whole fruit issue, was still on-off about it. Mrs Firth wanted a full report on the day. Jared even went so far as to open a bottle of champagne from MK's wine cellar so they could toast the two rosettes and the riders and ponies who had earned them. Gemma indulged in several glasses, having pleaded exhaustion and thus bagged a second night at The Paddocks and no doubt in Jared's bed.

Bet she's not too exhausted for that, Izzy thought sourly.

Throughout the meal Izzy continued to brood on what Marc Jones had said. She was aware she had no leg to stand on when it came to judging Jared and Mrs Firth. Yes, she'd been deceived but then she'd also done her fair share of deceiving. Also, she'd accused them of not caring enough about her to find out the truth behind her situation and yet she'd done the exact same thing. She'd been so wrapped up in her misery that she hadn't wondered about the mysterious MK. She had never thought to do any digging.

As soon as Taryn was in bed Izzy seized the laptop out of the winter den, retreated to her room and scoured the internet for information. She Googled Mika K and was astonished by the pages and pages of results.

> *Mika Konstantine,* she read, *is a Greek shipping magnate. Owner of Konstantine Shipping, est. 1949, being the business he inherited from his father, Spiro Konstantine, upon his death in the mid 1990s.*

Jaw hanging slack, Izzy went on to read how Konstantine Shipping, which had offices in London and Athens, manufactured ferries, tanker vessels and other smaller ships, was keeping afloat despite the Greek economic crisis, and how Mika himself had an estimated personal fortune of approximately two hundred and fifty million, which was apparently quite modest by all accounts.

That'd be enough to keep a pony in oats over the winter, Izzy thought irrationally. She read on.

Mika Konstantine was the widower of an up-and-coming Italian model called Marisa Pellacani, and father to two daughters. The article was accompanied with a picture of a stunning woman, naked and pregnant, and which had been one of *Vogue Italia*'s most controversial covers. It had been taken just months before her death. She'd only been twenty-eight. The girls, Carlotta in particular, were the absolute spit of her.

It must have been taken whilst she was pregnant with Taryn, Izzy thought, choking up.

Further stories went on to report that he was on remand for GBH by contract, awaiting trial, although he had repeatedly insisted on his innocence.

In her head she replayed Marc Jones's words.

*'It said he was being ridden by someone called Stanton and that threw me.'*

Stanton.

Kon*stant*ine?

'Konstantine?' Izzy muttered to herself. Where had she heard that name before? Her recall wasn't great so it took her a while. Then the penny dropped. With a clang.

Izzy was straight on the phone to Caro, being careful not to use the landline in case Jared or worse — Carlotta — picked up at the same time and started listening in. With a certain degree of irony she acknowledged how she was forced to use her 'emergency' phone given to her by Jared on her first day seeing as her own mobile had no signal. At least she now had a fair inkling why she'd been given the bleedin' thing in the first place.

'What do you know about Mika Konstantine?' Izzy demanded as soon as Caro answered.

'Traditionalists still prefer to use the term 'hello',' Caro said sarkily. 'Why?'

'Because I'm living in his house, taking care of his kids,' Izzy said. She found the sound of Caro nearly choking to be a satisfactory response.

'What? Are you sure?' Caro said.

'Pretty much. We were at the Great Yorkshire Show today and someone let it slip. I've done a bit of digging on the 'net and this Mika geezer is indeed widowed, having been married to an Italian model called Marisa Pellacani, and does indeed have two daughters, coincidentally enough called Carlotta and Taryn.'

'How come you're only finding out about this now?' Caro asked. She was back to her usual unflustered self.

'I was told his bleedin' name was Stanton. I had no reason to doubt. I thought MK stood for Michael Kevin or Malcolm Keith or something. How was I supposed to know it was his surname and it stood for Konstantine?'

'Here I am busting my buns trying to form a connection to the case and all the while you're living in his house, taking care of his daughters. Jesus! You couldn't make it up if you tried.'

'So what else can you tell me?'

'Not much you won't have read on the 'net. Multi-millionaire shipping magnate, inherited in the '90s from his father, Spiro Konstantine, who up until his death was considered to be the last great playboy private owner in the mould of the likes of Onassis and Niarchos. Mika revolutionised the company, which was struggling at the time, by relocating its head offices to Britain and introducing an ethos based on family values and discretion in direct contradiction of his father's remit. Unassuming, shy and private, he married for love, I understand, but was widowed within seven or eight years. More recently he hit the business headlines when he was arrested at the end of last year on a charge of Section 20 GBH. He'd paid a person five grand to beat up an ex-member of his staff and was caught out because of monetary transaction evidence in his bank accounts. Bail was refused; he'd be held on remand until next spring. The fellow is still critical and is being fed his food through a tube. His life is hanging by a thread. He's currently looking at a maximum of five years. If the victim dies your 'MK' will be charged with murder, joint enterprise law rendering him equally complicit in the assault, even though there was no intention to kill.

'Listen, I'll ring you back later once I've done a little digging. You sit tight and don't do anything stupid. Izzy, do you hear me? Keep out of this,' Caro said, her voice thick with excitement.

'Like hell I will,' Izzy said as soon as she'd rung off. Instead she pulled on her boots and ran downstairs to see if Jared was kicking about. She'd have this out with him! Alas, she was denied. He was in the stables with Carlotta and Gemma and not even she dare raise the subject in front of them. She was left to brood overnight.

She woke in a combative mood but was instantly disarmed upon discovering Interflora had made a delivery for her. A beautiful and clearly expensive display of the palest pink rosebuds intertwined with snow-white gypsophila, encased in a crystal vase filled with magenta coloured glass pebbles, stood on her place at the breakfast table. Everyone watched in bootfaced silence as she opened the card.

*To the charming Miss Brown. Till our next meeting.*
*Marc Jones*

On the back was a mobile phone number. Jared peered over her shoulder. A small part of Izzy hoped the flowers' arrival might make Jared realise she was worthwhile and attractive. But, alas…

'Blimey! What didya do to make an impression like that? Give him a quick hand shandy behind the collecting ring? And doesn't he know the word 'til is spelled apostrophe-tee-eye-ell. That sort of till is one that a greengrocer would use to tally up a basket of veg.'

Carlotta was simply furious that any member of the hated Jones family was infiltrating her home.

'Ceridwen will have put him up to this, just to piss me off, I hope you realise. I wouldn't start thinking you actually do have an admirer,' she said disparagingly. Hurt, Izzy bore the flowers off to the safety of her own room. She didn't entirely trust Carlotta not to hurl the vase to the ground out of sheer spite. Nevertheless, both Jared and Carlotta's words took all the pleasure out of the flowers to such an extent that Izzy couldn't even bring herself to send a thank you text. Each time she looked at them their undeniable beauty was diminished and embittered. Even Mrs Firth had been unimpressed and had, unbeknownst to Izzy, raised her eyebrows at Jared behind her back. Taryn, being too young to pick up on all the snide undertones, thought they were pretty and saw them for nothing more than what they were, that being a nice bunch of flowers. Gemma too thought it was a nice gesture and read the card with interest.

None of which improved Izzy's mood. Still brooding on Marc's words of the previous day, she privately plotted her next move. Should she confront Jared head on, or wait until Caro could provide her with some more info? Then fate intervened and granted her an irresistible opportunity. As Jet and Jester had been granted a day's grace from being ridden to recover from the exertion of the show, there wasn't a horse for Izzy to ride. With no envy whatsoever, she watched

Carlotta and Gemma, on Vega and Ghost respectively, and Taryn, looking minute on The Tank, head off to the far paddock to do some cross-country jumping. Returning to the stable block, intending to give poor Mini Cheddar a cheering scoopful of pony nuts as he was confined to his stable with a touch of sweet itch, she noticed a keyring on the oat bin in the feed store. Drawn like a magpie, Izzy couldn't help but pick it up. She studied it. It was solid silver and engraved with the Greek flag. It held two keys: one heavy and ornate, the other a simple Yale. She herself had a bunch of keys like the Warden of Alcatraz but none were either the same weight or colour as these. There was only one possible door that these keys opened.

It took Izzy less than a minute to make her decision. Mrs Firth was indulging in a baking frenzy in the kitchen and Jared was ankle deep in brassicas in the vegetable plot. She was pretty certain she wouldn't be disturbed. And anyway, what if she was? It wasn't as though everyone had been up front and honest with her.

MK's private suite could be reached through his bedroom. It was a revelation. A full-sized and fully equipped sitting room plus a vast office, a second personal bathroom and even a small kitchen complete with oven, fridge (empty and switched off, Izzy noticed) and sink. Izzy peered into every room but focused her interest on his office. The same neutral shades as the rest of his suite, it contained an enormous leather-topped desk and matching chair and an entire wall of filing cabinets, stacked with files. A large window overlooked the lawn and the vegetable plot. Izzy could see Jared digging. He was wearing long khaki shorts and green wellies, and nothing else. Izzy allowed herself the luxury of watching him work for a few moments before turning her attention back to her surroundings.

Photographs covered two of the four walls. One wall was covered in full colour prints of fishing vessels and oil tankers that Konstantine Shipping had built. The other was covered with photographs of MK with the great and the good. Izzy gazed at these. MK with Dame Judi Dench. MK with Sir Richard Branson. MK with the Crown Prince of Bahrain. There was also a picture, right in the centre, of MK with Jared. Both were in their military regalia, arms across each other's shoulders in unmistakable symbolism of their brotherhood. They both looked so young and handsome.

A file of correspondence between MK and Jared was lying on the desk top and had quite clearly been referred to recently. Izzy flicked through it. It contained handwritten letters, mainly concerned with Carlotta and Taryn, and photocopies of school reports and such like, and also several official looking forms and documents. Izzy noticed her name was mentioned several times but it wasn't clear what this was in connection with. Maybe it was to do with her wages. As it didn't appear to be particularly riveting Izzy set the papers back down and turned back to the bookshelves.

In between several boxes of boring old accounts was a large photograph album containing pictures of MK's wedding day. The quality of the photographs and the mountings were unmistakable. Izzy settled, cross-legged, on the thick cream carpet to look at them. As she turned the pages she felt she was being drawn into some magical world of wealth and celebrity the likes of which she'd only ever seen in *Hello* magazine. The album itself was sheer luxury, crafted from the softest white leather and surely that was real gold thread it was embossed with. The gossamer-esque sheets that separated each photograph were finest Chinese silk and the register of best wishes and messages of congratulations were like a charity event line-up. The signatures alone — Robert Palmer, Bryan Ferry, Joan Collins, Bobby Robson — would have guaranteed the album's worth as a collectors' item. The photographs were even more breathtaking. The fact that

Italy's most promising young model was marrying the heir apparent of one of Greece's most infamous shipping magnates was impressive enough, but the guest list was equally mind-boggling. And there, amidst almost every picture, was Jared. Fully kitted out in military dress, he looked young, happy and completely at ease. And that ridiculously pretty woman in the wide-brimmed hat he was glued to must be his wife. Not even the garish early '90s fashions could mar their beauty.

So engrossed was she in the album, she didn't even notice that Jared had entered the room.

'What the fuck do you think you're doing in here?' He looked livid.

Izzy jumped but, to Jared's utter amazement, didn't look guilty.

'Finding out some answers, seeing as no one was going to give them to me. Shit, is that Demi Moore?'

For once Jared was nonplussed.

'By stealing my keys?'

'I didn't steal them. You left them on top of the feed bins and I merely picked them up.'

'Don't lie!'

Izzy tore her eyes away from the album and looked at Jared with raised eyebrows.

'How very dare you!'

'I haven't been in the feed store since yesterday and those keys—' he pointed to the keyring laid by Izzy's left foot. '—Were locked in the safe overnight.'

'Nevertheless, that's where they were, just sitting on top of the oat bin, all shiny and bright.'

Jared looked disbelieving.

'With such secrets to hide,' Izzy waved airily at the walls, 'perhaps it's for the best it was me who found them.' She picked up the file she had taken off MK's desk and threw it at Jared's feet. 'MK's not abroad on business, is he?' she asked, speaking as though to a five-year-old who'd been caught stealing from the sweetie jar. Jared gaped at the file.

'Where did you get this? It was locked away.'

'Well, in that case, someone unlocked it again and left it out on the desk top for me to see. Probably the same person who left the keys on top of the feed store for me to find. Very accommodating, our mystery helper. My money's on Carlotta, personally. Not sure what her motives are but then, when do we ever truly understand what she's thinking?'

'Why would Carlotta do that?' Jared demanded.

'Why does Carlotta ever do anything?' Izzy countered. 'She might have been feeling anticlimactic after yesterday's triumph. She might have been feeling rebellious after you told that young lad to bugger off. She's already pissed off with her father for not buying her that second horse, and with me for receiving those flowers.'

'You weren't supposed to know about this,' Jared said.

'Well then, what a pity Ceridwen Jones's father let the cat out of the bag yesterday. He told me to my face that MK was in the shovel and pick. Quite chatty, he was, in fact, before he realised he'd put his size nines in it. Did you really think I wouldn't ask questions?' Izzy looked up at Jared with expectation. Even she had no idea why she was being so cold and clinical. 'So, what did naughty MK do? Fraud? Embezzlement? Didn't he pay his tax bill on time? Or did he, I don't know, pay to have one of his minions beat the tar out of someone he didn't like very much?' Defensiveness was making Izzy aggressive.

Jared looked at Izzy through narrowed eyes.

'There's no way on Earth MK gave that order. You can trust that, if nothing else. He hated violence. That's why he left the military the moment his obligation to his father expired. He doesn't have what it takes to kill, even in warfare.'

Little things the girls had said suddenly made sense, such

as Carlotta intimating that MK lived with dozens of other blokes and how he wasn't contactable by phone. How could she have been so blinkered?

'I can't handle this right now,' Izzy said, standing up. 'I'm going for a walk.'

'Get back here!' Jared barked. Izzy stood her ground.

'I'm not one of your platoon, *Jarhead*,' she said, echoing Carlotta's nickname from weeks ago, and which now made perfect sense. Wasn't a Jarhead some reference to the military? 'I can't be court-martialled for not obeying your commands. I'm going for a walk to get my head round it.'

---

THINGS REMAINED TENSE. For two days neither party made any mention of what Izzy had discovered but simply carried on with the usual routine. However, by the time they reached the third day Taryn, Carlotta, Mrs Firth and Gemma had all cottoned on that something had happened, and started to ask indirect questions in the hope of finding out. Realising that it had to be dealt with Jared sent the girls out on a long hack before dragging Izzy down to Philippa's Kitchen for a cream tea and some privacy. As they were on their way out Mrs Firth hurried after them.

'Could you ask Pippa if she would lend me a couple of gelatine leaves? I'd planned on making a strawberry cheesecake but I've run out.'

The proprietress, Pippa Newton, was delighted to see them but was wise enough to sense tension and, taking note of their stony expressions, ushered them over to one of the more private tables and advised her part-time waitress that she'd attend to them personally. Once seated, Jared ordered tea for two and three cream scones, two for himself and one for Izzy. Pippa jotted everything down in her notebook. As she turned to leave Izzy remembered Mrs Firth's request and flapped her arms in panic.

'Oh, and Mrs Firth asked if she can borrow some gelignite,' she said. 'She needs some for a pudding,' she added by way of helpful explanation, having mistaken Pippa's expression of astonishment for ignorance.

'Is she making a *bombe*?' Pippa asked, her face solemn.

'No, I think it was a cheesecake,' Izzy said, completely serious. Jared could see Pippa's shoulders shaking as she walked away. It was the afternoon's one and only moment of lightness.

Izzy and Jared managed to look at everything and everyone in the café and not once at each other for the duration of the wait for their food. Both were still furious, each believing they'd been lied to and that it was the other who was in the wrong. It was only once Pippa had placed their scones and tea on the table and melted away to attend to another customer that Jared began to speak.

'I know you feel you've been deceived but I can assure you there's a good explanation,' he said.

'So it's true that MK, or should I say, Mika Konstantine, is doing porridge and won't be coming back any time soon?' Izzy asked.

'Keep your voice down,' Jared hissed. 'It's not exactly something he wants broadcasting from the thatched rooftops.'

'Or to his staff—' Izzy said, upturning her palms in a sarcastic gesture. Nevertheless, she lowered her voice to a loud whisper.

'I can see how confusing and frustrating this must be for you—' Jared began.

'Actually, it's as black and white as the kitchen floor. You never intended to tell me my employer is up on a criminal charge or that you have no idea whatsoever for how long I will be required. As far as I know I could still be expected to ferry Taryn to and fro when she's attending university,' Izzy said. She paled at the prospect. God, she wasn't ever going to get back to her real life in London, was she?

Jared looked bleak.

'I appreciate it's not ideal but MK's legal team is working round the clock to find a way to prove his innocence. We're still hoping for a full acquittal.' He looked straight into Izzy's eyes. 'He didn't do what he's been accused of. If you can trust nothing else, you can trust that. I'm not permitted to discuss it in detail, disclosure and all that, which is why you weren't told. It's the best explanation I can give.'

'That isn't an explanation, good, bad or ugly.' Izzy said. 'And anyway, where do you fit into this? You're only the gardener. I'm the one paid to look after the girls. I'm the one who should have been kept informed.'

'I'm not just the gardener, or the handy man. Firstly, I'm the girls' official guardian and protector. Secondly, I'm MK's oldest and closest friend, which means that, in his absence, I'm the top of the chain of command. So when you ask me what gives me the right to tell you how you look after those girls, that's why.'

Izzy looked at him through slitted, suspicious eyes.

'It's no coincidence you were in the army, is it?'

'I wasn't in the army.'

'Come off it! Mrs Firth said—'

'She will have said I was in the military, she wouldn't have mentioned the army, not that she should have mentioned that either. I was in the Navy. I was a Green Beret.' Even though he was confessing Jared still looked blatantly proud. Izzy's jaw clanged, all the arguments and indignation shocked out of her.

Jared had been a Commando Officer in the Royal Marines' 3 Commando Brigade. He joined at the age of eighteen, having just finished his A Levels, and continued his education whilst he trained, obtaining a degree in Politics and Psychology, often undertaking his studies whilst he was deployed. He went on to obtain the rank of captain, having served for eighteen years, then retired at the age of thirty-six with an honourable discharge.

'My first campaign was aged twenty-two in the Gulf War.' Izzy gawked. 'Iraq,' he explained as though she were five.

'Even I know where the Gulf War was,' Izzy snapped.

'After that I served in Kuwait in '94, Bosnia in '95 and the Congo in '98. Since then I've also served in Kosovo, Oman and Afghanistan. On occasion I hopped over to Northern Ireland too.'

Izzy simply gaped.

After that Jared opened up a little about his life in the Marines. He spoke of the Commando spirit, of courage, determination, selflessness and cheerfulness in the face of adversity. That pretty much summed up Jared all right, Izzy thought, moved. He spoke of the ethos: unity, adaptability, humility and fortitude. All the things he expected of her. He also spoke of the famous Commando humour which was to offer gentle ridicule rather than sympathy. Izzy thought back to her early days at The Paddocks, how she'd thought Jared was being mean and picking on her. Now she understood that was just his way, and if he'd wanted to be mean to her she'd really have known about it.

'I met MK during my first year of training. He was my superior officer. We served together for three years until his father's death and he was required to take over the family business.'

'But MK's Greek. Don't you have to be British to serve in the armed forces?'

'Wrong! MK's mother is as Yorkshire as I am. He has dual nationality. He was educated here and entered the Navy at graduate level. It was his choice. Either military training here or conscription back in Greece.'

'So MK employs you as a bodyguard?'

'Lord, no! I may have been a marine but I don't hold the

requisite qualifications to be a bodyguard. MK employs me as a gardener,' Jared said, but the dry expression on his face told Izzy that his insidious job title was purely for the benefit of the outside world.

'Bloody well-paid gardener, I bet. I once read in *Heat* that a celebrity bodyguard can earn anything up to six figures in one year.' Jared couldn't meet her eyes. 'Jesus Christ, you earn that much money and you still dress like *that*!' Izzy scoffed. She remembered bleakly how money, and how he'd believed that having lots of it increased a person's attractiveness, had meant the world to Scott. Jared was impressed at how unfazed she was by his salary.

'Just shows how appearances can be deceiving, eh?' Jared said, composure regained. 'And as far as MK is concerned, no price would ever be too great for the safety of his daughters.'

Izzy was thoughtful.

'But Gemma and I are often on our own with the girls. I take Taryn to school every day; Gemma takes them out hacking. I know you think you're the God of Yorkshire but not even you are omnipresent.'

'Both MK and I are confident the girls are in safe hands with either of you.' Upon hearing such a compliment Izzy goggled for a second time. Then she considered something else.

'Hang on—' she said thoughtfully. 'Did no one think to tell me there was a potential security risk? What if someone tried to swipe Taryn whilst we were on the school run? What about my safety?' Izzy became indignant once more.

'You were never in any danger. It's all about the girls. If anything should happen to MK they each stand to inherit millions. That makes them very attractive to the lowlifes of this world.'

'I understand that. I also understand that I would be the expendable entity inconveniently in the way.'

'Has anyone approached you thus far? Have you ever felt

in danger during the course of your duties?' Jared asked sharply.

'No, but—'

'Then trust me to get on with my job, and you get on with yours,' he said. 'Everything's under control.'

'What about the dead animals?' Izzy asked.

'It's gone very quiet on that front. I'm still monitoring the situation closely but my gut tells me there's no immediate threat.' And with that Izzy had to be satisfied.

'Do you miss being in the forces?' she asked. 'Isn't this life a bit quiet for you after travelling all over the world?'

For a few moments Jared looked bleak.

'Not really. I think every soldier has an expiry date and I reached mine. I was one of the lucky ones though. I chose to walk away. Many of my colleagues were killed, transported back home in temporary coffins, whilst others remain the unseen dead of war, their bodies never fully recovered. I've been the one sitting in the middle of a bloody battlefield, left holding a dismembered arm that had once been attached to a friend. Not everyone recovers from the fog of war. I know plenty of ex-servicemen who'll be on meds for life. Often a soldier becomes removed from reality. It's not unusual to have entire chunks of time blacked out from memory. I was tough enough mentally to deal with it. Not everyone is.' He checked his watch. It was a deliberate change of subject. 'Christ, is that the time? We'll have to get back.' He surveyed the untouched scones in front of them as he stood up. Clearly neither had felt like eating. He handed a twenty pound note to Pippa who, not one to take umbrage and who was more than used to the quirks of her regular customers, knew Jared hated to leave food and merely scooped the uneaten scones into a white paper bag. She handed this to him along with his change.

'I've popped a couple of gelignite leaves in there too, so do take care,' she said, smiling innocently.

The bell jangled as they exited the café. The mid-afternoon sunshine was such a contrast to the soothing cool interior of Philippa's Kitchen that they both had to scrunch up their eyes until they became accustomed to it.

'Why gardening?' Izzy asked, rootling in her handbag for her sunglasses as they started to stroll down Cherry Tree Avenue.

Jared shrugged.

'After all the terrible things I've seen… and done, I figured that growing something of beauty, nurturing new life rather than destroying it, was a much better way to make a living. Besides which, I've always liked it.'

'You're lucky, doing something you love for a living,' Izzy said, sliding her glasses on, referring to her last job. She'd never enjoyed working in law. It was something good to tell new acquaintances but that was about it. The profession certainly wasn't anything like it was portrayed on the telly.

'Don't you like it here?' Jared asked. He looked askance at Izzy, idly wondering if she was aware of how glamorous she looked in her aviator sunglasses. Izzy misinterpreted his scrutiny and instead viewed it as yet another probing look.

'Of course. But then I remember that this isn't my real job and, sooner or later, I'll have to go back to London.'

There was a brief silence before Jared spoke again.

'What do you mean?'

'I thought we'd just had this conversation. If everything you say is true then MK will be let off the hook, thus rendering me instantly surplus to requirements. Plus, I can only stay until November in any event. As soon as the sublease on my flat runs out I'll be heading home.'

'So you're making bonds with Taryn and Carlotta only to leave them. They've had enough upheaval in their short lives already. Don't you think you're being a bit selfish?'

Now it was Izzy's turn to shrug.

'I wasn't the one who lied about this being a permanent

position. The agency woman told me it was for just eight-months until MK returned from business. How was I to know he was in the slammer? As far as I'm concerned I've fulfilled the terms of the contract I signed. I've done nothing wrong here.'

'Don't you care about the girls at all? Taryn clearly adores you. Don't you think it would break her heart if you just upped and left?'

'Of course I care. I love those girls, and Mrs Firth and—' For some reason she couldn't bring herself to include him too. '—Everything about being here. You've been like a family to me. It's just that... My life is in London. My friends, my family, my career—' her voice faded away. Even she could detect the lack of conviction in it. Nor was Jared prepared to let it go.

'I've always known you were a bonehead but I never took you for an out and out bitch. When your marvellous friends and family couldn't find time for you when everything went to shit it was Mrs Firth and me and the girls who pulled you through.'

Izzy didn't speak but kept walking. Jared's words were a little bit too close to the truth and only served to send a shiver of discomfort through her.

'Just answer me one thing, Izzy. If you love everything about being here why are you so keen to leave? I told you we were a family regardless of blood. Whether or not you want to become a part of that family is up to you.'

Jared strode off at his briskest parade walk, leaving Izzy staring after him. He avoided her for the rest of the afternoon. Izzy took refuge in the kitchen where Mrs Firth, at least, was in a good mood. She was relieved, she told Izzy as the bag of gelatine was handed over.

'At least it's all out in the open now, love. The number of times I nearly let slip. Plus I've always said to Jared that you can't expect folk to understand the situation here unless they know exactly what that situation is.' Even Izzy had to concede these were wise words.

Despite Jared's reassurances, Izzy found that for at least the next two weeks she was constantly on the lookout for assailants and kidnappers. Every bump and creak in the night caused her to cower under her duvet, alert but frozen into immobility. The fact that Steptoe was wholly untroubled by such noises was no reassurance to her. Whilst out on hacks, she continually looked from left to right, half expecting some balaclavaed maniac to leap out from behind a hydrangea and drag either her or one of the girls off their pony. As soon as Jared realised what she was doing he took to lurking behind doors and in cupboards only to spring out on her as she passed. He never seemed to tire of hearing her shrieks of terror but instead simply wandered off, chuckling to himself each time. Whether or not he had been indulging in some freaky reverse psychology Izzy never knew, but she soon learned not to be so suspicious and gradually life at The Paddocks returned to how it had been before.

---

AT THE OFFICIAL beginning of the summer holidays Carlotta was scheduled to pack up her bags and her pony for a week-long showjumping masterclass at Bishop Burton College in the East Riding. Gemma, who would be accompanying her, insisted that she and Carlotta study recent video footage of her best and worst competition results in order to identify where her strengths and weaknesses lay. As no one had yet viewed what had been shot at the Great Yorkshire Show it was decided it would be premiered in the winter den straight after dinner on the night before they were due to depart.

Everyone settled into their favourite chair as Jared plugged the camcorder into the TV. He would commit it to DVD at the same time. Taryn curled herself up in between

Izzy and Jared on the larger of the two sofas whilst Carlotta and Gemma made do with the two-seater. Even all the dogs funnelled through the doorway, vying for position. Steptoe curled himself up on a scatter cushion by Izzy's feet but only after scratching himself so vigorously his collar spun round his neck three times.

'Stop scratting,' said Jared in exasperation. Pongy wiped his arse on the floor, back legs akimbo like a porn star, front legs clawing at the carpet as he dragged himself along, before being yelled at by everyone to pack it in. Disgruntled and resentful, he then forced his way into the smallest of gaps between Izzy and Taryn, used one of the sofa cushions as a face towel, then lay down with a breathy grunt, his breath akin to that of a thousand camels. His crusty bum he directed towards Jared.

'I've fared no better,' Izzy countered in response to Jared's complaints. 'His breath is arguably worse than his farts.'

Mrs Firth had provided freshly popped corn and cookies for all. Jared had his requisite bottle of beer whilst Izzy and Gemma shared a bottle of Chardonnay. No one would be drinking much; both Carlotta and Gemma would be riding for all of the following day and as usual it fell to Jared to drive them to the equestrian college in the horsebox. Only Izzy was at liberty to get merrily pissed.

The footage commenced. They laughed and pointed as they remembered the events of the day. Taryn's sixth place in the showing class came on first. Izzy cringed as she saw how blue Jester looked even though everyone else thought it hilarious, even Taryn. They then watched the junior jumping. Gemma wanted to pause and rewind at critical points but was unable to do so as it would have skewed the recording.

Both Carlotta's rounds were good, Gemma critiqued, but on occasion she was still allowing her lower leg to swing backward ever so slightly at the point of take off. It was a tiny observation but Carlotta listened intently and pledged to work on it. The only time she took criticism well was when it was in connection with her riding, such was her single-minded focus on being better than her competition.

'If for some unbeknownst reason Jet put in a stop or stumbled, you'd go straight over the handlebars. You all need to be listening to this, in fact. That includes you too, Izzy,' Gemma said.

Izzy looked up, horrified.

'Haven't I hit the deck every possible way yet?'

'Have you broken anything yet?' Gemma asked, eyebrows raised.

'No.'

'Then no, you haven't.'

Taryn noticed that Jared's arm was stretched out behind Izzy, his arm resting along the back of the sofa and his hand almost, but not quite, touching her hair.

'Izzy, are you going to be Jared's new wife one day?' she asked in innocence. Jared choked on his bottle of beer. No one knew where to look.

'What makes you think that, sweetheart?' Izzy asked, her mouth dry. She was painfully aware of Gemma's green eyes boring into the side of her face. Unnerved, she fidgeted and stretched her bare feet out only to mistake Steptoe's warm fur for her slippers. As she tried to put her feet in him, Steptoe grumbled and mooched off to the safety of a nearby armchair. Jared, watching, shook his head in disbelief.

'I overheard my teacher saying all she ever did with her husband was argue,' Taryn explained. 'So I thought that seeing as all you and Jared ever do is row you might as well get married.'

An astonished silence hung in the air for a few seconds until Jared demolished it with a loud guffaw.

---

After an uneventful week had passed Carlotta returned home from her course, bringing with her several rosettes, a plethora of new knowledge and experience together with the news that she'd acquired a boyfriend. She announced, over dinner on her first night back, that she was going out to the cinema with him and some friends of Gemma's the next day.

'Who?' Jared demanded

'Some friends of Gemma's,' Carlotta repeated ominously. 'We're all going to see the same film so I'll be constantly chaperoned.'

'And where did you meet this Romeo?'

'A group of Gemma's friends came over to watch the competitions on the last day and he asked me out then,' Carlotta said, bottom lip out.

'Well, I want to meet him before you set off so I can decide on whether it's acceptable. That's non-negotiable so don't even think about trying to sneak past me.' And Carlotta had to be satisfied with that.

'I don't like it,' Jared later confided in Izzy. 'I'll have to run it past MK next time I visit him. I can't imagine he'll be best pleased either. Neither of us were keen to let her go on the wretched course in the first place but the benefits seemed to outweigh the detriments, plus it had already been paid for and, essentially, it was no different from her being at school. I'd hoped that once she was safely home I could stop worrying.'

'Surely you can't think she'll come to any harm with Gemma there though,' Izzy said. She herself was slightly irked that she hadn't been included in the invitation but didn't reveal this to anyone for fear of appearing petty or needy.

'I suppose you're right, but I still don't like it.'

Jared liked it even less when he clapped eyes on Carlotta's 'young man' (as Mrs Firth referred to him). He was driven to The Paddocks by another one of Gemma's friends. Carlotta, hovering by the intercom, made a big show of buzzing them in before going outside to meet them on the driveway. Jared followed, surrounded by dogs in an attempt to appear menacing. Izzy also tagged along out of sheer curiosity. A grotty-looking Clio slowed to a halt in front of them and a scrawny, spotty, shuffling youth climbed out of the passenger side.

'This is Alan,' Carlotta said, accompanying him over to where Jared was standing. She eyed Jared with a look that clearly said 'do not embarrass me'. Gemma also got out of the car and followed them over.

'Christ!' Jared muttered to Izzy out of the side of his mouth as they all approached. Izzy could do nothing but stare. This wasn't what she had expected Carlotta to roll up with at all.

Alan was not in any way what could generally be considered as attractive. He had pasty, tight skin and hollowed, black-bagged eyes that together gave the impression of a decomposing skull. It didn't help that he had a chin like Bruce Forsyth, vampire teeth and a suitably unpleasant frame of long, greasy hair with a centre parting. His one redeeming feature was that all the dogs, after a cursory sniff, seemed to be rather taken with him and bounded round him, tails wagging.

'What do you do?'

'I'm at college, studying 'orticulture. Carlotta fort you might be able to give us some tips,' Alan said. His accent was so broad it made Jared sound like Richard Burton.

'He's a Scorpio like me,' Carlotta said. 'Come on, I want you to meet my ponies.' Which Izzy had to concede, was one hell of a chat up line.

'If a horror like that was actually born on October thirty-first the irony will be too much for me to bear. He must save a fortune on Hallowe'en masks,' Jared hissed sideways at Izzy, who had to turn away so as not to giggle.

'Who the hell is this lad? And who are these friends that you're supposedly going out with?' he demanded of an unperturbed Gemma as Carlotta bore Alan off to the stables. 'You know MK doesn't want her gadding about any more than necessary. How could you let this happen?'

'I do have a life away from here, you know,' Gemma replied, exasperated. 'A bunch of us go to the cinema in Loxley every Wednesday and he asked Carlotta if she'd like to come along too. She won't come to any harm and I'll have her home by midnight. It'll probably do her good to get out with some kids closer to her own age. I honestly didn't think you'd mind. Alan's the brother of one of my friends from school so I can vouch for him. He's harmless enough.'

'He's Plug ugly,' Jared continued. 'You're friends with his sister, you say? Are you absolutely sure she isn't also his mother? He looks like a Catherine Cookson book plotline gone wrong.'

In the end Jared had no real grounds to forbid Carlotta not to go. Instead he insisted on checking over the car in which Gemma's rather plain friend had driven over. Jared couldn't see any family resemblance other than she was as unattractive as her brother. Carlotta could do nothing more than stand and watch, half mortified, half furious, as Jared checked the tyre treads and even checked over the engine.

'For God's sake, stop fussing,' Gemma said, impatiently tapping her foot. 'We'll miss the start of the film if we don't set off soon.'

Still unsettled, Jared retreated to the kitchen with Izzy in tow.

'What the bloody hell Carlotta sees in a specimen like that I'll never know,' he said to no one in particular.

'Aye, he's got a face only a mother could love,' Mrs Firth observed, having had a good gawp from an upstairs window.

'I know I've seen that face before, too. I just can't remember where,' Jared mused, still talking to himself.

'Well, it weren't on the cover of a magazine, that's fer sure,' said Mrs Firth, leaning over to set the table.

'Not unless it was *Gargoyles' Weekly*.'

Jared didn't relax until Carlotta was back home. As soon as he heard the front gates whir into action he was out of the front door like a rat out of a trap.

'No snogging in the car,' he was heard to mutter. He all but hauled Carlotta inside the house.

---

WITH MUCH TO REPORT, Jared drove over to HM Prison Leeds to visit MK for his next scheduled visit. Built in 1947, Armley Gaol, as it was then known, was the physical embodiment of the fashionable Victorian fantasy that if prisons were built to look like dark, Gothic castles it would act as a deterrent to would-be criminals. Whether such a vision was successful was questionable but there was no doubt that each time Jared drove past the crenellated gatehouse and high, grime-blackened quarry stone walls he felt a little piece of his soul disintegrate. As he drove into the visitors' car park Jared shuddered, as he always did, still unable to believe his peace-loving friend was incarcerated inside such a grim, foreboding place.

Having been trained to protect Queen and country, Jared had once despised the criminal fraternity, truly believing that if they were locked up they must have done something to deserve it. Now he couldn't be so sure. Every fibre of his body told him MK was innocent of the crime he had been accused of. He shouldn't be being forced to live here.

At least he was visiting alone today. Those occasions when Carlotta and Taryn accompanied him, dressed so sombrely in smart dresses and shoes, filled him with horror. He hated to expose them to the atmosphere in the prison, steeped with the living evil it encased and at the same time haunted by the ghosts of the inmates that had been executed or had committed suicide. Even if MK, as a remand inmate was subject to less stringent regulations than those who had been tried and convicted, it was still a gruelling ordeal for them to set foot in this place. Then for them to see how their father had changed from the dapper, handsome, tanned and well-groomed man he was to the pale, defeated, more unkempt stereotype of an inmate was even worse. Such visions would be indelibly printed on their memories. God knows what damage they could do in the future if left to stagnate. It was no place for children.

Jared handed his visiting order and identification over to the guard, together with the photographs he'd taken of Carlotta and Taryn at the Great Yorkshire Show and a packet of chocolate digestives, simply because he knew MK liked them. After stashing his belt, mobile, wallet and other personal effects into a locked tray, he was accompanied into the visiting room. MK was waiting for him. Their one hour had commenced.

MK was handed the photographs. He flipped through them, his eyes greedy to see his daughters. When he first saw the snap of Taryn being presented her purple rosette and the one of Carlotta clearing the last fence of the jump off, his seal-brown eyes filled with tears. God, he missed them.

'Izzy took that one,' Jared said, pointing to the picture of Carlotta. MK detected the trace of pride in his voice and sighed. There were unpleasant but necessary discussions to be held within their allocated short space of time.

'This must be Izzy?' MK asked, holding up a picture of Izzy with the girls and Gemma. It had been taken at the end of the day, just before they left. All four girls were smiling happily, their arms linked behind their backs. It was such a good picture that Mrs Firth had pinned a copy up on the corkboard in the kitchen.

'We need to talk about this Izzy,' MK said, pushing the

photograph back so that it was exactly half way between them. He then swivelled it so that they could see it. Both men looked briefly at Izzy's open, smiling face. 'What do we actually know about her? I wrote a letter to Merle Miller, who replied in writing admitting she didn't do a DBS check on this girl. Apparently she walked in off the street, no experience, no references... So why did she want to come to us?'

'She was desperate,' Jared said. 'We were her only option.' He was perplexed. MK had never before questioned the circumstances behind Izzy's appointment or his own judgement in continuing to employ her. Jared had only ever relayed back to MK how well she had settled in and how much the girls liked her. He had perhaps told MK tales of some of Izzy's more ridiculous actions, but he had always been amused by those, giving great shouts of laughter that made the watching guards jump suspiciously. What could possibly have brought on this sudden doubt? 'Is something wrong?'

MK spread his hands out in front of him.

'My head accountant visited last week. There are anomalies in the books again. Also, some deals that should have been a mere formality have fallen through for no reason. He believes someone has infiltrated my accounts and is helping themselves,' MK said. Jared was aghast. Then common sense kicked in.

'But what's this got to do with us at The Paddocks? The office in London runs everything to do with the business,' he said. 'You don't keep any business records at home.'

MK raised his eyes and looked directly at him. His expression was sober.

'The accountant has cross-referenced all the anomalies. They were all in connection with my private income: shares, bonds, equities, property, that sort of thing. None of them were accessed via Konstantine Shipping. The common denominator is that all these files are locked in my office.

None of these were major international matters, all personal deals, all easily covered up. Thousands of pounds have been siphoned out of my accounts, taken bit by bit so as not to raise suspicions. Someone in the house has been in my office and seen, and possibly copied, those files. Someone in the house is stealing from me. Someone in that house cannot be trusted and that means the girls could be in danger. I need to know who it is.'

'And you think it's Izzy?' Jared asked.

'It fits. When did she first appear?'

'February.'

'And these incidents commenced in March.'

Jared shook his head in disbelief.

'It can't be Izzy. She's not capable of carrying out a covert operation. She's gormless. She'd make the worst snoop ever.'

'But there's no one else. Are you telling me you really think Mrs Firth is getting out her night vision goggles and secret ink?'

'Carlotta's attached herself to some youth from the next village. He only materialised last week but he's still worth checking out. And what about Gemma?' Jared asked. He simply couldn't believe Izzy was the mole.

'Are you serious? Gemma's been with us since Taryn was a baby. She's like a sister to the girls.'

'I'm just considering all the possibilities. Gemma's been acting a bit strange since Izzy's arrival. Mebbe she doesn't like there being another young woman in the house. The girls have really taken to Izzy. Taryn adores her. Carlotta, not so much, but then Izzy isn't terribly strict with her so she certainly doesn't *dis*like her either. Mebbe Gemma feels threatened. It a tenuous motive, but it's a motive nonetheless.'

'Has something occurred between you and this Izzy that could have sparked some jealousy in Gemma? I'm aware that you and she had an indiscretion last year. Is something going on?'

'Nothing is going on,' Jared said emphatically. 'I haven't touched either of them.'

'It must be the nanny then. Everyone else has been ruled out.'

'I'm still not sure. She didn't even want to come to The Paddocks. Her story checked out. Her referee was from the Inns of Court.'

'Were you a military man or not? Their stories always check out. I want her watched. She's the last one in so she has to be the prime suspect.'

Jared still looked unconvinced but accepted that he had to agree to watch Izzy. Anxiety was making MK more abrasive than usual and Jared was an old enough friend of his to appreciate this and not take his bluntness personally. His own military instincts were directing him away from Izzy but, if MK wanted her watched, that's what he'd do. He stretched his hands out in front of him in a gesture of submission.

'Okay, I'll watch her but I still can't believe it's her.'

'You like her,' MK said, giving Jared a searching look. 'Well I must say it's about time someone made you stop brooding over that wife of yours. It's just a shame it's this particular girl.'

'My judgement hasn't been wrong before,' Jared said, still adamant.

'Your judgement hasn't been tainted in this way before. You can't accept that the nanny, this Izzy, is probably our mole because you don't want to.'

'So what do you want me to do? Send her away?'

'No. Keep her close where you can monitor her. If she's as idiotic as you say she'll soon hang herself if given enough lunge rein.'

'I'm sure it's not her, MK, I'd stake my life on it.'

'That's your choice. But are you prepared to stake the lives of Carlotta and Taryn on it?'

Put that way, Jared didn't feel he had a case to answer.

'Has she done anything at all that could justify suspicion?'

Jared felt his cheeks flush. He recalled how Izzy had lied so blatantly and elaborately when she'd first arrived at The Paddocks, and how he'd found her, just the week before, rifling through MK's private papers in his office. He had no option but to tell MK of these events.

'And you still believe she's here by lucky coincidence?' MK asked, eyebrows raised. It was plain to him that Izzy had been planted in the household. 'I don't like it. Watch her. You might as well do a bit of digging on this lad Carlotta's seeing too. No harm in covering all bases.'

At that point the harsh buzzer sounded, communicating in no subtle manner that the hour was up. A warden came to accompany MK back into the bowels of the prison. It tore Jared up to see his vibrant, life-loving friend cooped up in such a way. He didn't like to think of what went on behind secured doors and was just thankful that with his military training MK would be able to defend himself in the event of an unexpected attack.

'You know I'll do everything I can,' he called after him. MK's only response was to look over his shoulder at Jared, his dark eyes sad, and nod.

---

Jared returned to The Paddocks to find everyone on the manége. Carlotta was executing perfect figures of eight in canter, changing legs with flawless precision at the crossover. The afternoon sunshine was reflecting off Vega's gleaming golden coat like a mirror. Gemma was riding Ghost, concentrating on getting him to accept the bit. Whenever they passed each other it was like watching the sun eclipse the moon. Izzy was leaning on the gate, watching intently. Taryn was nowhere to be seen and was probably in the stable with Jester.

Izzy was in fact suffering from a severe bout of inferiority. It was sobering in itself to watch two such talented jockeys at work. It was even worse that Gemma and Carlotta were both riding in shorts and sports bras. Both were wonderfully brown and buxom. Izzy, self conscious about her lack of boobs, only ever went as far as a vest. Both looking ridiculously sexy, the two riders encapsulated both femininity and power as they bounced round the school, sitting astride these powerful beasts in a disturbingly primeval way, controlling them through an empowering combination of gentle empathy and sheer strength of leg. They were the personification of any hot-blooded man's fantasy. How could Jared possibly not fancy either of them? Or even both?

Feeling uncomfortable, Izzy forced herself to analyse Jared's relationship with Carlotta. He was always watching her very carefully and was very possessive of where she went and with who, more so than he ever was with Taryn. Yes, Carlotta gave him more cause for concern but on the other hand he had certainly overreacted about Alan. It wasn't beyond the realms of possibility that Jared did indeed fancy Carlotta. It was a revolting and grotesque thought, but Carlotta was gorgeous and did look a lot older than her fifteen years.

In October she'd be legal, thought Izzy with a stab of pain. The thought of Gemma and Jared was bad enough, but Carlotta and Jared…? That was unbearable.

Guilt riddled at being caught entertaining such unsavoury thoughts, Izzy coloured up when she noticed Jared hovering by the barn. God knows what he would think of her if he knew what she was thinking. How long had he been there anyway? Unnerved, not trusting herself not to say something stupid, she ignored him and instead turned her attention back to the activity in the school.

Standing twenty feet directly behind her, Jared also remained stationary. He couldn't put into coherent thoughts how very much he didn't want to corroborate MK's theory about Izzy, but then she had just looked so guilty when she'd turned round. It was obvious she hadn't expected him to be standing there. Was he going to be forced to re-evaluate his opinion of her? Was Izzy really as harmless as she appeared? And what had she really been doing sneaking round in MK's office?

If MK had presented him with the seeds of doubt, Izzy had just prepared the ground for their sowing.

---

STILL FEELING INVISIBLE AND MEDIOCRE, Izzy decided to take drastic action. She was sick and tired of being the butt of everyone's jokes. Plus she felt a bit jaded with her appearance. She hadn't had her hair either cut or coloured in months and was looking a bit wild and woolly. However, instead of taking the time out to pay a salon visit, she decided to use a do-it-yersen (as Jared would say) dye kit from the chemist in Greater Ousebury. Taking into consideration Jared's penchant for redheads, Izzy deliberated long and hard over her choice of shade and eventually plumped for a subtle coppery-blonde which she hoped would complement what was left of her caramel highlights.

Mistaken in the belief she'd chosen a semi-permanent dye, Izzy slapped the dye paste on her hair with enthusiasm, not realising until afterwards that she'd managed to blather two towels and the bathmat in her en suite at the same time. Looking down and seeing the mess she'd made, she shrieked for Carlotta, who when she finally appeared was no help at all but just stood in the doorway gulping with laughter. Worse still, Steptoe, attracted by all the noise, mooched in, sat on the sodden bathmat and ended up having a salon day himself. Covered in itchy dark orange dye, he promptly sat down and proceeded to groom himself.

'Don't let him lick himself. It'll poison him,' Carlotta shrieked, picking up the little dog and racing downstairs, holding him at arm's length as though he were a bomb. She left Izzy in the bathroom, desperately trying to rinse out every last drop of the thick red paste. It was only when she'd managed to dry and brush her hair that Izzy realised just how great a mess she'd made. Her hair was the same orange-red as a clown's wig, and as brittle and unmanageable as the straw she bedded Jester down with. Ironically, the towels and bathmat had ended up matching the colour swatch on the box perfectly.

'Jesus H Christ! What have you done to yourself? You look like a fucking Tweenie,' Carlotta said, reappearing fifteen minutes later. 'You'd better make yourself scarce. Jared's on the warpath. Poor Steptoe's got more orange patches than a nicotine addict.'

'Blue ponies, red dogs! What messed up Nickelodeon world do you live in, woman?' Jared roared when he tracked her down.

'Don't call me woman,' she had yelled back, close to tears.

'You're right, it's completely inappropriate,' Jared said. 'Infant child would be a more fitting description.' Even Mrs Firth was cross with her because she'd left a tannin-red tidemark round the bath. She could be heard chuntering as she scrubbed away with a jaycloth and a tube of Vim.

Nevertheless, Jared took Izzy into Loxley to have her hair reverted to its shiny caramel stripes. She dove into the glass-fronted, chrome and black themed salon with her orange hair battened down by one of Mrs Firth's ghastly headscarves.

'I'll be back for you in an hour. I need to go and buy some underpants from Marks's,' Jared said, backing out of the salon at speed. He couldn't remember the last time he'd set foot in a hairdressers and he certainly didn't intend to be talked into having a cut and blow today. His hair was cut by an old biddy in the village who charged him a tenner for a trim, and he was quite happy with the arrangement, thanks very much.

A wonderfully flamboyant stylist with precision trimmed facial hair and a bottom like two pomegranates in a fabric shopping bag sashayed over. His gasp of shock as he whipped off the headscarf caused every beautifully-styled head in the room to turn.

'Darling, what did you do? This is horrific.'

'I tried to dye it myself with a kit from the chemist,' Izzy confessed. Reflected in the walls of spotlit mirrors, her hair looked even more radioactive than ever.

'I don't know. Give someone a pair of rubber gloves and a bottle of Nice 'n' Easy and suddenly they think they're Daniel Galvin. What do you do for a living, sweetheart?'

'I'm a sort of nanny,' Izzy said.

'Right, well I'll make you a deal. I promise I won't try and look after small children if you promise to never try and do my job again. Now, let's get rid of this ragu.' He was so friendly and complimentary about her 'superior skin quality, darling' that within ten minutes he and Izzy were cracking jokes and comparing bad boyfriend stories. It was such a confidence boost.

Just over an hour later Jared reappeared. He didn't seem to care that Izzy was still in foils, looking rather like a space age Medusa, but simply plonked himself down in the reception area and rummaged round in the pile of magazines until he found a decrepit copy of *Gardener's World*. Izzy's stylist was agog.

'Is he your honey, honey?'

'Nah, he's my boss.' There was something in the way Izzy's eyes flickered that revealed her feelings. 'I'm not seeing anyone right now.'

'I see. Hmm, I wouldn't say no to working under him but I don't think I'm his type. Butch, isn't he?'

Izzy giggled. The stylist asked her permission to try a

brand new cut. It was fresh from New York, he told her, and was a sleek fringed bob with an asymmetrical cut. It would be nothing radical, he assured her, and certainly not as controversial as her own disastrous effort.

Streaked, straightened and styled, Izzy was finally done.

'What do you think?' she asked shyly, standing in front of Jared, who tore his eyes away from an article he was reading on the benefits of peat-free compost. He assessed the bias cut of the hair. It suited her perfectly but he was damned if he was going to tell her that. Instead, he couldn't resist having a dig at her.

'You look like Phil Oakey from The Human League. I'd ask for my money back on the grounds that they haven't finished the job.' The stylist shot Jared a look of quivering, outraged loathing. 'It's no use looking at me like that. You didn't see what she did to my poor dog. He was even more orange than she was.' He turned to Izzy. 'Come on, you. I suppose I'd better take you out for some dinner so you can show yourself off.'

Behind Jared's back the stylist stuck his thumbs up at Izzy. Half an hour later she was sitting in a cosy Italian restaurant with a bottle of Chianti and a well-stocked bread basket in front of her.

'What made you decide to go all Ginger Spice anyway?' Jared asked, perfect white teeth tearing into virgin olive oil soaked ciabatta.

'I don't know really. It just seems to me that redheads seem to garner a lot of respect. Caro, Pippa… Gemma.' Izzy tried to keep her tone light.

'Huh! More trouble than they're worth, redheads, in my opinion. I haven't met one who wasn't barking mad.'

'Mrs Firth said your wife had lovely red hair.'

'Did she now? And did she mention that she had a lovely red temper to go with it?' Jared asked drily.

'You never mention her,' Izzy said.

'You never mention Scott,' Jared countered.

'Touché!'

As they enjoyed their main courses Jared opened up to her a little about his marriage.

'She didn't like being a forces wife. She hated all the travelling. She cried buckets when I was drafted to Afghanistan and then cried even more when I came back alive, mainly because she was petrified she'd be forced to say goodbye to her lover and a considerable Navy pension. I guess she eventually got fed up with waiting and by the time I came home, she'd moved on. The irony is that as soon as she buggered off I was given an honourable discharge from the Marines. If she'd had a bit of patience she'd have got exactly what she wanted.

'She couldn't have picked a worse time. My mother lost her battle with cancer not long after I was discharged and then MK asked me to join him at The Paddocks. My life was in such a two and eight, as you would say, that I couldn't find any good reason to not accept his offer. They say that death, divorce and house moving are the three most stressful things a person can go through in their lifetime and I had all three in the space of two years. I didn't have this before that.' He pointed to the streak of white hair on his head.

'Isn't it worth contacting her to try and make a go of it,' Izzy asked. The words nearly choked her.

'Nah,' Jared said. 'It's been a long time since I've wanted her back. Whether it was the consequence of her betrayal, how she did it and the timing of it, or whether we simply weren't meant to be and she saw it first... I guess we'll never know. There were other issues too. She didn't want kids, I did. That's a big thing for someone to make a compromise on. There won't ever be reconciliation. I guess I really should find the time to go and see her and officially start divorce proceedings.'

'Why have you never done that?'

'At first I didn't want to.' Jared had never been so candid with Izzy. 'If we'd have got solicitors and courts involved I would have had to have accepted it was over. After that it was a simple case of never getting round to it. I'd moved into The Paddocks, she was living with her lover. Neither of us wanted to remarry. She didn't have the inclination and I had no prospects. It was just left to stagnate. I know I'll have to deal with it at some point in the future but it would be nice to have a reason to do so.' Jared looked at Izzy intently as he spoke, as if trying to convey some secret meaning to her. Or was that what she was hoping for, reading signs that weren't there? She guessed that was something she would never know.

They returned to a for once peaceful and ordered house. The girls had eaten their dinners with little fuss and were in their respective rooms, Mrs Firth told them, and there was a message for Izzy to ring someone called Caro.

'It isn't looking good,' Caro told Izzy, having picked up on the first ring. 'From what I can gather there's been talk of the victim's family agreeing to switch off the life support. Unless something drastic happens, Konstantine is going to be looking at the business end of a twenty-five year life sentence, or even longer if the judge decides to make an example of him.'

'It just doesn't fit, Caro. Jared is convinced of his innocence. He says MK is the most peaceable, non-violent man he's ever known.'

'If that's the case, I hope he has a good barrister. It's just a shame it isn't me.'

# JEALOUSY

August broke like a furnace. The entire country was gripped by a two-week heatwave. Hay bales started to appear in the fields early in the month, much to the delight of Taryn and Carlotta. Hay bales meant stubble fields, and stubble fields meant a good, uninterrupted gallop, although it was so hot that the horses could only be ridden in the evening when it was slightly cooler. Hacks through Prickett's Copse were simply amazing. The oaks and hawthorns provided a thick green canopy overhead, protecting them from the early evening heat. The horses clearly loved these rides. Their ears, pricked as they made their way through the peaceful little wood, twitched and swivelled like radars as they detected the clandestine sounds of wildlife in the undergrowth. On one occasion a young red deer cantered across the pathway a few yards ahead of them. Everyone reined in and gazed in silent wonder. Izzy had never experienced anything like it before in her entire life. Then any feelings of competence she might be harbouring were snuffed out courtesy of a brown pant moment when she lost both stirrups halfway through a mad gallop across the water meadow. How she stayed on she would never know!

Much to Mrs Firth's disapproval, Jared let the Aga fall dormant. Meals were instead cooked on the vast brick barbecue, and the rich Mediterranean aromas of grilled meat and fish constantly drifted through the now perpetually open back door, permeating the whole house. They ate as a family outside on the decking as the sun went down. The air was steeped with the natural perfume of night blooming stocks, phlox with its rich almond scent, honeysuckle, jasmine and the sweet aniseed smell of escallonia apple blossom, resulting in the redundancy of scented candles.

Not that the temperature dropped much at night time either. Izzy resorted to sleeping on top of the covers.

'You'd think someone as looted as MK could afford to install air conditioning,' she grumbled. Despite the heat Steptoe insisted on sleeping right next to her, fur from his hot little body pressing into her skin, making her itch, or with his legs stretched out so they prodded her in the back. Not having the heart to move him Izzy suffered in silence.

Then came the storms, both literal and metaphorical. One unbearably hot mid-month Wednesday, the temperature reached eighty degrees by mid-morning and the air was thick and close. Everyone had been tetchy all day. Taryn wanted constant entertainment. Carlotta had stropped off to see Alan after being snapped at by Mrs Firth for having a pigsty of a bedroom. Even Jared had yelled at the dogs for cocking their legs up the wellies he'd dumped by the kitchen door simply because they couldn't be arsed to walk any further than the back step. Pongy took idleness to another level and simply did his business in the house. As a result the kitchen and utility stank of hot pee, which annoyed Mrs Firth further. She could be heard chuntering a bucketful as she dug rags and disinfectant out of the cleaning cupboard. Izzy bore the brunt of all this ill temper and had finally escaped by declaring Jet needed some exercise.

Carlotta and Izzy had been taking it in turns to ride Jet on alternate days so as not to overreach him. It was really too hot to ride but Izzy knew he hadn't been schooled in almost a week. Since the arrival of Alan into her life, Carlotta had become much less precious about her pony and was quite happy to let someone else look after him. As Gemma was far too busy with the other horses this meant it was left up to Izzy.

She rode in a strappy vest and shorts but was still sweating cobs within minutes. Jet was for once amenable, subdued by the heat. Izzy schooled him on a twenty-metre circle. The reins slipped through her damp hands. She only gave him half an hour and even then restricted his work to walk and trot.

Once she'd turned Jet out, watching him amble unenthusiastically across the paddock to where Jester was shading under a leafy horse chestnut, Izzy wandered round the side of the house and flopped onto the parched lawn. She knew she should really go inside and shower but instead she lay on her back, letting the sun warm her bones, and closed her eyes. The strong, high midsummer sun penetrated her eyelids, creating trippy, psychedelic shapes in colours of strawberry red and mango orange. London seemed an age ago. Izzy wasn't even sure she missed it anymore. She shuddered to think what the city would be like in this heat. No one would be allowed to slow down or take time off. As the temperature rose, so would tempers. The streets would be overrun with crabby workers and impatient tourists. Pavement cafés would reduce space even further and all across the capital prices would be hiked for anything remotely connected to the heatwave: sun cream, cold drinks, parasols, nasty sun visors with green plastic beaks and Union Flag patterns. No doubt someone would be attempting to sell fresh ice out of a coolbox on a street corner. The Tube, buried deep beneath the hot city like the first Circle line of hell, would be filthy, claustrophobic and suffocating.

Feeling thankful to not be a part of all that, Izzy stretched. All around her the air was thick with the scent of cut grass, mint and bay. She could hear Jared beavering away in the vegetable plot, trying to manhandle it into some sort of order. He was singing *Wichita Lineman* in a slightly off-key baritone as he worked.

After the summer rains of July and then this heat, all the plants had gone berserk. In the orchard the fruit trees had started to produce tiny fruits. In another couple of weeks they would be overrun with food.

Izzy dozed off for a few minutes only to be rudely woken by Sprite and Nugget, their usual placid temperaments also altered by the weather, scrapping loudly not ten yards away from her. The snapping and snarling sounded much worse than it actually was but it was enough to startle her. She sat bolt upright.

'What the bleedin' hell—!'

Jared appeared brandishing a hosepipe and proceeded to soak both dogs and then Izzy too.

'Bastard!' she shrieked at him, holding her hands in front of her face as he continued to jet water at her, roaring with laughter. Never would she have admitted out loud that the impromptu cold shower had been most welcome, and almost pleasant. She'd be dry within minutes anyway. Jared grinned down at her, his body a giant black silhouette against the dazzling sun.

'Bloody dogs,' he said. 'Usually means a brewing storm when they start carrying on like that.' Izzy scoffed at him at first but then noticed a few petulant clouds gathering in the distance. She also considered how intense the humidity had been and had to wonder if he did indeed have a point. Later that day a sudden hot wind blew up only to drop away to an eerie stillness. Minutes later the heavens opened. The storm raged until the sky darkened. Steptoe hovered by the back door, growling, as though to say 'lemme out, I'll fight it'.

Nor were storms restricted to outside the house either. Relations between Carlotta and the rest of the household had reached an all time low. Jared insisted on voicing his unflattering opinion of Alan, who seemed to be round at The Paddocks on a perpetual basis.

'Nice 'ouse. Can I 'ave a tour next time?' he had asked Carlotta on one of his earlier visits. Jared, who had been hovering within deliberate earshot, eyed him with suspicion.

'Why would such a young lad be interested in fixtures and fittings?' he'd asked Izzy, who had merely shrugged.

'Perhaps he was trying to appear more grown up,' she said, not really interested.

'Hmmm!' had been Jared's only reply. Instead he took to demanding to know Alan's whereabouts at all times, in his own inimitable style.

'Where's freak of nature boy?'

Quickly forgetting how easy she found it to take the piss out of other people, Carlotta was surprisingly touchy on the subject of Alan's looks.

'Don't call him that! If I want to look at something pretty I'll look in my mirror,' she raged.

Jared invariably walked away chuckling, which was all very well, thought Izzy crossly, but she was the one who Carlotta vented her spleen on. The ultimate irony was that when Carlotta acted out Izzy then got it in the neck from Jared too.

'I just can't win,' Izzy grumbled to Mrs Firth one afternoon. As usual, Mrs Firth chose to remain neutral.

Izzy may have felt some sympathy towards Carlotta if it hadn't been for the fact she agreed with Jared that Alan was a hopeless loser. After all, Izzy had had more than her fair share of unsuitable boyfriends. However, she simply couldn't understand what Carlotta saw in the strange young boy who was neither attractive nor intelligent. His only redeeming quality seemed to be that he was prepared to fawn over Carlotta upon command.

A further and more sinister development was that Carlotta started to indulge in spontaneous disappearances, sometimes leaving fake running away notes. The discovery of the very first one had caused quite a stir. Izzy, in total panic at having found the scrawled note, had burst into Jared's room not realising he was just exiting the shower. Wet and naked, his face obscured by a towel as he rubbed his hair dry, he advanced towards her. God only knew what he'd been thinking about in the shower, because his cock was as big, hard and upright as a puissance wall.

'Oh! Oh! Oh!!' cried Izzy, holding the note in front of her eyes.

'Fuckin' 'ell, Izzy!' Jared shouted, hastily wrapping the towel round his waist. Eyes still shielded, Izzy handed over the note. Jared's face darkened several shades from embarrassed pink to furious crimson as he read it. 'Right,' was all he said, his tone sharp and determined. Three minutes later he was fully dressed and scorching up the drive in the Golf. Within half an hour both he and Carlotta were back at The Paddocks. He had found her and Alan drinking cans of tramp's lager in the village churchyard and, having dispatched the young lad with a truly ferocious series of threats, hauled Carlotta back home, literally kicking and screaming.

The whole fiasco had two clear consequences. Firstly, Carlotta's already well-developed malevolent streak matured into pure, concentrated venom. She prowled round the house looking for someone to torment, which resulted in Izzy shadowing Taryn's every movement simply to protect her. Both girls found this frustrating, but for totally different reasons. Nor did Jared's threats of further punishments prevent Carlotta from repeating what she clearly saw as being a very successful exercise over and over again until Izzy took

Carlotta's disappearances with a pinch of salt, refusing to rise to her or her badly-written notes.

'At last you're showing a bit of gumption,' Mrs Firth said after Izzy had scrumpled up yet another angry, threatening screed and chucked it in the recycling.

'What's gumption?' Izzy asked. Sometimes it really did seem they spoke a different language up here.

'You know, nouse, mettle… common sense?'

'Oh!' Izzy hadn't known what to say. Perhaps that was what had been wrong with her life thus far, why she had made such a bleedin' mess of everything. She suffered from gumption deficiency. What a shame she couldn't simply nip into Superdrug and buy a tub of supplementary capsules, rather like vitamins, to remedy the problem.

Secondly, and once he'd got over the initial shock of Izzy catching him in the buff, Jared took great delight in teasing her, calling her a voyeur and announcing to the room whenever he intended to strip off just in case Izzy fancied another opportunity to 'feast thine eyes'. Izzy's cheeks were perpetually scarlet, but never more so than when Jared loomed in to query whether she'd seen anything she'd liked. Izzy wondered what he would do and say if she, in all honesty, replied in the affirmative. Not for any sum of money would she ever admit how many times she'd drifted into a steamy daydream in which she hadn't had the enforced distraction of Carlotta's note and had instead plucked away Jared's towel, pushing him back onto his bed, glorious in all his damp nakedness. With no corporeal lover to appease her lust Izzy resorted to cold showers and self-service, although neither was ideal, especially as Taryn had a nasty habit of barging into her room unannounced at crucial moments.

'What *are* you doing?' asked the little girl, bemused to find Izzy lying under her comforter on such a hot day.

'Migraine,' Izzy improvised, through gritted teeth as she whipped her hand out of her jeans. No wonder little Hobbit and Breeze were so crabby when they were on heat. She had the utmost sympathy for them, poor bitches.

It first occurred to Izzy that she was finally over Scott one warm sunny day. She had wandered down into the village for a couple of pints of milk and a birthday card for Caro, enjoying the chance to stretch her own legs rather than Jet's for a change. As Steptoe had nattered to join her she'd clipped his lead on, not being as confident in his recall as Jared and not trusting him not to bugger off at high speed if he saw a cat or a squirrel.

The village was a hub of activity. Because it was the school holidays the air was punctured with the sound of kids playing in back gardens, accompanied by the faint drone from several lawnmowers. Cottage gardens were in full bloom, rich with roses, fuchsias and hollyhocks. Not a single cloud marred the perfect blue sky. Through the wide bay window of Philippa's Kitchen Izzy could see Pippa icing a tray of cupcakes with pastel pink, blue and yellow frosting. As Izzy passed by Pippa looked up and waved. Izzy waved back and carried on walking, deep in thought. Carefully hooking Steptoe up outside the village shop, Izzy knew she had precisely ninety seconds to make her purchases before he started howling for attention. She threw two bottles of milk and a birthday card into her basket and headed towards the counter, but was distracted by a placard on the freezer cabinet advertising a new, limited edition Magnum. Unable to resist, she reached in and grabbed one. Outside Steptoe, being a very vocal creature who would yowl whenever the phone rang or the intercom buzzed from the front gate and invariably set off all the other dogs into a barking frenzy, was now bored at being tied up and demanded Izzy hurry up via a series of high pitched, shrill, ear piercing yips.

'You'd think he'd get on his own nerves,' Izzy complained to the girl on the till, wincing, as she paid. She settled on the shaded bench on the village green to eat her ice lolly. Taryn and Carlotta would only demand to know where theirs were if she wandered back to the house with it. Steptoe settled underneath the seat to chew on the Jumbone she'd bought for him at the last minute in the hope it would keep him quiet for five minutes.

It was whilst she was sitting here that a shiny black Corsa with sports trim pulled up outside the village shop and a slim young girl, casual and summery in a black vest, denim miniskirt and espadrilles, ran into the shop. She emerged a few minutes later with her arms laden with packets of crisps, cans of Coke and chocolate bars. She looked so happy and was smiling so prettily at the driver of the car, who was quite obviously her boyfriend, that Izzy found herself staring. As the car drove away she felt a stab of loneliness, no longer for Scott, who, she realised with a jolt, she hadn't thought about in weeks, but just for that closeness, the togetherness of being in a relationship. Her thoughts kept veering towards Jared, who continued to feature heavily in her fantasies, but he gave no indication of reciprocating her interest. So determined was Izzy not to make a fool of herself, she kept her thoughts to herself. Plus, Izzy wasn't even certain he wasn't still having it off with Gemma in secret, and friends didn't skank other friends by hitting on their blokes. Then there was Marc Jones, but Izzy had heard nothing from him since she hadn't texted or phoned to thank him for the flowers. She was forced to accept that she only had herself to blame for that one. With a sigh she stood up, chucked the empty wrappers in the bin and headed back to The Paddocks.

The full realisation hit Izzy several hours later, whilst she was bringing in a basket full of dry dog blankets from the whirligig. It was the cusp of the day, just as afternoon turned into evening, and the high sugar-frosted skies were Elizabethan rose pink and pale turquoise. Over on the lawn Jared was chugging along on his ride-along grass gobbler. As she unclipped another peg Izzy recalled her moment of introspection on the village green and realised she couldn't actually remember the last time she'd thought about Scott before that afternoon. She no longer hoped he would get in touch, or wondered if he ever thought about her. He no longer featured in her dreams as she slept and she no longer woke yearning for him, devastated to realise all over again that he wasn't there. No one was more surprised than Izzy was to discover she was over him. There had been no clues, no bells and whistles or gradual realisation. It had simply happened. She felt a twinge of regret at having fallen to pieces so spectacularly and yet at the same time so needlessly. Like a fool she'd been so sure she couldn't live without Scott and that he'd been the one, and yet space and time had proved her so wrong. It had all been for nothing, a mere miscalculation of judgement. Then she chose to brood on it no longer. She acknowledged she had made a mistake, but that was something she couldn't change. It was time to let go, and move forward.

---

IT WAS ALSO around the beginning of August that Taryn started to natter about her birthday, which that year fell on the bank holiday. She wanted to have some sort of event, perhaps a gymkhana for her Pony Club friends or a fancy dress disco. At the mention of fancy dress everyone grimaced.

'But I want to go as Tinkerbell,' Taryn said stubbornly.

'More like Smee,' said Carlotta.

'Shut up, 'Lotta,' Taryn said. 'What do you think, Jared?'

'I couldn't give a Captain Hook,' said Jared, and roared at his own joke.

'Is that more of your Yorkshire rhyming slang?' Izzy asked. She had been subjected to several variations including Jared announcing with relish that he was going to the bog for a Forrest.

'Aye, and I could also do with a good Orson,' he had added. Izzy had heard this cryptic declaration before and had spent far too many fruitless minutes wondering what the hell rhymed with Welles. It was only when Jared raised one butt cheek from the kitchen chair and let rip with a long, voluminous fart that Izzy finally realised what the missing word was.

'That's released the beast,' he said, looking pleased with himself. Taryn and Carlotta emitted sniggers and cries of disgust respectively.

'Orson cart?' Izzy asked, appalled and disapproving. 'Really?' Taryn exploded into giggles.

Eventually, and after all the 'hilarity' had ceased, it was agreed that there would be a small gymkhana-type gathering which would please all Taryn's pony-mad friends. It would also involve Carlotta who, still gloating from her second place at Harrogate, had immediate visions of winning everything in sight.

'You can have a tack and turn out, a showing class, a jumping class for the little ones and a Chase-Me-Charlie for the bigger riders. That should accommodate all levels of competence,' Jared said, pouring over a page of handwritten notes. 'No more than a dozen friends and their families though, Taryn. You know the rules. We can have a barbecue and play CDs from Taryn's ghetto blaster.'

'They're called boomboxes now,' said Carlotta scathingly. Jared ignored her.

'Can we have gymkhana games, like bending and a Gretna Green race?'

'Who do you think I am? Raymond Brooks-Ward?' He then turned to Izzy. 'Would you fancy entering the showjumping on Jet? I think it would do your confidence good. The jumps wouldn't be any bigger than two foot six.'

'Wha-a-a-t!?' cried Izzy and Carlotta in unison. It was debatable who was louder.

'She's not riding Jet,' snapped Carlotta. 'I plan on winning the jumping on *my pony* and I don't want him ruining beforehand by a novice.'

Despite hate, hate, *hating* to let Carlotta have her own way or seeming to be intimidated or influenced by her in any way, Izzy also had something to say.

'No fear. I think I'll have enough to concentrate on without the added distraction of competing,' she said. She didn't add that she had every intention of tarting herself up to her best ability and was already mentally planning her wardrobe, which certainly didn't include ruining her hair with a riding hat. Perhaps Gemma would be up for another shopping spree in Loxley. She must ask her straight away. Then a thought occurred to her.

'What about Gemma? Won't she want to ride?'

'Gemma doesn't compete,' Carlotta said with such a tone of finality that Izzy chose not to press the matter further.

Having interpreted Izzy's refusal to jump as a lack of big match temperament, Carlotta had curled her lip in contempt. However, this soon turned to fury as Jared told her that, as co-host, it would be unsporting for her to win any of the events. It would be a case of Family Hold Back.

'Well I'm not bloody well entering at all then,' she snapped, scraping her chair back. 'No bloody point,' she could be heard fuming as she stormed outside.

Izzy supposed it was inevitable that what had been intended as a small gymkhana for Taryn's friends was soon eclipsed. What started out as a compact gathering soon escalated into a three ring circus, or rather three ring gymkhana. The guest list doubled within the week until it was evident that a cosy barbecue and a few records played wasn't going to be enough to entertain everyone. Nor were matters helped by Taryn and Carlotta writing to MK for authorisation every time one of their ideas was vetoed by Jared. Continually overruled, a very irate Jared added a bouncy castle (to provide some entertainment for the non-riding contingent) and outside bartendering onto his to-do list. Each time the phone rang or the postman delivered handfuls of RSVPs it meant more and more parents were confirming the attendance of their children.

'And could we possibly bring a plus one?' seemed to be the catchphrase *du jour*. Even the ubiquitous Alan had wangled an invitation, as had several families from the village.

'I don't remember sending half these people an invitation,' Jared said, both annoyed and bemused. Little did he know, Carlotta had printed off and mailed invites to everyone she either knew and liked, or knew and wanted to impress. Taryn hadn't been quite so sophisticated and had simply pinned up a hand-drawn poster in her classroom. Worst of all, both had posted the event on Facebook.

'From a security point of view, it's a nightmare,' Jared confided in Izzy as he contemplated the escalating numbers. 'I can't possibly keep an eye on this lot.' Never before had she seen him so discombobulated.

'Can't you call for backup?' Izzy said. 'You must have some mates you can count on.' Jared suddenly grinned. Filled with new vigour he sprang up from the table, grabbed Izzy and planted a loud kiss on the top of her head.

'You,' he said as he sat back down, 'are an absolute genius.' He reached for the phone before it rang again. Engrossed in activity once more, he didn't notice Izzy drifting out of the kitchen, her hand touching the spot where he had kissed her in wonder.

---

PREPARATIONS BECAME everyone's main focus. Jared enlisted the help of several burly fellows from the village, including the local farrier and his son, plus a few local farmhands used to calving heifers and heaving bales of hay around with their bare hands. Happy to work for the fee of a free feed and as much ale as their livers would tolerate, they would appear to mingle as normal guests but at the same time would keep a general eye on proceedings and act as chucker-out in the event of any aggro. Izzy's main responsibility would be to shadow Taryn, Jared told her. He and Gemma would keep an eye on Carlotta, seeing as it was a two-person job. Upon hearing this Izzy's exhilaration from the kiss he had given her evaporated. He always picked Gemma over her.

A show ring had been marked out in the near paddock for the showing class and tack and turn out. The showjumping and Chase-Me-Charlie would be held on the manége. Carlotta had been appeased slightly by being asked to design a course of eight fences for the minimus jumping. She would also be a co-judge with the vicar's wife for the tack and turn out. The local huntmaster had agreed to oversee the jumping events. Izzy and Gemma had fun jazzing up the stable yard with lengths of bunting.

Crates of Veuve Clicquot, outers of Pimm's and kegs of beer would be delivered over the course of the bank holiday weekend. Freshly baked bread rolls, cheese straws, beautifully iced cupcakes and an enormous birthday cake baked and decorated in the shape of a skewbald pony jumping a red and white wall had been ordered from Philippa's Kitchen. Mrs Firth would prepare bowls of pasta, rice and tomato salads and several cheese, pineapple and pickled onion 'hedgehogs' upon Taryn's special request. The Sainsbury's van could have driven itself to The Paddocks as it delivered crisps, bottles of pop and paper plates and napkins on continuous loop as the guest list continued to grow. Hundreds of beefburgers, stacked like miniature towers of tyres in the fridge, ribs, steaks and sausages had been bought from local farmers. Enough chicken drumsticks to service a steel drum convention were marinating in three vast casseroles on the pantry's cool shelf. Mrs Firth spent an entire morning assembling onion, pepper and mushroom kebabs 'for the vegetarians'.

Calling in to Philippa's to increase the order once again, Pippa asked Jared and Izzy if they would be interested in having Drew, her husband, do a half hour hypnotist's turn for the parents.

Izzy and Jared had turned to each other in glee until they realised that MK, who had suddenly regained his business nouse and had started to ask for a balance sheet, probably wouldn't be prepared to foot the appearance fee and said that, very sadly, they would have to decline. It was a very kind offer but they had already gone way over budget

'Oh no, it would be a freebie,' Pippa said. 'Kind of a birthday present for the little girl. We absolutely insist. The event is turning into such a highlight for the village and you've brought so much business my way. It's hardly even a favour from our point of view.'

Even Carlotta was impressed by the news. 'He's a seriously good act, and he's bloody gorgeous too.' She then eyed Jared with a witch's glare. 'I do hope I get something equally as fab as, no — actually better than — this do for my birthday.'

Ignoring her, Jared started muttering about not having enough chairs for everyone.

'Email them all telling them to bring their own, or picnic rugs,' said Izzy. 'They can sit round the show ring whilst they're eating their lunch.'

'Not a bad idea,' said Jared. 'But what if it rains?'

'It won't,' said Izzy, Taryn and Carlotta all at the same time. They all stared at each other in amazement before bursting out laughing. It was the first time in weeks the three of them had all agreed on something.

---

Endless preparations proved to be exhausting. Even the tireless Jared found he was knackered and took to having a fly kip in the hayloft on an afternoon.

'Isn't it too noisy up there?' Izzy asked, fascinated.

'Hardly. After a tour of duty in Iraq a few whinnies aren't going to make me lose sleep.'

Everyone was kept occupied. Direction signs had to be made for the toilets, collecting ring and refreshments. Raffle prizes were cadged off local businesses. Rosettes and certificates to five placings had been ordered and collected from Pets & Ponies. Izzy, Carlotta and Taryn had even spent an enjoyable, spat-free afternoon trawling round the shop choosing prizes for the winners and bickering happily over which little equine-themed novelties should be included in the party favour bags. Not even Carlotta grumbling 'the winner of the jumping should get a cup' could douse Taryn's excitement. All the while everyone kept one eye on the sky, hoping the incessant drizzle that had dampened the previous week would finally show some mercy and abate.

Not that everything went according to plan. A week before the big day Jared was unnerved to discover another butchered animal, a rabbit this time, on the premises. It had been dumped by the electric gates. Jared would have put its demise down to a fox or other predator if not for the clean, precision cut of the wound on its neck. Alas, there was no denying that a knife had been used.

It couldn't have come at a worse time.

'Should we cancel the party?' Mrs Firth asked. The two of them were huddled by the back door, talking in whispers.

'Probably, but it's too late now, plus it would break Taryn's heart,' Jared replied. He couldn't remember the last time he had been so on edge.

---

KEEN TO LOOK THEIR BEST, Izzy, Gemma and Carlotta managed to cram in a whistlestop shopping trip to Loxley at last minute. Every shop was scoured for the perfect party outfit. Lunch was a noisy two-hour affair which pleased Carlotta, especially as Izzy, egged on by Gemma, allowed her to drink as much Pinot Grigio as she wanted. The three of them giggled their way back to Greater Ousebury on the train. They drank the buffet car dry of miniature bottles of white wine.

Jared, having been summoned by badly-keyed text message to 'puck them up' from the halt at Greater Ousebury, had not been impressed at having found the platform abandoned and the three women, all both drunk and comely, ensconced in The Green Dragon being chatted up by a large percentage of the local football team. Surrounded by eleven randy men all celebrating a well-fought victory, the women — auburn, brunette and caramel — made an extremely attractive trio.

'You three look just like Charlie's Angels,' leered the goalkeeper, looming over Carlotta like a giant until Jared had barged through and oicked them out.

'Whadyer do that for?' Carlotta demanded, trying to wriggle free from his grasp. Izzy and Gemma were thrusting beer mats covered with phone numbers into their handbags.

Jared ushered them all, chuntering, into the Range Rover. They had no sooner passed the last house of the small market town when Izzy let out a curdling scream.

'What the fuck—!' Jared almost drove the vehicle into the village name sign.

'I've left my shopping in the pub,' wailed Izzy. Furious and cursing, Jared one-eightied the car and drove back. Even from the confines of the car, they could all hear the roar of delight as Izzy re-entered the pub. Jared swore again. His fingers drummed against the steering wheel. After what seemed to be an age, Izzy re-emerged, laughing and waving, her lipstick smeared and hair dishevelled.

'They formed a guard of dishonour as I left, each one gave me a kiss,' she laughed as she climbed back into the Range Rover. She had barely slammed the door shut before Jared screeched off.

'Jesus!' screamed all three girls as they were flung backwards into their seats by the g-force.

Back at The Paddocks, Izzy and Carlotta proudly displayed their purchases in the kitchen. Mrs Firth was keen to see what they had bought. Jared wasn't so enthralled. Still feeling the effect, Izzy bobbed into the utility room and changed into a pair of Quality Street-purple harem pants, high and broad waisted by a black cummerbund with baggily cut legs gathered in at the ankle by strips of black silk.

'What do you think?' she cried, pirouetting into the kitchen, causing the fabric to billow out. 'I'm going for the Cheryl Cole look.'

By this time thoroughly pissed off with all three of them, Jared could curb his anger no longer.

'Cheryl Cole?! More like a sack of coal. They look like MC Hammer's cast-offs,' he snapped. Izzy looked distinctly put out and would have retorted if a distraction hadn't been caused by Carlotta, having finally succumbed to the alcohol coursing her veins, throwing up in the Belfast sink.

---

DURING THE WEEK before the bank holiday weather fronts had stacked up like planes waiting to land at Heathrow. Eventually they changed course and flew westwards, away from Yorkshire and, as a result and to universal relief, Taryn's birthday dawned bright and sunny. A slight breeze rustled the tops of the poplars and leylandiis but even that was as hot as its Santa Ana counterpart. At least it had dried out the ground.

'It's like being blown by a bleedin' hairdryer,' Izzy could be heard grumbling as she helped Taryn catch and groom Jester. Because of the sheer volume of work that would have to be done she had been roused from her sleep at six thirty. Now, headcollar hidden behind her back in her right hand and shaking a bucket of oats in her left, she trudged across the far paddock towards Jester, who seemed to be grinning at her as he slinked away.

A flurry of washing and grooming followed until, finally, the ponies were ready. After that Izzy was pressganged into helping Mrs Firth put the finishing touches to the food. There was stacks still to do. The kitchen looked like a supermarket, complete with built in café. The fridge was filled to capacity with bowls and trays of salads. All the boxes, bottles and kegs of drink had been stacked in the utility and were being carried outside to the 'bar' by some of Jared's mates from the village. Borrowed trestles were being assembled in the stable yard. Several bottles had already been cracked and the atmosphere was genial. In the midst of all this Mrs Firth gave a shriek of horror and started to mutter about tablecloths. The ironing board was dragged out.

All the while Izzy was chopping up apple, cucumber and mint, all fresh from the garden, and distributing it into the dozen complimentary plastic jugs which had been sent with the Pimm's order, when Jared wandered into the kitchen looking for more bottle openers.

'More jugs than at a page three girl's hen night,' he said drily, looking down the line. He pinched several pieces of apple as he passed.

'Not helping,' Izzy snapped.

At last all that was left to do was carry the jugs out and add lemonade and ice. Izzy could at last have a shower and make herself up. Not that she fared much better from then on as she was constantly interrupted from her hair and beauty regime by Carlotta or Taryn obsessing about something or other. Taryn couldn't find her tweed jacket whilst Carlotta simply complained about everything and anything. Worse still, guests started to arrive three-quarters of an hour before they should. Hearing Jared bellowing for assistance, she eventually gave up and, with only one eye made up with eyeliner, which gave her a sinister look like Malcolm McDowell in *A Clockwork Orange*, and slippers on instead of shoes, she huffed downstairs and began to help Mrs Firth cart the dozen or so coolboxes of raw meat out to the barbecue. Col the Landlord had brought the industrial-sized gas-fired griddle from the pub and was already happily flipping burgers whilst taking great swigs from a bottle of Black Sheep. Predictably, neither Taryn nor Carlotta were now anywhere to be found. Jared was fully occupied helping to unload ponies left, right and centre and directing them from the driveway to the gymkhana field. They emerged in bays, greys, and chestnuts, each one more sleek and polished than the last. Izzy was pleased they had taken so much time over Jet and Jester. Yard by yard, inch by inch, the lawns were covered in tartan picnic rugs and fold-up chairs as fond parents, aunts, uncles and godparents scrimmaged for the best spot.

Izzy and Mrs Firth were desperately trying to ensure everyone was greeted with a full glass. As they handed out plastic beakers of wine, ale, lager and Pimm's it became evident that, despite most people bringing their own coolboxes of booze, they still wouldn't have enough food or drink, not even by half.

'There's just not enough food. I rang Pippa in panic and she's bringing everything she's got but we can't offer them only bread and desserts.' Mrs Firth was uncharacteristically agitated. 'We'll have to eat and drink the raffle prizes.'

'Shit! The raffle tickets!' Izzy said, turning pale. Where the hell had she put them? Everyone was supposed to be handed one as they arrived.

Just then an attractive, and vaguely familiar man, dragged a large and fully loaded foldable trolley up to them.

'Hello again, Izzy,' he said.

Who the bleedin' hell was this? And how did he know her name?

'I figured you might not be expecting such masses from Ceridwen, so I've brought extra supplies.'

Of course! Marc Jones, Ceridwen's father. The Pacer-mint jacket man from the Great Yorkshire Show. He was wearing an equally bizarre blazer today too. A chintzy affair, it reminded Izzy of Mary Poppins's carpetbag. Despite this he did look a lot better today in a white linen shirt and no trilby, although Izzy didn't think he looked as good as Jared who looked casual and relaxed in black Crocs, khaki coloured combat-style calf length shorts and a plain white tee shirt that showed off his tanned arms.

Marc began to stack cases of wine and several cheese truckles the size of car wheels onto the food table.

'There's red, white and rosé wines plus Cheddar, Stilton, Wensley and a large brie.' He also produced half a dozen boxes of assorted crackers and two large jars of onion chutney.

'That's so kind of you!' Izzy cried, thinking he was so much more attractive than she remembered from the first time she'd met him. 'You're a lifesaver.'

It had also been kind of him to drop hints as to his identity to save her blushes.

'Why don't I assist this charming young lady with these refreshments—' Mrs Firth simpered at Marc's compliment. '—Whilst you finish getting ready? Despite that make-up making you look like a disturbingly sexy pirate we can't be having you subjected to jokes about parrots and doubloons all afternoon.'

Izzy didn't need to be told twice, and fled. She returned ten minutes later, fully mascara-ed and wearing the right shoes to find Jared searching for Carlotta.

'Where is she?' he raged, resorting to ringing her on her mobile. 'You can get all that bloody slap washed off your face,' he said to Carlotta as soon as she materialised. She looked absolutely ravishing in the same hot pink jacket and white breeches she'd worn at the Great Yorkshire Show. Her face was made up like a Girl's World doll. 'I've seen less make-up on an England fan with the St. George's Cross painted on their face.'

'Izzy's wearing more make-up than me,' Carlotta snapped, taking note of Izzy's peacock-blue and sunset-pink eye make-up and pale coral lip gloss.

'Izzy is a grown-up,' said Jared.

Even Izzy raised her eyebrows at this questionable statement.

'What time's Gollum getting here?' Jared continued, referring to Alan.

'Don't *call* him that,' Carlotta replied through gritted teeth. Desperate to change the subject she turned to Izzy and gave her a rare compliment. 'Nice outfit.'

Izzy had abandoned her plans to wear the purple satin pantaloons as Jared had never tired of singing '*Stop! Hammertime!*' each time she mentioned them. Instead she was wearing her best and favourite mid-blue jeans, which were beautifully cut with a kick flare to elongate her short legs, wedged sandals which would allow her to walk on the grass like snow shoes and which showed off her recently pedicured toes, each painted a different colour like jewels of the sea, and a new top which was composed of two diamonds of shimmering sea-green silk held together by three gleaming gold circles and which showed off her tiny sylph-like figure. She wore no bra underneath. Her caramel hair was straightened and her make-up was now flawless.

She was glad she had pulled out all the stops as Gemma too had made a massive effort and was looking femininely gamine in a floral tea dress, cut low to show off her fantastic knockers and tiny waist, and red ballet pumps.

'There are still people arriving in droves, Jared,' Gemma said as she walked up.

Then Izzy jumped as Carlotta gave an angry hiss. Turning, she saw Ceridwen Jones leading her two palominos across the stable yard.

'Who the fuck invited her?'

'This is going to be hell to monitor,' Jared snapped. Then, catching sight of Marc Jones striding towards his daughter, he added: 'that is a shocking blazer.'

The driveway was soon crammed bumper to bumper with horseboxes, Range Rovers and Audis. Even more competitors arrived on horseback, having hacked from nearby farms and villages. Poor Mrs Firth, by this time completely tattered, was valiantly still trying to get everyone a drink whilst at the same time fretting about the bowls and trays of food that still needed bringing out to the buffet table. The landlady from The Half Moon had originally agreed to man, or rather woman, the bar but had cried off at last minute, citing a brewery visit as her excuse. Izzy, desperately trying to keep track of Taryn whilst at the same time handing out raffle tickets to each guest, was only able to sympathise in passing. In the end it was Pippa who proved to be an absolute angel. As soon as she arrived she despatched her absolutely gorgeous husband Drew, who had floppy jet-black hair and wore black nail varnish and eyeliner like a rock star whilst performing, together with the food she had prepared, into Mrs Firth's command before rolling up her sleeves and taking charge of the bar. Instantly freed from her barmaiding duties, Mrs Firth proceeded to tell everyone who would listen how marvellous Pippa was.

Lunch would be served first then everyone would settle

down for the gymkhana events. The booze never stopped flowing, mostly because once all the bottles were opened everyone took it upon themselves to help themselves. Jared and Col the Landlord presided over the barbecue. Everyone agreed that Mrs Firth and her team of grunts had prepared 'a good spread' as they piled their paper plates high. Pop music pounded out of Carlotta's boombox.

'What a wonderful party,' cried the vicar in his Sunday sermon voice, waving a cracker loaded with Stilton in the direction of the show ring where the entrants for the first class were warming up. 'You should make it an annual event.' Upon hearing these words an appalled Jared beat a hasty retreat before he could be roped in to join the parish committee or some other equally heinous prospect. He sought out Izzy, who was holding court at the bar with Pippa. Still pouring drinks for latecomers, they were being fawned over by a flank of dads and uncles who were tripping themselves up to refresh their glasses or bring them another burger.

'I can't imagine you eat at all with that lovely slim figure,' one of them leered. Inexplicably annoyed, Jared felt the need to quell these presumptions by informing them how she'd earlier eaten three burgers and two hotdogs in quick succession 'just to make sure they were okay'. Izzy, who had indeed gobbled down a large and clandestine lunch had only done so as she'd been so busy that morning that she had missed breakfast and had been starving, was furious by this revelation.

At ground level the dogs circled, scouting for manna from above. If it hit the floor, it belonged to the paw. Not that Steptoe restricted himself to this doctrine. He'd been dragged back to the house once already by an embarrassed Jared, having crept up behind an unsuspecting toddler and sucked the hot dog out of its bun before proceeding to eat it in two great gulps whilst both the child and its mother had hysterics.

Gemma appeared just as two husbands were referring to

Izzy as a cracker to Jared. They then referred to Gemma as the same.

'I don't know how you concentrate on your work,' one laughed.

Jared made some reference to wives. Bootfaced, the fathers drifted off.

'I'm not married,' said a voice behind Izzy. 'I'm delighted to report that Ceridwen's mother and I are very happily divorced.' It was Marc Jones. 'Walker.' He managed not to look at Jared as he greeted him. Instead he gave Izzy an approving glance. 'You look even prettier than you did earlier.' He pressed yet another glass of Pimm's No. 1 into Izzy's hand. Or should it more accurately be Pimm's No. 6, Izzy found herself wondering as she accepted it with a smile. It was so flattering to be chatted up. She couldn't remember the last time anyone had shown any genuine interest in her.

'I'm sure you won't object if I steal her away for half an hour, Walker? Poor little mite hasn't stopped since the party began,' Marc said. Unable to object to this proposal without seeming churlish, Jared had no option but to acquiesce.

'That was easier than I expected,' Marc growled huskily into Izzy's ear as he led her away. 'He guards you like a pit bull. I did wonder if he'd already staked his claim on you so I checked with Gemma first. I was thrilled when she confirmed that you were gloriously available.' Izzy was still busy processing Marc's comment about Jared guarding her to fully digest Gemma's involvement.

Marc Jones wasn't bullshitting. Not only had he found Izzy's slim figure and natural, open face very attractive from the moment he'd first seen her at the Great Yorkshire Show, he had been further impressed by her obvious skill with the kids. It was so important that any new woman in his life was suitably equipped to deal with his wilful daughter. If she could cope with that harpy Carlotta she would be more than well qualified to contend with Ceri.

He led her over to a prime spot by the makeshift show ring where a fold-up chair was awaiting.

'Hi Izzy!' Ceridwen greeted her with a pretty smile which made Izzy slightly on edge. If Carlotta saw her fraternising with the enemy she would be ostracised for life. She was still brooding on this when Marc whipped away her plastic beaker of now flat Pimm's and replaced it with a champagne flute of Moët.

'I thought you might like to actually watch your young charge from the ringside rather than from behind the scenes.'

The afternoon events kicked off with the tack and turn out. Into the ring filed all the little darlings. Izzy was most amused to see that any pony that was grey or had any grey points or markings had been dyed pale blue in honour of Taryn's win at Harrogate. They all looked so beautiful, thought Izzy, taking a slug of champagne, as she watched them go round and round. In the centre of the ring stood the vicar's wife and Carlotta, looking stunning and professional in jodhpurs and white shirt having temporarily discarded her red jacket.

No one was more pristine than Taryn on Jester, tack cleaned to perfection and mane beautifully plaited. Jester, now reverted to brilliant white and brown, caused all the copycats to gaze in dismay at their own out of fashion blue ponies. Jared, watching both Taryn and Izzy from the other side of the ring, thought it was a good job the vicar's wife had been instructed to not award Taryn a prize as she was easily the most dazzling. However, it had all been moot as the vicar's wife's vapid head had been turned by a pastel blue pony whose plaited mane, tail, bridle and stirrup leathers had all been threaded with a violent clash of summer blooms. The whole effect was hideously and ostentatiously topped off by a buttonhole the size of a Savoy cabbage which she promptly presented to the judge. The vicar's wife was duly charmed and wanted to award first prize to the little darling. Carlotta, however, was not so easily swayed. A closer inspection showed that the wealth of flowers distracted the eye from unpolished hooves, a grubby numnah and a grass-stained bit.

'You can't give her first place. Her tack's filthy and anyway, it's not a fancy dress competition,' Carlotta said. She'd plumped for a pretty little rider in a tweed jacket, cream breeches and jodhpur boots on an immaculately turned out perky bay mare with a white (not blue) blaze.

'She's not in fancy dress. It's just some flowers. I think she looks charming.'

'She looks like the fucking Royal Gardens at Kew,' Carlotta stormed to the edification of the onlookers. 'You've only been seduced because the pony's coat is the same colour as your blue rinse.' Izzy was drunk enough to find this funny. Over on the opposite side of the ring, Jared put his head in his hands, partly to hide his shame and partly to hide his shaking shoulders from laughing. No matter how inappropriate Carlotta's comments had been they hadn't been without truth.

The showing class was next. Ceridwen shot off to retrieve one of her ponies from the groom she'd forced to work for the day. Marc, who'd had to pay the poor girl double time as it was a bank holiday, wasn't overly thrilled about this. Carlotta, looking sulky but perfect, on Jet followed Ceridwen into the ring. The vicar's wife, married to a representative of God, put aside her Christian beliefs and refused to either forget or forgive Carlotta's earlier comments and promptly put her on the back row. To add injury to insult, she then awarded Ceridwen the red rosette. Livid, Carlotta exited the ring before the class had finished, not caring that it was terribly bad form.

'Oh!' said Izzy, dismayed. Marc merely filled up her glass.

'Let her stew,' he said. 'Teenage girls, honestly.'

During the interval the raffle was drawn. The ever-accommodating Drew Newton agreed to be master of ceremonies for the occasion and happily plucked several winning tickets out of the hat. Winners crowded round the table to see which prize their ticket correlated to. The booty was amazing. One tattered-looking mother won a well-deserved access all areas day pass to the beauty spa in a local hotel. Another parent won a three course meal plus wine at The Half Moon. There were also boxes of chocolates, bouquets of flowers and bottles of plonk to be won.

A great cheer went up when Izzy's ticket was the last to be drawn. Ever the showman, Drew made a big song and dance before handing her the last remaining prize, explaining how hard Izzy, and the other members of the household, had worked to put on such a wonderful event. A little round of applause followed and Marc could even be heard shouting 'bravo!' from the sidelines. Even Jared was smiling at her. For a few moments Izzy basked in her moment of triumph. This had never happened to her before. Then she looked down at the prize Drew had plonked into her hands. It was a plate of raw meat: steaks, a great round sausage like a Catherine wheel, bacon and even what looked like a slab of liver.

'What the hell is this?' she heard herself ask before she could stop herself. The applause turned to gentle laughter. 'Seriously, are you having a giraffe? It's just… meat.' Someone in the crowd guffawed. Izzy was genuinely bemused. She looked balefully at the woman next to her who had won a bottle of Piper Heidsieck. And what had she won? A plate of innards. And now everyone was laughing at her. Izzy's moment was over. Default settings had been restored. It just wasn't fair. Jared appeared at her side. He too seemed to be highly amused at her reaction.

'It's called a navvy's breakfast,' he explained loudly. The onlookers tittered. Izzy looked at him with suspicion. 'It's a good prize,' he assured her. He looked thrilled with her win and proudly bore it off to the now empty fridge in the kitchen.

The minimus showjumping followed. As Taryn was competing, Izzy could quite legitimately keep an eye on her from the side of the manége. Marc Jones never left her side and continually kept her glass filled to the brim. They hung over the manége fence as all the entrants did a parade circuit for the benefit of all the doting parents. Then the fun began.

Izzy had only had experience of the shows Carlotta entered, those being serious competitions with all the riders having serious aspirations of a career in equestrianism. Here, today, all and sundry had entered their ponies. Some were marvellous riders on well-groomed ponies; identikit children with outstanding talent and hideous attitudes.

'They're worse than Hitler's super race,' Marc hooted.

Others weren't so polished. One young lad from the less salubrious area of the village, wearing jeans and trainers, had borrowed a cobby bay (ungroomed) with a brutish face from somewhere. Alas, he couldn't ride for toffee and tried to whip the poor pony round the course, looking both surprised and put out when it wouldn't jump. Everyone watching cringed until the huntmaster felt compelled to eliminate him on the grounds of cruelty, which nearly started a punch up between him and the boy's father. Unfortunately, this was one of Jared's chucker-outers and Jared was called upon to side with his pal. Stuck in the middle, Jared tried to mediate... and failed. The end result was that the angry father dragged his son and the unaccommodating pony off and wasn't seen again. The audience was agog throughout the episode.

Another young rider couldn't make her pony jump the first fence at all and proceeded to drop her reins and sob uncontrollably until her father retrieved her. After this the standard improved, culminating in Taryn showing everyone how it should be done with a lovely, bouncy clear round. Jester looked so happy with his tail swishing and his little two-tone ears pricked that Izzy felt herself choke up. As she exited the ring Taryn gave the crowd a merry little wave before smothering Jester with pats and kisses. Everyone watching responded by giving her a round of applause interjected with a few 'happy birthdays!'.

The only person not enchanted with Taryn's charming display was Carlotta. She'd had no intention of entering the jumping class, believing it to be both childish and beneath her. However, as a result of everyone cooing over her sister, and being humiliated both in her capacity as a judge and a competitor, she felt she had a point to prove. Not caring that her name wasn't on the handwritten entry sheet, she mounted a hastily tacked up Jet and barged into the ring. She then proceeded to jump the tiny course of fences at collected canter. Her disdain was evident. In order to make it look less bad, Gemma bundled Ceridwen onto one of her palominos and told her to do the same. Hoping to trounce Carlotta, Ceridwen was happy to be accommodating. She also went clear.

'It's not fair,' one grown-up could be heard complaining. 'Those two girls compete on the national circuit. I thought this was supposed to be a friendly little gymkhana.'

Overhearing this, Izzy exchanged glances and a few brief words with Marc before shooting off to the huntmaster to ask if there could be a two-tiered jump off, with one for the smaller ones and a second, bigger course for Carlotta and Ceridwen. The huntmaster thought this was a splendid idea, as did the watching parents who were appeased by such a fair decision. The prize for the winner of the second jump off, the huntmaster improvised, would be a private riding lesson with him at the hunt stables. Knowing this was a prize well worth winning, Carlotta and Ceridwen eyeballed each other like championship boxers.

An über-brat from Taryn's school on a blood pony that clearly cost an absolute fortune won the first jump off and was presented with the splendid boxed grooming kit that Carlotta and Izzy had so merrily selected for the winner.

Taryn, on Jared's recommendation, had been advised to bow out of the jump off in a last ditch attempt to show that at least one of the two sisters had decent manners. It also gave her the opportunity to shove Jester in his stable and quickly change into her party dress in time for her cake to be cut.

The audience clapped lethargically as the rosettes were awarded for the first jump off. What they really wanted to see was what Carlotta would do next. Jared and Gemma raised all the fences to four foot whilst Carlotta and Ceridwen exchanged insults in the collecting ring. Izzy daren't look at Marc. Of course, she wanted Carlotta to win, but on the other hand she didn't want to appear to encourage her frightful behaviour. Marc, to her surprise and also considerable relief, didn't appear to give a shit.

'If she wins, all well and good, although it's not as though it's an important qualifier. If she doesn't win she needs to look at what she did wrong and suck it up,' he said. He gave a jolly laugh. 'Either way, one of us is in for a tough time tonight. I suppose I should be chivalrous and cheer on Carlotta just so you're spared the fallout. Shame on either count, as I can think of a far better way to spend this evening than listening to the bitter rantings of a pissed off teenager.' His meaning couldn't have been clearer. Izzy could feel her cheeks start to colour up. She didn't know what to say.

Thankfully, Carlotta chose that moment to cannonball into the ring. Clearly meaning business, she rode like a lunatic with little consideration for form, safety or technique. Usually such an organic, gentle rider, she abandoned everything she believed in and fair yanked Jet round the course. Her hands were almost touching his bit as she hauled him round the turns at forty-five degrees. She didn't care if she had to dismount and chuck Jet over the fences. Her one remit was to win.

And win she did. The time she set was scorching. Not even the supersonic Jonah could match it. Thrilled to have won, Carlotta's smile returned. Alas, it wasn't destined to stay for long. Jared, by this time at the end of his lead rope, had taken one look at the exhausted, bewildered Jet and vociferously forbade the huntmaster to credit Carlotta with the win. It was with sadness, but also an element of understanding, that the huntmaster accepted that Carlotta's excellent horsemanship over the course of the day couldn't be awarded a prize and not even him telling her thus made up for her not being announced the winner. Instead Carlotta had to watch Ceridwen shaking hands with the huntmaster. No doubt she would be goaded about it each and every day when term started. Her eyes narrowed further when she saw Izzy coffee-housing (or rather champagne-housing) with Ceridwen's cretinous father. It must have been Izzy who had invited the Joneses. Well, she'd suffer for that later.

Concerned at what she'd just witnessed, Izzy was in fact winding her way through the throng to get to Carlotta. She found both her and Jared in the now deserted stable yard. Jared was in full rant.

'I forbid you to ride this pony in the Chase-Me-Charlie,' He was saying as he ran his hands down Jet's forelegs. They were red hot. 'You'll be lucky if I don't have to call the vet out to see him. What the hell possessed you to ride him in such a careless, selfish manner? You could have lamed him for life, hurtling round corners like that. I don't need to tell you how disappointed I am with you right now.'

Carlotta stared at him with a poker face, feeling resentful of the constant attention Taryn was getting, not to mention the mound of gaily wrapped presents accumulating on a groaning, bow-legged trestle table. She, Carlotta, wouldn't get the benefit of either a lorry load of gifts or endless limelight and yet had still been banished from winning any prizes by virtue of her, quite frankly, superior equestrian skills.

'Go and hose his legs down,' Jared ordered. He gave her a piercing look. 'I know you don't care much for any human being, but I never once imagined you'd treat your beloved pony so cruelly.'

'Jared—' Izzy protested faintly. Now who was being cruel? She couldn't bring herself to look at Carlotta, who looked shattered by his words. Silent and pale faced, Carlotta took hold of Jet's bridle and led him into the stable yard.

'And you can shut up.' Jared turned on Izzy. 'Perhaps you should spend a bit more time doing your job rather than guzzling champagne and flirting with other people's husbands.'

Indignant and offended, Izzy turned on her heel and stormed back to where Marc was waiting for her with yet another opened bottle. He was filled with unrepentant excitement at all the family drama.

'Makes such a nice change for it not to be my family making an exhibition of themselves,' he said, absolutely without guile. Izzy couldn't help but smile. She then found herself wondering if he knew why his son wouldn't play with his Nintendo Wii, and blushed. At that same moment Ceridwen, once more mounted on Jonah, entered the manége for the Chase-Me-Charlie and Izzy's blush deepened. There were some things one never needed to mentally visualise, she considered silently.

The Chase-Me-Charlie was the final competition of the afternoon. Here all the riders would follow each other round in a large circle, jumping one solitary fence in turn. Once everyone had jumped the fence it would be raised, and round everyone would go again. If any rider refused or knocked the fence down he or she would be disqualified from the next and all consequent rounds.

Carlotta, still stinging from Jared's castigation, had sobbed for a few minutes into Jet's plaited mane whilst she ran cold water down his legs before her resentment flared up once more. Bloody Ceridwen Jones! Bloody Jared! And bloody Izzy too, come to think of it. In fact, bloody well the whole bastard lot of 'em. She'd show 'em. All of 'em!

A seed of an idea began to sprout. Jared hadn't forbidden *her* to ride in the Chase-Me-Charlie, he'd only forbidden her to ride Jet. He hadn't said anything about her riding any of the other horses. Giving Jet a last apologetic pat, Carlotta latched his stall and considered her options. Ghost, The Tank, Vega and even Mini Cheddar had all been kept in for the afternoon to prevent them from causing havoc in the paddocks. But who should she choose?

Rather like the Highlander, there could be only one.

Not only was Vega the best jumper and the most dazzling and impressive equine resident at The Paddocks, nothing would anger Jared more than if Carlotta rode her that afternoon. Carlotta had her tacked up within minutes.

Jared gave a hiss of disapproval as he saw Carlotta riding an already thoroughly overwrought Vega through the crowd, scattering kiddies and dogs in their wake. Barging her way into the chain of remaining riders she then proceeded to annihilate the opposition by circling round and round the jump, consistently placing Vega perfectly at the ever heightening fence. Each time the angry mare cleared it by feet to gasps of awe from the crowd. Jared, however, was not prepared to be impressed, especially as Vega, by now bored by such a piddling little fence, lashed out with her off hind at the pony behind her. Dodging between cantering ponies Jared approached the by now beleaguered huntmaster and whispered something in his ear. Within seconds Carlotta had been called in and was duly instructed to leave the ring in the interest of the other riders' safety. A blazing row between the three of them took place until Jared seized hold of Vega's bit and all but dragged her out of the ring, hooves still flying in all directions. The audience, having watched all this take place in fascination, turned to each other to pass comment.

'You have to admit, they've put on a good show,' one spectator was heard saying.

'Aye, and not just in the ring—' added another.

This was followed by a laugh of nervous relief as Carlotta was lead out of sight. Hearing it, Carlotta leapt off Vega and ran round the side of the house, leaving Jared to untack and settle the frenzied mare. Carlotta's only consolation was that Ceridwen Jones had finally been beaten by another rider.

In the wake of all the excitement, Drew Newton's half-hour turn, where he trialled a couple of new magic tricks he was working on for his new show and hypnotised a couple of sober parents... ('Probably the only two sober ones remaining,' he hissed in his pretty wife's ear.) ...was something of an anticlimax. After that Mrs Firth produced Taryn's pony cake, complete with nine lit candles, and everyone sang happy birthday to Taryn and gave three cheers. By now completely exhausted and wound up, Taryn promptly burst into tears of over-excitement once she had cut her cake. Mrs Firth, Taryn on one arm, the cake in the other, traipsed back to the house where she would slice the cake into as many pieces as it would conceivably go. Not that it would be enough, she thought grimly.

If Jared had presumed that the party would disband once the birthday festivities were over, he was sadly mistaken. Instead he discovered that Marc had convinced a three parts cut Izzy and a thoroughly smug Ceridwen to drag Taryn's karaoke machine downstairs. First up was Marc himself, who sang with his local Tuesday Singers and was a decent tenor, who crooned his way through *I Get A Kick Out Of You.*

Making an exhibition of himself, Jared thought sourly as he looked on. Worse still, Marc seemed to be singing it to Izzy, who was clapping and laughing as she watched him, her eyes dancing. After that, everyone made a mad scramble for the microphone. From then on it was carnage. Parent after parent seemed hellbent on shaming their offspring by butchering whichever song they had chosen.

'They could have at least chosen something cool,' one absolutely mortified young girl could be heard complaining as her parents embarked on a cringeworthy duet of *Dead Ringer For Love*, complete with x-rated gyrating. After that all the kids prayed their parents would choose something cool by Nelly Furtado or the Black Eyed Peas. One girl got her wish and lived to regret it as she was forced to watch and listen in undiluted horror as her father attempted to rap his way through an Eminem song, complete with profanities and hand gestures. Finally, one extremely pissed dad ambushed the CD player then seized the microphone.

'One…step…beeeeyoooooooond!' he roared before whipping off his tee shirt to reveal a flabby, hairy white belly, and attempting to stage dive onto the surrounding parents. All the fathers then proceeded to do the turkey dance as the Madness track played out. One fourteen-year-old girl hid her head in her hands to try and blot out the image.

More booze was drunk. Piles of empties rose.

'Your bin men aren't going to be thrilled,' one father pointed out to no one in particular.

Jared, having finally adopted an 'if you can't beat 'em, join 'em' approach to the afternoon was the biggest surprise of all as he got up to do an energetic if not very tuneful rendition of Kenny Loggins's *Danger Zone* from *Top Gun*.

---

CARLOTTA, still seething at being disqualified from the Chase-Me-Charlie, raged round the kitchen like a tornado. Alan, unused to seeing her in such a glorious rage, watched her in lust-fuelled awe. He had never attracted anyone as stunningly beautiful as her. She was magnificent. Suddenly a sinister calm came over Carlotta. Reaching for a pad and paper she started to write, a rictus grin on her face.

'This'll give 'em a jolt,' she said, folding up the piece of paper. 'Come on, you!' she said to Alan, giving him a hot look. Grabbing the last unopened bottle of Clicquot from the fridge, she dragged Alan outside. Scanning the scattering of kids around, Carlotta honed in on the youngest, most bullyable munchkin she could see.

'You! Come here!' she commanded. Terrified, the kid scuttled over. 'I have a mission for you. Are you up to it?' As short, plump and round as a Thelwell kid, she gazed in awe at Carlotta, nodding. 'Take this to one of the grown-ups who live here. Do you understand? It's very important and I'm putting a lot of trust in you. Now scoot!'

## REAL GONE KID

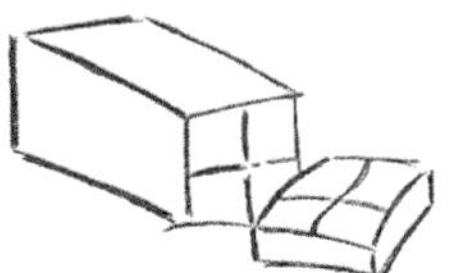

Izzy was just winding up a rousing rendition of Deacon Blue's *Real Gone Kid*, her signature karaoke song, to a chorus of *'woahoo woahoo woahoo woahoos'* from the drunken fathers, when Mrs Firth ran across the lawn. She was brandishing a cake knife in one hand and a sheet of paper in the other, like a homicidal Neville Chamberlain. Wobbling and gasping for breath, her capacious floral bosom heaving as she ran, she made a beeline for Jared.

'She's gone. Carlotta's run away,' she panted. Jared snatched the note out of her hand. His eyes raked over the scrawled message. It was short and to the point. Carlotta had had enough with being picked on and was going somewhere where she would be appreciated a bit more. It gave no clues as to where this somewhere was. Even more worrying were the last five words she had scrawled in bold capitals.

*I MEAN IT THIS TIME!!!*

'Where was it?' Jared asked.

'I'd just gone back to the kitchen to cut the cake and a little girl handed me this. She said Carlotta told her to deliver it to one of us.'

The music had stopped as soon as Mrs Firth's entrance had parted the crowd like Moses by the Red Sea. Above their heads, Izzy stood on the little stage, microphone hanging loosely from her hand, listening, aghast. Jared's eyes searched for hers above the throng. Without a word needing to be spoken, Izzy jumped down from the stage and ran over to him. She felt instantly sober as she read the note.

'We must find her,' Jared said. Izzy nodded. Jared's worried expression mirrored her own panicked one.

'Another one of her hoaxes?' Izzy had to ask.

'Can't be certain,' Jared had to admit.

Marc had followed Izzy across the lawn, having picked up the gist of what had happened.

'Is there anything I can do to help?' he asked. Jared gave him a look of scorn but Izzy shot him a grateful look.

'Could you just have a look round for Carlotta?' she asked, almost casually.

Jared, Izzy, Gemma, Taryn and Mrs Firth convened in the kitchen. Jared dithered over whether to inform the police or not. Eventually he decided that a quick call to the village bobby would at least cover his back.

'If she doesn't turn up in the next hour he's going to send a car down. In the meantime he's going to put a call out. He knows her well enough to not need a description,' he said, pressing the red button on the receiver. 'He said it's always better to be safe than sorry.'

Bit late for that, was everyone's first thought, although no one could bring themselves to voice it. For a few moments everyone did nothing more than stare at each other, uncertain as to what action to take next.

Marc entered the kitchen.

'No sign, I'm afraid. No one's seen her plus folk are

starting to leave,' he said. His words seemed to galvanise Jared.

'That's probably a good thing. Once everyone's gone we'll be able to tell if she's gone on foot, on horseback or by car,' he said, pacing and thinking as he spoke. 'Gemma, can you check the stables? Make sure all the horses are here. Izzy, you do a full sweep of the house. Mrs Firth, could you please stay with Taryn and make sure she doesn't get too excited?' Then Jared addressed Taryn directly. 'Don't worry about your sister. She'll be back before you know it.' Taryn, already tearful, bit her bottom lip as her face creased. 'Taryn, you know you can trust me to find her,' Jared said. Taryn nodded. Jared turned to Marc. 'If you could give me a hand checking the grounds—'

Marc nodded. 'Of course.'

Every square inch of The Paddocks was scoured. There was no sign of Carlotta. To keep herself occupied Ceridwen had loaded her own ponies into their horsebox before helping Gemma attend to the horses in the stable yard. She wasn't particularly worried about Carlotta who, she knew better than most from personal experience, was more than capable of taking care of herself. Plus, if she was seen to be helpful it would earn her Brownie points with her father, who she was desperate to live with full time rather than her overbearing, criticising mother. Drew and Pippa stayed behind to help simply because they were lovely, genuine people. They stacked all the empties in the stable yard and tidied round a bit before leaving.

'Do let us know when she turns up,' Pippa said, giving Izzy a quick hug. 'And don't hesitate to ring us, no matter how late, if you need any help with anything.' She wanted to add that she was quite prepared to search the countryside with a torch, if asked, but didn't like to mention it out loud in case it seemed a bit morbid, or insinuated that they might be looking for a body rather than a person.

Almost an hour later, and by which time all the guests had been dispersed, gently ushered out by Jared's makeshift bouncers, and the last horsebox had trundled out of the gates, Jared was reluctantly starting to accept that Carlotta had indeed done a runner and he would have to get the police involved in earnest. Despite all the attempts to remain anonymous, Carlotta was still a high profile target.

Across the fields the sun was sinking behind a row of poplars. It must be about eight o' clock, Jared estimated. He dragged himself back up the driveway towards the house in utter despair. He didn't even want to contemplate how he was supposed to explain this, or indeed himself, to MK. Some fucking protector he was, he berated himself. The finger of blame could only be directed back at himself. He should never have agreed to hosting such a ridiculously oversized circus. It had been far too big for one man to police. He'd been far too harsh with Carlotta too. And he had let himself be distracted by Izzy flirting with that walking teddy bear, Jones, although he couldn't even bring himself to despise him any more after he'd been so helpful in trying to find Carlotta. No doubt he understood what it was like to have to take guardianship of a stroppy, hormonal fifteen-year-old girl. God, what a mess!

But then…

'We've found her! It's all right, she's okay!'

Jared ran towards the voice. Never in all his life, or his military career, had he been so relieved. Gemma had finally tracked down Carlotta, and Alan, in the hayloft. Izzy, Marc and Ceridwen watched in silence as Jared climbed the ladder and disappeared through the trapdoor.

All trace of self-blame vanished as Jared took in the sight before him. No one was responsible for Carlotta's selfish actions but herself. Pissed as a rat, she'd shed her riding boots, pink jacket and had yanked her shirt outside her jodhpurs to allow Alan easy access, and was wrapped round him like a soft tortilla on a bed of straw. Both had lit cigarettes in their hands. A plastic cup, melted to a pungent brown mass around the rim, contained a dozen more burnt out cig ends. Taking in her unkempt hair, glazed eyes and the fecklessly discarded empty champagne bottle, Jared hit the hayloft roof. Everyone on the ground floor jumped, such was the force and volume of his roar of fury.

Carlotta was hoisted, wriggling like an eel, through the trapdoor into the safety of Marc's strong arms before being handed over into Izzy's custody. Alan, looking suitably terrified, was pushed through after her. Then came Jared, after hurling down Carlotta's discarded clothes and the makeshift ashtray. The empty bottle he carried. He would have dearly liked to have flung it at the wall, shattering it into smithereens in an attempt to purge his rage, but knew he had to think of all the animals' welfare. Paws and hooves had to be considered.

Izzy had never seen Jared so angry. Alan pinned himself to the barn wall, arms akimbo, like the man stuck to the board on the Solvite advert.

'Get him out of here,' Jared snapped at Gemma, who obeyed without question.

'I'll make sure he gets home. See you tomorrow,' she said.

Carlotta fought her way out of Izzy's grasp only to come face to face with Ceridwen. This only served to incense her further. A stream of expletives poured out of her mouth until Jared barked at her to pack it in.

'Everyone has been looking for you. The police have been notified. It's ruined Taryn's party,' he yelled.

'So!' Carlotta slurred.

'So? *So?* You could have burnt the fucking barn down, you stupid, selfish bitch! That's what's so! Even if you don't give a toss about us or your sister, I'm surprised you'd risk the lives of your beloved ponies. Jet could have been burnt to a cinder.'

Drunk and emotional, Carlotta burst into tears. 'Oh for fuck's sake!'

A long, embarrassed silence was ended by Marc.

'Right, Ceri, let's make a move,' he said, trying to inject an element of normality into his voice. 'Give me a call if you need any extra help.' He held out his hand to Jared, who for once didn't hesitate to shake it.

'Thanks, mate. Appreciated.'

Izzy walked Marc and Ceridwen to their horsebox whilst Jared led a still weeping Carlotta towards the house.

'Quite a day, Miss Brown,' Marc said.

'You don't say,' Izzy replied with feeling. She felt absolutely knackered. Ceridwen climbed into the passenger seat and closed the door behind her. Shadows were starting to creep across the slate driveway but despite the half-light the evening air was still warm. Izzy had a feeling she knew what was coming.

'Listen, I was wondering if you might like to join me for dinner one night this week?' Marc asked, casually.

Yep, she'd been right on the money. And weirdly, she felt really pleased about it.

'I'd like that,' she answered.

'What about Thursday? That'd give you a couple of days to recover from all the excitement.'

'Sounds like a plan,' Izzy smiled.

'Great! I'll pick you up at seven thirty. See you then,' and before Izzy knew it Marc had leaned down and kissed her, firmly yet gently, square on the mouth. Taken aback, Izzy didn't respond immediately, and yet as soon as she did, Marc pulled away. It was the first time she had been kissed in months. Since Scott. It had been a nice kiss. Marc grinned at her before springing into the cab of the horsebox. Izzy watched it trundle down the driveway, setting off the underground sensors, and out of the automatically opening and closing gates, before she returned to the house. She wondered what she would walk in to. Had Jared calmed down any? Would Carlotta be distraught? Rabid? Both? Was Taryn still traumatised? Who was angry with who? It also occurred to Izzy that, with Carlotta pissed and resentful, Jared livid, Mrs Firth cream crackered and Taryn overwrought, she, Izzy, was likely to be the only member of the household anywhere close to being happy.

Inside it was calmer than she had expected. Jared had already deposited Carlotta on her bed with strict instructions to drink the large mug of black coffee he'd plonked on her bedside cabinet.

Downstairs in the kitchen Taryn, no longer tearful but furious that not only had her day been truncated by Carlotta's selfish actions but also that her party had been completely overshadowed by all the drama, was being distracted by Mrs Firth. An obscenely large pile of gifts had been stacked on the kitchen table.

'Let's get these up to your room, eh? Then, after you've had a bath, you can open them all in bed whilst eating your supper.'

Later Izzy, Jared and Mrs Firth had fun helping Taryn open her gifts and cards. Mrs Firth wrote a list of who had given what to enable thank you letters to be sent. Carlotta, slowly sobering up, refused to attend, instead choosing to sulk in her bedroom.

The booty was astonishing, ranging from quite frugal offerings like new riding crops and gloves, HMV, Lush and New Look vouchers, to Royal Doulton figurines of ponies and horsey themed sterling silver jewellery shaped like horseshoes, snaffle bits and stirrups. Some cards simply contained that most marvellous gift of all — fivers and tenners.

MK had instructed Jared to buy gifts on his behalf and had chosen a memory foam saddle cover together with a matching brand new rug for Jester with Taryn Konstantine printed on it.

'Just a pity she can't use it until all this business with MK has been resolved,' said Jared to Izzy in an undertone as Mrs Firth tucked in Taryn. Izzy noticed that he looked absolutely done in.

Taryn lay in bed, sleepy, her mountain of presents happily within sight.

'It was a good party, wasn't it?' she asked.

'The best,' said Izzy, giving Taryn a quick kiss on the top of her head. 'And Jester was much the best pony and would definitely have won the top prize if the rules had been different. Sleep tight.'

Downstairs in the kitchen, Jared poured himself, Izzy and Mrs Firth a large glass of Scotch. Izzy accepted it, despite not wanting any more alcohol, as it seemed singularly appropriate to have a stiff drink after everything that had happened.

Jared nodded at Izzy.

'You did well today,' he said. Izzy realised with a jolt that she hadn't done anything stupid all day.

---

Izzy woke the next morning feeling as rough as ten tigers.

'How much did I *drink* yesterday—?'

Groaning, she dragged her carcass downstairs to find another vase of flowers, this one twice the size of the one she had received after the Great Yorkshire Show, sitting on the kitchen table.

*Until Thursday...*

...was all the card read. It helped Izzy to forget all about her hangover.

'Bloke must have more money than sense,' Jared grumbled, taking in Izzy's dreamy smile. 'You'll soon have enough vases to open your own John Lewis's.' He snatched the card out of her hand. He handed it back with a look of disdain. 'Don't tell me you actually agreed to go out with that soft shite?'

Izzy ignored him and instead concentrated on texting Marc straight away to say thanks. Halfway through typing she paused. Should she put kisses or not? A quick scan of her present company made it apparent that there was no one's advice she could ask. Mrs Firth? Jared? Carlotta? *Hardly!* Eventually she plumped for one 'x' and pressed send.

Carlotta, also feeling fragile, glowered at Izzy from across the table. Taryn hadn't materialised yet. Mrs Firth was cooking the Cumberland sausage, black pudding and gammon steaks from Izzy's navvy's breakfast. Izzy helped herself to a mug of coffee from the percolator. Carlotta continued to stare at Izzy. She didn't move her head, as that required effort plus it hurt too much, only her eyes, sliding them from side to side to mirror Izzy's movements. After five minutes of this silent observation Izzy found herself unable to keep quiet any longer.

'Wot?'

'You invited that Jones bitch,' Carlotta said accusingly.

'I bleedin' well didn't,' Izzy said. 'I was as surprised as everyone else when they turned up.'

'Well, who did then?' Jared asked. He suddenly looked more cheerful.

Everyone exchanged blank looks. At that moment Taryn drifted into the kitchen. Her hair was sticking out at right angles and her face had a long red crease down the left cheek where her sheet had tattooed her. Her eyes were like pin pricks. Despite all this she looked calm and happy.

'Did you invite Ceridwen Jones?' Carlotta said before anyone else had the chance to say good morning.

'No,' Taryn said huffily. 'Why would I do that? You hate her.' Turning she smiled up at Mrs Firth, batting her eyelashes like a coquette. 'Darling Firthie, can I have eggs and soldiers instead of that nasty meat?'

'Course you can, pet,' said Mrs Firth.

'I'm not eating it either then. And get that horrific pigs' blood away from me,' Carlotta snapped, referring to the disc of black pudding Mrs Firth was trying to force on her. She pushed her plate towards the middle of the table.

'Gerrit down yer. It'll do you good,' Jared said. He made no attempt to hide his lack of sympathy.

'Good? It's practically vampiric,' Carlotta growled into her coffee mug.

Taryn dragged one of the newspapers towards her having noticed an article about children's ponies and knackered racehorses being killed for horsemeat and sent to France. This disturbed her.

'If Papa ever sells Mini Cheddar or Jester I shall file for emarzipanation.'

'Why would he do that?' Jared asked, wondering what TV Taryn had been watching now to learn about such things.

'What if he has his arse frozen and runs out of money? He'll have to sell stuff. He can't work if he's in prison.'

'That isn't going to happen,' Izzy said automatically.

Carlotta was contemptuous.

'What do you know about anything?' she spat before turning to Taryn. 'Don't you mean if he has his *assets* frozen? Anyway, I wouldn't worry yourself, shrimp. Papa's assets are divided between his personal and business ventures, so even if Konstantine Shipping did go under we'd hardly be destitute.' Jared shot Carlotta a sharp look. Since when had she become an expert on her father's finances? It had always been his belief that so long as the Bank of Papa remained open for business Carlotta didn't care where the money came from. 'Anyway, even if he does come home he'll still have to work in London all week. Eventually he'll get a new girlfriend and we'll be forgotten, stuck here with Jared and Firthie and Nanny McPheeble like the lost boys.'

'That's enough, Carlotta,' said Jared, still annoyed with her over her disappearing act of the day before.

Once breakfast had been cleared away, with most of the meat eventually being enjoyed by a row of slavering dogs, the Big Clean Up began. The mess was colossal. A mass of equipment including the gas barbecue from The Half Moon and at least a half dozen trestle tables had to be returned to their rightful owners. The Newtons came to collect their kitchen gear. The rightful owners of several items of lost property had to be tracked down. Jared stood and looked balefully at the state of the grass in the paddocks which was now peppered with thousands of hoofmarks and interspersed with enough spent cig ends to fill the tack room bucket. Then the barn and stable yard had to be swept from end to end and the manége returned to a usable state. Izzy even found a used condom in one of the bushes lining the driveway and just hoped and prayed that it had nothing to do with Carlotta — or Jared. She finally fell into bed exhausted for the second night running, thankful she hadn't agreed to meet Marc until Thursday.

Izzy spent a great deal of time preparing herself for her date with Marc, including positioning Taryn in the hallway like a sentry to ensure that Jared couldn't interfere. His piss-taking had been unbearable since Izzy had told him she was being taken out to dinner.

Marc rolled up promptly at seven thirty in a mint-green Z4 with the top down. After ringing the doorbell like a prom date, he presented Izzy with a box of white chocolate truffles (—'you are not to feed these to the dogs whilst I am out, Taryn'—) and admired her MC Hammer trousers, which she had worn in defiance of Jared. He then made a big song and dance of closing the convertible's roof so as not to reduce

Izzy's carefully styled hair to a haystack before whisking her away to the soundtrack of Michael Bublé.

'Flashy bastard,' said Jared, who had been surreptitiously spying on events from within the downstairs bog. 'Give us those sweets, Tar. I fancy summat sweet for my pudding.' Giggling, Taryn handed them over. If she played her cards right she could blackmail Jared into letting her have some. And they did look *delicious*!

Marc had booked a table for two in an exclusive little bistro called Warwick's in a nearby market town. It was charming inside and out, with yellow roses trailed round the rustic porch and a basketful of chopped logs in the vestibule entrance. The waitress led them to the one remaining empty table which was adjacent to the open fireplace. As the weather was still so warm the grate had been filled with twinkling white lights. Light, acid jazz was being piped into the room, but only quietly so as not to impinge on anyone's conversation. When the waitress brought the menus over Marc ordered a bottle of Taittinger for Izzy and a bottle of Perrier for himself.

'Couldn't possibly risk even one glass of plonk whilst I have such a precious cargo in my car,' he said with a quick grin as he poured her first drink. Izzy saw this for the cheesy line it was, and didn't care. It was so nice to be wooed.

'Cheers!' They clinked glasses.

Once they had chosen their courses the waitress returned with a basket of bread rolls and a little white dish which contained curled butter, to tide them over until their starters arrived. It hadn't escaped Izzy's notice that Marc hadn't ordered anything heavily flavoured with garlic. Clearly she was on course for a goodnight snog at home-time. Or did he think she would be going home with him? No, surely not. He'd only met her twice. On the other hand…

To curb her rampant thoughts Izzy gazed round at her surroundings. The eponymous Warwick was an antique glass collector and had filled his bistro with beautiful, unusual objects from around the globe, including fiery amberina scent bottles and Venetian glass that was as carefully blown and fragile as a Hubba Bubba bubble.

One side of the room had been sectioned off and had clearly been reserved for an evening wedding reception. Tables had been covered with pristine white cloths and pink and silver metallic confetti in the shape of champagne bottles and horseshoes. A simple two-tier cake decorated with a single frosted grey rose was being kept cool in a glass bell jar cake stand. Izzy wondered if the cake was Pippa's handiwork.

'They only have half the covers on tonight so I had to pull a few strings to get us a table, but I was determined. This place is worth it for the vanilla and pistachio cheesecake alone. Trust me,' Marc said.

By that time I'll be pistachio-ed, Izzy thought, taking another slug of champagne. She must get a grip. She didn't want to end up shitfaced and start acting like a hussy. As it was, the bubbles from the champagne were taking great delight in congregating in her oesophagus and she kept having to pretend to be looking at something just so she could crane her head away from Marc and eke out a sly burp.

Just as the main course arrived the wedding party came in. Both in their sixties, the bride wore a dove-grey shift dress and kitten heels and looked as radiant as a twenty-one-year-old as she handed her bouquet to her granddaughter, who could have been no older than Carlotta. It was a small wedding party, clearly only family and the closest of friends, with the women in Monsoon dresses and the men in light linen suits. Champagne corks popped like fireworks.

'Ahhh,' said Izzy, by this time well down the bottle of Taittinger and whose innards had turned to goo in the face of such romance. 'I guess there really isn't any age limit on love.'

'I do hope not,' said Marc. His meaning couldn't have been clearer. Izzy didn't know where to look.

They didn't leave the bistro until well after eleven. Izzy found herself talking about Taryn and Carlotta and how she'd never had to deal with youngsters before. Marc responded with accounts of Ceridwen's antics.

Back in Nether Ousebury, Marc pulled up outside the electronic gates, switched off the engine and turned to face Izzy. He was flatteringly nervous.

'Don't be alarmed, but I'm going to kiss you goodnight here rather than at the doorway. I don't trust Carlotta and Taryn not to spy on us like a peep show nor that bloody ex-Navy gardener of yours to be watching us with his night vision goggles,' he said. He then proceeded to kiss her thoroughly. He then pushed back his blonde hair, which had flopped over his forehead in all the ardour, and switched on the engine. 'Better call it a night before we get too carried away. Are you busy at the weekend? Do you fancy a day trip to Rievaulx Abbey? We could take a picnic and make out in the cloisters and desecrate the sanctity of the place.'

Izzy let herself in as quietly as she could. She had expected that everyone would have retired to bed but the alarm warning hadn't sounded so someone must still be up. She'd just poured herself a glass of water and was about to creep upstairs when Jared called to her from within the winter den.

'Had a good night, Cinderella?'

Izzy pushed the door open to find him sitting on the sofa. His bare feet were propped up on the occasional table, something that he always forbade anyone else to do. At least seven empty Stella bottles were lined up next to his feet. Not one of the many scented candles in the room had been lit. Steptoe was lying next to him in prime position whilst all the other dogs were sprawled out on the rugs. Three open DVD cases were scattered in front of the player and the screen had been paused. He'd clearly been there for some time.

'Yeah, it was nice,' Izzy said, reluctant to go into details. She couldn't interpret the expression on Jared's face.

'Okay,' said Jared and pressed play on the remote. He turned his attention back to the screen.

'Goodnight, Jared.'

''Night.' His eyes didn't so much as flicker but stayed fixed on the telly. Only Steptoe moved, jumping off the sofa and following Izzy upstairs.

'Bloody four-legged traitor,' Izzy thought she heard Jared say, but she couldn't have sworn to it. Ten minutes later she heard the alarm being set. There was no doubt about it; Jared had waited up for her.

---

A WEEK later term started and Izzy had the unpleasant job of packing up a fearsome Carlotta. As the end of the holidays had loomed closer Carlotta had reverted to dark and sullen moods, which worsened once she had returned to school. Still riddled with furious resentment and jealousy, Carlotta proceeded to give her headmistress several coronaries by running away from school twice to meet Alan in secret trysts. Unable to be complacent in the face of such a security risk, the school had no option but to contact the police on both occasions. The police were, in turn, singularly unimpressed to have their time wasted by such a silly little girl. It wasn't long before MK stuck his two drachmas in. Jared was summoned to Armley for a discussion about what to do.

'MK has requested that Carlotta no longer has contact with this Alan character. He's asked if you could deal with it,' Jared reported back to Izzy upon his return.

'How?' Izzy asked, full of indignation. 'Does he even know his own daughter? Doesn't he know how unreasonable she is? 'Dealing' with Carlotta is easier said than done. If I ask her nicely she'll ignore me. If I yell at her, she'll strop. If I give her an order, she'll disobey me.'

Jared was already walking away, shrugging his shoulders. He needed a beer.

'Well? What do you suggest, smart arse?' Izzy shouted after him.

'You'll think of something. It *is* your job.'

Refusing to be dismissed so cavalierly, Izzy stalked after him. The fact that his head was buried in the drinks chiller didn't dissuade her. She was sorely tempted to bang the door shut on his thick skull. Mebbe that'd make him listen to her.

'Is that a fact? 'Cause I have to be honest with you, I'm a little hazy about what my job actually is. Perhaps you can tell me. Am I a nanny, groom, cleaner, riding companion, maid, cook, gardener, dog walker, small animal carer, taxi driver, or just a general dogsbody?'

Jared continued raking in the chiller.

'I'm sure there were some Buds left in here. Ah!' Emerging from the chiller he gave her a sarky smile. 'Fact is, so long as you continue to pipe down and just crack on with everything, no one cares what your job title is.'

Jared grabbed a bottle opener and pushed past her. Pig, thought Izzy.

'Why don't I shove a nice big broom up my arse and sweep the stables whilst I'm at it?' she screamed after him.

'If you like.'

Seething, Izzy sought solace in a phonecall to Marc and allowed her battered self-esteem to be soothed somewhat by his endless flattery, but deep down she was hurt by Jared's constant griping.

---

THE MORE IZZY learned about the Konstantines and their situation, the more she grew to understand Carlotta and how her bloody-mindedness and histrionics were a direct result of both the sacrifices she had been forced to make and of her worries about her father.

Carlotta was driven in a way that Izzy never had been. Addicted to red rosettes, the only thing Carlotta wanted to do was showjump and, moreover, she was prepared to put in the hours to achieve this. She was a grafter. She would ride for hours on end if she believed it would improve her technique. Nor was she a mere glory hunter either. It was this that she despised about Ceridwen Jones, with her fleet of minions who schooled, groomed and trained Jinx and Jonah on her behalf. Carlotta had genuine affection for all her father's horses, not just Jet and Vega, and was just as happy to attend to their stable management as she was to competing.

Nor had Carlotta had it all her own way. Despite her privileged upbringing she'd had to suffer hardship, just never the financial variety. Izzy discovered that Carlotta had good reason to believe she'd be selected for one of the junior national teams, because she had been so previously. The year before she and Jet had been asked to join the under 18s on a tour of the European circuit but had been yanked out at the eleventh hour by her father, both as a punishment for her unacceptable behaviour but more pertinently to keep her safe until her father's mess had been sorted out. Bitter, not able to understand either why her father would be so cruel to her or why she had to suffer just because of something he had (or rather hadn't) done, Carlotta expressed her feelings in the only way she knew how. By acting out.

After giving this new information serious consideration Izzy decided to take a proactive approach when it came to the problem of Carlotta. She acknowledged that when she'd been going through tough teenage times she would have liked adults to treat her like a grown-up and talk to her, rather than simply doling out punishments. Therefore she, Izzy, would try and reason with Carlotta in private, she told Jared, rather than have everyone lambasting her at once. Jared pooh-poohed this idea as New Age claptrap and overruled her. Instead Carlotta would be hauled home for the weekend, allowing everyone to air their grievances round the kitchen table at a family meeting.

'I want to get to the bottom of all of this,' Jared said, sternly. 'You can't keep running away like this, Carlotta. You know how dangerous it is. You could be picked up by any sort of nutter. What's the matter?'

'Izzy likes Taryn better,' Carlotta said, sulking. 'Everyone does. She's everyone's favourite.'

Izzy was astonished at this jealousy.

'Are you insane?' she said. 'Of course I don't have a favourite. I love you both the same. Mind you, sometimes you don't half make it an effort.'

'You love us?' Taryn asked. All eyes swivelled to Izzy. She was silent for a few moments. She felt uncomfortable. She didn't know what to say. The matter of her affection for the girls had never been raised before and her words had come as much of a surprise to her as they had to everyone else. But that didn't mean it wasn't true.

'Of course I love you.' Izzy gave a smile as Taryn leaped from her chair and flung her arms round her neck. 'How could I not?' she asked truthfully, hugging the little girl back.

'Both of us?' Carlotta asked, her face still sulky. Unsurprisingly, Carlotta hadn't copied her sister's actions.

'*Both* of you. In equal measures,' Izzy stressed.

'Gross,' Carlotta muttered, but Izzy knew she was pleased.

---

MARC DIDN'T GIVE Izzy a moment's trouble. Whenever he was with her he behaved like a perfect gentleman and had the added benefit of being exactly her type; a clean cut, smart, well-educated rugger-bugger type. Everything about him was smooth, from his very blonde hair and youthful, smiling face, which was wrinkle free courtesy of a happy, stress-free life. Both Izzy and Taryn thought he was quite handsome but Jared and Carlotta disagreed. Jared was the most disparaging, claiming that with his pale blonde eyebrows and eyelashes and slightly flushed pink cheeks, Marc looked like a pig in a very nasty blond wig. This sent Carlotta off into peals of laughter.

'And what's your opinion?' Izzy snapped, turning on her. Carlotta looked taken aback for a few seconds before replying that she thought he was a cockwomble. 'Sorry I asked,' Izzy said, still cross. 'And I don't know why you're laughing,' she said to Jared. 'Marc once called you a gnarly old bastard and, at this present moment in time, I'm inclined to agree with him.'

'Charming,' said Jared, but the smile was wiped from his face nonetheless.

Within the four walls of The Paddocks Jared didn't make any secret of the fact that he loathed Marc Jones. When pushed, he couldn't cite a justifiable reason but instead said it was just a gut feeling. He didn't bother adding that he had always felt that Marc, who he had come into contact with several times at school events, looked down on him because he had a broad Yorkshire accent, instead of speaking like a plummy toff, and hadn't been to public school. He had managed to make a good show of friendship at events such as Taryn's party purely for the sake of appearance but now he had to be polite to the straw-haired cretin all the time. But what really rankled Jared wasn't only that Izzy was the happiest he'd seen her since her arrival at The Paddocks but also that she was no longer at his beck and call. He hated to admit it, even to himself, but he was jealous.

If Jared had been outwardly accomplished in hiding his

dislike of Marc, then Marc was equally adept at hiding his loathing of Jared, and MK too.

Marc had built his business, a regional wine warehouse, from scratch and yet everyone still showed MK more deference. MK ran a very successful company, granted, but he had inherited it from his father. All he had to do was keep an eye on it to make sure it didn't go under and, after all, he had a board of directors to do that for him. Marc's achievement was so much greater, in his own personal opinion. Marc didn't admire jealousy as a character trait in others and so had no desire to encourage his own feelings of resentment towards either man, which had been borne of years of indifference and exclusion from their world, but he couldn't help but derive some pleasure at the prospect of claiming Izzy as his own. Despite all his wealth and influence, Marc would finally be able to take something away from MK, and Izzy, who he did genuinely like, was the perfect trophy. He was also aware, even if Izzy was blissfully ignorant of the fact, that Jared was furious about him dating her. Everyone who met Jared seemed to adore him, finding him witty and charming despite his inherent commonness. This annoyed Marc, who felt the gardener looked down on him just because he had been a bloody marine and knew he could kick his arse six ways to Sunday if he so wished.

Marc was never late, instead always turning up with a bottle of 'something nice' from his very extensive wine cellar. He never swore, broke wind, teased Izzy or made her feel stupid. He was well groomed and always took great pains with his appearance, wearing chinos, nice shirts from Jermyn Street and Marks & Spencer, and eccentric blazers, and *never* left his stubble to grow as he didn't want to cut her face to ribbons. He brought horse themed gifts for Carlotta and Taryn, having done his research by subtly interrogating Ceridwen as to what young horse-mad girls would like. Carlotta refused to accept these on principle and sent them back. Taryn had no such misgivings and happily grasped anything offered in her grubby little hands. Marc always took Izzy nice places: a back street blues bar in Harrogate, the Theatre Royal in Loxley, cosy little restaurants with great menus and wine lists longer than the Book of Job, and always brought her home safely, delivering her right to the front door after quarter of an hour's snogging by the electric gates. Always the gentleman, he never tried it on with her.

Marc's one flaw was that he was a wine snob and didn't bother to hide his disapproval if Izzy ordered a bottle of lager or a cocktail whilst they were out, dismissing them as less sophisticated drinks. Izzy was the first to admit that, much as she enjoyed drinking it, she knew sod all about wine other than the red stained her teeth and the pink stuff gave her a shocking hangover. Not for anything was she prepared to admit she'd always mistakenly believed that any old bottle of wine continued to increase in vintage, flavour and worth when left in the wine rack for a couple of years (and let's be honest, that had never happened). She was therefore apprehensive when Marc suggested they dine in The Half Moon one evening so that he could discuss wine suppliers with Col the Landlord.

Wearing one of his trademark flamboyant blazers, this one blue and cream striped, with a well-tailored white shirt, cream slacks and brown brogues, Marc looked just a little bit too fancy for a week night in The Half Moon. At least he had left his trilby in the Z4, Izzy thought as all eyes turned to look at them as they entered. Thankfully, it wasn't quiz night either. But worse was still to come.

Just as they'd settled down with their drinks, and ordered their food, Jared materialised, looking as rough as a badger's arse in ripped jeans and a filthy tee shirt. Despite the state of him, Izzy felt her insides reorganise themselves. She watched him surreptitiously as he ordered himself a drink before wandering over to their table, reckoning he'd fancied a pint of real ale as opposed to the light beers he stacked the chiller with. Izzy, however, wasn't convinced he hadn't turned up on purpose just so that he could spy on her. Feeling cornered, Izzy felt she had no option but to invite him to join them for a quick drink until their starters arrived. Marc, who had ordered a bottle of the pub's most expensive Sauvignon Blanc and was keen to show off his knowledge and palate, forced a glassful on Jared who, never one to refuse a free drink, accepted it. Alas, their truce didn't last long.

'Is he wearing Farahs?' Jared hissed at Izzy as Marc, having discarded his striped blazer, went to the bar for another bottle. 'Or has he just got a really fat arse?'

'Will you pack it in?' Izzy hissed back, quickly turning her look of fury into one of happiness as Marc turned round to smile at her. No one was more aware than she that Marc's round backside could not in any way compare to Jared's Michaelangelo-esque rear end. She was most relieved when her and Marc's starters arrived and Jared, bored because he wasn't causing as much friction as he would like, excused himself and mooched back to The Paddocks for a proper drink from the chiller.

When Izzy returned home after her date she found Jared waiting for her, as he always did whenever she went out with Marc. His official party line was that he didn't trust her to set the alarm properly but Izzy suspected she was being monitored. He also mocked her ceaselessly.

'Where's Housewives' Choice taking you next time? A flower show? A cookery school? A tea dance? I hope he does realise that you're not an adult yet and that all this sophistication is wasted on you.'

'So where would you take me on a date?' Izzy finally snapped. Jared gave her a carry-on leer.

'I'd take you anywhere you wanted, sweetheart,' he mocked. 'Absolutely anywhere.'

Spitting, Izzy stormed out of the room.

The next day she poured out her angst to Caro over the ether.

> *Marc is so sweet and treats me like a princess, but Jared does his best to ruin it,* she typed furiously. *Marc and I have such a nice time when we go out, but Jared is always waiting for me when I get home, like a Victorian father. He's exactly the same with me as he is when Carlotta goes out with that ghastly Alan, which would be fine except she's half my age and a minor in his guardianship. Honestly, I don't know what his problem is.*

Izzy stared at the email she had just written. She didn't know what her problem was either. She was so confused. She enjoyed her time with Marc. He was everything a woman could want: successful, available, kind, attentive, thoughtful, generous. Plus she couldn't afford to be picky. He was the first decent bloke she had met since her arrival at The Paddocks. She felt she should at least give him a chance. If only it weren't for those two words she found herself repeating over and over again.

But Jared…

> *Let me know what you think. Take care of you, Iz xx*

If that weren't enough for Izzy to consider, Marc then threw a flaming curve ball at her one evening whilst he was driving her back home after dinner.

'Rhys has just received notice from his games master that he has been picked for the first XV for the first time. It's something of a big deal for Rhys as he'll be the youngest player ever to have been selected. Plus it's the first big match of the season against the local rival school. I'd be thrilled if you'd come along too. They're going to put on a bit of a 'do' for the parents afterwards and I'd really like to show you off. Plus you'd get to meet Rhys.' Marc paused, as though carefully thinking about how to word his next sentence. 'I wondered if you'd like to make a weekend of it and stay in a hotel for the night.'

In other words, was Izzy's first thought, Marc was fed up with mere snogging in the driveway and wanted to progress onto full blown shagging. And probably full blown something else too. She didn't know what to say. In many ways she was happy with the way things were going. Izzy didn't know if it was because it had been so long since she had been to bed with anyone or if it was because she had 'father' waiting up for her back at The Paddocks, tapping his foot and checking his military-grade wristwatch, but she couldn't help but feel that her relationship with Marc was rather like those she'd had when she had been a teenager, with racing hormones and clammy hands and moonlit gropes in cars, but no suggestion of commitment. Admittedly the standard of car had improved considerably, not that that was relevant. Now Marc had changed all that with his proposition and Izzy had had to drag herself back to the real world. She wasn't a teenager, but an adult in an adult relationship. And there were other people to consider too. To her shame Izzy had never given Ceridwen's role in all this much thought. She had always been there or thereabouts, somewhere in the periphery, and Izzy couldn't help but view her as Carlotta's nemesis first and foremost and Marc's daughter only as an afterthought. Now he was keen to introduce her to his son also. That was serious. That was like she was being assessed as potential stepmother material. Jesus! That scared the shit out of her.

'Izzy?' Marc's voice cut through her thoughts.

'I… err… I,' she struggled to find words. She plumped for the first thing that came to mind which was, of course: 'I'd need to check with Jared first.'

'Why?' There was the faintest trace of irritation in Marc's voice.

'Well, I've never been away from the girls overnight and, technically, he is my boss.'

'But Carlotta will be at school and I've heard you complain that you haven't had a full day off since you started.' Marc didn't sound pushy or petulant, but hurt, which automatically pulled on Izzy's heartstrings.

'I just need to make sure it isn't Mrs Firth's weekend at her sister's before I give a definite yes. That's all.'

That seemed to appease Marc. Izzy made a note of the date and promised to let him know as soon as possible. The following morning she checked the kitchen calendar to see if Mrs Firth would be at The Paddocks that weekend before approaching Jared. Yes, she would be. Izzy didn't know whether to feel thrilled or disappointed.

On edge, she tracked Jared down in the vegetable plot. He was shovelling compost from a wheelbarrow into a deeply dug trench and was wearing nothing but shorts and wellies. Determined not to be distracted by his tanned flesh or taut muscles, Izzy ploughed straight in.

'Marc's invited me to a do at his son's school which would mean an overnight stay. D'you think that'd be okay? It's not for a couple of weeks and it isn't when Mrs Firth is away.'

Jared stabbed the spade into the ground and studied it for a few minutes before facing Izzy. God only knew what he was thinking, Izzy thought.

'Can't see it being an issue. Just make sure you have your mobile with you and be prepared to come back at short notice should we have an absolute emergency.'

That seemed fair enough.

'Don't you mind?' Izzy heard herself say. She wasn't sure why but she'd expected he'd have something more to say than that. He didn't even make a derogatory remark about Marc.

'Why should I?' he said, his expression blank. 'It's nothing to do with me. The only person who should have any input on your decision is you.' He picked up the spade and returned to shovelling soil. The conversation was clearly over.

Izzy returned to the house and rang Marc. He answered immediately, which made Izzy wonder if he had been waiting for her call. She felt an unbidden flash of irritation.

'So, what did the Green Reaper say?' Marc asked. Izzy grimaced into the receiver. Somehow Marc didn't have Jared's gift for injecting humour into an insult.

'Not a problem. I'm good to go.' Oh crap, why had she said that?

'Wonderful. I can't wait.'

After a few minutes of random chat Izzy fabricated a reason to say goodbye and rang off. She was more confused than ever. What the hell had she agreed to? Did she even want to sleep with Marc? Oh God! Then she calmed herself. It wasn't for another couple of weeks. She might have a completely different approach to it by then. The only reason she was feeling so mixed up was because Jared was spinning her head. Marc was a perfectly nice, sweet man who wouldn't do anything to hurt her. There was no good reason for her to throw what they had away just because Jared was being obstreperous. She was overreacting, thinking about it too much, just being silly. But on the other hand Jared had managed to tune in to her own misgivings and his comment about the decision being hers and hers alone brought her some comfort.

After all, if when the time came she didn't want to sleep with Marc she could always just say no.

# THE WINCIDENT

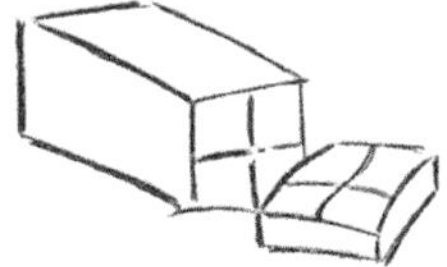

Of course, the piss-taking came later. Jared insisted on referring to it as Izzy's 'dirty weekend' and openly encouraged Mrs Firth, Gemma and even Carlotta to do the same. Carlotta went so far as to ring up from school asking to speak to Izzy.

'I can't believe you're going to have sex with Ceridwen Jones's dad. It's repulsive. He's older than Treebeard. Ugh! How you can even consider having that pink and white face looming over you as he heaves away, I'll never know.'

None of which helped.

Nor did the passage of time offer Izzy any enlightenment. With less than a week to go she was still wrestling with her emotions. Even more disturbing was the fact that the more time she spent with Marc, the more similarities she could see between him and Scott. Not wanting to replace Scott with another man who would tire of her when he realised she, Izzy, was a code red disaster zone, she mentally compared the two men for hours. Both were successful in their chosen field, loved expensive things and spending money. Izzy also suspected Marc was a little bit of a show off. Appearances were everything. Scott had always been obsessed with his looks, fashion and, most pertinently of all, other people's opinions. Marc at least lacked Scott's absolute vanity although he did like to be well groomed at all times. Izzy couldn't remember ever seeing him in jeans, not even designer ones. Jared lived in his jeans. Uninvited, he had managed to creep into the equation yet again. He bore no resemblance to Marc or Scott. Jared couldn't give a shit what people thought about what he did, said or wore. He wasn't shallow and would rather die than see his friends hurt, both metaphorically and literally if his military record was anything to go by.

Such was the atmosphere in the house, it was only a matter of time before things came to a head. It came out of nowhere. Taryn, in her innocence and who like a magpie was attracted to pretty, shiny objects, had been questioning Izzy about Marc's mint green Z4.

Jared entered the kitchen just as Izzy was waxing lyrical about its features.

'—And it even has its own docking station for your iPod,' he heard her say.

'Big deal. You get those in new Fiestas now,' he interrupted, reaching into the fridge for a can of Coke. 'There's summat similar in the Range Rover too. It's called a radio. He's just showing off so he can get in your pants.'

Looking back, Izzy had to concede there had been no reason for the row to escalate as it did. Jared's comments had been no more combative or insinuative than usual. It was just that Izzy was twitchy about her weekend away. So, it seemed, was Jared.

'Why do you insist on being such a gorilla?' Izzy snapped.

'Aw, don't I stack up against that Welsh marshmallow? I'm devastated. Oh wait, no I'm not.'

'You're just jealous because Marc is everything you're not: suave, sophisticated, successful. He owns his own house and business whilst you just play at Lord of the No Manners whilst MK bankrolls you.'

'You're one to talk. You swan around, doing fuck all but taking everything you can in your grabbing, gold-digging little hands. I hope your Tim-Nice-But-Dim lookey-likey realises what a leech you are.'

'Leave Marc out of this. At least I work for my wages. You just swan around with a piece in your pocket pretending to look all mean. Oh, and you dig up a few carrots for appearance's sake.'

Jared's only response was to let out a great, rasping fart.

'Oof! Get out and walk, ye bitch,' he said, fanning the air behind his backside with his hand.

Taryn exploded into giggles.

Izzy stared him out, disgusted. 'Couth is just something that applies to other people, isn't it? If you can't eat it, or take the piss out of it, what use is it?'

'By that yardstick you have at least one use then,' he said, slamming the chiller door shut and strolling back out of the kitchen. 'Anyway, let's not forget that you're nothing but a moaning, whinging southerner.'

'Well there's no need to pop a vein on my account. My flat will come free at the end of October, I bleedin' well hope, and then you'll be rid of me forever,' Izzy screamed after him. Jared spun on his heel and poked his head back round the door.

'Thank fuck. And speaking of which, I hope your man's planning on using a johnny. He could catch a nasty bout of stupidity off you.'

'D'you know what? I think you are just a vile, chauvinistic pig.'

'Nowt new there.' And this time he really did leave, leaving Izzy standing in the kitchen, absolutely foaming with rage.

It was the worst argument they'd ever had. Izzy was

accustomed to Jared mobbing her up, but this was something else, filled with spite and needlessly cruel. She'd said such terrible things in return, and all in front of Taryn too. Both knew they'd behaved unforgivably, but still neither was prepared to be the first to apologise.

---

SEPTEMBER CONTINUED to succumb to an Indian summer. The weatherman on the lunchtime news had quoted some blurb about how it hadn't been thirty-two degrees since 1949, over sixty years ago. The last time it had reached thirty degrees so late in the year had been 1999. The word he had used was freakish.

It had been a hot day, probably one of the last hot days of the summer. Izzy had had a busy day ferrying Taryn to and from school. It was so hot that she, Gemma and Taryn had given up on their hack after only half an hour and had had to hose the horses down before turning them out into the paddocks. Jared had driven over to the nick to visit MK, which meant that they would have a late dinner. Taryn was, for once, happily submerged in her school prep up in her room having been allowed to pick her own project topic which had, of course, been ponies. All of which had left Izzy with a free couple of hours. Tired, aching and sticky, she opted for a quick shower before enjoying a quiet drink outside in the warm evening air.

Dressed in clean white cotton clothes, she wandered into the kitchen where Mrs Firth was chopping salad veg at the same time as watching *Eggheads* on the portable telly. The comforting smell of fresh bread emanated from the Aga.

'Aren't you boiled?' Izzy asked, fanning herself. The kitchen was stifling despite all the doors and windows being flung wide open.

'Used to it, love,' Mrs Firth said. 'Jared rang whilst you

were in the shower. He'll be back about half seven, he said. He gave instructions for you to open a bottle and mekk the most of the heat as it's due to break this weekend. We'll eat once he's home.'

Such a thoughtful message caught Izzy off guard and disarmed her. Relations had not been good between her and Jared since their big row, if not since Taryn's party if she were really honest. Perhaps he would be less grievous about her weekend away with Marc from now on.

Outside Izzy settled into one of the recliners on the decking with a large glass of White Zinfandel in her hand. The remainder of the bottle was in a cooler jacket in the shade beneath the lounger. MK never scrimped, even with her and she was a stranger to him. What lovely, generous people they were, she thought with every passing glass of wine. In less than an hour the sun would sink beneath the horizon and the temperature would drop at last, if only by one or two degrees. Cats and dogs were milling round, looking for a suitable spot in which to bask. Steptoe was already asleep by her feet, heat pulsating off his body. Izzy could just see the ponies in the field. Jester was lying down, his chin resting on the parched grass as though thoroughly pissed off at being so overheated. The others were standing in the shade of a couple of great oaks, hind legs cocked lazily.

Izzy didn't read or write lists of the chores she needed to do. She didn't even plug in her earphones and listen to music. It was too hot even to think. Instead she let her mind empty and allowed herself to be peaceful. Occasional sounds drifted across the fields: the whistle of a train and the merry chime of church bells heralding the commencement of evensong. From their cool sanctuary within the orchard, a dusk chorus warbled a lullaby. Izzy had never felt so relaxed and contented. It was the most perfect evening she had ever known. It was inevitable that the combined effect of the heat, the alcohol and Izzy's tiredness caused her eyelids to lower.

She drifted off, dreaming about long stretches of golden sands with Arabian horses galloping along them ridden by jewel-laden, silk-clothed, ebony-haired princesses that looked curiously like Carlotta, and handsome, well-sculpted men whose faces all merged into Jared's.

Footsteps on the decking woke her three-quarters of an hour later. She'd know that gait anywhere. Jared was home. Steptoe, suddenly unaffected by the heat, was so thrilled to see his master he leapt off the sun lounger and began to circle Jared's legs in glee.

'I am not a maypole,' he told the dog, bending down to give him a quick pat. On seeing Izzy lying on the sun lounger with a near empty bottle by her side he turned on his heel and disappeared back into the house. Izzy's heart sank. He couldn't even bear her company now.

Two minutes later he reappeared with a glass and another bottle and, after pouring himself a generous glassful, settled in the hammock which spanned between two trees on the lawn. He seemed to be in a good mood.

Perhaps if Izzy were especially nice to him he might not be so moody.

'That's a nice aftershave. Smells citrusy,' she called over to him.

'It's insect repellent spray,' Jared said. Izzy felt herself blush to precisely the same shade of pink as the wine in her glass. A loud high-pitched honking above them made them both look up.

'Pink-footed geese,' Jared said. 'They'll be on their way to their wintering areas in Norfolk.' They watched in silence as a great flock in spearhead formation crossed the sky high above them. 'A sure sign autumn is on its way. They can sense the change of the season before we can.'

For a few minutes they partook in idle chatter, mostly about MK and the girls. Jared was lying with his arms behind his head, swinging slightly. His white tee shirt contrasted against the dark hairs and brown skin of his arms and was cut with such finesse that it revealed, to glorious effect, the power and strength of his biceps. Izzy found herself mesmerised by Jared's forearms. She imagined herself running her hands up and down them. Would the hairs be coarse or soft? What would his scars feel like? What would happen if she slid her hands all the way up, inside the tight fabric of the sleeves, across his chest...? God, she had to get a grip.

Behind the orchard the sun was retreating into the horizon. It must be nearly eight, thought Izzy. She had never known such a long, hot day. She was still warm in her floaty boho skirt and strappy camisole. A full bottle of chilled wine had done nothing to lower her temperature. Afterwards she never knew what made her stand up and walk over to the hammock. She never knew whether it was the wine, the sultry night air, the chirruping crickets or the heady scent of the summer flowers. All she knew was that she bent down, lacing her fingers into the holes of the hammock for balance, and kissed Jared bang on the mouth. He merely looked at her, his expression unreadable, not responding with either word or action. Undeterred, she lowered her mouth for a second kiss and this time his arms clamped round her, pulling her down onto him. His kiss was urgent rather than tender. Beneath her, through his jeans, Izzy could feel the hardness of his erection pressing into her crotch, almost but not quite where it should be. She wriggled into position then gasped as a bolt of pleasure ricocheted through her. Now Jared was tangling his hands in her hair as he trailed a line of kisses down her neck. He could smell her scent, intensified by her hot skin. His hands lowered, gently skimming over her breasts with the lightest, most tantalising touches, before encircling her once more. They never stopped kissing. The hammock swayed precariously as Izzy wrestled Jared's white tee shirt over his head. She kissed every inch of his scarred arm then ran her hands over his chest, deliberately letting her fingers and her rings catch in his chest hair so that it pulled and snagged. Liking the sensation of pain it caused, Jared cursed and swore endearments at her. Pulling down at her cami he released one of her breasts, tracing his fingertip, and then his tongue, gently over the nipple. Izzy's gasps and moans were both reassuring and flattering.

Risking tipping them both on to the ground, Jared flipped them both over so Izzy was underneath. Beneath his weight she could feel her skin being crushed against the fabric and holes of the hammock. The sensation was uncomfortable, almost painful, but pleasurably so. Izzy fumbled for his belt buckle, struggling for a few seconds to undo it before sliding her hands inside his jeans, running them over the firmest buttocks in Yorkshire, sinking her nails in so that Jared thrust against her.

'We shouldn't do this.'

'Don't you want to?' Izzy wrapped her legs around his back. Stronger from months of horse riding, she was able to grip him, pull him down towards her, causing him to groan.

'You know I do, more than anything, but what if someone sees us… Mrs Firth… Taryn—?' Jared said, unconvincingly, his eyes dilated, his mouth still assaulting her neck with hot kisses between protestations.

'No one will see us. Firthie will be embroiled in *Midsomer Murders* by now and Taryn is in her room pouring over *Horse and Hound*. There's no reason for either of them to come out here,' Izzy replied.

'Are you sure?'

'I'm sure. Shut up.' Izzy let her hands roam round the side of his hips, across his pelvic bone… Jesus, he was big! Jared's sharp inhalation of breath let Izzy know he wanted her as much as she did him. His hands slid up her legs, pushing up her skirt. Thank Christ she had shaved her legs in the shower!

Desire coupled with too much booze made Izzy reckless.

'I've never done it on a hammock. Mebbe next time we

can do it in the Roller, and I'll ride you like Jet, like you did with—'

Jared jerked away from her with such force that Izzy fell off the hammock. She landed on the grass with a thud but only her ego was bruised.

'I can't do this, not again,' Jared said, scrabbling to button up his jeans. 'I've already caused a problem by sleeping with one member of the staff here.'

For a nanosecond all Izzy's sense and knowledge escaped her.

'Mrs Firth?' she said in disbelief. Then she remembered Gemma. Of course not Mrs Firth, idiot girl.

An uncomfortable silence hung in the air. She stared up at him, her breast still exposed from her top. Confused and embarrassed, she covered herself up, yanking up the neckline of the camisole. Scrambling to her feet she backed away from him, her face pale and her eyes huge, filled with horror at what she had initiated and the manner in which she had been rejected.

Jared watched her run across the lawn. It took all his self-control not to sprint after her, catch her, drag her down onto the grass and fuck all the idiocy and nonsense out of her, all the while releasing his own frustration and confusion about who and what she was. Only when Izzy had made reference to that stupid, reckless night with Gemma in the Rolls Royce did he consider how foolish he was being. How could he have let this happen? How could he have responded to Izzy's advances like that? God only knew what sort of dog's supper it would make of the atmosphere in the house. MK had made it clear on several occasions, including yet again that very afternoon, that Izzy was off limits, plus she wasn't even available anymore. One final question had yet to be answered. Why on Earth had he made himself stop when he had? Talk about Stop! Hammocktime.

Up in her room Izzy was bouncing off the walls from a

combination of mortification, sexual frustration and confusion. Jesus, what had possessed her to launch herself on Jared like some rampant maniac? What the hell must he think of her? She was supposed to be Marc's girlfriend. They were going away together at the weekend. She was nothing more than a slut. A duplicitous, cheating, shameless slut.

She didn't want to acknowledge the niggling voice telling her there was no way on the green and blue planet she would have been able to keep her kit on for almost a month if she and Jared were seeing each other. And yet all the while she couldn't help but dwell on the enthusiasm of Jared's response to her touch. She had been so certain he'd wanted her, in many respects she still was, and yet he'd backed off with such conviction as soon as she mentioned his involvement with Gemma. Oh God, Gemma! She must never know what Izzy had done. Some friend she was. At least no one had witnessed her ignominious rejection, seen her sprawled out on the orchard lawn with her tit hanging out of her top. And thank God for that! At least the whole sordid incident would remain between her and Jared and no one else need ever know.

But Izzy was quite wrong about that. A pair of angry, tear-filled eyes had watched the entire performance from within the dark cover of the orchard.

---

GEMMA LOOKED up from the saddle she was cleaning when Izzy entered the barn the next morning.

'Jesus, you look rough. Heavy night?'

Izzy gave a wry smile but remained silent.

Only the most insular, self-involved person wouldn't have picked up on the uncomfortable atmosphere between Izzy and Jared in the stables. As soon as Jared appeared Izzy coloured up. Gemma noticed that Jared was wound tighter than a watch spring and that he and Izzy managed to hold a full five-minute conversation about Taryn without looking at each other once.

As soon as Jared had left Gemma turned on Izzy.

'Something's happened between you and Jared,' she said, accusingly.

Izzy tried to laugh it off.

'Don't be silly. Jared and I work together. Anyway, what makes you think he'd look twice at me? I'd drive him mad within minutes.'

'Don't deny it. And don't try to fob me off with a bunch of lies. I know something's been going on. Firstly, I'm not stupid. Any idiot could tell something was up from that unpleasant little encounter just now. Secondly, I know because I saw you.'

Izzy started at her words.

'What!?'

'Yes, I saw you, both of you, last night, and what a lewd little sex show it was,' Gemma spat. Her fury was extraordinary. 'Some friend you are. You chase after my man like a bitch on heat, then you have the nerve to lie to my face about it. I bet if I hadn't caught you out you'd still be lying about it. You know how things are between me and Jared and yet you threw yourself at him anyway. But he turned you down, didn't he? Oh no, not at first because he's only a man and what man doesn't get carried away when some whorebag hands it to them on a plate? But he couldn't go through with it, could he? I saw him dump you on the ground. I saw him send you away. I saw it all.'

Furious at being spied on and tricked into honesty, as well as with the whole situation, Izzy retaliated.

'Fine! I admit it. I had a skinful of wine and cracked on to Jared, and he rejected me. And I lied about it to you because I knew it would hurt you and plus I really didn't want to have to think about it and relive the humiliation. And now no one can stand the sight of anyone else anymore and everyone is pissed off. Moreover, everyone is pissed off with me and I can't even moan about it because I caused it all. So, as I pretty much feel bad about everything already you might as well heap your twopenn'orth on in giant scoops. Does that make you feel better? Does it help that I feel like a big fat fool? There, are you happy now?'

'Yes,' said Gemma, looking Izzy straight in the eye, her expression cold and hard. 'I am.' Turning on her heel, she strode into the stable block.

---

IZZY NEVER KNEW if Jared's rejection of her or Gemma's ostracism influenced her decision to sleep with Marc. She did know that after what she referred to in private as the 'wincident', because whenever she thought about it, it made her wince with shame and guilt, she felt like a social leper. Gemma refused to speak to her other than if it were absolutely necessary. Jared avoided her as much as he could, unable to look her in the eye. Even Mrs Firth had raised her eyebrows when she'd seen the grass stains on Izzy's white boho skirt during dinner that night. The days seemed longer than ever. Sharp as a tack, Taryn picked up on everything.

'Did you and Jared have a row?' she asked, looking worried. 'Are you going to leave us?'

'Of course not,' Izzy said, trying her best to smile naturally. Even so, she was concerned about where she stood. Both Jared and Gemma had been part of the household for many years. If they decided to be malevolent they could gang up and conspire to have MK fire her.

Thus it was with considerable apprehension that Izzy packed an overnight bag and stood waiting for Marc to pick her up on Saturday morning.

Jared had been almost accurate in his weather forecast.

The sunny weather did indeed cease on the Friday evening and was replaced with lashing rains and blustery winds that rattled the leaves on the trees and shook the apples from their branches in the orchard, but the temperature remained high.

Marc wore a snazzy tartan blazer when he came to pick her up.

'McGood McGod! He looks like a set of bagpipes,' Jared said.

Marc's fashion sense was something of a mystery to Izzy. She couldn't figure out if he wore such eccentric items, such as paisley cravats and patterned neckerchiefs, because he was deliberately trying to make a statement or because he honestly thought they were stylish. Today he was wearing moss-green cords that only served to make his chunky rugger legs look like two fields of baby crops and which didn't quite match his Black Watch blazer. As soon as they reached Rhys's boarding school he donned a matching waxed jacket and fishing hat, which at least was a different colour and style from her own coat. In order to contend with the growing maelstrom he also pulled on a pair of brand spanking new Hunter wellies. Izzy counted her blessings that neither Jared nor Carlotta had clapped eyes on this particular ensemble.

Never having been a fan of any sport involving a team of sweaty men and a ball, Izzy didn't really enjoy the rugby match. She clapped politely when everyone else did and was of course delighted on Marc's behalf when Rhys's team won but it was nothing compared to the thrill of watching Taryn show Jester or Carlotta winning a jump off. Worryingly, she had been just a little bit turned off by Marc as he became more invested in the game. He roared his opinion from the sidelines, his ruddy face becoming redder and redder and sometimes even spitting out a bit of saliva, such was his fervour. Nor was she impressed by some of the other fathers slapping Marc on the back as they referred to her as a 'fine filly'.

The evening do, which took place in Rhys's boarding school refectory, had been only marginally less tedious. She had worn completely the wrong thing, having opted for her purple harem pants again on the basis that Marc seemed to like them, and an almost see-through black gossamer top which pretty much let everyone know what make of bra she was wearing. All the other parents had worn tailored suits or tea dresses. Izzy could feel their eyes assessing her. They probably thought she was some sort of disco tart. How ironic that there wasn't any music whatsoever. The food had been nice enough, but fussy, and there hadn't been enough of it. Used to Mrs Firth's daddy bear portions, Izzy immediately tore into a packet of peanuts with her teeth as soon as they returned to their hotel room. Bugger, a peanut kernel had stuck in her teeth and she'd forgotten to bring any floss.

Another aspect of Marc that she had never appreciated before was his fastidiousness. Earlier that day, upon their arrival at the five star hotel Marc had booked them into, he'd inspected the room like Kim and Aggie before insisting that it was unacceptably dirty. Mortified, Izzy had skulked along the hotel corridor behind him as a stiff backed concierge led them to a room he hoped was more appropriate. Even more off-putting was the fact that he had insisted on taking a shower before bed. He emerged from the en suite reeking of toothpaste and aftershave, wearing a white hotel dressing gown and, to Izzy's horror, tight black briefs. He'd even put on the complimentary slippers, for God's sake. They did nothing to flatter his milk-white legs. Izzy couldn't help compare Jared's solid, tanned, taut body with Marc's white, rather wobbly one. Perched on the edge of the bed, still fully dressed and with red wine breath, Izzy wanted to run into the en suite and bolt the door after her. Unbidden memories of Jared's hard body and how his hot skin had smelled of lemons and Ralph Lauren's Polo Sport overwhelmed her. She closed her eyes and replayed the images in her head. It was like virtual erotica, and such a turn on. The next thing she knew Marc was kissing her and her traitorous, excited body responded. Then she was on her back, the gossamer top was being pulled over her head and her bra was being unhooked. As Marc swooped down to seal the deal, Izzy allowed herself to be transported back to memories of the hammock. If she closed her eyes she could pretend it was Jared's hand pulling down her knickers, then sliding his body between her legs. It was almost exquisite. Almost, but not quite. She just couldn't bring herself to imagine that Jared would make such a guttural, tortured, grunting noise as he succumbed to a shuddering, twitching climax. Afterwards Marc held her close until he fell asleep. Izzy got the very distinct feeling he'd only done this because he thought that was what she wanted.

Appalled by what she had just done, Izzy stared at the ceiling and wished she were in her own bed at The Paddocks. It had been so long and it was just nice to be touched, to be intimate with someone, but it had been with the wrong person. There was no doubt it had been a release, and that was the worst of it. Once she had got herself revved up it didn't seem to matter who it had been. She felt like a whore. She equated it to ordering a meal in a restaurant that had sounded splendid from the brief description but, when it was set in front of you, wasn't quite what you'd expected. It was satisfying enough, but just not exactly what she'd wanted. She remembered with bitterness that Scott had continued to shag her right up until the night before he dumped her, the randy bleeder. God, she was no better than he had been.

First thing Sunday morning Izzy escaped to the hotel spa before breakfast for both a literal and metaphorical cleansing. As she steeped herself in a jacuzzi that smelled of spiced apple and vanilla she couldn't stop thinking about Jared. Then she berated herself. What was wrong with her? Here she was with a perfectly nice man who treated her better than any of her other boyfriends ever had. He was kind, generous, and considerate; the list of his attributes was endless. She needed her thick skull looking at, she told herself sternly. She could do, and indeed had done on several occasions, a lot worse than Marc Jones. There was just the one characteristic missing from his list. He wasn't Jared.

Having insisted upon a room with a balcony, Marc had ordered breakfast via room service so they could sit and enjoy the view over the Dales. Returning to the hotel room, Izzy found Marc fully dressed and pouring coffee from a cafétière.

'Good morning, darling. Is the spa nice?'

'Yes, lovely, thanks,' Izzy said as she slid into her chair. Her appetite tainted by her disgust with herself, Izzy chewed on a piece of toast. Thankfully Marc was engrossed in one of the Sunday papers and didn't notice she was so quiet. Or was it all of the Sunday papers? Izzy had never seen so many different magazines and supplements. She peered round the coffee pot and did a quick scan. Sports, business, foreign affairs, culture, celebrity gossip. Nope, it was all one paper. Jeez, how much of it was there, and how long would it take for Marc to be done with it? No doubt he was a cover-to-cover sort of geezer. He hadn't proved to be precipitous the previous night. He'd had more stamina than The Tank.

Thinking about the horses made Izzy remember something else.

'How did you know about Taryn's birthday party?' she asked.

'Gemma invited me,' Marc said, not looking up from the article he was reading.

'Gemma?' Izzy was taken aback. Marc nodded, then folded up the paper and set it aside.

'She rang me up. She thought it would be nice for Carlotta to have some competition of her own standard, plus she tipped me off that you liked me, you know, after we met at the Great Yorkshire Show. And thank God she did.' He leaned over and gave her a tender kiss. 'You were amazing last night.'

The compliment bypassed Izzy. She was flabbergasted. She'd thought Marc was pleasant enough the first time she'd met him but then, on the other hand, she hadn't remembered who he was when he'd turned up at Taryn's party. Not once had she mentioned anything to Gemma about finding him attractive. Gemma must have filched the number off the back of the florist's card, which would have meant she'd snuck into her room. Izzy suddenly had the very distinct and uncomfortable feeling that she'd been set up.

'Listen, I have to go to France for five days next week to check out some promising new vineyards. Come with me?'

'For a week? I really can't. I can't leave Taryn for that long.' It may have been a welcome excuse but at least it had been a truthful one. For the first time in twenty-four hours Izzy felt like she could breathe. Marc seemed surprised by her answer. Plainly the encounter of the night before had left him wanting to see more of her, not less. For a few moments they simply looked at each other, neither knowing what to say.

Marc's phone rang and interrupted them. Even with the handset held close to his ear, Izzy could hear the high-pitched, hysterical shrieking of a female voice. After five minutes, having barely spoken in reply, Marc shut his phone.

'Ceri,' he said apologetically. 'She's suddenly decided she has issues with there being another woman in my life.'

Ceridwen did indeed turn her hog out, as Mrs Firth would have said, and had a hissy fit of such magnitude that Marc was forced to abandon the day of romance he'd planned in order to go home and calm her down. With much reluctance he dropped Izzy off at The Paddocks with earnest promises to devote more of his time to her once he was back from France. In the meantime he would ring her every day, even whilst he was abroad.

'I'll be thinking of you all the while,' he told her, looking deep into her eyes. Izzy waved him off, smiling happily, but not for the reason Marc thought as he watched her in the rear view mirror as he roared away.

Once she had returned home the cold war between Izzy and Jared ensued. In fact, it was worse than ever. He exited the room as soon as she entered and didn't speak to her other than to mob her up. Gemma did the exact same. Even Mrs Firth watched with keen eyes, trying to figure out what was going on. Izzy knew it was inevitable Mrs Firth would always support Jared, after all they had known each other for decades, but even so she still felt it was unfair that Mrs Firth didn't bother to ascertain her side of the tale before picking sides. Furthermore, she wished she could have confided with the down-to-earth housekeeper and drawn on her wisdom. Only her relationship with Taryn remained unchanged.

As it turned out it was just as well she'd turned down Marc's offer to travel with him to France as the week that followed was chaotic.

Yet another animal appeared, this time a tiny feral kitten, which looked so innocent and pitiful curled up in death that Izzy clamped a hand over her mouth as she fought back tears. God, she hoped it hadn't suffered. Worse still was the fact that Taryn had been with Izzy upon discovery of the little creature and had been terribly upset.

As if that wasn't bad enough, whoever the culprit was also broke into the barn, having smashed a small window at the back, hid a few lengths of barbed wire in the food bins, rather like a demonic bran tub, and scored Jet's saddle with a Stanley knife. Thankfully, the horses had all been out in the field overnight.

Jared studied the saddle with defeated eyes.

'I don't understand how this keeps happening and yet I know nothing about it. Why didn't the alarm go off? And why would anyone want to deface a saddle?'

'Perhaps it's someone with a grudge against Carlotta.

Who has she pissed off recently?' Izzy asked. Ceridwen Jones appeared unbidden in her thoughts.

'What makes you say that?' Jared asked, eyes narrowed.

'It's her pony's saddle,' Izzy replied. 'That might not be a coincidence.' Then another thought occurred to her. She also rode Jet. Could the vandalism have been meant for her? It was no secret that she was hardly in the running for any popularity contests. For the second time, her thoughts drifted to Ceridwen. But there was no way she'd have access to The Paddocks out of hours, Izzy reasoned. Then a truly terrible thought occurred to her. 'I hate to ask it, but could Gemma have done it?'

'Nah,' said Jared, straight away. He then mulled it over for a few moments before coming to the same conclusion. 'Nah, there's no way. She's been with us forever, plus she hasn't even been here since the weekend. Anyway, what possible beef could she have with Carlotta? She's her prodigy.' Jared's insistence of Gemma's innocence allowed Izzy to breathe a sigh of deep relief. She would have derived no pleasure if she'd been right in her accusation. 'What on Earth made you think that anyway?'

'We've had a bit of a falling out,' Izzy confessed.

'What about?'

'Not much. Just girl stuff,' she said cryptically, turning her scarlet face away. She was damned if she was going to tell Jared why.

'Well, sort it out. There's enough aggro in this house as it is,' Jared said impatiently. He contemplated the ruined saddle once more. 'This'll have to go to the saddlers before Carlotta gets back. I hope they can fix it.'

The week worsened. Not sleeping as a result of nightmares, Taryn succumbed to a bug that was circulating round her school and was not an easy patient. Jared was summoned to Leeds for yet another meeting with MK, no doubt to discuss what had happened. Then a call came, on that very same day, from Carlotta's school. Could someone please come and collect her straight away please? There had been another incident.

There was no one else. Izzy had no option but to climb into the Golf and set off for Queen Vicky's. Carlotta had been goaded by Ceridwen to such an extent that a colossal scrap had ensued. The two girls had wrestled on the dorm floor whilst the other occupants of the room had taken factions, yelling and cheering as they stood on beds and dressers to get a better look. After three photograph frames, two chair legs and Ceridwen's little finger had been broken, Carlotta had been dragged off by two butch members of the sixth form hockey team and despatched to the housemistress. Unrepentant and refusing to speak about what had started the fight, Carlotta was reminded of a long list of offences.

'Fighting, swearing, absconding, cheeking the staff, boozing, smoking, disobeying direct commands,' read the housemistress in an emotionless monotone to the head whilst Carlotta kept her eyes fixed on the school motto plaque hanging on the wall. Something about honour it read. She gave an audible snort of contempt which made the headmistress and housemistress exchange knowing glances. What did any of these silly bitches know about honour, Carlotta thought furiously. Not for anything would she repeat some of the terrible things Ceridwen had said not only about MK being a jailbird but also about Izzy, calling her a slag, a thick tart and a ho-bag and how shamed she was that her own father was boning the hired help, a scrubber in every sense of the word.

When Izzy arrived Carlotta was sitting outside the headmistress's office, packed bag by her feet, her eyes red raw. Izzy's interview was with the headmistress. A cool, well-groomed academic with a steely gaze and air of superiority, she immediately made Izzy feel it was she who was being judged, like she was back at school and being hauled in for a ticking off.

Carlotta was a bright girl, Izzy was told, but she simply didn't apply herself to anything. Every teacher, except the equestrian master, had something to complain about. All she thought about was horses and wasn't meeting the school's high academic expectations. Izzy, cruelly reminded of her own school day inadequacies and even more pertinently of her recent career failure in law, felt a curious sense of protection towards Carlotta.

'Carlotta is a very gifted horsewoman. Just this summer she won second place in the junior jumping at the Great Yorkshire Show against a field of sixteen-year-olds and in front of a BSJA selection committee. I'm sure when she's won team and individual golds at the Olympic Games and is World Champion this school will suddenly decide that it is proud to have her as one of their alumni.'

'No doubt. But we can't accommodate Carlotta's behaviour today on the slim promises of tomorrow's predicted accomplishments. Furthermore, her constant fighting and aggressive behaviour has made it impossible for us to continue with her education. Carlotta is very lucky the father of the injured girl has stated, quite firmly, that he doesn't intend to press charges.' Izzy daren't look at Carlotta. She was sorely tempted to tell this po-faced old bag exactly why Marc Jones wouldn't be pressing charges just to see the expression on her face — but didn't. 'I'm afraid we can no longer offer Carlotta a place here.'

'You're expelling me?' Carlotta asked, aghast. She thought she was in for another suspension, but expulsion?

'But she's just starting her GCSE year. You can't do this to her.'

'Despite what you might think, it gives me great pleasure to tell you, in the immortal words of Barack Obama, yes we can. Furthermore, looking at Carlotta's fourth year exam results, it's very doubtful we'd be able to consider her for A Level work. She simply isn't up to it academically. We'd be asking her to leave at the end of the summer term in any event. Carlotta has already packed what she can. The rest will be sent on in due course.'

Izzy stood up with all the dignity and composure her five-foot frame would allow.

'I can assure you it's this school's loss.'

'That's a risk we are prepared to take,' said the headmistress coolly. She looked Izzy up and down with undisguised disdain. 'If nothing else this incident has brought to light why Carlotta is so arrogant and overconfident.'

'Better that than negative and short-sighted,' Izzy said. Years later she couldn't be sure whether she was referring to Carlotta's headmistress or her own headmaster, but it had felt cathartic to say it at the time. Beside her Carlotta was muttering under her breath.

'Well, it's all fucking moot, isn't it, because next year I shall be too busy jetting round Europe with the British under 21s showjumping squad to worry about sitting stinky old A Levels. And I know which one sounds more exciting.'

'Sums it up, really,' Izzy snapped. She knew she shouldn't encourage Carlotta to be so rude to her elders but, as Carlotta had quite rightly pointed out, it was indeed all moot. 'Come on Carlotta, let's go home.'

On the car journey home they travelled in silence for several miles before Carlotta muttered a tearful thanks. It was enough to let Izzy know how much her blustering defence had meant to her.

Jared had beaten them back and was singularly unimpressed to learn Carlotta would be at home full time from now on.

'Telling MK about this latest transpiration is going to be big fun,' he said, his voice dripping with sarcasm. He eyeballed them both, his face set in much the same expression they'd encountered on the headmistress's face earlier that day. 'Get up to your room, Carlotta. You've caused enough trouble for one day.' He then turned to face Izzy. 'And as for you—'

'What the hell did I do?' Izzy asked indignantly.

'Mark my words, you've done plenty. If you spent a little more time doing your job rather than gallivanting to posh hotels with your boyfriend then mebbe shit like this wouldn't happen.'

---

A FEW NIGHTS later Izzy was back in Jared's arms. He crept into her room and under her bed sheet, deftly removing her pyjamas and muttering all the while about all the unimaginable things he was going to do to her. He was dominant, controlling, expert. Izzy had never known sex like it. It was so hot. The air was so still it seemed to slow them down. Outside the sky gave an ominous rumble, followed by a crack of lightning that shook the bed even more than they had.

'See the extent the universe has to go to in order to compete with us,' Jared whispered in her ear as he continued to drive into her. Izzy had never experienced anything like it.

A second bolt of lightning woke Izzy mid-orgasm. Still hopelessly turned on, sweating and alone, she sat upright in bed. The sheets were tangled round her ankles. A third bolt of lightning illuminated the room, casting shadows like a film noir. Disturbed and disappointed to have woken from such an exquisite dream, Izzy flopped back onto the pillows. Virtual sex it may have been but it had been exhausting. Divine, but exhausting.

Jesus! Would the real thing be just as extraordinary, she couldn't help but wonder. She'd never get back to sleep. It was already starting to get light. It must be almost half six, she guess-timated. There was no point anyway. Her alarm was due to go off any time soon.

Steptoe, for once asleep on the armchair due to the heat, sensed movement, woke, stretched, then begged at the door to go out. With a sigh Izzy climbed out of bed. Wearing only shorts and vest pyjamas and a pair of slippers in the shape of a monkey's head eating a banana, she accompanied Steptoe downstairs, remembering, for once, to disable the alarm at the top of the stairs before descending.

Izzy had no reason to be afraid as she stood at the open back door waiting for Steptoe to come back in. Nevertheless she found herself shivering for the first time in days. The storm had taken all the heat out of the air. It was the coolest it had been for weeks. A noise behind her made her jump.

'Everything all right?' It was Jared. Hair tousled and wearing only tracksuit bottoms which were barely skimming his pelvic bones, his expression was somewhere between concern at finding her roaming the house and annoyance at being disturbed. 'I heard noises.' His unexpected appearance reminded Izzy of her steamy dream and made her colour up. She was also aware how scantily she was dressed in her pyjama shorts that barely skimmed her backside and how much her innocent monkey-banana slippers, transformed by the half-light, now looked more like a very hairy man giving someone a blow job.

'Steptoe wanted to go out,' Izzy said, averting her eyes. When was the wretched creature going to come back into the house?

'That's not like him. Did something wake him?' Even in the middle of the night Jared was fully alert.

'Only me. I had a bad dream,' Izzy lied.

Jared stepped forward. 'Are you all right?' He extended an arm towards her. It was the first time in days he had spoken to her with any compassion.

Izzy shrank back. 'Don't touch me!'

Jared yanked his arm back almost before she got the words out. The tension between them was off the scale. An uncomfortable silence was broken by Steptoe running back into the house, in between the pair of them and straight back upstairs. I'm off back to bed, was the message he clearly conveyed.

'So long as you're all right,' Jared said, staring after Steptoe.

'Honestly, I'm fine,' said Izzy, staring at the back door as she locked it. They ascended the stairs in silence. Jared reset the alarm as Izzy returned to her room. Had it been hurt or contempt in Jared's eyes as she'd snapped at him to leave her alone? She hadn't meant to induce either but at the same time she knew letting Jared lay so much as one finger on her would be the biggest of mistakes. God only knew how she would react. Most likely she would molest him again, against his wishes, and make an already dire situation much worse. After that hot dream she wouldn't have trusted herself not to push him onto the black and white kitchen floor and attempt to seduce him. Maybe she'd better take a cold shower instead of going back to bed. She'd never sleep anyway.

In his own quarters Jared was giving himself a similar talking to. What the hell had he been thinking, reaching out to Izzy like that? He had already hurt her with his ham-fisted rejection. Any physical contact with her could only serve to open up that particular wound. Nor did he trust himself. She had looked so vulnerable standing in the doorway, wearing only those sexy shorts which suited her slender legs so well and what could only be described as pornographic slippers.

Fuck, fuck, fuck! He had torn himself away from her the other night so as not to cause an atmosphere between them, as he had when he had recklessly bedded Gemma two years ago. Fat lot of good his chivalrous deed had done. His unexplained rejection of Izzy had caused a far greater atmosphere and, worse still, hurt her into the bargain, and hurting her had been the last thing he had ever intended to do, at least not unless he was giving her equal proportions of pleasure at the same time.

Then there was MK to consider. He had warned Jared not to get too close to Izzy in case his gut feeling about her was wrong. Could she really be the mole? He found it so hard to believe she was capable of such duplicity and yet she had spun them all a right yarn when she had first arrived back in February. Jared gave a groan of frustration as he relived the moment Izzy had stepped off the TransPennine Express with her horrendous orange tan, streaked make-up and hair that had made her look like the lead singer of Whitesnake. He wanted to tell her he'd been attracted to her from the start, that he found the most inane things about her endearing, such as the way she sneezed, delicate atishoos, always in threes. And how she so clearly cared about Taryn and Carlotta too, refereeing between the pair of them and telling off any third party who dared to be mean to them, like that snooty bitch headmistress who had rung up and complained about how Izzy had offered no apology for Carlotta's actions but had instead supported her. If Izzy was indeed the mole and was merely playing the role of affectionate nanny then she deserved to win a bloody Oscar for the quality of her performance. Deep inside, despite how much he trusted and respected MK, he simply refused to believe she was an impostor. Which led to the question, why was he, Jared, letting Marc woo her so successfully?

The worst thing of all was he had a nasty, niggling feeling that through his indecisiveness and bitterness he had driven her straight into Marc Jones's arms, and, even more gallingly, also into his bed. When had things become so convoluted? Three staff members — he, Izzy and Gemma — were barely speaking to each other, instead communicating via the girls, which was a truly unforgivable crime. Then, although it was the last thing he wanted to admit, there was that fop Jones to consider. Where did he fit in to all this? Was he Izzy's boyfriend, or her fuck-buddy? And did he know what had happened between him and Izzy on the hammock? Questions, questions... and the most pertinent question of all, and the one Jared wanted to answer the least...

What the hell had Izzy *really* been doing roaming round the house in the middle of the night?

# PARCEL FARCE

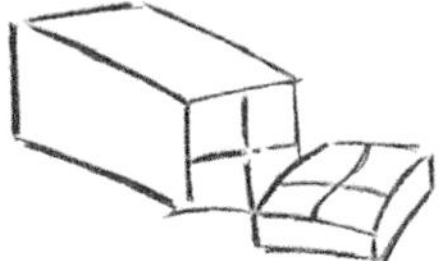

The backlash from Carlotta's expulsion was extraordinary. Both Mrs Firth and Jared yelled at Carlotta over her stubbornness over Alan, with whom she spent more time than ever, but to no avail. MK was apoplectic, Izzy garnered both from overheard conversations and Taryn's smug hints that Carlotta was in big bother. Plus, for the first time in their relationship there was an uncomfortable tension between Izzy and Marc. But then, Izzy considered, it was only understandable considering that her own charge had broken his daughter's finger. Normally not one to hold back, Carlotta was surprisingly button-lipped about the whole incident.

'She's such a bitch,' was her only comment about Ceridwen Jones. She wouldn't be drawn further and, when pressed for an explanation, barricaded herself in her bedroom with a two-litre bottle of Lilt, an eight pack of Tunnock's caramel wafers, all four *Twilight Saga* books plus all five movie adaptations on Blu-ray. She refused to come out.

Izzy tried to be cross too but, although Carlotta wouldn't say exactly what had caused her fit of temper, she'd assured Izzy she'd had good reason. Considering how intricately interwoven all their lives had become, Izzy had enough nouse to figure out that Ceridwen had instigated the fight with the sole purpose of driving a wedge between her and Marc.

A further consequence was that MK reiterated his demand that Carlotta be prevented from seeing Alan in the future. This was a buck which Jared promptly passed to Izzy. Unsure how Carlotta, already sensitive and volatile about her expulsion, would react to such a direct command, Izzy tried a different tack, instead offering support and a non-judgemental ear in an attempt to get on her good side. Carlotta's response was surprisingly affable. She had just started to watch *Twilight* on her fifty-inch HD TV when Izzy tapped on the door, two mugs of fresh coffee steaming temptingly in her hands.

'Can I come in?'

'Sure,' Carlotta replied. She didn't look away from the TV screen once. Instantly getting the message, Izzy didn't speak further but merely sat beside Carlotta on the bed. They watched the remainder of the film in silence.

'It's not really like that, is it? Love?' Carlotta asked as the end credits rolled. Izzy nearly fell off the bed in surprise, not only because Carlotta was instigating a conversation but also due to the intimate nature of her query. 'I mean, it must be rare to meet the man you want to spend the rest of your life with when you're so young. How do you know if it's the real thing?'

'The real thing,' Izzy repeated, with a bitter smile. 'I don't even want to remember how many times I've thought it was 'the real thing', only to have been mistaken in the very worst possible way.'

'How do you know when a guy is telling the truth or if he's feeding you a line?'

Izzy gave a hollow laugh.

'If I could answer that question I would be exceedingly rich. When I was at university—'

'You were at university?' Carlotta asked, unflatteringly surprised. 'I didn't think you were bright enough.'

'Thanks,' Izzy said, drily. 'As I was saying, when I was at uni this guy I really liked told me the song *Head Over Feet* by Alanis Morissette was exactly how he felt about me.'

'Did you believe him?'

'Course I did, like a fool. But he didn't really feel that way. I don't even think he meant it as a line. He probably thought it was a cool, romantic thing to say and never imagined I'd actually take his words at face value. It's a good example of how people choose to misunderstand each other. Anyway, I'm not sure I'm the best person to give you advice on relationships and I certainly can't guarantee its quality as my own track record isn't anything to boast about.'

'Pfft! I don't know about that. You seem to have men swarming round you like flies.'

Izzy considered this point, ruefully acknowledging that attracting the attention of potential boyfriends hadn't ever been an issue. It was hanging on to the bleeders that was the problem.

'How much does being heartbroken hurt?' Carlotta carried on.

'Ha! Why not ask an easier question, like explaining quantum physics or chaos theory?'

'I'm being serious!' Carlotta said.

'So am I!' replied Izzy, with feeling.

'But you were heartbroken when you first came to live with us. What's it like?'

'Is this about Alan?' Izzy asked, her eyes narrowed with suspicion.

'Might be.'

'Okay. Well, being heartbroken is one of the worst things in the world. It's painful, and cruel, and it hurts all the time. There's no reprieve. It invades your thoughts and your dreams and it finds ways to use your own mind against you, turning happy memories sad. Whilst your heart is broken you can find no peace. It's something you wear, like a new skin, and until you can shed it, you carry it around with you everywhere you go.'

'Is it like someone dying?' Carlotta asked. Izzy thought about this carefully, aware that Carlotta had known grief already in her short life.

'At its most basic core, perhaps, but they are quite different. Both is a grieving process but whereas with death one might have to deal with the cruelty of fate or come to terms with a horrific accident or a terrible illness, with a broken relationship you have to accept that the person you love doesn't love you in return. You have to deal with rejection, which usually results in over-analysis of what you could have done differently to prevent the break up. There may be self-blame. There may also be hope. When I first arrived here I prayed for a phone call or an email from Scott. Death is devoid of all hope. That the person you love isn't coming back is a certainty.'

'I remember when Mama died,' Carlotta said. 'After the funeral Papa locked himself away for a week, then threw himself into his work. He lived in hotels in London for weeks. We barely saw him. Even when he was home he couldn't bear to look at Taryn, and didn't spend much time with me either. Firthie looked after us. She said we shouldn't blame him and he just needed distance to sort himself out. After a couple of months he returned to normal. He made us all swear to secrecy that Taryn should never find out.' Carlotta glared at Izzy, as though holding her responsible for her revelations. 'You mustn't think he was ever a bad father.'

'I don't,' Izzy said. 'People deal with their grief in many different ways. Perhaps he had to distance himself in order to be able to cope. Perhaps allowing you to see the extent of his grief would have been more distressing for you and Taryn than his absence. I imagine he was trying to protect you, trying to keep things normal for you.'

'It was so awful. We were all so excited about the new baby. And then everything was different.' Izzy found herself suppressing the desire to cry. Carlotta had never confided in Izzy before and had never spoken so frankly about her mother. Although, Izzy couldn't help but wonder what had brought on such a wave of introspection.

'Do you have suspicions that Alan might want to break up with you?'

'No,' Carlotta scoffed, her tone expressing the impossibility of such an occurrence. She then paused, as if uncertain whether she should continue. 'But I might want to break up with him.'

Izzy took a few moments to digest this. Carlotta dumping Alan of her own free will would provide a simple and satisfactory solution to her own remit. It was imperative that she appeared to be supportive of Carlotta's decision whilst at the same time resist the temptation to be pushy. Tricky.

'You know, that might not be such a bad thing,' she said finally, hoping for lightness.

Carlotta looked daggers at her.

'Why does everyone have such a problem with Alan? Papa, Jared, Firthie—'

'You mustn't be too harsh on your father, and Jared and Firthie. They want what's best for you, or at least what they think is best for you.'

'How can they know what's best for me? What about what I want?'

'I can kind of understand where they're coming from—' Izzy said. Carlotta jerked her head. '—In that they want someone amazing for you. They want someone who is your equal in every way, someone who can match up to you.'

'But they don't know Alan. They've never bothered to get to know him. How do they know he isn't amazing? '

'Because everyone is comparing him to you. They see you — beautiful, clever, talented — and they think you should be with someone equally as beautiful, clever and talented. It's not a bad thing they're interfering, Carlotta. It's not that they want these things for themselves. They want these things for you. They want someone special, for you. Someone who can match up to you. Now, just imagine how much they must think of you to want all those things.' Carlotta looked marginally appeased by such flattery.

'That does make sense, I suppose. But I'm still sick and tired of being told I'm too young to have feelings. Or to be in love.'

'Who said that?'

'Everyone! My father, my teachers, Jared, Firthie. They say it's puppy love and I'll grow out of it. That I'm not old enough to know what real love is.'

'Well, they're all fools. I know that someone your age can love. Look at childhood sweethearts. They know their love is real otherwise why would they stay together and eventually marry and have families of their own. The thing is, the problem with being able to be loved is that you're also able to be heartbroken. And if anyone says that someone your age can't be heartbroken then they're a fool all over again. In fact, I think heartbreak could be worse for someone your age. Especially the first time. As people get older they learn. They learn how to deal with things, they can see patterns and signs. They learn that hurt goes away with time. It's like a natural process, like a tan fading. Some take longer than others, granted, but the formula is always the same.'

'Someone's going to end up heartbroken, aren't they, in any relationship?'

'Most times, yes. On rare occasions a couple may both decide separating is for the best. Usually one person wants to stay together, and the other—'

'Doesn't,' Carlotta concluded. 'It always ends in bitterness and resentment as well, doesn't it? I mean, exes don't normally get on afterwards. Someone always gets hurt.'

'Usually, not always,' Izzy said lightly.

'But you don't want to see your ex anymore.'

Izzy thought about this carefully. She had no desire to see Scott, that was quite true, but not because she felt any resentment that he no longer wanted her. It had been months since thinking about Scott had caused her unhappiness and she now felt nothing more than relief that he was no longer a part of her life. The passage of time had given Izzy not only the gift of perspective but had also eradicated the haze of false affection she'd believed she'd felt for Scott. With love removed, she was now able to see him for the cruel, narcissistic player he was. 'No, he's part of my past now.'

'Even if a couple stays together forever, one of them has to die before the other. Makes me wonder if it's even worth bothering with relationships at all.'

'You mustn't think like that. A good relationship can be the most wonderful thing of all.' Izzy's thoughts drifted to Caro and Jonty. 'Look at how happy your parents were. I know your father thinks it was worth bothering. Despite all the heartache and sorrow he still got you and Taryn. That can only be a good thing, can't it?'

'I'm so confused,' Carlotta said.

'I wouldn't worry. That just means you're normal,' Izzy said.

'Huh! Thanks.'

---

After the last September storm there had been a distinct change in the air. The wheel of the year had turned once more. Summer had eased into autumn, not with howling winds and tree-stripping storms, but with a gentle, inevitable resolve. The landscape had a washed out look courtesy of low mists and colder air. The sun, lower in the sky, retired each evening as though weary after the exertion of summer, leaving behind stunning skies of amber and pewter. Izzy was reminded of childhood autumns, walking to school with her big sister, kicking the leaves that had congregated on the roadside. Izzy invariably didn't see the high kerb hidden beneath the leaves and stubbed her toe. This never happened to her sister. She compared herself and her perfect sister to Carlotta and Taryn, and hoped Taryn had ceased to feel inferior but instead accepted she was equally as beautiful and talented as Carlotta, albeit a little less ostentatiously.

Sunrise was now around six thirty in the morning. With a sinking heart Izzy realised she would soon be getting up in the dark. The horses were now turned out in their rugs. Mornings were much colder. It surely wouldn't be long before the first frost of the year. In the garden, Jared brought in the fuchsias and geraniums, wrapping their pots in bubble wrap before storing them in the greenhouse. They wouldn't come back out until after Easter next year. He covered the barbecue and the garden furniture with their tarpaulins and pruned the roses and clematises. Leaves were starting to fall. Only a few fruits remained on the trees in the orchard. On the outbuildings the Boston ivy had turned from green to red and would eventually drop, leaving the brickwork beneath exposed to the coming winter elements. Only the ivy, firs and hollies retained their vibrant green but even they seemed blanched by the dropping temperatures.

Mrs Firth was equally busy inside the house. Summer bedlinen was replaced by high togged duvets and wonderfully comforting, brightly coloured, luxurious blankets that didn't scratch the skin. Great fabric snakes were placed on each windowsill in order to soak up any early morning condensation. Downstairs fireplaces were raked out each morning and stacked with kindling and the previous day's newspapers before being lit just after breakfast. The last of the produce from the garden was prepared and frozen, ready to be transformed into delicious pies and casseroles over the winter months. Izzy spent most of her free time in the kitchen with Mrs Firth, where she could huddle up next to the Aga and where tea and cakes were drip-fed throughout the day.

Some things hadn't altered, however. The horses still had to be mucked out and exercised, tack still had to be cleaned and dogs still had to be walked. Izzy dug out her fingerless gloves and fleece jacket and muttered constantly as she cleaned out the rabbit hutches. Hacks were less frequent than in the summer months but riding lessons continued as normal, whatever the weather. If riding in an incessant drizzle wasn't bad enough, Izzy found she had another reason to not look forward to her lessons these days. Whereas Izzy's relationship with Carlotta had reached a grudging truce, her friendship with Gemma had continued to deteriorate. Gemma never missed the chance to wind Izzy up and riding lessons continued to be her most profitable source of opportunity. By default Izzy became a much better rider as Gemma bombarded her with commands to perform ever more difficult manoeuvres, mercilessly barking instructions at her from her post in the centre of the school. If Izzy fell off, she was icily unsympathetic.

The latest craze in equestrian equipment was an inflatable body protector. Worn like a tabard, it was attached by a lanyard to the saddle, and which puffed up like a blow up doll within nought-point-one of a second of the rider separating from the horse. Always conscious of his daughters' safety, MK had immediately despatched Jared to Pets & Ponies to buy one each for Carlotta and Taryn. Considering Izzy's propensity for being repatriated to the manége floor, Jared also bought one for her. Alas, Izzy would forget she was wearing it and promptly inflated herself every time she dismounted.

'You always said you wanted a bigger chest,' Gemma said bitchily. She was careful never to be snide in Jared's presence, knowing he wouldn't tolerate infighting amongst the minions.

Not that Izzy could rely on Jared to defend her from Gemma anyway. Her rift with him hadn't eased either. He wasn't ignoring Izzy, but nor did he go out of his way to be in her company. He'd never been amused by what he referred to as her inanities, and inflating the body protector needlessly certainly qualified as such an example, in his opinion.

'That's another thirty quid to reset it. That's what it costs every time you decide to inflate it by accident, you know? I know MK is minted but he's not a bloody alchemist,' he said, his tone frostier than a January morning in a cold snap. And Izzy would slink away, belittled and hurt.

She resorted to watching him clandestinely as she tried to figure out both his thoughts and her own feelings. The worst of it was she still found him so unbearably attractive. Why didn't she feel the same way about Marc, whose girlfriend she was supposed to be? Carlotta wasn't the only one confused about relationships!

One morning, from her post at the kitchen table, Izzy watched Jared lugging boxes of groceries from the Sainsbury's delivery van on the driveway into the utility for Mrs Firth to unpack. She fixated on his muscles as he bent down, lifted and stretched, mesmerised by the way his biceps flexed and relaxed. He was so different from Marc, she found herself thinking. Marc was smooth and refined. Jared was neither of these things. He was rough around the edges. Tough too. He bleedin' well must be not to wear a jacket or even a sweater on what was plainly the coldest day in months. But he was also honest, and trustworthy and made her feel safe. She finally knew what her mother meant when she'd said she thought Sean Connery was 'all man'.

Mrs Firth was bustling around her. Did she want another

cup of tea? A sandwich? A cherry Bakewell? Izzy refused all offers but whilst doing so realised she knew absolutely nothing about Mrs Firth except she'd lived at The Paddocks since it'd been built and she had a sister in Leeds. Evidently she had once been married but where was Mr Firth?

'Firthie, what did you do before you came to work here?' Izzy asked. Mrs Firth seemed surprised but, at the same time, pleased to be asked.

'Not much really. I've lived all my life in this area. My father worked on the estate of what was referred to back then as the Big House and so we all lived in a cottage in the grounds. We were quite a small family, just four children. Two older brothers, my sister, then me. When I was a teenager the Big House was converted into a hotel. It's that posh one on the main road over the other side of Greater Ousebury that's popular for weddings and suchlike. Me dad stayed on as a handyman and got me a job as a chambermaid, but it weren't fer me, working in the hotel. Too impersonal. But, I can't complain as it was there that I met my Terry.'

'Your husband?' Izzy asked, engrossed.

'Aye, God rest his soul. He was a gardener just like our Jared. I've allus found gardeners to be decent folk, honest, they respect the earth and value life and growth. Like that Alan Titchmarsh on the telly. I like him. He always seems nice.'

'What happened?'

'We married, in this village's church would you know, lived in a little terrace in Greater Ousebury, had a son, and then Terry was taken ill with pneumonia. We didn't have any money for medicine and insurances and healthcare plans were unheard of in those days. Terry should have stayed at home and got himself better but we just couldn't afford for him to be ill and so he continued to work the fields. It was the death of him. I was barely out of my twenties when I was widowed. My father, he was well-respected in the community, fixed me up with a job as a cook at The Rookery, you know, where the Newtons now live. Me and our Terry — he's called Terry too — lived there until he was grown up. He was allus a bright lad, our Terry. He did well in school, went to university where he met the girl he married. She's a nice girl, a southerner too, but she takes life too seriously, like you used to—' Izzy was gobsmacked. She'd never considered herself to be the type who took anything seriously. '—And they decided to move down under for the good life. They live there with my two granddaughters.'

'My sister lives there too,' Izzy said, with a wry smile. 'She tells me it's quite marvellous. We never see her anymore. She used to come home twice a year, once in the summer and at Christmas, but since she's had kids she expects us to go over there. My mum and dad have been over a few times but I've never been able to afford it.'

'Aye, that sounds familiar,' Mrs Firth said. Izzy could detect the agony in her voice and felt terribly sorry for her. She'd been brassic because she'd pissed her salary away up the West End and in the fashion shops on Oxford Street; Mrs Firth would have worked hard all her life. 'I stayed at The Rookery well into the '80s. Then MK had this place built. I remember the workmen coming into the village, bringing truck after truck after truck. Very unpopular he was, at first but folk soon warmed to him. The people I worked for recommended me to MK as housekeeper and I've been here ever since. At first it was just the two of them, then Carlotta was born. She's so like her mother, you know. She was a lovely lady, was Marisa, very kind and generous but, my word, she was a fiery sort. You wouldn't want to cross her. Carlotta's the image of her, and like her in temperament too.'

'Do you have any regrets?' Izzy asked, completely fascinated by Mrs Firth's tale.

'None that I could do anything about,' Mrs Firth replied. 'I'd have liked to have had my husband at my side as the years went on. I'd have liked my boy to have lived near to me so I could see my grandchildren for Christmases and birthdays and school concerts, but it just weren't ter be. But I have to count me blessings. I've allus been very happy here, and Carlotta and Taryn might as well be blood family. Of course I have regrets, who doesn't? My grandmother always said to me that it's better to regret something you've done than something you haven't. It's a solid piece of advice that I'd pass on to anyone.'

Cringing as she recalled how she had cracked on to Jared, Izzy considered Mrs Firth's words and felt a little better. At least she'd found out where she stood. That had to be the one and only upside to the whole incident.

Later that day Izzy went to pick up Taryn who was outraged to learn that whilst she had been cooped up in school Carlotta had been out on a hack with Gemma. She moaned all the way back that Carlotta was having a much more fun time being at home all day. Why couldn't she? It just wasn't fair! As soon as Izzy halted the Golf in the driveway Taryn launched herself out of the car, slammed the door shut and stropped off to groom Jester, her little face set in a mask of furious resentment. Worn out, Izzy retreated back to the kitchen where she sat at the table reading *Wuthering Heights,* grumpily finding unfavourable similarities between Marc and the wishy-washy Edgar Linton, and eating peanut butter out of the jar with a spoon, which was forbidden. She was here when Jared received a phonecall from MK's solicitor.

'Shit!' Jared said as he hung up the cordless.

'What is it?' Izzy said, looking up and reading the look of horror on his face as easily as she'd been reading her book. Mrs Firth also looked up from the pot she was watching.

'It's not good. The victim's family have made the decision to turn off the life support. Prosecution are pushing to upgrade MK's charge to murder.'

The three of them exchanged looks of unmitigated horror. Izzy digested this information slowly.

'Are you going to tell the girls?' she asked finally. Jared shook his head.

'No. Not until I've spoken to MK.' He looked sternly first at Izzy and then at Mrs Firth. 'This goes no further.' Both women nodded.

Later that evening Izzy received a phonecall of her own from her mother. Surely it couldn't be more bad news, was Izzy's first thought as she took the receiver from Jared. Her mother hadn't rung her once since she had been at The Paddocks. Even now, deeply suspicious of anything technological, she'd rung on the landline. Puce with embarrassment, Izzy slid out the kitchen, the phone flush to her ear.

It wasn't bad news. Her mother was having a small party for her fifty-fifth birthday in the first weekend of October, Izzy was told. Because she'd played hookey the previous weekend, Izzy felt she couldn't leave The Paddocks again so soon and felt obliged to decline the invitation. It wasn't just that she'd been spending a lot of time with Marc. There was also Carlotta being at home to consider. And the news about MK... She really couldn't take any leave right now, not even for her mother's birthday. She knew her mother was disappointed; now she had two daughters she never saw. Instead Izzy set about finding a fabulous gift and the following morning called upon Pippa for some expert advice.

Izzy was pleased with the selection of jams and preserves she'd chosen. Pippa's advice had been invaluable in both her knowledge of her own produce and in how to package them up safely. Izzy always found herself in awe of the diminutive redhead who owned and ran Philippa's Kitchen. Despite her fractional height and friendliness she was a truly formidable woman. Not even the fearless Carlotta dared cheek Pippa.

Now Izzy carefully placed each little jar into a cardboard

box lined with bubble wrap and coloured tissue paper. Lime and coriander marmalade, strawberry and champagne jam, lemon cheese (whatever *that* was!), spicy chilli pepper chutney, North Yorkshire mustard; each one had been lovingly labelled and was gloriously bucolic. Izzy was in no doubt her mother would just love them.

As she was sealing up the box Gemma rushed into the kitchen. In her hand she also held a small package, not quite sealed

'Have you seen the Sellotape... oh!' she asked, and then stopped abruptly as she saw the empty reel on the kitchen table. Overcome with discomfort in view of the deterioration of their friendship, Izzy was once more besieged by guilt. It somehow felt as though the used-up Sellotape metaphorically represented Jared.

'I'm afraid that's the last of it. Taryn used the rest on some harvest festival project she's been assigned at school. I'm going to get some more from the Post Office and finish my packaging there.' Noting Gemma's crestfallen expression Izzy immediately offered to take her parcel too. Perhaps if she were doubly helpful it might go some way to mitigate the damage she had caused, even if only slightly.

'It's very important,' Gemma said, her voice slightly gruff.

Izzy rolled her eyes knowingly as she carefully wrote her parents address on a sticky label.

'Tell me about it! Is yours a birthday gift too?' At least Gemma hadn't thrown her offer back in her face, she thought. That had to be encouraging, surely?

'Yes,' Gemma croaked. 'Something like. I'd take it myself but the farrier is due any minute to take a look at the horses' shoes. It really has to go today.'

'Don't worry. I'm setting off just as soon as I finish up here. One thing I daren't do is miss my mother's birthday so this definitely has to go before the last post tonight. Write the address on one of those labels and I'll make sure it goes today.' She pushed a use-again label across the table towards Gemma. She thought she was doing a good job of being reassuring but Gemma didn't look wholly convinced. Her pen hovered over the address label.

'I don't know, Iz. Mebbe I'd better just take it myself. It's not that I don't trust you—' This statement was a clear indication to the contrary. 'It just has to go today.'

Izzy was just about to tell Gemma to suit herself when fate chose to intervene. The gate buzzer sounded.

'Oh *sod*, the farrier's here,' Gemma said, clearly agitated. She dithered for a moment then quickly wrote the address on the packing label. She handed both the label and the parcel to Izzy. 'Please, Izzy, make sure you tape it up properly and make sure it goes today. You can't funk this one up. It's—'

'I know, I know, it's very important. Honestly, Gem, I can be trusted to post a couple of packages.' Izzy was slightly irked. She gathered both parcels and both packing slips in a carrier, and headed down to the Post Office.

In the Post Office she bought a couple of reels of Sellotape and then spent a great deal of time making sure Gemma's precious parcel was secured on all edges. She had placed each label on its respective parcel and was just about to stick them on when the sub-postmistress dropped a box of greetings cards in the aisle and made her jump. Sellophaned packs of Christmas cards slid in every direction, some were stopped by the hessian doormat, others decided to hide under the dairy chiller and stoutly refused to come out no matter how vigorously the sub-postmistress prodded them with a rolled up *Radio Times*. Izzy rushed to help her pick them up and was soon distracted by a die cut card of fat robins perched on top of a row of spades — Jared would like that one —and other charmingly countrified snow scenes.

'Oh, how sweet!' she exclaimed, holding up a card depicting two overweight Shetlands ruthlessly decimating a rather scantily filled hay net. 'That one looks just like Mini

Cheddar. I must get these for Taryn to send out to her friends.' Izzy then stopped short. Would she still be at The Paddocks at Christmastime?

The postman arrived to collect the last post. Izzy hurriedly took her two parcels to the counter. All the while she was distracted by the Christmas cards. Then she had a brainwave.

'Can I send them recorded?' The sub-postmistress looked pained and insisted on sticking the labels on her behalf. Behind her the postman tapped his foot impatiently.

'I need a return address,' the sub-postmistress said. Izzy panicked. She pictured the front facia of Gemma's scruffy house but couldn't remember if it was number 16 or 18 and daren't risk a guess. To be on the safe side she put herself at The Paddocks on both.

Back at the house she handed Gemma her tracking slip.

Gemma looked relieved.

'So, it's gone?'

'Yep. I watched the postman carry it out to his van with my own eyes. 'I even sent it recorded, so it's doubly safe. I couldn't remember your house number so I put this address on.'

'Oh!' said Gemma. Izzy noticed she looked pale and drawn.

'I did do the right thing, didn't I?' Izzy asked, feeling insecure. Had she cocked up again?

'What? Oh, yeah, sure. I'm just feeling a bit under the weather. I think I've got a cold coming. Let me know if the parcel comes back.'

---

IZZY HADN'T SEEN Marc since Carlotta's fight with Ceridwen and her consequent expulsion, but knew that matters weren't going to resolve themselves. Jared had been a deliberate pain in the arse, keeping her busy with all manner of unspeakable chores to gobble up her free time. Finally Izzy had begged Mrs Firth to babysit so she could finally meet up with Marc in The Half Moon. It was an exercise in damage limitation to try and improve relations between them. It didn't start well. Marc had been expecting to have dinner but Izzy had already eaten at teatime with the girls. Thus she had to sit and watch as Marc tucked into a lonely plate of wild mushroom risotto.

'I'm sure I could manage a dessert,' Izzy offered bravely, despite having eaten half a tonnage of rice pudding only an hour earlier. She forced key lime pie down into her already groaning stomach. Matters weren't eased by Marc insisting on them trying the new range of rosés he had supplied to Col the Landlord. All of which was fine except because Marc was driving he only took the most perfunctory of sips from any bottle he bought before pushing the remainder in Izzy's direction. Already steeped with guilt over Ceridwen and her two-timing thoughts about Jared, Izzy didn't feel in a position to refuse his generosity, especially when that generosity was fifteen quid a bottle. The worst of it was rosé wine did tend to give Izzy a killer headache the following morning. Nevertheless, she swigged it down.

With three open bottles lined up in front of her on the table, Izzy was part horrified, part relieved to see Jared walk into the pub. He had developed a nasty habit of turning up uninvited whenever she was on a date with Marc so she wasn't entirely surprised to see him. Previously this had rankled but on this occasion she was glad of the distraction he presented. Marc was subjecting her to a detailed report on his recent trip to France, heaping on how marvellous it had been which Izzy was quite sure was a ploy to promote the lifestyle he could offer her. She also felt he was having a subtle dig at her for not accompanying him.

Jared was wearing his leather jacket and clean jeans. He walked straight up to the bar and ordered a pint of Black

Sheep. He didn't give the room so much as a cursory scan, which told Izzy that he knew exactly where she was sitting.

I must not fancy Jared, I must not fancy Jared, she chanted to herself.

Marc looked extremely put out. 'Christ, can't we go anywhere without your minder?'

'I'll have to say hello,' Izzy said.

'Why?' It was a valid question.

'He is my boss,' Izzy said, providing an equally valid answer.

'He doesn't have to be. You could always come and live with me,' Marc said, sliding his hand across the table. Izzy gave a nervous giggle. Yep, she'd been right on the money. 'What's so funny? Ceri has to get used to the fact sooner or later, plus she's at school for most of the year. You could hand your notice in at The Paddocks and be free to do whatever you wanted.'

Which should have been an irresistible offer, Izzy acknowledged ruefully, except that what she wanted to do was stay at The Paddocks with Jared and the girls. Christ, how did she manage to get herself into these messes?

The decision was taken out of both their hands because Jared walked right up to their table once he'd been served. Good mannered even in the face of his deep resentment, Marc waved his hand towards a vacant chair.

'Ta,' Jared said, licking froth off his upper lip as he plonked himself down. He looked both of them in the eye. 'I hope I'm not disturbing you both.'

'We were just talking about work,' Izzy said, in all honesty.

Jared raised his glass to her.

'Not surprised you're having a drink after the news we had today,' he said, alluding to the fact there'd been even more bad news from MK's solicitor. As he spoke he flicked his eyes at Marc, communicating that he and Izzy had conversations that Marc wasn't privy to. He then surveyed the row of bottles. 'Mind you, looks like you intend to have more than 'a' drink.'

'What happened today?' Marc asked quickly, refilling Izzy's glass. It was a counter act of possession.

Jared gave Izzy an appraising look. So you didn't tell him, it said. I'm impressed.

'Try this rosé, Jared. It's from the Loire Valley, very nettley,' Izzy recited, grabbing Col the Landlord as he passed by on a round of glass collecting and asking him for a third glass. It was a neat change of subject but alas played right into Marc's hands.

'Yes, Jared, you must tell me what you think of its bouquet,' he said, knowing full well that Jared had neither the experience nor the inclination to provide such an assessment. He poured Jared a glassful whilst at the same time sloshing a small measure into his own oversized wine glass, which he carried round with him wherever he went and whipped out of his blazer pocket like a magic trick, and swirling it round. Marc had a tendency to be pompous when it came to wine. He stuck his nose deep into the glass and inhaled like a bloodhound.

'I'm getting lettuce leaves, sweet and sour chicken and cola cubes,' he declared to the table. Beside her, Izzy heard Jared snort. She knew he liked to crack a bottle of beer on an evening as his first choice of alcoholic beverage but did enjoy a bottle of wine on occasion.

'I like wine, I can enjoy a bottle but I can't tell if it has aromas of beefy Pot Noodle, Jester's sweaty numnah or the aftertaste of Steptoe's farts,' he said disparagingly, setting his glass down. Izzy, who didn't have a nose for wine either, shot him a grateful look and took another large slug of her very expensive Shiraz-Sangiovese. It was going to be a very long night, she suspected, with each man indulging in an evident battle of territorial one-upmanship. If Jared began talking about something that had happened at The Paddocks, Marc would start reminiscing about one of their dates, and vice versa, until Izzy was just about ready to scream. It was a battle that was eventually won by Marc. As the bell rang for last orders he insisted on driving Izzy all of the three hundred yards back to The Paddocks' front gate where he proceeded to kiss her very publicly and in full view of Jared as he stomped past.

'Think very carefully about what I said,' were Marc's final words of the evening. 'You don't want to see out your best years here in Nether Ousebury.'

Izzy could do nothing more than nod mutely before scuttling inside. A heavy dinner, two puddings and a mixture of three half bottles of wine were sloshing around inside her uneasily. The contents of her head weren't making her feel any better either. No one was more aware than she that she had two men in her life and somehow she was managing to piss off both of them.

After a cursory check that Carlotta and Taryn were both asleep she crashed onto her bed without brushing her teeth or removing her make-up. As she closed her eyes the room spun.

The following day didn't start well at all. She woke feeling rough, nauseous and extremely unaccommodating. Everything irritated her and she wasn't overly concerned about being agreeable. The first thing to aggravate her had been her ever-lengthening fringe. Having driven her mad for days, she grimly took a pair of toenail scissors and cut it in her bathroom mirror. Alas, she accidentally cut her eyelashes at the same time and could have measured their straightness with a spirit level. They looked even more ridiculous once she had applied mascara.

'If that's the 'London look' Kate Moss is always banging on about, I'm not impressed,' said Jared at breakfast. She noted he looked annoyingly fresh and fit with not so much as a hint of a hangover.

After this she had to endure a torturous riding lesson with Jared, who offered no sympathy whatsoever that she was still hungover from her bender of the previous night or that there was a relentless downpour of stinging horizontal rain.

'Your problem is you don't concentrate on the job in hand,' he bawled as Izzy struggled desperately to get Jet on the bit. His hooves schlooping with every stride, Jet was no more in the mood for the intricacies of dressage than Izzy was, and hardened his jaw in defiance. Her only consolation was that Taryn and even Carlotta were also struggling with the elements although, Izzy noted sourly, they weren't being bollocked for it. That particular privilege was hers alone, it seemed. 'You're not even trying. For God's sake, woman, concentrate! What are you thinking about at this very moment? Is it your chinless boyfriend?' Jared continued to holler at her.

'I'm thinking about how I would prefer to be back in London where I wouldn't be forced to do *this!*' Izzy yelled back, losing her rag. Her head was pounding and the unending up-down-up-down of Jet's bouncy trot wasn't helping her stomach to settle.

'Flattering though that is, you really should be concentrating on the horse. Even in halt you're still riding and need to be thinking about what your pony is doing. Anything could happen, a pheasant could fly out of the hedgerow or a rabbit startle the horse and you need to be prepared.'

To prove a point Jared cracked the schooling whip millimetres behind Jet's hind legs. Startled, the pony shot forward, living up to his name with all four hooves off the ground like vertical launch. Izzy found herself eating sawdust, puffed up like the Michelin Man once more.

'You rotten fucker!' she shrieked, pounding the ground with her fists. She was sitting in a gritty puddle of water whilst Jared, Carlotta and even Taryn guffawed. To add to her humiliation Jet, having deposited her on the ground one time too many, turned round and bared his teeth as though in some sarcastic grin of amusement. Izzy responded with a tirade of extremely choice language that left Taryn and even Carlotta with their mouths agape. 'Can't you be serious about anything?' were Izzy's concluding words.

Jared dragged her to her feet and shook her so viciously that her inflated chest bounced off his own torso in a most undignified fashion.

'Of course I can be serious, when I need to be, and this isn't one of those times. I was pretty serious when I watched my comrades being shot to shit in the field in Afghanistan and when I was knocked unconscious and woke up in a hospital tent with my arm chock full of shrapnel. I was serious when my wife left me whilst I was recovering in hospital. I was serious when I buried my mother last year. Don't be such a clever bitch. You're not hurt except for your pride. You sitting in a pool of mud is pretty funny and you'd think so too if you could lose that poker from up your arse and instead find a sense of humour. There's no choice but to be serious sometimes. Believe me, there's nothing funny about war. Therefore, when I've a choice between being serious or not, I choose not. Life's too short. Now get up, and don't use language like that again in front of the girls. They're enough of a handful as it is and I don't fancy explaining to MK why his own daughters are using words like that.' He paused only to glance up at the ever-thickening rain. His mouth was a solid, straight line of discontent. 'This rain is getting worse. The lesson is over. Get these ponies inside and attend to their needs.'

Seething, Izzy dragged Jet into the barn, slung a red, black and gold Newmarket rug over his barely wisped withers and proceeded to muck him out in a wild fury, jabbing a two-pronged pitchfork into the fresh straw with venom. Alas, she miscalculated and in her rage stabbed it straight through her wellington boot and into her foot. Her yowl of pain brought everyone running to see what had happened. They all converged on Jet's stall where Izzy stood, propped up against the partition with the hand that wasn't still holding the secured pitchfork, her breath ragged and her eyes protruding. Taryn screamed, then hyperventilated.

Experienced with injuries, Jared wasted no time. He yanked the pitchfork back out and eased the punctured welly off whilst Izzy screamed with pain. Carlotta, who up until then had unsympathetically howled with laughter, paled and quietened as blood started to seep through Izzy's sock. Izzy, watching her foot turn red, felt her face turn white at the same speed, fainted, came to, then threw up all over the fresh straw.

Having entrusted Carlotta with the responsibility of bedding down the ponies and instructed Taryn to inform Mrs Firth of what had happened, Jared carried a sobbing Izzy to the Range Rover and bundled her in to the back seat. He covered her with a horse fleece before driving her to the nearest minor injuries hospital. Not caring two figs that he had abandoned the car in a tow-zone or about the appalled faces of the duty nurses as he marched up to them and presented Izzy to them still rolled up in the fleece like a very large, hairy fajita.

Jared stayed with her as she was stitched up. Despite the potential for piss-taking he desisted. He appeared to have lost all desire to wind her up and no longer seemed angry with her, just weary.

'You really are hopeless,' he told her bleakly as the duty doctor finished applying the dressing. Unable to disagree, Izzy could do nothing more than gaze sadly at him.

Izzy was surprised to find herself disappointed that she was banned from horse riding for several weeks. By some miracle she had completely bypassed her metatarsus, the doctor said, and would only have to wait for the flesh to heal, but in the meantime any strenuous activities were out of the question as this could rent the wound open. There might be some discomfort as the scar tissue healed, she was told, but she would be able to drive so long as she was careful. It was a credit to Jared's self-control that he didn't say something at this point. Instead he liaised with the doctor on her behalf with regards to her prescribed medication and what aftercare the local surgery could provide with regards to fresh dressings and such like. Whilst he did so Izzy sat on the bed, hands in her lap, childlike and chastised. She felt like a complete failure.

They travelled back to The Paddocks in silence. Jared listened to the radio, his hands drumming the steering wheel along with the bassline of the music, whilst Izzy gazed out of the passenger window at the countryside flashing past.

Just like my life, she thought gloomily.

Next morning she was left to lie in and didn't wake up until gone ten o'clock. She languished in bed for a further half hour, deliberating over her relationship with Marc. It had only been when she had curled up in bed the previous night that she realised she didn't want to tell him about her latest accident as he would only insist on fussing over her and she couldn't bear the thought of that. It was no use. She would have to end it before he became more attached to her than he already was.

She eventually materialised in the kitchen, not showered and in crumpled clothes, to find her parcel had been returned to sender. Mrs Firth had opened it and had lined up each of the little jars like a miniature firing squad in front of a loaf of bread and the butter dish.

'I opened it by mistake. I'm waiting for a delivery of oven cleaners from Lakeland.' She was very apologetic. 'I didn't read the address until afterwards. I'm so sorry.'

'Oh, that's my mum's present,' said Izzy, crestfallen. She

groaned. She'd never make the short journey to the Post Office with this foot. 'What's it doing back here?'

'It says it has an undeliverable address,' Mrs Firth said as she thrust a mug of coffee into Izzy's hands.

'What?' Izzy cried in disbelief. How the bleedin' hell had she managed to get the address of her own parents' home wrong? Jared was right. She was hopeless.

She picked up the empty box and turned it over, scanning the address with relief. 'Wait a minute! This isn't mine. It's Gemma's. Hang on, I'll go and get her.' Izzy limped round the side of the house in her slippers, which were the only footwear she owned with enough breadth and give to accommodate her padded bandage. Gemma was in the barn cleaning tack with Taryn.

'Gemma, your parcel has been returned. There's a note on it to say it was undeliverable.'

'What?!' Gemma gasped, setting down the saddle she'd been holding. She paled visibly. 'Where is it now?'

'In the kitchen. Mrs Firth opened it by mistake so you'll have to pack it back up.'

'*What*?!'

Everyone trooped back into the kitchen. Gemma looked down at the collection of condiments. Her expression was undecipherable.

'You must have bought the 'Pippa special' too,' Izzy said, surveying the array of jars and bottles on the kitchen table.

'Huh?' Gemma asked. She seemed distracted.

'You've got the exact same stuff I bought for my mum,' Izzy said. 'Are you okay? You look terrible.'

'What? Oh, yes, yes, I'm fine. I just really wanted my aunt to get her present on her birthday,' Gemma said. She scooped up all the jars and packed them back into the box. 'They'll just have to be a few days late.' She looked so despondent that Izzy felt sorry for her. At least her own parcel had arrived safely. A quick text to her mother had set her own mind at rest. A reply pinged almost immediately, which was an amazing achievement for her technophobic mother.

Yes it's here. Will open Sunday after party.

That evening Jared drove Mrs Firth to the halt in Greater Ousebury. From here she would catch the TransPennine Express to Leeds where she would stay with her sister for the weekend. She'd be back first thing Monday morning and had left a casserole for Saturday's dinner and strict instructions that Izzy was to get plenty of rest. Izzy did as she was bade on Saturday, watching back-to-back family films on the telly with Taryn and enjoying being waited on by an indignant, protesting Carlotta, but by Sunday she was crawling the walls with boredom. By now unused to inactivity, she decided to cook a nice simple corned beef hash on Sunday afternoon for that evening's meal, but forgot to take it out of the Aga. Four hours later all that remained of the hash was an inedible charred mass that resembled the charcoal innards of a barbecue pan. Three pairs of eyes, each attached to a hungry body, stared at her accusingly.

'The symbolic irony is not lost on me,' said Jared, reaching for the takeaway menus and his car keys. 'Talk about 'hash Brown'.'

After a late dinner of chicken chow mein and special chop suey, Izzy battled with Carlotta over getting her to do the geography homework the temporary tutor had set.

'This is crap. It's the sort of stuff kids Taryn's age do. I'm surprised I haven't been presented with a set of crayons and a colouring in book.'

Knowing that she was setting an uneasy precedent, Izzy practically did it for her. Jared loomed over her shoulders, surprised to see that Izzy was remarkably good on capital cities and flags.

'How do you know so much about geography?'

'Eurovision,' said Izzy, with no word of a jest. Unable to dredge up a suitably cutting reply, Jared drifted away.

'Can I ask your advice about something later? Will you have time for a chat?' Carlotta asked as she gathered up her books and pens. Mentally adding yet another chore to her ever-lengthening list, Izzy didn't feel she could refuse. But it would have to be once she'd finished everything else she had to do though, she said.

With Carlotta dispatched, Izzy all but wrestled Taryn into the bath, fed all the dogs and cats, loaded the dishwasher and prepared Taryn's school clothes and satchel ready for the start of a new week the following day. Of course everything took her twice as long to do as she hobbled round the kitchen at half-speed. At least she had been excused from stable duty since harpooning her foot. Still gallant despite his grievance with her, Jared insisted he would see to the horses if she could sort out the kitchen and the girls.

Izzy flopped into bed knackered just before midnight. She gulped down several painkillers in the hope her foot would stop aching. Her last thought before she was enveloped by sleep was that she never did get round to having that chat with Carlotta.

---

JUST OVER TWO hundred miles away, Izzy's mother's birthday party was reaching its conclusion. Most of her guests had left, having had a marvellous time and having feasted on a delicious buffet courtesy of Marks & Spencer and the Tesco Finest range. Barbara Brown did not cook! Only Caro and her parents were still present.

'I'd forgotten about Izzy's present,' Barbara said, unearthing it from beneath the sideboard where she'd put it to keep it safe.

Caro tried not to notice as her parents exchanged knowing

glances at the mention of Izzy's name but even she leaned in, intrigued to see what Izzy had sent.

Barbara slit open the box with as much dramatic flair as a cake slice could provide, expecting to see pretty tissue paper and perhaps some champagne bottle confetti. Instead she was faced with crumpled up balls of newspaper. Caro glared at her father as he failed to silence a derisive snort then became entranced as Barbara started pulling items out of the box, a look of bewilderment on her face. After Barbara had extracted a thick pile of what looked like bank statements, a bundle of at least a dozen keys and a cigarette packet full of bank cards, Caro sensed something was wrong.

'Don't touch anything else!' she cried, peering over her own mother's shoulder and taking a good look at the items that were still in the box. Her jaw dropped. 'Holy shit!'

## NEW WOUNDS

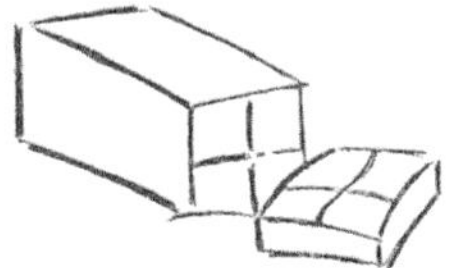

That night Izzy dreamed about Jared again. He'd crept into her room and had pulled the bedclothes back from her face. He was whispering in her ear.

'Izzy—' he was saying. Izzy smiled in her sleep and languorously pushed her head against the hand touching the side of her face. 'Izzy, wake up, sweetheart—'

Wait a minute! She wasn't dreaming. Jared really was in her room. She opened her eyes to slits. It must be early; it was still dark. He was barely a silhouette, a dark shape against the meagre light her open bedroom door offered. Beside her Steptoe thumped his tail against the duvet.

'Wha—?' she managed. The hand continued to stroke her hair, very gently.

'I've been called to see MK. Something urgent. I don't know much else. The timing couldn't be worse with Mrs Firth away. I hate leaving you in this house on your own.'

'What time is it?' The meds she was on for her foot made her dopier than ever.

'Half four, ish,' Jared said. 'Listen, Mrs Firth will be back around lunchtime and I'll be back as soon as I can, hopefully with more info. No need to tell the girls, just carry on as normal.'

'I have a nurse's appointment at lunchtime.'

'That's fine. Just make sure you all have your mobiles with you and keep yourself locked in whilst you're here. Try to keep Carlotta on your radar.'

'Is something wrong?'

'Not sure. Just sit tight and I'll see you real soon.' Then he looked down at her with such tenderness that Izzy began to wonder if she was dreaming after all. 'Go back to sleep. I'll set the alarm on my way out.'

'Be careful.' Izzy had no idea what compelled her to say that. It was just a feeling, a niggle, that something wasn't right.

Jared slid a rough hand down her cheek. 'Get some rest.' He looked like he wanted to add something, but didn't. Instead he gave Steptoe a quick pat and left the room. He closed the door quietly. A few minutes later Izzy heard the slight quadruple beep of the alarm being set, the front door being locked and footsteps on the driveway. Izzy didn't know why but she felt very vulnerable.

Two hours later she was awake again. This time the radio alarm shocked her awake with some horrendous song. Izzy was exhausted. She was expected to see Marc that evening and had been planning on telling him it was over but she would have to raincheck once more. She knew it had to be dealt with and she couldn't continue to put it off, but today she had far too much to do.

Hobbling, she wandered round the house performing the usual morning routine, opening blinds, making breakfast, feeding the dogs and rousing Taryn from her pit. Never before had Izzy fully appreciated how hard Mrs Firth worked or how smoothly she ran the household. She must buy her some flowers or chocolates on her way back from the school run.

Of course, the first thing Taryn asked was where Jared was. Izzy bluffed her way through that one, instead encouraging Taryn to concentrate on her breakfast. Usually subjected to porridge or muesli, it hadn't escaped Taryn's notice that she'd been allowed Coco Pops instead. Taryn, desperate to get to school early so she could be the first to sign up for the end of term nativity, started to heap pressure on Izzy who, due to that awful niggle in her stomach, was reluctant to leave Carlotta in the house on her own. Carlotta, pathologically lazy, was never at her sunniest first thing and refused to get up. Instead, having lost her affability of the night before, she effed and jeffed at Izzy from beneath her duvet. Izzy tried cajoling, bribery and threats but nothing worked. Eventually Izzy accepted defeat. She didn't have the time to act as counsellor and friend at that precise moment. If Carlotta wanted to speak to her so badly, she would. In the meantime, all Izzy could do was damage limitation. She was quite happy to let the little upstart stay in bed and deliberate on her expulsion.

'Fine, you can stay here on your own but I'm setting the alarm and you are not to set foot outside the four walls of this house. I'll be back in about an hour and a half.'

Izzy was at her wit's end by the time she returned to Nether Ousebury that morning. Sharp as a tack, Taryn had insisted on chattering ceaselessly for the entire eighteen-mile journey and had asked some very uncomfortable questions both about her father's incarceration and Izzy's relationship with Jared. Izzy had fielded these questions as best she could but by the time she reached the electronic gates of The Paddocks she felt weary and had a thumping headache. Her foot ached. All things considered, she was relieved to have received a brief call from the surgery asking if she minded postponing her appointment with the nurse until later that afternoon. Now she could get a few chores done over lunchtime. There was so much outstanding. How did Mrs Firth do it all? Damn, she'd forgotten the chocolates!

Just as she pulled up outside the house, Gemma ran up to her, her knee boots clacking on the driveway. Izzy thought Gemma looked very pretty in the same floral tea dress she'd worn to Taryn's birthday party and a faded denim jacket.

'Thank God you're back! I'm late for an appointment in Loxley and have missed the bus. I hitched a lift from Greater. Can I take the Golf? I promise I'll be careful.' Izzy knew Jared would have plenty to say about Gemma taking the car but she looked so stressed and desperate that Izzy didn't have the heart to refuse.

'I'll need it back by three though. I have to go to the doctor's. Jared has taken the Range Rover and I can't see MK being thrilled about me taking the Roller.'

'Absolutely. I promise,' Gemma said. Izzy took a good look at her. She was very pale and was holding her left forearm with her right hand, as though it were causing her some discomfort.

'Everything all right?' she asked, giving the arm a pointed look. Gemma nodded quickly, releasing the arm with exaggerated nonchalance.

'Everything's fine, just a bit bruised from a riding toss. I'm really late.' With no reason to doubt her, Izzy slid the car key off her keyring as she got out of the car and tossed it to Gemma who caught it deftly. Within seconds Gemma had leaped into the driver's seat and scorched up the driveway. Izzy watched her for a few moments before turning towards the house with a shrug. She couldn't blame Gemma for being suspicious of her. Maybe this kind gesture would go some way to fixing their friendship. Not that Izzy would forgive any woman who'd tried to steal Jared away from her.

Thoughts of Jared and whether he would be home soon distracted Izzy as she entered the house but even so she couldn't help but notice how messy it was. Clothes and shoes were scattered all over the hallway, the hatstand had been knocked over and several ornaments had been smashed. As Izzy picked her way through a gauntlet of coats and umbrellas she wondered if this was Carlotta's handiwork and, if so, what the hell had angered her so much for her to embark on such a campaign of destruction. Evidently she had disobeyed Izzy's command not to leave the house as the alarm had been deactivated.

'Carlotta!' Izzy called up the stairs in what she hoped was a friendly, non-combative tone. Perhaps Carlotta would have defrosted sufficiently for her to open up about what was troubling her. 'I'm back. I'm making a pot of tea. D'you want a cup?'

Silence.

Izzy gave another shrug. Maybe she was in the stables or maybe she was simply sulking and deliberately ignoring her. Izzy no longer worried herself about Carlotta's moods. There was nothing she could do about them and she'd long since learned not to take them personally. Instead she wandered into the kitchen, flinging her handbag onto the scrubbed table before heading towards the kettle. The kitchen, like the hallway, looked like a tornado had gone through it. Muffled barking diverted her attention. Why the hell had Carlotta banished them to the lounge, Izzy thought irritably, stomping back out of the kitchen. As she opened the lounge door all the dogs funnelled into the hallway. Except Steptoe. Izzy frowned. It was unlike him to not come racing to greet her as soon as she set foot over the threshold. Maybe he was outside with Carlotta. Izzy followed the pack of dogs into the kitchen, intending to head outside and yell for Carlotta to come in, when a furious scraping interrupted her thoughts. Hobbit and Sprite were both pawing frantically at the utility room door.

'For God's sake. You've already been fed,' Izzy grumbled. Softhearted as always, she relented quickly. 'You can have some Bonios and that's all.' She reached for the utility door handle and pulled.

Then she screamed.

Lying on the tiles was Steptoe. He was on his side, perfectly still, his eyes open, staring, frosted. His mouth was slightly open and a thin gossamer thread of red saliva was suspended from his exposed teeth to a half gnawed slab of steak that lay on the floor next to him. The meat had been studded with slug pellets. With leaden legs, Izzy ran to his side, tears streaming down her face, sobs erupting from her throat. With shaking hands she stroked his little white body, desperate to detect some indication of life. There was none. He was cold.

'Oh my God! No, no, please wake up, Steptoe. Wake up, *wake up*!' Izzy shook the little dog, desperate to elicit some, any, reaction. There was no response. 'Please. Please,' she pleaded, still shaking him, unable to stop, unwilling to accept the intolerable facts. A wail of undiluted anguish ripped from her body. Not Steptoe. Not her little furry first-day friend. It couldn't be. It just couldn't. Then she was shocked back into panic as a couple of the other dogs barged into the utility behind her, almost knocking her into the washing machine, and made a beeline for the steak.

'*Leave it*!' Izzy screamed, panicked. Startled, the dogs stopped in their tracks. Crying all the while, Izzy shunted them all out of the kitchen. After scrabbling in her handbag for her mobile, she ran back into the utility and grabbed a carrier bag from the dispenser on the wall. With great care she used it to pick up the steak and flung it into the sink. Still shaking, she scrolled down to Jared's phone number.

*The telephone you are trying to contact is switched off. Please leave a message after the tone.*

Izzy groaned with frustration as the irritating voicemail

woman continued with her robotic blurb. All the while her trembling hand ran over Steptoe's white fur. 'Come on, come on,' she muttered. At last, there was the tone. 'Jared, come home quickly. Steptoe has been poisoned—,' she wailed. 'Please come home right now! I don't know what—' Words dried up on Izzy's lips as something occurred to her. 'Shit!' She slammed the phone down on the utility workbench, still connected to the voicemail.

Carlotta!

Izzy sprinted back through the kitchen, into the hallway — running the gauntlet of frenzied dogs once more — and up the stairs. Mess was everywhere and for the first time Izzy noticed some items were missing also. An original picture from here, a priceless ornament from there.

*'Carlotta!'* Izzy shrieked as she stumbled along the landing, bouncing off the walls in her panic. Why the hell wasn't she replying?

The door to Carlotta's room was wide open. Izzy cannoned off the doorframe and into the room, grinding to a horrified halt as she surveyed the devastation. This room had been trashed too. Bedclothes had been ripped from the bed, the dresser chair was on its side, cabinets and bookcases swiped clean of ornaments and the entire room was thick with the reek from several shattered perfume bottles. An overpowering, cloying amalgamation of scent hung in the air. It hit the back of Izzy's throat as she inhaled, causing her to splutter as she backed out of the room. Beneath her feet something crunched. It was Carlotta's iPhone, rendered useless by a well-aimed boot. An avalanche of horror was crashing over Izzy, almost unbalancing her with its force and velocity. This wasn't Carlotta's doing. She was far too self-serving to destroy her own stuff. She would trash Taryn's, her father's, Izzy's… but never her own. Something terrible had occurred here.

Overcome by a need to vomit, Izzy lurched back

downstairs, falling down the last few steps in her haste. Snatching up her phone from the utility work surface she redialled Jared's number. Voicemail again.

'Jared, come home, please come home. Carlotta's gone. Looks like there's been a struggle. Please ring me as soon as you get this. Please hurry. I don't know what to do.' Izzy paused, desperately trying to collect her thoughts. The police! She should ring the police. 'I'm going to ring the police now but please come home as soon as you get this.' She paused again. 'I'm really scared.' She rung off and stared round at the utility with unseeing eyes. After all the hoaxes and false alarms that Carlotta had caused over the past three months the police would have her life. They had warned that no further claims of Carlotta's abscondments would be tolerated.

Izzy jumped as her phone rang. Her merry, jangling ringtone of *Take That and Party* seemed inappropriate to the point of obscenity amidst all the horror. Izzy answered it after just half a bar of music without looking at the textscreen.

'Jared?'

'Izzy, Izzy! It's Carlotta—'

'Carlotta! Thank God! Where are you?' Relief flooded through Izzy. Surely Carlotta must be safe to be able to make a phone call.

'—Izzy, I'm at the abattoir, I can't get out and I'm scared. Please get Jared! They came whilst you were out. They had keys!' Carlotta's voice was high and thin with panic. 'Izzy, it was Alan. *Alan and Gemma*!'

The words 'Jared's not here' died on Izzy's lips as she was forced to endure the sounds of a scuffle. She could hear Carlotta screaming 'No, please, no!' before there was an eardrum-piercing crunch and the connection went dead. Whoever's phone Carlotta had managed to swipe, it had now been destroyed. Izzy dialled out immediately.

'I'm ringing from The Paddocks in Nether Ousebury.

We've had a break-in and one of the children has been kidnapped.'

'Calm down, please. What is your name?'

'Izzy Brown, I'm ringing from The Paddocks in Nether Ousebury and Carlotta Konstantine has been kidnapped. She's been—'

'One moment, please!' Izzy was incensed to have been put on hold. Holding the phone away from her face at head height, she stared at it in disbelief. Jesus, someone was talking again.

'Hello, hello? You said Carlotta Konstantine, yes?'

'Yes, she's been taken to—'

'We'll send someone round to your home to discuss this.'

'No, listen—'

'Madam, we've been instructed to view allegations of one Carlotta Konstantine's disappearances as low priority. We understand there have been several false alarms.'

'This is not a hoax. Why won't you listen to me, you ignorant pig?' Izzy howled, not realising exactly what she was calling the officer.

'There's no need to be abusive. Police officers don't appreciate being referred to as pigs.'

'I'm sorry, but please hurry. She's been taken to the old abattoir just outside the village—'

'An officer is on their way to your house—'

'No, they need to go to the old abattoir on Loxley Road, not here.'

'They'll be with you shortly. Please try and remain calm. Thank you for your call.' The line went dead. Frustrated, Izzy stamped her feet like a toddler. Muttering, she dialled Jared's mobile for a third time.

'Jared, it's Izzy, again. The police wouldn't listen. If you pick this up please call them and convince them it's not a hoax. Carlotta's at the abattoir. She said Gemma and Alan took her. She sounded really frightened.'

If Jared didn't pick up her message and convince the police it wasn't a prank she was screwed. She would just have to drive to the abattoir and hope to retrieve Carlotta herself. Mebbe she could create a blockade or something. Anything.

Flinging her mobile into her handbag, Izzy raked around in the key cupboard for a set of keys. They were all missing, even the Roller's. Izzy groaned as she recalled how Gemma had torn away in the Golf, taking the last set of keys with her. Horror upon horror dawned upon Izzy. Gemma had known about the trashed house, and Carlotta's kidnap and Steptoe's cruel murder. And she had the bloody temerity to stand there and act as though they were friends.

'*Bi-i-itch*!' Izzy screamed at the ceiling in sheer enraged frustration. She was trapped in the house with no means of transport. No, that wasn't strictly true. There were several forms of transport standing idle… in the stables. 'Bleedin' Christ!' Izzy shrieked as she realised what her last option was. As if taking great glee in mocking her, her pierced foot reminded her with a stab of pain that she had been forbidden to ride. Of course, why wouldn't it? The doctor had told her not to partake in excess activity, as this would prevent the tissues from knitting, and yet here she was, gallivanting all over the house like a blue arsed fly. Wincing with pain, Izzy hobbled to the stables and yanked open the door.

'Fa-a-arcking hell!' she roared as she surveyed the inside of the barn. Each and every stall door was swinging on its hinges. The horses had gone. Izzy spun on her one good heel and squinted out at the paddocks. There they all were: Jet, Ghost, The Tank and Jester, all grazing peacefully in the farthest field, happily unaware of the storm breaking in the human world. It would take too long for her to catch one of them. Far too long. The sound of hooves behind her caused Izzy to spin once more. Mini Cheddar was trotting towards her at double speed. Izzy only just managed to jump out of the way as, with a great whinny, he barrelled past her in his keenness to join his buddies, who all neighed in reply. Then another horse neighed. The noise came from behind her. Izzy turned once more and stumbled along the stable block. In the very end stall stood a horse which stared back at Izzy with an expression that gave her a chill.

Vega.

'Of course,' said Izzy to herself out loud. 'Of course.' It was the only moment of self-doubt that she allowed herself. Concentrating her thoughts only on Carlotta, she heaved Vega's saddle off the wall and snatched the bridle off its hook. Mothering Christ, it was a double bridle. As if matters weren't complicated enough she now had to navigate two bits, four reins and a curb chain. As Izzy unbolted the loose box the mare flattened her ears against her poll and swished her head towards her like a cobra.

'Give over!' Izzy snapped, administering a light slap to Vega's twitching withers, attempting to imitate Jared's brusque, no-nonsense approach to equine discipline. It appeared to work. Vega's ears shot forward in surprise. Limping painfully, fingers fumbling, Izzy managed to tack Vega up through sheer dumb luck and brute force rather than skill, and led her outside to the mounting block. Wishing dearly that it was Jet, The Tank or even Ghost that she was about to ride, Izzy realised her crash cap was upstairs in her bedroom. It would be madness to ride Vega across country without headgear — Jared would kill her — but there was simply no time to go and get it.

Handbag slung diagonally across her shoulders, Izzy climbed the mounting block, constantly dodging Vega's snaking head as she tried to take a bite out of her arse. Vega jibbed and danced at every little sound. On any other horse Izzy would have been tempted to give her a quick slap with a whip but, with Vega, she was keenly aware that this would result in her being carted out of The Paddocks in a wooden box with all her friends and family looking on to the mournful tones of *Ave Maria*.

A further complication arose. Her left foot was considerably enlarged courtesy of her padded dressing and lodged itself in the stirrup as she mounted, probably never to be released. It was imperative her bum stayed glued to the saddle. If Vega tipped her off she would be dragged for miles. No sooner had Izzy picked up the reins than Vega accelerated into a fast canter, clattering out of the stable yard, thankfully in the direction of the main gates. Which were, of course, closed.

'Shit! Shit! Shit!' Izzy squealed as they advanced on them at increasing speed. There was no way Vega's weight would be heavy enough to trigger the underground sensors and she didn't trust the mare not to try and jump them, all five foot of them. She'd be a goner for sure. Four reins in one hand she raked around in her handbag for the blipper. Thank Christ! Her fingers curled round the little black device and, by the magic of infrared, the gates eased open. As they passed through them Izzy realised that she hadn't locked the house. Well, it would just have to remain open. Hopefully the dogs would do their canine duty and protect it from any opportunistic intruders. Hauling on the reins like a scurry driver, she successfully turned Vega right onto Cherry Tree Avenue. Behind her the gates glided back together. Praying to the dear Lord that they wouldn't encounter any tractors, Sunday drivers, dog walkers or happy hackers, they cantered through the village, Izzy clinging onto the pommel of the saddle for extra grip. Philippa's Kitchen, The Half Moon and the village green whooshed past in a blur. Izzy was filled with the unpleasant notion that she should be bidding a last, fond farewell to them all.

At the cusp of the village, where the wide avenue met the main road, Izzy hauled the other way on the reins, causing Vega to veer sharply to the left at forty-five degrees, tilting like a pendolino train. Izzy thought her last moments had come. Vega was now up to full speed and was utilising every inch of her long, smooth stride along the main road with little concern that her shod hooves were skidding on the tarmac. Izzy wouldn't have been surprised if they were throwing up sparks in their wake. Her mobile was ringing in her handbag but Izzy daren't let go of the pommel long enough to grab it. A quarter of a mile ahead was a turn off to the right. Leading first to a gathering of smallholdings and then onto the disused abattoir, it was nothing more than a glorified bridleway but would at least hold less potential danger than the main road. Despite their ever-increasing speed, it remained stubbornly and frustratingly out of reach.

They had now acquired a tailback of cars. Thankfully, the lead driver had enough sense not to overtake and had moved as close to the central white line as possible so as to keep all other vehicles safely behind them. Not so the drivers of the oncoming traffic. Lorries and saloons failed to slow their speed as they passed her in the opposite direction, drivers gaping out at her with blank faces. A comedian in a souped-up SEAT thought it would be funny to toot his horn and gesticulate as he approached. A thumping bassline shook the car as it passed by. Vega swerved like a formula one car in a chicane, first to the left, then to the right.

The turning was now looming. If there wasn't a break in the traffic flow they wouldn't be able to turn and, if that were the case, God only knew where they would end up. But luck was on Izzy's side for once. After a little hatchback trundled past them a gap formed. Reins like washing lines, Izzy stuck her right hand out and flapped like a maniac to indicate that she intended to turn. Fortune was again benevolent as Vega, by now thoroughly bored with the main road, had spotted the turning and veered over.

Just as well, thought Izzy as she reeled in the reins. She'd never have managed to turn her otherwise. Behind her she could hear the sound of traffic speeding up. Above, black and white clouds chequered the sky. It looked like a squall was heading their way. That was all she needed! Within minutes diagonal rain was cutting Izzy's face to ribbons. Visibility had been reduced to mere feet. At least she could just make out the outline of the disused slaughterhouse through the downpour. Boxy and metallic, it looked like an oversized corrugated Monopoly building. Vega had already gibbed at every rustle in the hedgerow since they had left the stable yard. Now, the closer they got to the former abattoir, she was even more skittish than ever. Little wonder Jared had always forbidden them to go anywhere near it. It gave Izzy the creeps.

Vega slowed to a canter as they crossed the perimeter of the dilapidated complex. A large, square concrete forecourt, criss-crossed with fissures, was edged by a basic post and rail fence. Weeds were forcing their way up between the cracks. There was no other vehicular access other than the single track Izzy had taken.

Two cars were parked outside the main entrance of the building. One was a battered hatchback. The other was the Golf. Its driver's door had been left wide open. Izzy felt rage bubbling up inside her. She'd had her ups and downs with Gemma but would never have imagined she was capable of harming Carlotta. Carlotta had always viewed Gemma as her best friend. It would be like Caro betraying Izzy. It was unthinkably painful to even contemplate.

Struggling to slow Vega to a trot, Izzy circled round and round the enclosure in ever decreasing loops. She deliberately didn't call out. What if that prompted them to do something rash? Better to stay outside, undetected and not taken into account. If she could at least block the narrow, gateless exit she could at least scupper any plans to cart Carlotta off and perhaps cause enough of a delay until the police arrived. But Vega was by now thoroughly worked up. Unsettled by the faint smell of disused machinery and animal carcass, she began to buck, neighing and snorting like a rodeo pony. As Izzy yanked on the reins she could hear Carlotta screaming her name from inside, her shrillness amplified as the sound bounced off the stark, metal walls. Undistinguishable faces emerged, pale and ghost-like, at the whitewashed windows. They watched her with malevolence. Which one was Gemma, Izzy wondered. Still circling, she knew she wouldn't be able to stay on board for much longer. Desperately trying to tug her bandaged foot out of the stirrup before her inevitable ejection, she gave no thought as to what would happen to her once she was on the ground, when they captured her too.

Then finally, reprieve. Sirens, gradually getting louder, could be heard in the distance. Craning her neck like a tawny owl, Izzy could just make out flashing blue lights on the top road. The faces at the window disappeared, then a small group of people poured out of the abattoir, piling into the little hatchback. Carlotta wasn't one of them but Izzy caught a slight glimpse of Gemma's distinctive red mane. Police cars flooded into the forecourt. Attempts to drive away were abandoned. Everyone scattered. In the mêlée no one noticed a small, slight figure evaporating into the dark anonymity of the thick copse that shadowed the building. On the very edge of her peripheral vision, Izzy saw Jared's Range Rover bouncing along the bridle path and felt an immense sense of relief. She slumped in the saddle. It was her undoing. Vega, who by this time had had more than enough and who could sense weakness, gave a final almighty buck. Afterwards Izzy would have liked to have said she saw the ground rise up to meet her, but it wouldn't have been the truth. The post and rail fence got in the way. Crashing through it was Izzy's last memory.

---

Izzy woke to find Mrs Firth sitting by her bed. It wasn't her bed at The Paddocks though.

'Welcome back, love,' Mrs Firth said, smiling. Izzy gazed round at her unfamiliar surroundings. She was the sole occupant of a small but bright and airy room. The bed was single and the furniture minimal. A television was bracketed to the opposite wall. Beside her was a bedside cabinet. On this was a basic telephone, a jug, a stack of plastic cups, an angle-poise lamp and several greetings cards. Beside her an electrical device on a tall stand beeped hypnotically. Jesus, it was attached to her! She must be in hospital.

To her right was a large window that stretched the entire length of the room. Outside the sun was shining. Gone was the wintry shower of the previous day. Izzy could see birds slaloming round established oaks and beeches. Up above them a pastel pink vapour trail inched across the clear sky. It all looked so peaceful. To her right was a chair, covered in boxes of chocolates, fruit baskets and stuffed toys. Every other possible surface was smothered in fresh flowers. The underlying aroma of disinfectant in the air was sweetened by the perfume of roses, lilies and stocks. Her arm was in a cast and her punctured foot shielded by a plastic bridge that kept the weight of the bedding off her injury. She ached all over. What had she done to herself now? Then it all flooded back with overwhelming clarity. Izzy grabbed Mrs Firth's arm with her uninjured hand.

'Carlotta? Taryn? Are they both okay? How did Taryn get home from school? What about Vega? Where am I?'

'You're in the Nuffield, love, and everyone's just fine. You took the brunt for everyone. You've been out fer't count since yesterday. Eeee, you went with a reet wallop. We could do nowt but look on in 'orror.'

*We?*

Jared!

She looked around for him, saw he wasn't there and

promptly burst into tears. Then she pictured poor little Steptoe, cold and alone on the utility floor, and the tears turned into sobs.

'Oh my God, Steptoe! I left him on the utility floor. What about the other dogs?'

Before Mrs Firth could respond a nurse, hearing the racket, bustled in and immediately ordered Mrs Firth to leave.

'We can't have our patient getting overexcited,' she explained.

'No!' shrieked Izzy. 'I want her to stay.'

'Now, Isabel, be sensible.' The nurse attempted reason.

'You be sensible,' Izzy screeched. 'I want her here. It's not her fault. It's the bleedin' bastards who kidnapped my Carlotta and killed our dog that have overexcited me. I… want… her to *stay*!' She turned to Mrs Firth in panic, her tone low but urgent. 'Stay here. Don't leave me. Please.'

Mrs Firth patted Izzy's free hand. 'I'm not going anywhere, love. I promised Jared I'd stay by your side. And don't you worry about anything. It's all been sorted. Little Steptoe's been given a hero's burial. Jared wrapped him in his favourite blanket and buried him in the pet cemetery with all his old friends. He's at rest now.'

Sensing that reason wasn't an option, the nurse backed out of the room. Izzy turned her attention back to Mrs Firth.

'Where's Jared?'

'I'm sorry, love, he was demented with worry but he had to leave. He insisted I stay with you until you were well enough to come home.'

'When will he be back?'

'I don't know. Honest, I don't. He had stuff to do.'

Tears flooded again. God, she couldn't stop them.

'Why isn't he here? I want him to be here. I need him here.' She then realised what she was saying and turned to face Mrs Firth. 'Please don't tell anyone about this,' she sobbed.

'I think everyone knows, love. The only two who haven't cottoned on yet are you and 'im.'

It was in that moment Izzy had to accept that she loved Jared. Previously when she'd met a guy, she'd fancied him, been taken out on a few dates and gradually got to know him and fall in love whilst the relationship evolved. With Jared it was different. They had already despatched with the preliminaries and as a result Izzy knew him inside out. Carlotta had asked her about the real thing. Well, this was it all right.

'Who's with the girls now?' Izzy heard herself say.

'They're with MK.'

'He's back!?'

'Oh yes, he was back last night. The CPS received some new evidence that was inedible or something. I don't really understand the ins and outs. Anyways, they chucked out his case and he's home safe and sound.'

'What's happened? Please tell me. I'm going mad not knowing.'

'I'm not sure you should be overexcited—'

At that moment a police officer peered round the door.

'Do you feel up to going through what happened?' he asked. Izzy shrugged.

'Only if someone will fill me in on the bits I was too knocked out to remember,' she said.

The young officer pulled up a chair and unfurled a notepad.

'Is this a formal statement?' Izzy asked.

'Do you want it to be?'

Izzy shrugged again. 'Why not?'

She was encouraged to start from the beginning and recounted how Gemma had been waiting for her, and had taken the last of the transport. Then how she had found the house trashed, and Steptoe...

'She was nursing a rather nasty bite on her left arm. I gather the little dog took quite a chunk out of her,' said the officer.

'Good Steptoe,' Izzy said, jaw stiff from the effort it took to keep her lip from quivering.

The interview continued. The police had rounded everyone up whilst Jared had raced over to Izzy's side. A policewoman released Carlotta from her restraints. She'd been bound to a disused machine in the main body of the slaughterhouse. Mrs Firth proudly recalled how she had marched up to Gemma and slapped her face.

'I would have done it twice but the policewoman restrained me.' She stared at the young police officer in defiance, as though daring him to judge her. He didn't dare.

'Errr—'

Izzy turned to Mrs Firth.

'How were you even there? You were visiting your sister,' she said, confused. Mrs Firth went on to explain whilst the officer continued to take notes.

Jared had received a panicked call from Armley. Could he please come immediately? Jared drove straight to Leeds only to be turned away at the front gate. MK hadn't made any such request, Jared was told. Realising he'd been duped, he was already well on his way back to The Paddocks, having made a brief detour in order to retrieve Mrs Firth on the way, when he picked up Izzy's messages and rang the police.

An ambulance had been called and Izzy and Carlotta carted off to hospital; Carlotta for a check-up and Izzy with a broken arm and a concussion. A police officer had taken Mrs Firth back to The Paddocks and arranged for Taryn to be brought home from school by the parent of a classmate from a nearby village. Vega had simply gone home. Fed up with all the drama, she'd taken it upon herself to find her own way back, jumped into the paddock and stood there, still tacked up and with broken reins, until someone attended to her. This task had eventually fallen on a hysterical Taryn and Mrs Firth.

'I'll need to get this typed up and then you'll be asked to sign it,' the young officer explained after he had run through everything briefly a second time for accuracy. 'Feel better,' he added, nodding a goodbye.

After he had left, Mrs Firth, the eternal mother, fluffed up Izzy's pillows and poured her a fresh cup of squash.

'You must be shattered, love. Try to rest. I'll be right here with me *Woman's Weekly*.'

Exhausted, Izzy slept. She dreamed Jared was with her, holding her hand. She could feel the rough skin. When she woke, the broad, bright window had been transformed to a theatrical sequinned curtain of midnight blue. A sympathetic moon watched over her. She must have slept all day. She could still feel the pressure where Jared was holding her hand, but when she turned her head she realised the hand holder was Marc. Disappointed to the point of devastation, Izzy burst into tears.

'I want my mum.'

'Your mum knows where you are, Izzy, but she couldn't make it up here. She's so sorry and sends her love. She sent a card and some flowers too. We've been keeping her updated as to how you're doing. We said you'd give her a ring when you were feeling up to it.' He indicated to the white telephone on the bedside cabinet. Izzy wished Jared would make it ring for her.

Marc seemed to read her thoughts. He and Izzy stared at each other for a good long time. Marc looked knackered, Izzy noticed. Knackered and resigned. Izzy realised he already knew.

'Why are you here?' she said, not unkindly. It was a fair question.

'I don't like loose ends,' Marc replied. 'Although I do wish it could have been different.' He seemed sad rather than angry. 'I've always known that it wasn't going to work, ever since I saw you and Walker on the hammock in the summer.'

'That was you? But Gemma said—'

'No, it was me. I was angry and upset. I'd parked up by the pub and snuck round the back of the house, hoping to surprise you. I was the one who got a surprise. Serves me right for creeping round someone else's property, I s'pose.' His words were laced with double meanings. 'Gemma was the first person I saw as I was walking back through the village. I confided in her not knowing that there was history between her and Jared. She went spare. I had to get a drink from The Half Moon to calm her down. I thought she was going to have an embolism. I'd never have opened my mouth if I'd known. Afterwards it all made sense. She saw how keen I was to meet you at the Great Yorkshire Show and invited me and Ceri to Taryn's party, hoping I would lure you away from Jared. She must have pretended she was the one who had seen you. No wonder she was so pissed off with you.' It was the only beration he gave her.

'I'm so sorry,' Izzy whispered.

'So am I. I really was quite taken with you, Izzy Brown. I should have known it was always Walker. In retrospect it was quite obvious from that first day I saw you at the Great Yorkshire Show. The two of you seemed to naturally gravitate towards each other. He's always been territorial about you. Anyway, Carlotta would never have forgiven you if you'd become Ceri's stepmother. I'll let Mrs Firth know I'm leaving.' He gave her an affectionate kiss on the top of her head before he left, letting his lips linger slightly before saying goodbye.

Once he'd gone, Izzy took a short break from the guilt and self-loathing she felt with regards to Marc and instead contemplated the mess she had created. So many people had been hurt because of her stupidity. She couldn't help but believe her duplicity had been the thing that had caused Gemma to finally snap. Carlotta could have been hurt, as could Taryn. Steptoe had suffered the worst. Izzy couldn't bear to think about him. Instead she packed his memory up in a little metaphorical box, padlocked it and buried it deep inside her thoughts where she couldn't easily access it. It was only when others mentioned it that she had to acknowledge its presence. It manifested as a sharp, painful reminder, deep in her gut. Of all the dogs at The Paddocks, why did it have to be Steptoe? And yet another part of her accepted that it had been inevitable. Steptoe was Jared's dog, and had been her favourite too. If fate was doling out an element of justice for Gemma in recompense for the perfidy she and Jared had committed against her then it had chosen well. At the end of the day it was a mercy the only casualty had been a dog and not one of the girls, but that didn't make it any less hard to accept.

As for herself, for the second time within nine months she was boyfriendless, no doubt jobless and thereby homeless, and again all in the same day. Her track record was beyond shocking but at least she was consistent, she reflected miserably.

'Go home, Mrs Firth. I'll be quite safe here.'

'But I promised…'

'I know, but I'm really okay. I'll be home in a couple of days.'

---

THE CONSULTANT, a suave individual with a Cote D'Azur tan and a Tag Heuer peeping out from his white coat, carried out her assessment.

'I gather you took quite a toss,' he said, smiling down at her, revealing excellent white teeth. Izzy, having whiled away the hours reading the brochure for the hospital, wondered if he'd had to pay full whack to have them done or if he'd had them done by the house dentist for a tummy tuck or a course of lipo quid pro quo. 'I don't know, you horsey types. Always getting into scrapes. Anyway, it's not all doom and gloom. You've broken your right arm but the good news is it's a simple transverse fracture.' Izzy looked at him blankly. 'A clean break,' he explained. 'Nice and uncomplicated and easily healed.'

Oh, the irony, thought Izzy.

He gave Izzy's collection of cards and gifts a breezy wave. 'You're certainly very popular.' Izzy gave a weak smile. Earlier that day an auxiliary nurse had sat with her and passed her each card in turn so she could read them. Not only had there been wonderful messages from Taryn, who also sent a fruit basket and her beloved iPhone in case Izzy got bored, both intended as a private joke, and Mrs Firth, who'd left a tin of home-made fudge, but also a very grateful offering from MK himself. Her parents and Caro also sent their love. More surprisingly were the tasteful card and enormous basket of muffins and cupcakes from Pippa and Drew from the café. There was even a violently pink card from Col the Landlord and his wife, Tania, which contained what looked like the good wishes of most of his regulars. Unbeknownst to Izzy, several of the locals had witnessed her mercy dash through the village and applauded her bravery. The dizzy Londoner had proved herself. She was no longer a southern softy but an honorary Yorkshire lass. There were also messages of best wishes from the parents of Taryn and Carlotta's school friends, prompted by the intense relief that none of their offspring had been subjected to such an ordeal. The biggest and most flamboyant card had been from Marc, but of course that was all irrelevant now. She asked that the flowers, chocolates and stuffed toy he had bought her were pushed to the back, where she couldn't see them.

Izzy had been so affected by such unexpected affection

that the kindly auxiliary nurse had had to help mop up the streams of silent tears that had poured down her face throughout. Even more upsetting was the fact there was nothing from Carlotta, which she could justify, or from Jared, which she couldn't. It was as though he had vanished into thin air.

The consultant was still checking her over.

'I think you're mending quite nicely, young lady. You're young, fit and healthy and that always helps. You'll need to keep this pesky pot on for about six weeks and then it'll be a course of physio for you. We have a good programme here. You're in good hands. Until then we can liaise with your local GP to have the practice nurse keep an eye on your dressings. Broken bones, pierced feet and other such trivialities aside, you're not in bad shape. No more stunt riding for a while though.' He gave her another megawatt smile. 'You'll be out of here tomorrow.'

Having been assured arrangements would be made for her to be taken home, Izzy was instructed to get a good night's sleep.

As if.

Instead she plugged in Taryn's iPhone and fretted about which home she would be taken to. After her escapades with Vega, she wasn't even sure she would be welcome at The Paddocks anymore. It was such a good job the sleeping tablets she had been instructed to take were starting to kick in otherwise the temptation to scroll through Taryn's iPhone and find Jared's number would be too great to resist. As she drifted off a song by Goldfrapp, about ending up in accident and emergency instead of being taken out on a date, seemed to sum up how she felt.

# GUMPTION

After another night's observation Izzy was allowed back home. Beetroot with shame and embarrassment at all the fuss, Izzy was aided downstairs by two nurses and ushered into a waiting chauffeur-driven midnight-blue Bentley Turbo R with a private plate and blacked out windows. She sank into the luxurious champagne-coloured upholstery whilst the chauffeur attended to 'madam's' comfort, adjusting the armrest and footstools and covering her knees with a lambs' wool rug.

Her overnight bag and a carrier bag full of stuffed toys and get well soon cards were strapped into the seat beside her as though as precious as a living entity. She had purposely left behind the fruit basket, cakes, chocolates and fudge, pressing them onto the fleet of nurses that had looked after her as a thank you. Before handing them over she had extracted the little message cards and tucked them into her handbag like treasure.

'All settled?' the uniformed driver asked, turning to give her a brief smile. Izzy nodded. She hadn't expected this. On the opposite side of the road shiftworkers from a red-bricked chocolate factory were queued at the bus stop. Spotting such a posh car, they stopped complaining about the state of the nation, the youth of today and the weather, and gawped and pointed as though she were a celebrity. The air smelled of petrol fumes and chocolate mint. The nurses waved her off as the Bentley glided into the non-stop traffic.

From the route taken there was no mistake that she was being driven to The Paddocks. Izzy returned home to find a huge banner across the driveway. 'Welcome home, Lizzy' it read, with the L in Lizzy being added in garish red paint and in a deliberately scruffy, last-minute font to indicate it was a personal, private joke between them all. For the first time in days Izzy gave a genuine laugh. Carlotta, Taryn and Mrs Firth were waiting on the front door step. Her driver must have called through and advised of their arrival.

No sooner had Izzy been helped out of the car than Taryn launched herself at her, throwing her arms round her waist in a ferocious bear hug. Mrs Firth hurried after her and dragged her off.

'Come on, missy. Let her catch her breath,' she berated kindly whilst at the same time gently squeezing Izzy's good arm. 'Welcome home, love.'

'Firthie's planned a special celebration dinner for you. I'm gonna be allowed to stay up for it,' Taryn chattered, refusing to let go of Izzy's hand. Above Taryn's head Izzy could see Carlotta watching her. Carlotta remained silent, her expression indecipherable.

From behind them MK appeared. Having only ever seen him in two-dimensional photographs, Izzy was taken aback by the extent of his persona and charisma. Tall, taller even than Jared, and broad, he wore a beautifully cut pair of slacks and shirt. He had swarthy Greek features, immaculate teeth and was dripping with gold jewellery. He looked as though he had recovered from his year in jail pretty quickly. Only his tan had faded. Izzy had no difficulty in imagining him hosting a yacht-full of bikini-ed beauties as he sailed across the glimmering Aegean Sea, playboy stylie. Although, Izzy conceded, whilst it was almost a certainty that MK did indeed have a luxury yacht moored somewhere in the Med, whether or not he entertained the ladies was very doubtful. Taryn resembled him more than Carlotta, she noticed. MK had a quiet confidence about him. Izzy felt like he knew exactly what she was thinking, and could see where Taryn got her calm intuitive nature from.

He looked serious. Expecting a bollocking, Izzy cringed inwardly. She would have liked to have melted into the driveway beneath her feet, metamorphosing into a crunchy golden leaf and disappearing into the masses with comforting anonymity. She was therefore astonished when he leaned in and kissed her on both cheeks.

'*Efharisto, efharisto*,' he said, adding that his debt to her would never be repaid. Izzy called him Mr Konstantine but MK brushed this aside.

'Only my business associates call me that. Acquaintances call me Mika. My friends call me MK, which is what I hope you will call me.' He summoned his daughters. 'Now, let us get this poor creature up to her room. We have had strict instructions from your singularly scary surgeon at the hospital that you must rest, rest and rest again. We will do all we can to help. Your recovery is our highest priority.' Leaning down, he picked up her luggage.

Her stomach in ropes, Izzy looked round for Jared. He wasn't there. Unable to raise her voice to ask where he was she allowed herself to be led inside. All the chaos that Gemma and Alan had left in their wake had been tidied up. The house was as serene and ordered as ever. Upstairs, her bedroom had been cleaned and filled with flowers. The air smelled of fresh bedlinen and lavender. Never before had her bed looked so inviting. She wanted to crawl under the duvet and not come back out unless time managed to magically reverse itself and make things the way they were before that horrible day had taken place. Mrs Firth seemed to pick up on her change of mood.

'Look, the poor girl's done in,' she said, ushering everyone out of the room before turning back to Izzy. 'I'll bring you up a nice cup of tea and then you can have a little rest before dinner.'

Taryn wanted desperately to stay with Izzy and had to be practically dragged out of the room. Izzy was left with her thoughts and teacup. She didn't need to read the leaves to know that her heartbreak wasn't going to go away any time soon. Nothing in her life had ever hurt as much as this did. Having forced down her drink and taken a couple of the diclofenac she had been prescribed to ease her pain and reduce the swelling in her arm she drew the bed clothes over her. Just as she was drifting off something jumped up onto the bed, startling her. Reminded of Steptoe, Izzy's unforgiving subconscious gleefully unearthed the metaphorical box buried deep in her thoughts and smashed open the lock, letting heartbreak and retribution pour out like Pandora's tribulations. Pushing down the duvet she saw that her new companion was Hobbit, the pretty little Border Terrier bitch. Always second fiddle to Steptoe, she had seized her chance to be pack leader. She bestowed on Izzy a quick lick before settling down next to her, her back pressed up against Izzy's thigh. Izzy reached down to stroke her, drawing comfort from her company. At least it hadn't been Pongy, she thought with the slightest ghost of a smile. Then she slept.

She woke just as it was getting dark. She could hear the sounds of people and animals moving about. Jared's absence aside, The Paddocks had returned to normal. Temporarily rested, she joined the others for dinner. For the first time since Easter, it was served in the dining room. There were six place settings and Izzy's eyes kept sliding towards the empty chair where Jared should have been seated as Mrs Firth served up a splendid roast chicken dinner. MK carved then he encouraged everyone to raise their glasses in a toast to Izzy's bravery. Embarrassed, Izzy wanted to climb into the sideboard and hide. Fortunately for her, Carlotta had no intention of letting Izzy's heroics monopolise the conversation.

'Can we have a swimming pool?' she asked her father as soon as everyone started eating. Being crafty to his daughters' ways, MK had ascertained within mere hours that Carlotta had realised she could use the trauma of her kidnap to manipulate everyone to her own ends. He had already agreed to buy Nicola Ward's amazing grey showjumper, Polo, for her as an early birthday present but wasn't prepared to be taken for an absolute mug.

'What for? You already have a stable full of ponies, and dogs, cats, and rabbits. Not to mention every gadget known to man, or rather to child.'

'It would help me heal,' Carlotta said, looking pious.

'I thought that was why I bought you that new horse.'

'Suky Fellowes's parents have just installed an indoor pool,' Carlotta said sulkily, feeding all the chicken off her plate to the dogs.

'Well, Suky Fellowes's parents must have more money than sense. You are spoiled enough as it is so forgive me if I decline your pitch.'

Izzy decided she rather liked MK. He spoke with a dry, amused tone that reminded her of Jared. No wonder they were such good friends.

'Why should you get a new horse *and* a swimming pool anyway?' Taryn asked. 'I haven't got anything.'

'You weren't kidnapped,' MK said.

'I could've been,' Taryn said, her serious little face scowling. It was a valid point, Izzy had to concede. 'It's just bloody typical.'

'And what's that supposed to mean?'

'You don't love me as much as you do Carlotta,' Taryn said, her face set.

'Whatever makes you think that?' MK's astonishment was apparent to all.

'It's so obvious. You're always saying how much Carlotta looks like Mama and you're always sad on my birthday. Everyone is.'

'Sweetheart, if I'm ever sad on your birthday it's not because it's the day you were born, but the day your Mama died. It would never be because of you. You are your Mama's last gift to me and that makes you the most precious thing in the world.

'What about that picture in your bedroom? It's only of Mama and Carlotta. You don't have any pictures of me.'

MK was shocked into silence. Taryn's bottom lip began to quiver.

'But you are in that picture,' MK said, finding his voice at last. 'You just hadn't been born yet. That picture is the only one ever taken that has all three of you in it. And that's why I chose it.'

Taryn was only half-appeased.

Izzy realised her earlier assessment of The Paddocks couldn't have been more wrong. It hadn't returned to normal at all.

---

IT WASN'T until after dinner that Carlotta came face to face with Izzy. Izzy was dragging herself back to bed at the same time Carlotta was exiting her own room. They met on the landing, where they stared at each other in silence, united in their horror at what had happened. Carlotta's eyes kept darting to Izzy's sling, as though she couldn't drag her eyes away. Izzy noticed Carlotta was pale and subdued. Clearly all the bravado at dinner had been mere fronting. Instinct encouraged Izzy to draw her into a tight hug. Carlotta clung to her.

'I'm so sorry,' Carlotta said, her voice low.

'Whatever for?'

'Because if I'd said something before, about how worried I was and how domineering Alan was being… maybe none of it would have happened. I wanted to break it off with him but he wouldn't take no for an answer. Instead he kept asking to come into the house. He wanted to stay over and was pushing for us to go all the way. I didn't like it and said I was telling Jared but then Alan said if I told anyone I'd be sorry, so I didn't. I ended up sorry anyway.'

'Is that why you wanted to talk to me the night before it happened?'

'I was going to, but I bottled it.' Carlotta shook her head as though trying to force any unpleasant thoughts out. 'I was so frightened. That's why it's all my fault.'

Izzy shook her head.

'You mustn't blame yourself, and nor should I. Gemma's the one who should be bleedin' sorry. I'm just so glad you're okay. I'd never have forgiven myself if anything had happened to you.'

Carlotta pointed to Izzy's arm. 'Does it hurt?'

'No,' Izzy lied.

Carlotta wandered into Izzy's room and over to the dresser. Here she studied the array of cards. She picked one up, read it, then set it down before turning to face Izzy.

'I didn't send you a card, or a gift. Not because I didn't care but nothing I wrote would be special enough. I didn't want to thank you by proxy. I wanted to see you in person. It was really brave of you, you know, what you did.'

'I didn't really have a choice. I had to do something,' Izzy said. Carlotta gave the smallest of smiles.

'That was some piece of riding. Good job you're a natural. No novice could have stayed on Vega all that way, and especially near to that awful place.' There was no greater stamp of approval coming from Carlotta. It also gave Izzy an in to a conversation she knew they would have to have sooner or later.

'Was it really horrible? Inside there.'

Carlotta shuddered.

'They tied me to this big piece of equipment. I can't even bear to think about what it did to those poor animals. The whole place had this weird metallic smell of blood and machinery. I haven't been able to eat meat since.'

'Do you want to talk about it?'

'Not really.' A pause. 'Not yet.' And with that Izzy had to be satisfied.

---

IT WAS ONLY a matter of time before MK called Izzy into his office 'for a chat'. They sat opposite each other in the big, squashy tan leather chairs. Mrs Firth had provided a cafétière of coffee and a plate of biscuits. Clearly the meeting was intended as being informal but Izzy felt as though she were going to the gallows. Still convinced there had been something else she could have done to prevent Carlotta being nabbed, she fully expected a bollocking from a like-minded MK. She was therefore stunned when MK seemed more nervous about their discussion than she was. As soon as Mrs Firth exited the room he leaned forward, rocking slightly on the edge of the seat, his fingertips pulsing together.

'Firstly, I want to thank you for taking such good care of my two babies,' was his opening, and instantly disarming, sentence. As he spoke he poured a large mug of coffee and handed it to an astonished Izzy. She had expected him, with all his success and millions, to treat her with subservience and here he was pouring her beverages for her. 'You went far and beyond what anyone would have expected of you, and I want you to know how much I appreciate that.'

Izzy didn't know what to say. 'Thank you for sending the car for me. There was really no need. A taxi would have done just as well,' she babbled.

'Nonsense! Nothing but the very best for the young lady who has been taking care of my daughters so meticulously.' MK paused, then looked mischievous. 'I do hope they were well-behaved.' He held Izzy's gaze for a few seconds before both of them grinned, each certain in the knowledge they had been anything but. It lifted the mood slightly.

'There is much to discuss. At the very least you deserve to know the truth about what has been going on here. My family has so much to thank you for: for looking after Carlotta and Taryn for the best part of the year, for your selfless bravery, for your wonderful barrister-friend's involvement in my release.'

Ever enterprising and self-serving when it came to her career, Caro had managed to involve herself in the dismissal of the case. In the heavyweight light of Gemma's box of evidence, there had been no case to answer. The CPS had no option but to drop all charges. In the end Caro's involvement had been liaising with MK's appointed legal representation about the box's contents and could barely be described as work, but even a cursory mention in the case notes would look great on her CV and send her closer to being a QC.

'Mrs Firth said something about inedible evidence,' Izzy said. MK gave a wide grin and a shout of laughter before becoming instantly sober.

'Indeed. The contents of Gemma's parcel were truly incriminating. She had copy bank statements, account numbers and passwords, copy keys, alarm codes… These she used to undermine Jared and the security of the house. More disturbing were the blood-stained knives and skewers she'd used to torture and kill small animals, which I understand she then left as macabre gifts for my children with the intention of terrorising them. Worst of all were the photographs of Carlotta, Taryn, Mrs Firth and myself each defaced with crude, childlike depictions of us being stabbed or maimed.' MK paused, as though uncertain as to whether he should continue. 'Snaps of you suffered a similar fate, except added to these were words of hatred. She called you a whore and a bitch and wished you dead. Only the pictures of Jared, mostly taken without his knowledge, were left unmarked.'

There were a few moments of silence as this news was processed. The depth of Gemma's hatred was a new horror to have to deal with.

'I still don't understand why she chose to do such dreadful things,' Izzy said quietly.

MK filled Izzy in on Gemma's story. A teenage equestrian prodigy, Gemma had won, amongst many other things, the Pony of the Year competition in the late nineties and had been earmarked as a talent for the future. Destined to fast track to the senior circuits, her bright future had been mapped out and all but writ in stone. Then disaster had struck. A horrific road traffic accident involving the horsebox she had been travelling home in from another show shattered these hopes and plans. Not only had Gemma's professional riding career come to an abrupt end courtesy of a shattered shoulder but her beloved prizewinning pony had had to be destroyed having suffered breaks in not one but two legs. Gemma would be able to continue riding, in time, but only for recreational purposes. Her ruined shoulder would never be able to withstand the rigours of the professional circuit. Never before had the old adage 'those who can, do; those who can't, teach' been more pertinent. Instead of pursuing a glittering career in showjumping, Gemma resigned herself to a life of teaching other young talents, ensuring that they achieved what had been so cruelly snatched from her own grasp. Izzy remembered Carlotta telling her back at the time of Taryn's birthday how Gemma didn't compete. It all made sense now.

'Her parents divorced just after her accident too,' MK continued. 'Guilt is a terrible thing. It drove them apart, Gemma included, and she became all but estranged from them. All this, in addition to the accident, the loss of both her pony and her promising career was too much. In retrospect it seems clear that the threads of her mind were already unravelling at this point. Perhaps the boundaries between reality and fantasy were becoming smudged. Perhaps all the pressure and expectation that had been heaped upon her, the accident and the consequences thereof unhinged her,' MK said. 'Either that or she felt so bitter about having her destiny so cruelly changed that she felt she was owed something in exchange. Either way, she saw nothing wrong with using this family for her own ends.

'It's clear that she fixated on Jared, believing they were a couple and having read far too much into their one brief fling, which took place just after he'd first arrived at The Paddocks. He was just back from Iraq, very raw about what he'd seen and done and dealing with the breakdown of his marriage and the loss of his mother on top. It should have been no more than that. Evidently, Gemma saw it otherwise.

'It lasted for a couple of weeks. Then the headiness wore off and common sense returned, for Jared at least. But in Gemma's mind they continued to be a couple.'

'When I first arrived Gemma took great pains to let me know it was still ongoing,' Izzy confessed. 'She said it had to be a secret because you didn't want the girls to know.'

'I see. That explains a great deal. In retrospect, I suppose I shouldn't be surprised. Clearly she really believed it. From her own warped perspective it wouldn't have even been a lie.'

Then things had become more convoluted. Jared had broken it off, telling Gemma, quite truthfully, that MK would disapprove. Unable to accept this Gemma began to feel resentful. Then opportunity struck.

'One of my security staff caught a disgruntled ex-employee trying to key my car, the Rolls Royce, and punished him a bit too enthusiastically with tragic consequences. Seeing the chance to punish me for splitting her and Jared up, she implicated me by accessing my personal accounts and transferring a considerable sum of money from me to my employee, and then tipping off the Inland Revenue. It was enough to incriminate me in the crime. I don't think she meant for me to be arrested and accused of GBH. She only wanted to inconvenience me, blacken my name. Everything she did was for her own benefit. It was quite cold, quite calculating and completely without conscience. It's almost as though she couldn't differentiate between right and wrong. She didn't care that my accountants couldn't prove what the money had been used for because there had been no instructions, or that I couldn't provide a reasonable explanation. From a tax perspective alone it was disastrous. My security guard admitted full responsibility, but the damage had already been done. I was hauled in, and refused bail.'

Izzy was aghast.

'So all along she knew you were innocent, and let you rot in prison? She knew how painful it was for the girls and yet didn't speak up. It's incomprehensible.'

MK nodded sadly.

'She must have been terrified by this point. She could hardly admit to what she'd done without implicating herself and losing Jared forever. It started a downward spiral. Our only saving grace was she was still obsessed with Jared and that caused her to procrastinate. I also think she was torn by some genuine, if warped and territorial, fondness for the girls. It would appear it was your arrival at The Paddocks that forced her to emerge from her fantasy.' MK was closer to the mark than he could have imagined. What he hadn't known was that Gemma, believing there to be a growing attraction between Izzy and Jared, had tried her best to push Izzy towards Marc Jones. When that too failed, she gave up hope.

'She began to feel resentful. Not only about having to share Jared with another woman in the household, but also the girls' affection. She was already helping herself to whatever she wanted. It seems she took a pincode here, a borrowed key there. Almost like a collection. She was very discreet. She extracted small amounts of cash from my personal accounts, small enough to be written off as anomalies, but to my immense shame I still don't know how we missed her involvement. Maybe she just got lucky. Perhaps her greatest ally was our trust. Yes, she was remarkably efficient in covering her tracks, but I admit that I never suspected her. In my defence, it was an inconceivable as suspecting Jared or Mrs Firth. I had people scouring my companies. I never dreamed it was someone in my own household.

'We'd always believed she'd come here to help Carlotta achieve what she could not. It's very sad. If it hadn't been for Gemma this family would have barely coped. We had just lost Marisa, Taryn was a baby. Gemma and Carlotta became best of friends. She'd been part of this family for almost seven years. It's still so hard to believe she could be so duplicitous.

'Unfortunately, if the desire for Jared's approval was the one thing keeping Gemma honest, the one thing that could turn her was the thought she would be usurped in his affections by another. It didn't matter that her love for Jared was totally unrequited. As I've said, she truly believed they were in love. And then you turned up and her worst fears came to pass. Gemma was forced to accept that Jared did not love her. I don't know exactly what happened but Gemma had to face reality. Something provoked her into a panic. It must have been quite a reality check.'

Izzy coloured up as she remembered the 'wincident'. She was pretty sure that had provided the swing vote.

'We'd had some problems with the other nannies — stealing, the girls locking them in cupboards,' MK said.

'All Gemma? But Jared thought it was the girls playing tricks.' Izzy remembered how Jared had told her about her predecessor being locked in the wine cellar and how horrified she'd been at the prospect of suffering the same fate.

'So it seems, and I'm sure they were willing accomplices, believing it to be humorous. Gemma's motives were far more self-serving. She simply didn't want another woman in the house. Unfortunately for her, you stuck around.'

'She probably didn't see me as a threat, at least not at first,' Izzy said gloomily, recalling her disastrous first few weeks at The Paddocks. Gemma wasn't the only one who would have presumed she wouldn't stick it for more than a fortnight. Any sensible person would have backed her for a quitter.

'Gradually a large amount of evidence had been amassed. Something made her panic so she packaged it all up, then asked you to post it to a made-up address. She must have hoped it would never come back.'

'And then I screwed up her plan not only by adding a return address but worse, by mixing up the parcels,' Izzy said. She was pretty certain it had been Carlotta threatening to spill the beans to Jared about Alan that had prompted Gemma to act. This she relayed to MK. He nodded in sage agreement.

'That's most likely. Gemma must have nearly died when it was returned to sender. What went through her mind when she discovered it was full of preserves, I can't imagine. At this point she would have known you'd posted her box of tricks to your mother. At that point there was no preventing the inevitable, and so she panicked. She sent Jared a bogus message from me. Mrs Firth was already away—'

'But I still don't understand why or what she hoped to gain.'

'There is no explanation. As Carlotta's success grew, so did her resentment. It's highly likely she just wanted to make us suffer in the same way she had. Her obsession with Jared was her last link to sanity. Once that was removed… In many ways Carlotta played right into her hands with her constant running away and tantrums.'

'But if I hadn't messed up the parcels her hand wouldn't have been forced. It's because of me that Carlotta was taken and Steptoe was killed,' Izzy wailed.

'I can see why Jared says you're a lunatic,' MK said wryly. The warm glow Izzy had felt when MK had hinted at Jared's feelings for her dissipated. 'Quite the contrary,' MK continued, his voice hardening. 'It's because of you that all this has come to light, and that can only be a good thing. You intervened, be that intentionally or via the hand of fate, and the evidence was misdirected. You were the one who got the police there so quickly, you were the one who got Jared there so quickly too. I know you think they didn't listen to you but Jared rang the chief inspector at the local police station and corroborated your story. It's the most exciting thing that has ever happened in the history of the Greater Ousebury constabulary.

'So you see, you mustn't blame yourself in any way. If you hadn't managed to mix up those parcels it's likely I would never have been exonerated. No jury would have found me innocent. I owe my freedom entirely to you, and so does Carlotta. You chose to ride Vega — something I've never dared do, I might add — and that choice ensured the failure of Gemma's scheme. You must love my daughters very much to so willingly put yourself in such danger.'

'I'd never let anything happen to them,' Izzy said fervently. MK gave a bark of laughter.

'Now that I do believe,' he said. 'And it's another reason why I wanted us to have a chat today. I want you to stay, permanently. No one could possibly take better care of my daughters than you. Everyone wants you to stay. *Everyone*. Jared told you right from the start that this family hasn't been formed on blood ties alone. You are as much a part of this family as Jared and Mrs Firth—'

'And as Gemma used to be,' Izzy said thoughtfully.

'Was she?' MK asked bleakly. 'I wish I could be sure of that. Although,' MK spread his hands out in a gesture of hopelessness. 'I have no doubt she loved the girls in her own misdirected fashion. She must have been very confused. She risked a lot to leave Vega in the stables. It would have been far more sensible to isolate you completely.'

'She still poisoned Steptoe,' Izzy said. She still had nightmares about finding him stone dead on the tile floor. 'And killed all those other poor creatures. She still chose to do that.' Izzy covered her open mouth with her hands to conceal the horror she was experiencing. The animals had gradually increased in size, culminating in a dog. Would one of the ponies, presumably either Jester or Mini Cheddar, have been next if she had continued uncurtailed? The thought made her feel sick.

'Yes,' MK said. 'She did. It would seem that every time Jared showed you affection, she retaliated with an act of violence.' It all made sense. The incidents started the day Izzy fell off Ghost and Gemma had taken the rap for it.

'So the scored saddle had been directed at me, after all,' Izzy said slowly.

'It's a truly frightening thought. She had copied keys, gate blippers, alarm codes, passwords, access to everywhere. All the safety precautions were for nothing. She could have entered the house at any time. She was often alone with either of my daughters, sometimes both. It makes me shudder to think how vulnerable you all were for so long. We must remember Steptoe with honour. He put up a good fight. He took quite a chunk out of Gemma's arm, I gather. It shall be his last hurrah. It's no coincidence it was Jared's dog she chose to kill.'

Izzy couldn't help but dwell on those awful words. Chose to kill…

'What will happen to her now?' she asked. She was aware that Gemma was being detained in the psychiatric ward of a women's prison. Once confronted, Gemma had signed a full confession detailing how she had broken into MK's office and sent the electronic payment. This had finally provided the answer to the one aspect of MK's alleged crime that had never made sense. Why would he send such a payment so blatantly with no attempt at inscrutability?

'I feel very torn. Part of me would like to see her slung in jail and the key thrown away but, having just spent almost a year rotting in a prison cell, I cannot in all good conscience subject her to the same fate. Clearly she has been very unwell for some time and we may also have to accept that matters here have exacerbated that.'

'I think you're very generous, under the circumstances,' Izzy said.

'It is very complicated but I cannot forget that, whether intentionally or not, she has done as much good for this family as she has bad.'

'Is Carlotta really all right? Did they hurt her?'

'They slapped her about a bit. She's okay though. She's tough. Just like her mother was.'

'What did they intend to do with her?'

'No idea. I don't think they gave it any real thought. Alan? He was just a paid pawn who Gemma saw fit to exploit. He was lodging with her since the spring. I'm not sure if she promised him riches, or adventure or sex… but what a job for him! Even as a proud parent, no one can blame me for proclaiming Carlotta a beauty. She has confessed that Alan fed her a sob story about how his family was poor and all he wanted to do was ride ponies and she fell for it. It was a simple case of pity mistaken for affection.'

Izzy finally understood what had attracted Carlotta to him in the first place.

'There can be no doubt that Gemma was deeply jealous of Carlotta on so many levels,' MK continued. 'Her talent, her beauty, her able body and the ample wealth and upbringing that enabled her to pursue her career in equestrianism. It must have seemed to Gemma that Carlotta had been handed everything she had been robbed of on a silver platter.

'Taryn has been affected by the events as a whole. She's less bothered by Gemma's duplicity than Carlotta. Carlotta is resilient in general, but cannot forgive Gemma for betraying her trust. She hero-worshipped her. Taryn was fond enough of her, and is very upset at her betrayal, but Carlotta…? She is devastated by what Gemma has done.' MK rolled his eyes. 'No doubt it will cost me a fortune to heal her wounds.'

'She told me she's been having nightmares about the abattoir,' Izzy said. 'I think it has affected her quite badly.'

MK's face contorted with fury.

'I have already made plans to acquire the land and buildings. It will be razed to the ground the instant it's in my possession. It is another reason why I'm keen for you to stay. There's been enough disruption to this household over the past year. The girls trust you. You bring an element of normality.'

That was a truly remarkable first! Izzy thought.

'Jared has been under a great deal of strain, as has Mrs Firth. Constantly supervising the girls with this hanging over them has been difficult.'

'Why didn't they share the burden with me?' Izzy asked. 'I found out anyway.'

MK had the grace to look embarrassed.

'I said we have much to thank you for. We have much to apologise for too. I have to confess that I was suspicious of your motives,' he admitted. 'How wrong could I have been? We now know that the increase in Gemma's underhand behaviour was in no way coincidental to your arrival here. To my jaundiced eye it seemed evident that you were the cause. Merle Miller was no use whatsoever. She admitted, after I applied a certain amount of pressure, that she never did process your DBS check. She justified herself by saying that her gut had told her that you would be a success and this negated any guilt she felt at not processing the search. She must have been desperate to bring money in to be so cavalier with my daughters' safety. She considered me to be one of her more generous clients. She didn't find me so generous when I started proceedings against her for negligence. I am not a vengeful man but I was incensed. It's no reflection on you,' he told Izzy. 'We were so lucky it was you and not someone who could be tempted to manipulate the situation.

'Jared was instructed to keep an eye on you. He told me over and over again that you were trustworthy, he was adamant. So you see, the decision not to involve you further was deliberate,' MK said. 'I must confess that we, or rather I, wasn't sure you were genuine.'

'I see.'

It didn't escape MK's experienced, business eyes that Izzy winced every time Jared's name was mentioned.

'I know you're wondering where Jared is.'

Izzy flinched again.

'One of us had to mention his absence at some point. I understand the two of you have become close friends. I asked him to take some leave. He has some… err… matters he needs to sort out. He's also worked non-stop for the past two years without taking a break, so he needs time and space to reconcile his feelings about all of this. Understandably, he feels guilty. He had no idea Gemma was so unhinged and he feels responsible, to blame. If you feel you also need some leave, or perhaps some counselling to help you come to terms with what has happened, I'm happy to take care of all the arrangements.'

'I'm okay,' said Izzy, truthfully. She couldn't help but wonder what matters Jared had to deal with. Clearly the secrets continued.

---

IZZY MOPED ROUND The Paddocks for several days. What with her foot in a bandage and her casted arm suspended in a sling, she was in permanent discomfort, which didn't help improve her state of mind.

Daily activities were a nightmare with only one arm. MK brought in a mobile hairdresser to wash and style her hair every other day. Taryn and Carlotta helped her with everything else. She literally wanted for nothing.

'The locals wanted to throw you a party at The Half Moon but I didn't think you'd be keen.'

MK also declined any interview requests on her behalf.

'As much for my family's sake as for yours.'

Instead a brief statement would be issued.

One of the broadsheets picked it up and ran a brief column on one of the central pages.

*Konstantine Magnate Exonerated: Groom's Vendetta Foiled By Nanny,* it read.

It gave a clinical breakdown of the series of events and was accompanied by an old school mugshot of Izzy looking gormless and dishevelled. A similar snap of Gemma showed her to be smiling and glamorous. Izzy compared both pictures and tutted. Even in glory she was still characterised as the idiot. Nevertheless, the newspaper article made her feel twitchy. She'd always dreamed of being someone important, someone people would recognise, but now she'd had a taste of fame she found she wanted nothing more than to remain anonymous. At least it hadn't been one of the tabloids.

---

In Jared's absence the veg plot went berserk. MK brought in the nephew of the local bobby to help in the gardens and stables as a temporary measure.

'If we can't trust him, then God help us.'

Despite knowing full well it would be nothing more than self-torture, Izzy let herself into Jared's room and lay down on his bed. Mrs Firth had changed his bedding so the sheets and duvet smelled of nothing other than fabric softener.

Upon opening his wardrobe, Izzy saw that his clothes were folded and hung with military neatness, and all shoes polished and neatly paired up. Izzy gave a small smile. That figured. She ran her hands over his tee shirts, remembering what he had been doing when he had worn each one. That black one he had worn on her first day, and the navy one when he had taken her to The Half Moon for her supper back in February. This was the tee shirt he'd been wearing at the Great Yorkshire Show and that white one was the one he had been wearing on the night of the 'wincident'. She unhooked it from its hanger and carried it over to the bed, where she sat down. Holding it to her nose, she breathed in. It still had the faintest smell of the aftershave and the insect repellent from that evening. Izzy was transported back to that hot September night in an instant. It made her feel dizzy with longing. After that she sat, threading the tee shirt through her fingers as she tried to figure out where it had all gone wrong.

Carlotta found her there. Izzy looked up at her, her face the picture of guilt at being caught snooping.

'Don't think badly of me.'

Carlotta waved this aside.

'I don't. I went through your stuff when you first came here. Missing J-boy, eh? Don't look so surprised. Everyone knows you've got the screaming hots for him. It's *sooo* obvious. I reckon he fancies you too. He was demented in the ambulance. Not that I blame him for that. It was awful. You were just lying there. I thought you were dead. Anyway, he never let go of your hand once.'

'So how come when I woke up in the hospital he was gone?'

'Because Marc chucked him out, dumbass.'

'*What?!*'

'Marc barged in, saw Jared sitting by your bedside and shouted at him to 'get the eff away from my girlfriend'. After that they just stared at each other across your body, eyeballing each other like Sprite and Pongy do when they're arguing over a bone.' Izzy raised a small smile at this. 'After that Marc told Jared to piss off and leave you alone. I think his exact words were... 'Where the fuck were you with all your flash military training? She could have been killed."

'So what did Jared do?' Izzy asked, her throat constricting.

'Just upped and left.'

It was all Izzy needed to know.

'Here, you forgot this!' Carlotta chucked the white tee shirt at her. Shaking her head, Izzy crossed back over to the wardrobe and hung it back on its hanger.

'No crutches this time.'

---

TWO WEEKS after her return from hospital Izzy found herself alone in the house except for Mrs Firth and the dogs. Carlotta and Taryn had been taken to the Horse of the Year show by MK, who was keen to spend some quality time with his daughters. Both girls had wanted Izzy to join them but she'd chickened out, claiming she wouldn't be able to navigate the crowds with her brace of injuries. This had been only partly true. The truth was that Izzy had wanted to steep in her own misery for a few days. She herself acknowledged it probably wasn't the healthiest decision but on the other hand she felt she needed to allow herself time to recover. Time to absorb what had happened over the past few months before she let go. A further consideration was that she simply couldn't bear to be around happy people at the moment and MK and the two girls were dizzy with joy following their reunion.

As she lay on her bed watching some chick flick or another, Izzy was aware of the intercom buzzing faintly. It was probably the milkman calling for his bill or the postman delivering one of the many mail order gifts MK had bought to spoil the girls. Either way, Izzy saw no reason to disturb herself. She was surprised therefore to find herself summoned by a very excited Mrs Firth. There was someone asking to see her. A gentleman. He was waiting in the winter den. Izzy was invaded by a swarm of butterflies, or perhaps stinging bees taking into account the sudden pain in her stomach.

*Jared!*

He'd come back at last. He always hauled her into that room when he wanted to speak to her.

In her own mind she raced, but in actuality she hobbled, down the staircase and into the study. Six dogs followed her. There she found herself looking at the impeccably suited back of a well-built, tall man. But it wasn't Jared. Izzy knew this even before he turned to face her.

Gutted by disappointment, Izzy found herself two feet away from Scott. He was smiling at her with that cheeky, sexy grin which she had once found irresistible. Today it left her numb.

'Izzy! Thank God you're okay. I've been hearing dreadful things about you being hurt.' After engulfing her in an uncharacteristic hug, which Izzy did not reciprocate, Scott gave a short laugh and waved his arm around the room. 'I can't believe you live here. This is an amazing place. Look at that view! And the kit in here, and in the hallway! I'm sure I saw an original Monet on the staircase. I was grilled at the front gate by some old troll before I was let in. How on Earth did *you* manage to land such a cushy job?'

Trust Scott to see only the material rather than the emotional wealth of The Paddocks.

'So flattering... as always. What do you want?' Izzy asked, easing herself down onto one of the dark red leather sofas. The dogs formed a protective circle round her, all eyes fixed on the stranger. Some lay on the floor. Others, including Hobbit, jumped up onto the sofa and settled next to her. Since Steptoe's death the little terrier had become her constant companion. Izzy found their presence comforting, reassuring. Only Pongy kept his distance, instead sitting amusingly close to Scott's legs, gazing up at him with an expression of innocence. Both Izzy and Pongy knew it would only be a matter of time before an unpleasant stench reached Scott's nostrils.

Taken aback by such an unexpectedly frosty reception, Scott stalled for a few moments. He stared at her, wrongfooted.

'I've... er... been worried about you, baby doll—' he began.

Izzy truncated him. 'No you haven't. And don't call me that. I'm not your baby doll and haven't been for quite some time.'

Scott went for the boyish, charming approach to disarmament.

'I know. I was such a fool. I've done nothing but miss you since you left.'

It didn't work.

'I didn't *leave*. You kicked me out, remember? That was

just before you changed all your contact details so that I couldn't track you down. Plus, it's taken you over nine months to realise this. So, I'm afraid I don't believe you.' Izzy stared up at him from the sofa.

It was at this point that Scott took a good long look at Izzy. He saw the newly curvy body, wonderfully accentuated by a rugby-style eventing shirt, which had alternate broad hot-pink and white horizontal stripes which made her boobs look bigger, and a pair of flatteringly cut dark grey flannel track bottoms. Her face had also filled out and her skin and hair, stylishly cut, were in obviously great condition. There wasn't a hint of fake tan but instead a good, healthy country-life glow. Izzy had never looked better, fitter or sexier. He also noticed the bandaged foot and the arm, still in its sling.

'You're injured,' he said, stupidly.

'Well spotted!' was Izzy's dry reply. Then, to amaze him further, she added: 'I fell off a horse whilst galloping across country.' She wasn't going to give him the satisfaction of knowing she'd also stabbed her own foot with a pitchfork.

Scott gave a short, unpleasant laugh.

'Pull the other one. Since when did you learn to ride?'

'Since February. Since I came to live here after I lost everything I loved in London.'

'That's why I'm here. I finally realised how happy you made me. I've come to take you home.'

'I am home.'

'But you just said… about everything you loved in London.'

'Yes, emphasis on the word *loved*. Past tense.'

'You've changed,' said Scott.

'Yes, and thank God for that,' said Izzy. She was suddenly overwhelmed with fatigue. 'Are we done here? I really need to get on with my life, and you don't feature in it.'

It was at this point that Scott abandoned all pretence of

congeniality. Denied his prize, the return of his trophy girlfriend, he decided to put the boot in.

'I read about you in the paper. It said you'd foiled an attempt to kidnap the daughter of Mika Konstantine. I mistakenly believed you might have grown up a bit, having gone through a bit of trauma, but I can see I was mistaken.'

Izzy laughed at this. Suddenly everything was clear. Scott had read about her heroics and decided that, finally, she was worthy to be paraded on his arm. At last she'd become someone he could boast about. How ironic that, now that she'd become exactly what Scott wanted, she no longer needed him to want her.

'So, I'm finally someone you can respect,' Izzy said. 'What sweet irony that now I respect myself I don't need to look for you for approval and justification.'

'Has all this got something to do with the Jared character that sent me a cocky letter months ago? I bet it has. Where is he? I want to speak to him.'

'He's away on business right now, but if he were here he'd kick your arse.'

'I very much doubt that. I do work out,' Scott replied, scornfully.

'Yeah well, he used to work out… in Iraq, as a marine, so I wouldn't fancy your chances. Go home. There's nothing for you here.' Then a thought occurred to Izzy. 'Oh, wait here. Yes, there is.' She hobbled out of the room, returning a few minutes later with Scott's blue tee shirt that had caused such a row when she had first arrived at The Paddocks. She chucked it at his chest. 'I don't need this anymore.' It was her final piece of closure.

Mrs Firth was hovering by the door.

'Should I make a pot of tea?' She was practically dancing from foot to foot with suppressed nosiness.

'*Oxhi, efharisto. Archimalakas.*'

Mrs Firth simultaneously raised her eyebrows and suppressed a smirk.

'Are you speaking Greek?' Scott asked, astonished. It was apparent he didn't want to leave but Izzy had already pushed past him.

'Scott was just leaving, Mrs Firth. Please show him out.'

---

TIME SHUFFLED on at The Paddocks. Everyone returned from the Horse of the Year show in good spirits. Carlotta in particular was delirious with happiness, having been earmarked by the selectors for a trial at the David Broome Event Centre in November. Already aware of Polo's showjumping credentials this, added to Carlotta's undeniable talent, was an amalgamation that couldn't be disregarded. It was just a matter of seeing if they gelled. Their only concern had been Jet's unsuitability for the junior circuit. Undoubtedly a great competition pony, at 14.2hh he was a little on the small side and wouldn't have the scope for the bigger courses, but with both Polo and Vega Carlotta would have two top class horses. Her face clouding, Carlotta mentioned she had a lot to thank Gemma for. It was a sad acknowledgement.

'I'm gonna ask Papa if he will put the Team Konstantine logo back on the horsebox before we go. If I meet Ellen Whitaker I'll wet my knickers with excitement. You really should enter a couple of novice competitions on Jet next summer. I think you'd really enjoy yourself.' There was something touching about the way Carlotta presumed Izzy would still be around next year.

MK threw himself back into his home and business lives with gusto. He spent most of the hours of daylight in his office but still found time to pull more strings than a puppet master to get Carlotta accepted into an equestrian school close by. She would be allowed to take both Polo and Vega with her and train them in conjunction with studying for her upcoming mocks. It was hoped the school would coax the best out of Carlotta both in the classroom and in the saddle. She would start after Christmas, at the beginning of the spring term. Until then MK agreed to continue rolling in an army of personal tutors to get her up to speed with her studies. Showjumper or not, GCSEs were still expected to be passed.

Taryn struggled more than anyone else to come to terms with the events of the past weeks and clung to Izzy more than ever. Her hyperventilation attacks were more frequent and she had even begun to whinge about fruit again. None of this escaped MK's notice so he called Izzy to the winter den for a brief interview.

Coincidentally, Izzy received a letter from her letting agent that morning advising her that her tenants had given notice on their sublease and her flat would soon be vacant. She could move back to London at the beginning of November. Still clutching this letter in her hand, she joined MK in the den. As though by psychic abilities MK knew what the letter contained.

'We all want you to stay. Everyone here loves you.' Embarrassed, Izzy scoffed at this. MK looked at her meaningfully. 'Mrs Firth, the girls, *everyone*.'

Izzy turned away. It was still too painful to think about Jared and his abandonment. Izzy couldn't believe he hadn't been back to see Carlotta and Taryn yet, even if he didn't care about her.

'There's no place for me. Eventually you'll meet someone and remarry and they won't like their position being usurped by a scatty nanny.'

'You're not the girls' nanny. You're their friend and the closest thing they've had to a mother in years. Let's be honest, Taryn hasn't ever had anyone at all. Even if I did meet someone, and believe me I have no prospects at all, especially since I've spent the past twelve months living with hundreds of blokes—' MK gave a wry smile that made Izzy feel more at home. '—They would have to fit in with this family. And that includes you. I know I am repeating myself but when Jared—' Izzy dropped her eyes at the mention of his name. '—Told you that this household is a family regardless of whether there is a blood tie, it was a great truth. You're a member of this family now. Please stay.'

'I promise I'll give it serious thought,' said Izzy. MK sighed. 'I realise you'd like an answer, and the right answer, straight away, but that's the best I can offer. I hope you understand.'

'After experiencing loss myself, and considering what has happened here, I'd be a hypocrite if I didn't. Take all the time you need.'

Izzy had promised MK she would give him her answer by the end of the week. She woke on Friday morning consumed with misery, still undecided. By arrangement, she and MK had agreed not to tell either of the girls until a decision had been made. If she made her mind up to leave, Izzy realised that her answer would break Carlotta and Taryn's hearts. Well, they say these things come in threes, she thought to herself.

Izzy went for a walk and brooded on all this as she watched a leaf being blown across the stable yard.

Just like me, she thought sadly. All her old problems had returned except she had swapped her love for Scott for an even more hopeless love for Jared.

It had been a mild October, leaving the leaves on the trees the chance to turn gold, ochre and red before they fell. Only a few were scattered across Cherry Tree Avenue. Boston ivy and Virginia creeper, purple and red, still clung like an ex-girlfriend to the sides of houses and walls and brought beautiful brickwork, roadsigns, postboxes and house nameplates into high relief. The misted air was damp and close, almost claustrophobic, and was steeped with the sharp tang of gardeners' bonfires and decomposing foliage. It would soon be Hallowe'en. Izzy felt that the weather suited the month, being clandestine, full of secrets, easy to hide within. During the last week frosts had threatened. When the first severe one hit all the leaves would be stripped. Autumn would be over. Winter was just a breath away.

She had witnessed the trees turn from naked brown skeletons to the full bloom of summer only to shed their leaves once more. She felt that she had become part of the scenery, almost a part of Yorkshire herself. She was also amazed at how much she would miss the place if she left. God's own country, she had heard the locals say. Lucky God, she thought. She wished it were her own.

Just before it got dark Izzy visited Steptoe's grave in the little pet cemetery and laid some Bonios on it. She took some time to shed a private tear for the little dog who had been her first friend at The Paddocks. Almost a month had passed and she was still having nightmares about finding him in the kitchen. Above her a rusty sky stretched across the firmament. No doubt Steptoe was chasing balls in doggie heaven. Over by the church spire a fat hunter's moon was starting its ascent into the evening. It promised to be a cold night. The horses had been turned out in their rugs, their winter coats woolly. They'd need to be clipped soon. She was still amazed at how much she'd learned since she'd been here, both about horses and about herself. From the house she heard the sounds of Carlotta's pop music and could smell the faintest waft of the tagine Mrs Firth was cooking.

Over on the manége Taryn had just finished schooling Jester and had dismounted. Now she was leading her pony over to where Izzy was standing, grabbing the last of the apples off the trees and feeding them to him along the way. Izzy smiled as she remembered how terrified Taryn had been of fruit. At least she could walk away knowing she had done some good things.

'Are you coming in? It's nearly dinner time.'

Izzy gave Taryn a special smile and nodded. 'Shall I help you untack?' She indicated to her arm. 'Rather, shall I come and watch whilst you untack?'

'Please!' Taryn said. She shovelled yet another apple into Jester's eager mouth. Izzy gave her a disapproving look. 'He's been ever so good. He did a perfect full pass for me today,' Taryn protested.

In that moment Izzy realised how badly she wanted to stay. How could she possibly be thinking of leaving?

Half an hour later Izzy followed Taryn into the house. MK and Mrs Firth were in the kitchen deep in conversation. They ceased as soon as Izzy walked in, leaving her with the unpleasant notion they had been talking about her.

'Taryn, please don't sit in the kitchen in your riding gear. You know the rules. Go and shower before dinner.' Huffing, Taryn left the room. MK turned to Izzy. She felt very cagey suddenly.

'Are we still okay to have a chat after dinner?'

Izzy nodded but said nothing. MK gave her a searching look. Mrs Firth hadn't yet spoken. She was too busy preparing what seemed to be a vast feast. How many people were eating, Izzy thought, irrationally.

'Can I do anything to help?'

MK and Mrs Firth exchanged glances.

'Just go and relax. Have a nice hot bath.'

Izzy was relieved to leave the tension of the kitchen. She didn't feel like a bath. Instead she went along to the winter den and opened the door. The fire had already been lit. The laptop was open on the occasional table. Izzy eased herself round the table and onto the sofa and pulled the computer towards her. She might as well check her emails before dinner.

There were several tabs already open. Not wanting to disrupt anything anyone else was doing, Izzy began to minimise them — she could put it back as it was once she was done – and that's when she saw it.

Clearly MK had been doing some work and, having been called into the kitchen, had left his email open. At the top of the inbox was an email from J. Walker entitled *Coming Home*. Despite the chorus of voices in her head telling her not to look, Izzy clicked on the email to open it. And immediately wished she hadn't. With one eye on the screen and one eye on the door, Izzy read that Jared had arranged a meeting with his wife to 'put things right once and for all'.

> *I've no idea if it can ever work out properly but I at least have to try everything I can to give it its best shot,* Izzy read. She felt sick to her stomach. *Fingers crossed, I'll be back with you by the end of the week.*

Unable to read further Izzy closed the email and did some panicked calendar maths. It was Tuesday today. He could be back at The Paddocks within four days, complete with wife. No doubt that was what MK and Mrs Firth had been discussing in the kitchen. No wonder they'd fallen into an uncomfortable silence as soon as she'd appeared. She couldn't bear the thought of it. It was no use. It would be too painful to stay here. Her answer to MK would have to be no. Carlotta had been wrong. She herself had been wrong. All her secret hopes were dashed as she had read the paragraph. There was nothing between her and Jared, and never had been. She had to accept that otherwise she was no better than poor, deluded Gemma. She would have to do the adult, sensible thing and walk away. Immediately.

Not wanting to be caught doing the visual equivalent of eavesdropping, Izzy quickly maximised all the windows and slid out of the winter den.

Somehow she maintained a fixed, brittle smile throughout dinner. Afterwards she told MK that she'd made her decision. She would return to London before the end of the week. She felt like a louse.

'Can't you stay until Jared is back?' MK asked, aghast. Izzy shook her head. She could barely speak. MK tried a different tack.

'But you can't go back to London with your arm in a sling.'

Izzy gave a small wry smile that contained the slightest hint of pride along with some self-respect.

'I'll cope.' For the first time in her life, Izzy believed herself too. 'I need to sort out my flat.'

'I can arrange to have it taken care of on your behalf.'

Izzy shook her head. During the first weeks after Scott had dumped her everyone at The Paddocks had dragged her through it. This time it was up to her to look after herself. 'I need to do this myself. For me.'

MK gave a heavy sigh that somehow conveyed that whilst he was deeply disappointed he also understood.

'Okay. But if you need anything, anything at all, all you have to do is ask.'

She had finally done it. She finally had gumption.

---

Two days later Izzy left The Paddocks. She had packed the smaller of the suitcases Caro had given her back in February. MK had insisted that the remainder of her items would be boxed up and couriered down to whichever address she wanted. Even as Izzy packed, she couldn't believe how much stuff she had acquired in so short a time. There were several new items of clothing, including the ill-fated harem pants and the beautiful, shimmering sea-green silk top she had worn for Taryn's birthday party back in August, as well as a host of new photographs and trinkets that each held a painfully exquisite memory.

MK himself drove Izzy to the halt. Taryn came along too but Carlotta refused to go, instead choosing to stay at home and sulk over the maths homework her tutor had set her.

'Please come home soon,' Taryn had begged as she had given Izzy a tearful hug goodbye. Even MK kissed her on both cheeks.

'You may be London born and bred but you belong here with us. Please remember, this will always be your home.'

Not trusting herself to speak, all Izzy could do was nod silently as the train rumbled towards the platform. Then she was climbing onboard and finding her seat. Looking out of the window she could see Taryn sobbing, the very picture of heartbreak as she clung to her father. Was she really doing the right thing, Izzy thought in a sudden panic. But the train was already pulling away.

## IT'S GRIM DOWN SOUTH

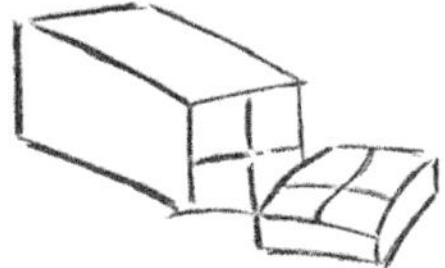

Izzy returned home to a city that was alien to her. As the East Coast Express cut its way through the outskirts of London, Izzy stared out of the windows at the building rush hour traffic, watching normal people stare listlessly back at her from within their 12 plate Zafiras as they waited at traffic lights and slip roads. She had difficulty understanding how she hadn't noticed before how built up and claustrophobic the city was. The further to Central London they got, the more hemmed in she felt. It was as though the high-risers and office blocks were looming in on her, gradually moving closer, the spaces between the buildings ever decreasing until she was trapped. There was no space, no air. All over the city streetlights, headlamps and houselights were being switched on earlier than usual now that the clocks had gone back. Football teams were playing evening games on floodlit Astroturf. Every so often a premature Guy Fawkes firework rocketed into the air, making everyone crane their necks towards the window to see. Even the darkness was closing in on her. She could almost hear Mrs Firth's voice: 'Put the big light on, love.' God, she missed The

Paddocks. She had only been gone for a matter of hours and it was torturous already.

King's Cross was even worse. Having grown used to the gentle undulation of rural life, Izzy was aghast at the sheer mass of people and the speed with which they pushed past her as though she were invisible.

Unable to face the Tube, she took a cab to Uxbridge, pretending to doze so the driver wouldn't ramble on at her. The lights were off in her flat. It had been empty for about a fortnight now. Cold and dank, it was much smaller and more threadbare than she remembered. Exhausted from having lugged her suitcase up two flights of stairs with her one good arm, she lit the electric fire and flopped onto the sofa, staring round at what had once been her lounge. It was a far cry from the luxury of The Paddocks. All her personal possessions were still boxed up and stored, half at her parents, half at The Paddocks. Save for a few bills and junk flyers on the side table there was no indication that the flat had ever been lived in, and certainly not by her. Unable to remain inactive she wandered into the kitchen. It smelled of turned-off fridge and disinfectant. The management company must have come in to do a cursory clean. Opening cupboards, she realised she didn't even have so much as a jar of instant coffee. Unpinning a takeaway menu from the corkboard, she ordered a pizza she had no intention of eating. It was something to do and at least they would also bring her a bottle of Coke.

The bedroom was as spartan as the lounge and kitchen. The only furniture was a wardrobe, one bedside cabinet and the bed. Even then the duvet had been stripped of its cover and there were no slips on the pillows. It was liveable and clean enough but offered no comfort whatsoever. The flimsy voile curtains she had put up so happily the previous summer did absolutely nothing to mitigate the Locket-yellow glare from the streetlamp just outside the window. There was no way she would be able to sleep with such light, especially as it periodically flickered on and off. It'd bring on a migraine before morning. When she had first arrived at The Paddocks she had found the country nights too dark. Now they were too light.

All of which she could have coped with if only it hadn't been so quiet. It was noisy enough outside. She could clearly distinguish the familiar hiss of tyres on wet tarmac as incessant traffic droned past and the roar from the 747s taking off from Heathrow. People were shouting to each other and laughing in the street as they walked home from the local pub. It was the human noise inside the house that she missed. Having lived with so many people for so long she felt bereft with loneliness. She was used to Jared always being around, strong and safe, the girls' constant chatter and squabbles and Mrs Firth's solid, sensible company, not to mention all the dogs and cats and horses. For the first time in almost nine months Izzy was truly on her own. Not that the girls were a subject she wanted to dwell on either. Izzy had respected them too much to fob them off with false hopes or lies and had therefore told them the truth, that she would be returning to London for a while at least, probably permanently. Neither had understood. Taryn had clung to her, begging her to stay, great racking sobs shaking her tiny body, whilst Carlotta had simply shrugged, expressing neither anger nor sadness. But Izzy knew Carlotta well enough to know that her immobility indicated how deeply betrayed she felt.

Mrs Firth had been philosophical, and just a little bit cryptic, about it.

'You've got to do what you feel is best, love,' she'd said. Which hadn't made Izzy feel any better.

At least the telly worked. On *EastEnders* and *Coronation Street* there were several new and unfamiliar storylines and characters. She watched them without paying any real attention. The same applied to the programmes that followed: a gritty drama set in an inner city university, Newsnight and then a shockingly bad '90s martial arts film. Still bothered by the excess of light in the bedroom, she slept on the sofa, covered by the coverless duvet and a fleecy throw she rooted out of the airing cupboard. With not even a stuffed toy to act as a substitute for Hobbit she resorted to clutching a faux fur cushion. Thank God for all night telly, she thought as she finally drifted off. It was her only company.

It came as no surprise that she *didn't* feel better after a good night's sleep. Woken several times by vivid, fractured dreams she rose at dawn, having finally admitted defeat, devastated to realise she was back in her flat and not at The Paddocks. She showered, dressed, applied her make-up as best she could then sat on the sofa, staring blankly at the television, until it was late enough for her to leave the flat.

Unable to face breakfast, she battled her way to Holborn on the Tube, standing like a zombie with her one good arm gripping the pole as it trundled along the Circle line towards Blackfriars. Half an hour later she was standing in the Treasury Office of the Inner Temple, waiting for the administrator to tell her if Caro was in her chambers or in court. Izzy closed her eyes and crossed her fingers that it was the former. The administrator looked at her bandaged arm with suspicion as she muttered into the telephone receiver. Probably thinks I'm one of Caro's clients who has been in a scrap, Izzy thought. There was a time when she would have been concerned by the opinion of a stranger and would have tried to appease them. Now she didn't care. Instead she concentrated on reading a plaque on the wall whilst she waited.

'Izzy?'

Izzy spun round. Caro had entered the Treasury Office. She looked stunned. 'It is you!'

'Surprise!' Izzy said weakly. The sight of her oldest friend made her feel quite emotional.

'Oh my God!' Caro cried, hugging Izzy, taking care not to

jar her arm. The administrator watched surreptitiously. Caro was both formidable and to be respected. Good job she hadn't curled her lip at her visitor, who must be important for Caro to collect personally instead of sending her clerk.

'How are you here? I thought you were living the good life with your rugged marine. At least that's what Scott told Jonty.' Caro stepped back and studied Izzy carefully. 'You look amazing, injuries aside.'

'That's what country life does for you,' Izzy said wryly. It was true that she had never had a better figure. Eating three square meals a day, plus Mrs Firth's home-made goodies on top, had filled out Izzy's slender frame. Daily horse rides and manual chores had then honed her muscles so that she was now slim and athletic rather than skinny and undefined. Her skin had also never been in such good condition due to the combination of such a good diet and plenty of exercise.

'Don't take this the wrong way, because it's great to see you, but what are you doing in London?' Caro asked.

Izzy glanced quickly at the administrator, who was still eavesdropping. Caro read her mind.

'Come along to my chambers. I'll ask Ian to make us a pot of tea. It'll have to be a quick cuppa though as I'm due in court in an hour.' Ian was Caro's longstanding clerk. A quiet, subtle brain, he subsidised his considerable clerk's income by frequently winning cash prizes on the London pub-quizzing circuit. He spent these earnings jetting himself and his boyfriend first class round the globe in order to watch groundbreaking opera. Always polite to Izzy, he never displayed any emotional extremes. He was one of the kindest, most contented people she had ever met. After producing two steaming mugs of tea, and a well-stocked Harrods biscuit tin, Ian melted into the background, immersed in legal papers. After a few self-conscious minutes Izzy forgot he was in the same room.

'Listen, why don't you come round for supper tonight,'

Caro said. 'Jonty's out on a works do so I'll be in on my Jack Jones anyway. Stay over and we'll have a bottle or two and you can tell me all about your adventures in the wilderness. What are you doing for the rest of the day?' Izzy had absolutely no idea. She had no plans, no commitments.

Caro checked her wristwatch and scooped up her briefcase. 'Why don't you meet me at Rah-Rah's at about six thirty? We can have a quick glass of wine and then go back to mine for a takeaway. God, it'll be fab to have a proper catch up.' They left the Inn together. It was still cold outside, and damp too. Izzy shrank into her old mac, one sleeve flopping loosely at her side. As she watched Caro stride away she felt very definitely envious. Even when she walked she oozed confidence. She, Izzy, would never walk like that.

Unable to bear returning to her flat she mooched round the West End for an hour or so, calling into shops to buy essential items such as a new toothbrush and paste and some make-up remover. Realising she wouldn't have to go back at all if she bought pyjamas and pants and such like, she kept herself busy by shopping. Early window displays in red, green and gold were a painful reminder that it would soon be Christmas. That thought was almost unbearable. Now she wouldn't know the joy of trimming the tree with Carlotta, or seeing Taryn as Mary in her school nativity, or hearing the bells of the village church ringing in the birth of Christ. She could only imagine what Christmas Day would be like at The Paddocks. There was no doubt it would be a joyous occasion and a distinct improvement on last year when MK had been on remand and had spent Christmas banged up. Goodness knew what sort of Christmas dinner Mrs Firth was capable of rustling up and Izzy was sure the girls would insist on all the usual traditions such as crackers, party hats and games. Izzy presumed she would spend it with her parents as usual. She didn't allow herself to wonder whether or not Jared would be back. Did he even spend Christmas with the Konstantines or did he return to his own family: sisters or aunts or suchlike? He had never mentioned them. It wasn't something they had ever discussed. She had always presumed he stayed at The Paddocks. It had been insinuated during conversations with Carlotta and Gemma about the Boxing Day drag hunt. Last year it had been a bright, crisp, frosty day, Carlotta had told her, with a cool winter sun glinting weakly off the tinsel the riders had threaded into their horses' tails. She, Taryn, Jared and the cussed Gemma had gathered with the rest of the hunt outside The Half Moon. She had continued to describe the scene in such detail that, in her mind, Izzy could see the masters in their red coats, and everyone else in blues, blacks and tweeds. The hounds, white, black and tan, milling around the horses' legs, some with their paws on the master's horse's side in the hope of a treat. If she had been there would she have dared to join them, galloping across the frosted countryside on Jet? Yes, she probably would.

To offer some distraction she had a lonely sandwich in a side street café before passing three more hours by watching a mediocre film in Leicester Square.

Six thirty crawled round eventually. Izzy stood shivering outside Rah-Rah's, a half dozen carrier bags propped by her feet. It had been hell carrying them all with her one good arm, which now ached more than her injured one, if that were even possible. Why did she never think these things through?

Unable to face waiting inside on her own she peered in through the embossed glass windows at the darkened interior. It was already heaving with young executives let loose from their jobs in advertising and marketing. The latest, hippest beats were thumping out of minuscule Bose speakers bracketed to walls. Waitresses were delivering trays full of squat vodka shots and designer bottled beers to groups of workers squeezed into booths and crammed round high-legged tables. The racket that emanated from them as they all talked over each other was deafening. They all seemed to be so manic, so keen to drink away the stresses and strains of their hectic lifestyles. It was beautifully hyperactive. Izzy couldn't even claim to have once been a part of it. She'd never really fit into this world. And she certainly didn't want it back.

Caro came bounding up. Her eyes gravitated towards the mass of bags.

'Retail therapy?' she asked, her eyes dancing. 'What did you buy? I'll get them,' she added, noticing Izzy struggling to pick them up with her one good arm.

'A few essentials and a decent winter coat,' Izzy said wryly, looking down at her thin belted mac. She missed the waxed jacket she'd borrowed on her very first day at The Paddocks. She never had got round to buying her own. 'This thing is no use at keeping out the cold.' She didn't like to add that since she'd returned to London she hadn't been able to get warm once. 'Listen, could we pass on the drink in the bar and just head back to yours? It looks really rammed in there and I just don't think I'm up to it.'

'Of course.' Caro frowned slightly as she considered Izzy's subdued tone.

Jonty was ambling through the hallway in his boxers when Caro opened the front door and ushered Izzy inside. His face at their premature arrival was a picture.

'I'm setting off in about ten minutes,' he said, looking startled. 'I think I'll wait downstairs for my... err... lift.' He was now shooting daggers at an embarrassed, cringing Caro.

'What was all that about?' Izzy asked after Jonty had huffed back into the primary bedroom.

'Jonty's going out on the pop with Scott,' Caro explained, not quite meeting Izzy's eyes. But Izzy didn't even flinch. She had no feelings left for Scott. So long as he didn't bother her in any way she couldn't care less what he got up to.

Five minutes later Izzy and Caro were settled in the lounge with a bottle of wine apiece and a large bowl of Kettle

Chips to share. The telly was on but neither woman paid any attention to it.

'So,' said Caro, tucking her feet beneath her. 'What's been going on? I know all about your brilliant mercy dash to save the wayward daughter of a banged-up multi-millionaire from the deranged machinations of a vengeful riding teacher, so we'll skim over all that. Scott came roaring back with tales of how you'd become all dignified, and just a little bit bossy, a bit like a schoolmistress. He was really pissed off that you turned him down, the arrogant shit, and couldn't stop going on about how much you'd changed and how you were shacked up with this butch Commando. Jonty and I were agog—' she stopped abruptly as Jonty, now fully suited and booted, entered the room. 'Are you heading out now?'

'I am,' said Jonty. He looked at the bottle of red on the table beside Izzy with suspicion.

'You sure you're not gonna knock that over?' he accused. He had spent many an hour scrubbing at his and Caro's prized white carpets after Izzy had been to visit.

'Nope,' said Izzy, looking him straight in the eye. Jonty was staggered by her audacity. 'But if I do, rest assured I know how to get it out with a jay cloth and some white wine.' Izzy turned to a sniggering Caro. 'Although that is a waste of good white wine.' At that moment Shuffle wandered into the room. He was the first animal Izzy had seen in a day and a half and she was desperate to get her hands on him. She instinctively made clicking noises to attract his attention, rubbing her thumb over her fingers as she did so. Shuffle regarded her with knowing yellow eyes and chose to ignore her. Sitting on a human's knee was only fun if it annoyed them.

This time both Caro and Jonty gaped.

'But you hate cats,' Jonty spluttered. 'You could never bear Shuffle to be anywhere near you.'

'I love animals,' Izzy said truthfully. For a few seconds

only, she allowed herself to think about all the creatures at The Paddocks. Caro noticed that as she spoke a flash of utter anguish crossed her face. Then it was gone. 'So typical that he won't come to me now that I want him to. That's such a cat thing.'

Jonty was still looking at her as though she was a stranger.

'Since when did you become an animal lover?' he asked. 'I can't believe you've suddenly become a country girl.'

'Jonty, I've *always* been a country girl,' Izzy turned to give Caro a slightly sardonic smile. 'I just didn't know before, because I'd never been to the country.'

Jonty gaped at her. Caro was grinning widely.

'Scott did say she'd changed,' she said, almost gloatingly. Izzy also grinned up at Jonty. He'd so often succeeded in making her feel inferior. It was such a simple joy to let him know that he wouldn't succeed again.

'Don't worry, Jonty. I'm still a berk. The only difference is that now I don't care if other people think I am too.'

'Right... err... I'll be off then,' Jonty said, totally wrongfooted by Izzy's easy admission.

Once he had gone Caro released her inner barrister and continued to grill Izzy about Jared.

'He doesn't sound like your usual type at all,' Caro said after five minutes.

'And that's a bad thing?' Izzy asked.

'What is it about him that you like so much?'

'He's real,' Izzy said simply. 'There's no bullshit, or vanity, or pretension. He doesn't care about appearances, or other people's opinions, or their past mistakes.'

Her tongue loosened by half a bottle of Shiraz, Izzy then told Caro all about Marc and the remarkable mess she'd made for all concerned. Red-faced, she concluded with a sordid recounting of the hammock indiscretion.

'I've made a right Henry Halls of it, haven't I?'

'Oh, I don't know,' Caro said. 'Although the irony is

extraordinary, if you think about it. When you left London you had nothing: no job, no home, no man, no life. Then you spend ten months in Yorkshire and come back with options galore. You've got three blokes in tow. I reckon this Marc chappy'd still have you. Plus I bet Scott would come slithering back in a heartbeat, if you'd be mad enough to let him. Each comes attached to a place to live, sometimes a job too. Hell, Marc's even offering you a life where you don't have to work. Honestly, in the nicest possible way, it leaves me lost for words.'

'Thanks for highlighting the blatantly obvious,' Izzy said wryly. No one was more aware of all this than she. In so many ways everything had gone so right, and yet she was still miserable. She really needed to have a word with herself.

But Caro hadn't finished with her yet.

'As for this Jared, if I were you I'd hotfoot it back to Yorkshire before someone snaps him up. He sounds like a prime catch to me.'

'No point. He's not there,' Izzy said. 'I saw an email he'd sent to MK. He's back with his wife, trying to make a go of it.'

Caro looked confused but desisted from further comment.

Izzy was safely tucked up in the spare room by the time Jonty rolled in. From beneath the duvet she could hear him and Caro bickering in the kitchen. No doubt he was demanding that she, Izzy, be ejected from the premises by breakfast.

'Oh do stop being such a callous beast. She's lost the love of her life,' she heard Caro snap as the argument was relocated into the bathroom.

'That was what she thought last time,' Jonty said nastily. 'She couldn't have got that more wrong if she'd tried. Scott says he was lucky to be shut of her when he was.'

'And that's why he legged it up to Yorkshire as soon as he learned that she was linked to a millionaire, I suppose. I don't know why you're the only one who can't see Scott for the arsehole he is. I think you'll find you've got it the wrong way round, and it's Izzy who's lucky to be shut of *him*.'

Mortified, and fully aware that she wouldn't hear anything good about herself, Izzy strained her ears to hear the spat's conclusion but was denied. Caro, realising that Izzy would be eavesdropping, dragged Jonty into their bedroom where she continued to bollock him for being an uncharitable grouse. Izzy was left to dwell on what she had heard. The fact that the last time she had slept in this bed was back in February when Scott had dumped her didn't escape her. She'd been near hysterical then, grieving not only for the loss of Scott but for the package he brought with him: the lifestyle, the friends. When she had split from him she'd thrown herself onto her bed and howled like a teenager who has discovered her favourite pop star was getting married, banging her fists against the pillow in childish frustration.

This was different. The lifestyle was still there if she wanted it, but she felt, without Jared to share it, it would be unbearable. Now she was stoic, resigned, calm. This grief was deep-rooted, dignified and all-encompassing. Surely she had changed?

On the other hand she was shamefully aware that she had spent the first half of the year whinging about Scott and the second half whinging about Jared. Maybe she hadn't changed at all. She was also surprised that Caro had referred to Jared as the love of Izzy's life. She had never called him that.

Her body clock reprogrammed during her time at The Paddocks, Izzy was now used to rising early and was wide awake at six-thirty. Jonty was astonished to find her clear-eyed and lucid at the breakfast table. He couldn't even mock her about her broken arm seeing as she had acquired it so heroically. Still smarting from Caro's tongue-lashing of the night before, he was forced to be more genial than he would have chosen, first asking if Izzy had slept well before extending her invitation to stay until the weekend. Izzy raised her eyebrows as she reached for the telly pages supplement without any feelings of inadequacy. It must have nearly choked him to utter those words, she thought drily. Perhaps Caro had threatened to deny him all nookie unless he played nicely. The irony was that, although she would have loved to have accepted his stilted offer out of sheer spite, she had to decline.

'I've stuff I have to do,' she said, not wanting to elucidate further.

'Does this stuff include ringing The Paddocks and at least asking if Jared is back?' Caro asked as she watched Izzy collect all her belongings together.

'Nope.'

It was only after Izzy had been shown out that Jonty cornered Caro, his eyes slitted with suspicion.

'What do you know that you aren't telling her?' he asked, with the depth of instinct that only years of cohabiting can craft. Caro stared back at him, her expression neutral.

'I have no idea what you mean.'

---

LONDON HADN'T CHANGED in Izzy's absence. There were still drab skies, bare trees and bitingly cold days. Darkness fell at the same time as it had in February. It was as though the seasons hadn't moved on. Izzy couldn't help but appreciate the symbolic irony. She had left in winter, and returned in winter. If she didn't know differently in her own mind she would have sworn that the spring, summer and autumn she'd spent at The Paddocks had been nothing more than a dream.

Also, being back in her flat with only one functional arm was hell. She managed as best she could but struggled to carry out normal day-to-day activities, such as washing her hair. She ended up clean enough but, with hair straightening out of the question, she did look a bit wild. Caro was a godsend and drove Izzy to the supermarket on the Saturday morning. Jonty and Scott had buggered off to play a round of golf, Caro explained as she manoeuvred her Mini Cooper between two badly parked hatchbacks. Shopping was a sobering experience. She was like a decrepit old relative that couldn't get out on their own, Izzy thought grimly, as Caro wheeled the trolley round the supermarket for her whilst she shuffled along beside it.

Even so, Izzy didn't buy anything with a long sell-by date. Aware she should be buying proper ingredients with which she could cook decent meals, she guiltily filled her trolley with ready meals and comfort foods. In her defence, she still hadn't decided what to do and some part of her clung on to the slender hope that Jared would appear, as if by magic like Mr Benn, and whisk her back 'oop north'. Under such circumstances there would be no point in stocking up with flour and herbs and spices only to have to throw them all out, was how she justified it to herself. Even so, somewhere in the depths of her subconscience she had to admit she wasn't convinced she would ever return to The Paddocks.

Desperate for company on the one hand but equally keen not to become a hindrance on the other, she deliberately turned down Caro's constant invitations to stay with her. Knowing that Jonty was as reluctant to encourage her as Caro was keen was a constant spur to Izzy's pride. Instead she allowed herself the luxury of three full days' moping in her flat. During the day she sat huddled beneath her duvet, equidistant between the television and the electric fire, watching endless programmes about everyday folk selling old junk for useful cash or upping sticks to their dream home in the country. To Izzy it seemed that they were all living their lives, taking it by the scruff of the neck and making it do what they wanted.

On one particularly galling afternoon *International Velvet* was on the television. Izzy remembered how she had grumbled about having to watch it, but now wished desperately that she was sitting in the winter den with Taryn and Carlotta beside her and a carpet of dogs by their feet. As the film reached its triumphant climax, Izzy found that her face was drenched with tears.

Sometimes she wandered down to the local library and logged on to the archaic computers to check her email for word from Jared only to slink back to her flat in despair when there was none. In the evening she lay on the sofa, misery eating and watching soaps.

Still sleeping on the sofa, she was constantly exhausted and longed for her queen-size bed at The Paddocks. She couldn't think about Steptoe without filling up and still had nightmares about his little white body, cold and stiff on the floor. She would wake up paralysed with terror and cold with sweat. On other occasions she woke up sobbing, tears of grief both for Steptoe and the life she had thrown away pouring down her cheeks.

Despite being in such a built-up area, she had never felt so alone. She recalled how exposed she had felt during those first weeks in the countryside. How could her perspective have changed so much in such a short space of time? Now her flat seemed different. It no longer felt like her home. There were fresh holes in the walls where the subtenants had hung pictures. She wasn't supposed to do that under the terms of her lease. No doubt she would either have to fill them up, or pay up. Not that she was sure she wanted to keep the flat on at all. She would have to let the landlord know just after Christmas.

During moments of weakness she would indulge in fantasies of Jared tracking her down in London. In her imagination there would be a knock at the door and Izzy would open it to find Jared standing in the cold November rain, filled with anguish because he had almost lost her. They would live at The Paddocks, and marry in the village church, and have kids of their own to whom Carlotta and Taryn would be like big sisters. Oh, she wanted children of her own. Occasionally drawn into her own fabrications, she jumped with hope every time the intercom sounded, thinking it might be him. But it never was. She opened the door to several intimidatingly over-sized trick-or-treaters, a couple of Jehovah's Witnesses and on one occasion a group collecting for a children's charity. Having shoved a rolled up fiver in the collection box in the hope it might elicit some good karma, Izzy closed the door, devastated once more.

The bald truth was that Izzy was lonely. She hated being alone. She had long since drifted apart from the few London friends she'd had, except Caro of course. Not that it was these people's company that she craved. She missed the noise and bustle of The Paddocks. She missed Taryn's girlish companionship and Carlotta's uncertain moodswings. She missed the space of The Paddocks, the clean air and the feeling that life didn't have to be lived all in one day. She yearned for Firthie's wonderful cooking and no one could have been more colossally surprised than she was to discover she was pining for all the animals. For Hobbit and Jet, who always pricked his ears when he heard her footsteps, and the cats, and even smelly Pongy. She missed village life and all her new friends such as Pippa, Drew and Col the Landlord. She could only imagine walking through the village. In her mind she could see people sitting outside the pub in weak sunlight, enjoying an afternoon pint, hear the clip-clop of hooves as horses were hacked along Cherry Tree Avenue and smell the comforting aroma of Sunday roasts as they billowed out from extractor fans.

But she missed nothing more than Jared, with his sarcastic wit and the continuous insults that, after months of taking offence, she'd finally realised were laced with affection. It had taken Izzy the trauma of separation to finally appreciate how accustomed she'd become to his company, and not just because she fancied him rotten. Jared was someone with whom she could truly be herself. For the past ten months he had been her closest, most reliable and, at times, most uncomfortably honest friend. Little wonder she missed him so much. If only she could ask his advice as to what to do about her feelings for him.

Then she had to accept that he hadn't bothered to even send her a text since her accident. He didn't know whether or not she was all right. The last time they had spoken had been on that fateful day when he'd crept into her room and stroked her hair so tenderly. She'd never imagined that it would be the last time she would see him. Yes, she had seen his Range Rover bouncing over the field but after that she'd been unconscious. She didn't remember travelling in the ambulance, or Jared even being at her bedside in the hospital. All she knew for definite was that he had walked out on her as she lay there, and not looked back. This stark and inescapable realisation was Izzy's final act of closure. As if a flood barrier had been breached, Izzy put her head in her hands and cried.

After three days of 'being a wuss', as she referred to herself, Izzy acknowledged that action had to be taken. She was very fortunate that since her wages had been stacking up for several months she could afford to take her time in looking for a new job. Her rent was taken care of until spring but, although Izzy knew she was in a very good place financially, she knew her savings couldn't fund her forever. She might as well start looking for something straight away.

She searched for a new job with zero enthusiasm, plodding from one recruitment agency to another. Merle Miller's was not one of them. It was all moot anyway. Not that Izzy would have trusted her to tell her the correct time never mind find her another job, but, and not surprisingly considering her dubious working practices, Merle Miller had been shut down. Ironically, Izzy had been her last successful placement.

Izzy knew MK would give her a glowing and impressive reference and that she would be able to confidently walk into any nannying job but instead she stared at the little white cards clipped into the notice boards and convinced herself there was a good reason not to apply for each and every one. She didn't fancy being nanny to some smug married couple who were out at constant business meetings and dinner parties, and she certainly didn't want to replace Carlotta and Taryn with some other kids she didn't know. Nor could she bear to think about going back to being a legal secretary. Instead Izzy wondered about the possibility of retraining in teaching or childcare. Yes, that was something worth investigating. And so back to the library and the archaic computers she traipsed.

On her second weekend back in London, Izzy arranged to meet Caro in Hyde Park. It had been Izzy's choice of location. She knew people rode in the park and longed to see some ponies. Other than the travellers' horses on Hillingdon Heath, which with their woolly piebald and skewbald coats reminded her so painfully of jaunty little Jester, she hadn't been within furlongs of a horse since her return to London.

She met Caro at Hyde Park Corner and they entered the park through the Queen Elizabeth Gates. The park was already busy with tourists and early Christmas shoppers. The day was cold and crisp, bright rather than sunny, and with the sheerest haze of mist just blurring the edges of the buildings on Park Lane and Knightsbridge, which were peeping over the tops of the oaks, beeches and plane trees. Beneath horse chestnuts children, wrapped up like presents in brightly coloured scarves and mittens on strings, were scrabbling in the fallen leaves for conkers. Izzy was glad of her new military style coat. Ankle length and pillar-box-red, she brought a wonderful blob of colour to the blanched landscape. When she had left Nether Ousebury the trees had been golden, ochre and red, emanating warmth and the promise of harvest fires. Now, here in London, the few remaining leaves were grey with early frost and hung, withered and woeful, before dropping to the hard ground below. Despite the chill, Izzy revelled in the fresh air as she and Caro strolled along past the bandstand. Hyde Park was vast enough for her to forget she was in Central London, for a couple of hours at least.

As they passed the boathouse the Serpentine was busy with boaters.

'Look!' Izzy said to Caro. Ahead of them a group of horse riders had turned off West Carriage Drive onto Serpentine Road. There were five of them, Izzy noted, keenly interested. Two bays, two greys (one dapple, one flea-bitten) and a chestnut with a broad white blaze and white socks. As the bridle path was quiet they were riding five abreast, chattering amongst themselves. The horses had their ears pricked and the riders all looked so happy and carefree. They looked beautiful to Izzy.

'Wouldn't you just love to be one of them?' Izzy asked, heading towards them.

'Not really,' said Caro bleakly. 'Not my thing, Iz. I've never been on a horse in my life.'

'You mean there's something I can do that you can't?' Izzy asked lightly, but Caro knew how important it was for her. Ahead of them the horses had stopped and one of the riders had dismounted. 'Must have picked up a stone,' said Izzy, watching as the rider picked up the horse's nearside hoof and inspected it. Drawn to the horses, Izzy approached them and asked if the riders would mind if she stroked the horses before rooting around in her handbag for a packet of Polos. Even that reminded her of The Paddocks. She wondered if Polo the wonder jumper had settled in yet and whether Carlotta had been for her junior squad trial yet.

Watching Izzy stroking and patting the horses' heads and necks, seeing how they responded to her touch with gentle headbutts, rubbing their faces across her shoulders, Caro was astonished. Who was this Izzy, who was so confident with these great beasts and who didn't care that they'd shed their coats all over hers? Now she was feeding them teeny-tiny mints from the palm of her hand. Considering the size of their teeth, how did she dare? And yet she seemed perfectly at ease in their company.

By this time the offending stone had been removed and the rider remounted. With one last pat, Izzy said goodbye and the riders moved off. She watched them go with a wistful longing. Caro, having kept her distance from the horses, now moved forward and stood beside Izzy, studying her intently. Izzy had been heartbroken when Scott had blown her out, but in the way a teenager would be. Now she was calm, but sad, almost resigned. Caro had watched carefully, impressed by the way Izzy had asked the rider if she could stroke the horse, and the way the horse responded to her touch, like it knew she wasn't a novice.

'You're different,' she said.

'That's what Scott said.'

Caro gave a hollow laugh. 'But I mean it as a compliment.' They wandered on towards Magazine Gate and the Serpentine Bridge. Halfway across the bridge Caro planted her feet and shouted at Izzy.

'When are you going to stop being so proud and ring him?'

'Not an option.' Izzy continued to walk on.

'Why not?' Caro stood her ground.

Izzy spun round to face her. Her face was contorted into a mask of anguished fury.

'Because his actions speak volumes, Caro!' she said, finally voicing the pain and hurt she'd lugged around since she'd left The Paddocks, and even before that if she were honest with herself. 'Believe me, I've had this discussion with myself a hundred times and I always reach the same conclusion. If Jared felt the same way about me as I do about him, he'd have been in touch, but I haven't had so much as one text. He's made it clear he doesn't care about me that way so I'm not going to make an arse of myself by grovelling.' She didn't add that she had mentally wrestled with the possibility of returning to The Paddocks with her feelings securely battened down but wasn't sure she had the strength to live in such close proximity to Jared and watch him build his life with someone else. That was a big ask for a person of substance, never mind a lunatic like her. Nor was the prospect of living at The Paddocks if he wasn't there much better. She wasn't sure she could bear that either. Her best option was to move on and try to build a life for herself back in London.

'It would be different if he'd given me even the smallest of signs but I've heard nothing, *nothing*! Not from him or from any of the others. It's over.' She stared across the water at the bronze of Isis on the opposite bank, taking a few moments to compose herself. 'Where are we going for lunch?' It was made perfectly clear the subject was closed.

'I have such a lot to thank you for,' Caro said, changing the subject after a few paces of silence. Izzy looked at her in disbelief. 'Well, you and the delectable MK. Don't look at me like that. He's a very attractive man and if I wasn't so sure that Jonty is my soul mate I would set my barrister's wig at him. The final paperwork on his case came through this week. It's officially over. Everyone knows I did bugger all on the actual case but I was still involved and that will look great on my portfolio. It might be the last ounce of added weight to my quest to be a QC.'

'That's fantastic,' Izzy said, trying to inject a suitable degree of enthusiasm into her tone. 'See? Maybe that was the reason I ended up in Yorkshire. Maybe I was fated to help you achieve your goals. What a good friend I am,' she concluded piously.

'Huh! Or maybe you were fated to end up there for your own benefit but you're too pigheaded to accept that,' said Caro sternly. Naturally tenacious, unused to losing an argument either in or out of court, Caro was more than prepared to be persistent. 'And I still think you should at least ring to see how the girls are doing. They must be missing you.'

'Well, I'm not gonna, so you're wasting your breath. And quit trying to emotionally blackmail me.'

'Damn! It would have worked twelve months ago, too,' Caro said, smiling. She linked an arm through Izzy's uninjured one as they walked on through the park. Izzy couldn't help but laugh at this.

'It would, wouldn't it? Look, see how much I've grown.'

---

THE FOLLOWING Monday morning Izzy found herself sitting in orthopaedic outpatients at Hillingdon Hospital. Today she would finally get her pot off. And thank goodness! She was sick and tired of lugging the wretched, heavy thing round.

She had an early appointment time and had to walk across the heath in the cold drizzle, which she hadn't appreciated one bit. It was one of those days that were so cold it made you feel that you'd never be warm again. She was chilled down to her bones. The doctor specialised in bones. Mebbe he could give her a shot or something.

The waiting room was full of screaming kids in fluorescent yellow and pink casts. Her head was pounding. She tried to read a celebrity magazine but had only got as far as the second page when an article about how Girls Aloud were going to switch on the Regent Street lights depressed her so much that she slung it back down. Because she was one of the first patients in, she hadn't had to wait long. A nurse inspected the pot before a doctor appeared. He was a stuffed shirt who insisted on asking her a litany of questions that she had no desire to answer as he cut away. Was she married? No, she wasn't. Was she looking forward to Christmas? She supposed so, she replied although in her head she answered with a resounding 'no'. Christmas could sod off. So could New Year's. Now the nosy sod was reading all the messages the girls had scrawled on her cast as well as the gushing screed Marc had added before he had dumped her. Were these her children? he asked. Unwilling to become embroiled in the complications of explaining, Izzy merely grunted. It was at this point that the doctor began to look stern.

'How did you break your arm, Isabel?' he asked. The cast was now off. He was studying it.

'I fell off a horse,' Izzy said dully.

'Are you certain that's what happened?' the doctor persisted.

'Err, yeah, I remember it pretty well. Why?' He was really starting to get on her nerves now. The doctor turned the cast over and held it out for Izzy to read.

*My precious Izzy. Please get better soon. I know these injuries are all my fault but I promise this'll never happen again. Please forgive me and let me make it up to you when I get back. I've got a couple of urgent errands to run but all the time I'll be thinking of you. Wait for me. Yours always, J. xxx*

Izzy gaped. Wordlessly she reached for the cast. It had been written on the underside, where neither she nor anyone else had been able to see it. Jared must have written it whilst she was still unconscious, just before he took off.

'Did someone do this to you, Isabel?' the doctor persisted,

interrupting her thoughts. 'Did this man, this 'J', break your arm?'

'No, I fell off a horse,' Izzy repeated dreamily. She felt really spaced out, displaced.

'—Because if someone has hurt you, you must tell someone. We can get you some help.'

Izzy flexed her hand. There was definitely atrophy in her muscles but otherwise the arm felt good. There was no pain, just a slight cold tingle as her skin became accustomed to exposure to the air again. Was it her imagination or was her right arm now thinner than her left? Her skin was clammy and pale, almost translucent. It needed to toughen up again.

'How long before I can ride?' she asked. It was the doctor's turn to gape.

'You'll need to complete a course of physio and I would be inclined to advise against any particularly strenuous activity until well into the new year. After that I don't see why you shouldn't partake in some gentle exercise. No galloping across country like a lunatic though,' he said, tittering at his own attempted joke.

'That's what got me in this mess in the first place,' Izzy said, pulling a comical face. She felt quite giddy, almost hysterical. The doctor was now looking at her with suspicion.

'I'm going to ask the nurse to fit you with a tubigrip. I want you to keep it on until Christmas. It'll give you a little bit of support.' He stood up and headed for the door, pausing just before exiting. 'Please think about what I said, Isabel. You don't have to suffer in silence.'

Izzy had had enough. She stood up, raised her chin and looked the doctor straight in the eye as she spoke.

'My name is Isabel Brown. I sustained this injury, together with a concussion, falling off a mental pedigree horse whilst attempting to rescue the daughter of a wrongfully imprisoned shipping magnate from a spiteful groom hellbent on vengeance. The man who wrote that message on my cast is, for want of a better explanation, my bodyguard, and he'd never hurt me. Sounds ridiculous, I know, but it's true. Isabel Brown, my name's right there on your sheet. Seriously, Google me!' The doctor beat a hasty retreat. Izzy was sure she heard him mutter something about 'unbalanced' as he briefed the nurse.

Izzy could barely wait to be discharged. She fidgeted as the nurse rolled the tubigrip up her forearm and danced from foot to foot whilst being forced to wait for her appointment card to be filled in, by the slowest receptionist *ever,* with her first physiotherapy session. At last she was freed and, once outside, practically ran back to her flat. Completely disregarding any medical advice she'd been given, she flung clothes into her suitcase with her duff arm whilst at the same time frantically texting Caro with the other.

> Have decided to go back to Yorkshire to tell J how I feel. Will explain why later. Wish me luck. Iz xx

It was only once she was seated on the thirteen-ten out of King's Cross that she began to question the sense of her actions. What had she been thinking? Jared had written that message six weeks ago and she hadn't seen or heard from him since. What if he'd changed his mind? What if he was over her and had moved on? Worse still, what if she had completely misread the entire situation and he had never felt like that about her in the first place. Either way she had to know. Well, it was too late now. She would be in Greater Ousebury by five o'clock. She would get a cab from the halt to The Paddocks.

Each time her phone beeped she jumped, her innards instantly relocating to somewhere in the vicinity of her oesophagus. With shaking hands she flipped open her phone only to give a howl of frustration as she read a standard infomessage from her network provider. She didn't care that she hadn't used up all her free texts for the month, for Christ's sake.

'Bastards, *bastards*!' she ranted, much to the disapproval of the mother across the aisle who promptly put her hands over her young son's ears.

It was beeping again. This time it was a brief message from Caro.

Bout time 2 :-) x

Textbook Caro, thought Izzy. Succinct, economical and typical of a person who charged by the word and the hour. Such encouragement buoyed her up, but only for half an hour or so. After that self-doubt kicked back in.

Fretful, Izzy bought three vodka and Cokes from the hostess trolley to calm her nerves, lining them up on her flip-down tray like popgun target practice. Mixed with the anti-inflammatory painkillers she had been prescribed and chased down by a considerable shot of nervous apprehension, the end result was stomach-churning nausea. Was she *insane*? If Jared did love her then surely wouldn't he have come to find her? The only thing that awaited her at The Paddocks was a big, fat, juicy rejection. And she couldn't even blame him for that. If it weren't a metaphysical impossibility she'd bloody well reject herself on the grounds of her being a disaster, a fool and an eejit.

Izzy was still mentally arguing with herself as she alighted the train at Loxley. Despite all her misgivings her feet continued to march with purpose towards the bread-bin train to Greater Ousebury. The previous train had been delayed by half an hour and was just about to depart. Never before in her life had she experienced such a seamless travel connection. It was as though it had been waiting just for her. Did that bode well or was fate simply having a good laugh at her expense?

Hand shaking, her stomach churning like a tumble dryer,

she presented her ticket to the conductor. Jesus, she'd be there in forty-five minutes. She allowed herself to daydream for a few moments. Jared would be thrilled to see her, he'd come running up the drive to meet her, arms akimbo. No, he'd be out on a hack with Carlotta and Taryn and would *gallop* up the drive to meet her.

Course he wouldn't, you berk, it's almost dark. Since when did horses have headlights? Now she was holding conversations with herself. She was officially crackers.

Then another thought struck her. What if Jared wasn't there at all? In all her hubris and enthusiasm she'd merely presumed he'd returned to The Paddocks. Come to think of it, she hadn't heard from any of them in ages. What if none of them were there? What if they were all in Greece? What if she turned up to locked gates and an empty house?

Then reason kicked in. If The Paddocks was deserted she would book herself into The Half Moon for the night or, better still, prey on the Newtons' good nature and blag herself a room at The Rookery. Surely they wouldn't turn her away? But what if they were away too...? She really must stop rambling to herself. Oh shit, they were here already. Izzy dragged her suitcase out from between the seats, wincing as her newly-fixed arm protested at the resistance.

Waiting in the vestibule for the train doors to open, Izzy couldn't help but cast her mind back to when she had first arrived in Nether Ousebury. That had been a cold, dark evening too. The door slid open and Izzy bounced onto the halt, nearly garrotting herself in the process as her handbag strap caught on the door handle. Chuntering as she unhooked herself, it took her a few seconds to get her bearings. At least it wasn't raining here. Instead the frosted air was thick with woodsmoke, bonfires and burnt out fireworks.

Now, where was the best place to get a taxi from? Izzy scanned her surroundings for options. Then she physically jumped, for standing next to the little swing gate that opened onto the main road was Jared. As their eyes locked he raised his hands. He was holding a card that said:

*IZZY WALKER?*

Its meaning was lost on Izzy. She was too busy coming to terms with the fact that everything was spinning, that the world was shrinking and that only the two of them were left standing there. Why had no one warned her? For a few moments they stared at each other. Izzy scoured every inch of Jared's face for a clue as to how he was feeling. He looked ghastly, even more haggard than usual. He allowed his utter anguish to show for mere moments before his expression reverted to type.

''Bout time you showed your face. Where the fuck have you been these past two weeks?' Jared said, dropping the card down to his side as he strode over to her. Izzy felt the corner of her mouth twitch. 'Everyone's furious with you,' Jared continued, reaching down for her suitcase.

Izzy's face crumpled. 'I don't blame them. I'm furious with myself. I've been hopeless, haven't I?' She began a self-deprecating diatribe.

'Eh? That's not why they're furious. They're cross 'cause you buggered off and they all miss you,' Jared said, but Izzy wasn't listening.

'If I hadn't sent the wrong package to my mother none of what happened would have. And if that weren't bad enough I handed Gemma the keys to the Golf that afternoon without a second thought. If anything had happened to Carlotta it would have been *all my fault*. I'll never forgive myself.'

'No one blames you. You were a bloody heroine.'

'I blame me. All my life I've wreaked havoc in my wake. My headmaster at school used to call me Incapability Brown. He thought himself such a comedian,' Izzy said with genuine hurt and bitterness. She turned her head away, unable to look at Jared.

'Funny that he should have called you Incapability Brown. Did you know that Capability Brown was a gardener, just like me?' Jared asked, lightly. 'Well, actually he was a landscape architect, which is a bit beyond my skills. He designed the gardens at Badminton House, Blenheim Palace, Chatsworth House and Burghley, amongst others, all which host international horse trials. Admittedly, that's eventing rather than showjumping, but nevertheless, still an equestrian connection. So, you see, your nickname means you're actually our perfect fit, for so many reasons. You're my perfect fit.' He placed his hands at either side of her face and turned it gently to face him. 'Look at me. Who rode Vega all that way just to protect Carlotta? And without a hat... did I teach you nothing?' That raised a small smile. 'Who got that singularly scary barrister woman onto Gemma's tail? You did. So there, incapable no more! MK thinks you're a marvel for protecting his girls so selflessly. And as for me? I've seen the best of you, and the worst, as you have me, and I think you're pretty bloody amazing.'

Their faces were mere inches apart. Izzy raked her eyes over Jared's face, looking for answers. Not once did he drop his eyes. Aware that her breath probably stank of vodka, Izzy took a step backwards. Jared didn't try to stop her.

'I came back to tell you that I love you,' Izzy said. It wasn't pleading or romantic but a statement of fact. From somewhere she found the courage to look directly at him as she spoke. 'And I don't think I'm going to stop loving you anytime soon. So, if I'm going to come back to The Paddocks, like MK and the girls want, that's something you'll just have to come to terms with.'

Jared's beautiful mouth spread into his trademark broad smile.

'I think I can handle that,' he said, reaching for her and

drawing her to him. They didn't kiss. It wasn't the right time for that. This was more sacred, almost hallowed. Instead Jared clamped his arms around her, pressing her face into his shoulder, muttering endearments into her hair. Izzy breathed him in, certain that never before had soil, horsehair and waxed jacket smelled so sweet. Despite the frosted air blowing in from across the open fields at the back of the halt, Izzy felt warm for the first time in weeks. It was as though Jared read her thoughts. 'Come on, let's get into the car. It's far too cold to be standing around on a draughty platform.'

Later, Izzy couldn't explain what had come over her but, as Jared pulled away and started to lead her through the swing gate, and at the culmination of such a romantic and much longed for moment, she thwacked him on his upper arm with what she had intended to be a stinging punch. Alas, she did so with her duff arm and managed only a feeble swipe. 'Why didn't you get in touch?'

'I wanted to, so badly, but MK and Mrs Firth ganged up on me and forbade it. They said I was to leave you to stew. That you would miss the girls, me, living here… and would come back once you'd sorted your head out. They said London would drive you bonkers and you'd have to accept you belong here with us.'

'They were right,' Izzy scowled, then gave a reluctant smile. 'Clever sods. But you just vanished. By the time I came round, you'd gone. No one would tell me where. I went back to London because I lost hope. I just figured you'd gone back to your wife.'

'Whatever made you think that?' Now it was Jared's turn to be incredulous. He goggled at her from across the roof of the Range Rover.

Looking sheepish, Izzy confessed. 'I saw an email you'd sent MK. By accident! I wasn't snooping. It said you intended to go and see her so you could sort things out once and for all.'

'Firstly, you should know better than to read mail that isn't addressed to you. Secondly, trust you to get the wrong end of the stick. I did go and see my now almost officially ex-wife in order to finally get a divorce, so that I could make a proper go of it with you, you dozy bugger! Not to get back together with her. Didn't you see your friend Caro when you were back in London? I thought she'd have filled you in.'

'Caro knew? I'll fill her in when I next see her!'

'She was the one who tipped me off you were on your way back. She also fixed me up with a shit-hot divorce lawyer.' Jared opened the passenger door, reached into the glove compartment and withdrew a large brown envelope. He handed it to Izzy. 'Open it.'

Izzy did as she was bade. Inside was a sheaf of papers. Legal papers. She may have been the most inept legal secretary to have ever disgraced a law firm but she would still have recognised them anywhere. It was a decree nisi.

'Oh!' was all she could think of to say. She'd been so stupid. Nothing new there, then.

'In six weeks I'll get my decree absolute and then you won't have the stigma of being the girlfriend of a married man. And to stop you from getting anymore ideas about running back to the big smoke you can give notice on your flat first thing tomorrow. Then I'm gonna hire a transit van and we're going to drive down to your parents' house, both so I can meet them and so we can get all your stuff. We can store it in one of the many empty garages at the house until we've bought our own place in the village. There's no way we're living in that asylum all our lives.

'I'm going to marry you, and then I'll give you lots of babies of your own so you don't continue to pander to those two hellions. Incapability Walker doesn't really have the same comedy ring, does it?' He grazed one rough hand down the side of her face, tracing the contour of her bottom lip with his thumb. 'I finally found my reason to let go of the past.'

Then he did kiss her, thoroughly and brain-meltingly, his hands wedged in her unstraightened hair.

'I don't understand how even you couldn't figure out how I felt about you. Didn't you read your cast? I left you a message.'

'You wrote it on the bit that was practically under my armpit. I'd have had to have been a contortionist, either that or possessed, to crane my head that far round. The first time I saw it was this morning when the bloody thing was sawn off. Very cryptic too, thank you very much. The doctor thought you were apologising for clobbering me and was desperate to usher me into therapy.'

'At least we're getting a chance to uncross these wires. Christ, what a mess. I had to write that message in a hurry, plus I didn't want to put it somewhere really obvious in case Marc scribbled it out before you woke up. Cheeky bastard slung me out of the ward. If I hadn't promised MK that I would track down and capture the ubiquitous Alan as a matter of extreme urgency, I would never have left you. I would have decked him too. MK knew where I'd gone, and why, but daren't tell you. None of you — you, Carlotta, Taryn, Mrs Firth, even MK — were safe until he was caught, and MK was so worried that Carlotta would be terrified knowing he was still at large. Took me the best part of three weeks to pin the slippery little sod down. It was as though he had just disappeared into the ether. I can't believe I didn't even recognise him as the young lad from the Great Yorkshire Show, the one I'd told to bugger off. He'd been sniffing round for weeks, apparently, waiting for an 'in'.

'I made MK promise to keep you here until I came back. Course, I should've known you'd do the exact opposite of what I wanted and if I'd known how long I'd be away I'd have instructed MK to clamp you in shackles. I'd have been back sooner if I hadn't had to track down my errant ex-wife too and demand that she sign the divorce papers.

'I gather I finally arrived back the day after you left. I couldn't believe it. I'd missed you by one lousy day. I tortured myself that Marc bloody Jones pursued you to London and seized his chance to win you back. Plus Mrs Firth said your ex had turned up at the house, full of smarm and righteous possessiveness. I went through agonies wondering if you'd gone back to him too. I wanted to jump in the car and drag you back but MK convinced me that I should be patient, give you a bit of space. Then Caro tipped me off that you'd been to see her and seemed to be as miserable as I was.'

'I'm gonna murder her,' Izzy growled, but good-naturedly. At least Caro's constant encouragements to get in touch with someone at The Paddocks now made sense.

'I brought you back a present too. It's in here—' Jared reached into the back of the Range Rover and brought out a yipping, squirming bundle of white fur. It was a tiny Jack Russell puppy.

'OMG! He's adorable,' Izzy said, throwing her handbag into the car so she could stroke its face. She was rewarded with several licks. He didn't have the same markings, and his legs were short and bowed rather than long, but there was something in the mischievous black eyes that reminded her of Steptoe. Jared handed her the wriggling mass.

'He's all yours. So now you have to stay to take care of him, and good luck to you 'cause he's a little bleeder. I even gave him a name you'd approve of.'

Izzy eyed him suspiciously. 'What?'

'Gary Barlow,' said Jared. His face didn't crack once.

'You did not!' Izzy said, laughing at last. But she knew it was the truth as the little dog pricked up his ears and looked expectant upon hearing his name.

'Are you ready to come home?' Jared said. 'The girls'll go mental when you walk through the door. Carlotta nearly did cartwheels when I got Caro's text. MK had to rugby tackle her to stop her texting you and letting the cat out of the bag.

Don't be surprised if they haven't badgered Mrs Firth to prepare you a six course celebratory dinner, complete with bunting as far as the eye can see.'

Izzy couldn't help grinning as she climbed up into the Range Rover. Gary Barlow made it as difficult as he could with his frantic scrabbling and with his back end gyrating independently and in the opposite direction from his front. Home at last, she thought happily. Then something occurred to her.

'You could have come to pick me up in one of the nicer cars,' she grumbled.

'I did think about it, but then I thought you might like to go out for a ride in the Roller sometime,' Jared said, flashing her an x-rated look.

Izzy pretended to not understand his insinuation. 'Can I have a go in it?' she asked, grinning widely. That'd wind him up.

Just as she predicted, Jared looked appalled. He turned the key in the ignition and pulled away from the kerb before casting her a quick glance. His love for her was written all over his face.

'The way you drive? Best not, eh?'

THE END

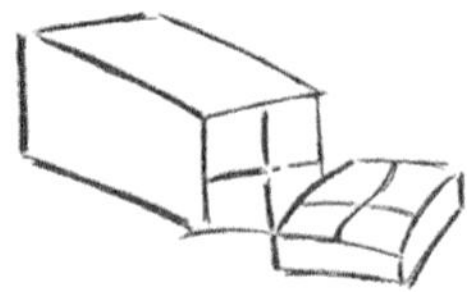

# 10TH ANNIVERSARY EDITION BONUS CONTENT

## MRS FIRTH'S BATTENBERG RECIPE

Nowt goes down better with a pot o' Yorkshire Tea than a slice of my home-made battenberg. Trust me, this lot are like vultures on baking days, barely waiting until I get the blasted thing out of the Aga.

A lot of folk are wary of baking a battenberg, wrongly thinking it's more complicated than it is. Here's my own foolproof recipe.

Ye only need use one baking tin, which means less washing up. If ye fold up yer baking parchment craftily enough, this creates two separate baking compartments, ye see.

The best jam for sealing yer marzipan to yer sponges is apricot, both for flavour and colour. Same applies for when ye're icing yer Christmas cake. Trouble is, no bugger in this household'll touch apricot jam at any other time of the year, nattering either for raspberry or, in Jared's case, marmalade. So whenever I used to open a jar of apricot jam for baking, it allus went to waste. Nowadays, I just ask anyone what's going to a posh hotel or guest house to sneak a couple of them miniature jam jars into their pocket or bag and bring 'em home. This is a useful tip — or life hack as Carlotta tells me they're called these days — if ye need to use runny honey in a recipe too, but have run out.

I can mekk marzipan from scratch, so don't be saying I can't, but who has time for that sort of faffing on? Just buy it in a block from the shops. All ye need to remember is to use a nice, bright yeller marzipan for a traditional pink and yeller battenberg, and the posh white variety for a coffee and walnut one. It just looks better, I'm telling ye!

Reet! Let's gerron wi' it, then…

Get yerself t'shop and buy this lot, if ye don't already have it in yer pantry. Also, I've converted the recipe into grammage, as I've been told by Taryn's cookery teacher that no bugger uses pounds and ounces these days. Tch tch, I don't know.

- 175g proper butter (not that margarine tripe), softened
- 175g caster sugar. Golden's best, but regular'll do if ye've nowt else in
- 3 nice big eggs, free range
- 50g ground almonds
- 140g self-raising flour
- ½ teaspoon baking powder
- ½ teaspoon almond extract
- Pink food colouring. Decent stuff, an all! Don't be wasting time with cheap stuff. It won't do t'job proper. Ye don't need yeller; sponge'll be reet of its own accord.
- Big block o' golden marzipan. Ye might need to hide this, if ye've got marzipan fiends in yer

household, like these three girls and Jared. Thieving magpies, they are! I once learned that Izzy, Carlotta and Taryn had taken a full block and divided it into three to make marzipan fruits. Fruits! I saw no fruits. I ask ye.
- Icing sugar, for rolling out.
- That apricot jam I was telling ye about…enough to coat and fill the sponges.

When it comes to food colouring, flavouring and seasoning, remember the cardinal rule… ye can allus add more in, but ye can't tekk it back out!

If ye don't have a battenberg tin, here's a crafty trick. Line an 8 inch… sorry, 20cm square tin with baking parchment, but big enough so's ye can make a good, straight pleat right down't middle. This'll mekk yer tin have two equal halves, one fer each colour.

Now, I don't have to put me oven on, unless it's a bloomin' summer heatwave, because I cook in an Aga, which is on all year round. Mekk no mistake, cooking on an Aga is a bit different from yer gas or leccy stove as ye have to use cooling sheets and all that carrying on to control the temperature. Anyone who has an Aga'll know what they're doing, so I'll write this 'ere recipe for regular ovens.

Preheat yer oven to 180c/160c fan/gas mark 4.

Sling all the cake ingredients, except the colouring, into a good sized bowl and beat until fully mixed and glossy. Ye can use a hand whisk, or even an electric whisk if ye're a big fanny. Me, I like to mix by hand. Keeps yer bingo wings at bay!

Tip half the mixture into one side of the baking tray. Ye're gonna colour t'other half pink, drop by drop until ye get the shade ye want. I prefer a nice rosy pink, not pink that's as hot as Barbie's best knickers. Once ye're happy with the colour, tip this mixture in t'other side o't tin. Gie it a few taps, to even the mixture out and get rid of any big air bubbles.

Bake for 25-30 minutes, keeping an eye on it, 'cause ye don't want the edges to catch, or until a metal skewer comes out clean*. Cool it in't tin fer 15 minutes, and only then transfer it to a wire rack to cool completely.

Once fully cooled, ye can cut each half up lengthways into two identical portions. That's two yeller sponges and two pink. Ye can be all precise with rulers and what-not but I like me cakes to look home-made, so if it's a bit wonky, that fine by me. I cook rustic, me. All tastes the same in the end.

Dust yer work surface or board with icing sugar and roll out yer marzipan into a nice, even rectangle big enough to go right round the cake. If it's a bit big, ye can always trim it to size, but if it's not big enough, ye'll be scuppered.

Heat a small amount of apricot jam in a pan or in't microwave and brush this over the middle of the marzipan. Place one of the four sponge rectangles on the marzipan and brush its sides and top with the jam. Place a different coloured piece next to it, and brush the exposed sides... If ye can't see where this is going, I'm not sure baking's fer ye, to be honest.

Once all four sponges are jammed up and in place — in a chequerboard pattern, otherwise it's not a battenberg, is it? — roll the whole cake up in't marzipan and smooth it out. Trim the marzipan as necessary — some gannet'll want to eat it, rest assured — and crimp the join with yer thumb and finger. There — ye've medd a battenberg. Now, tuck in and enjoy.

*I've asked every bugger I know why a red hot skewer can be dabbed against yer bottom lip and not burn, but put it anywhere else on yer body and ye'll know about it. No one knows. It's a bluddy mystery, I'm telling ye.

**QUEEN VICTORIA'S BOARDING SCHOOL FOR GIRLS**
**CARLOTTA ANDROMEDA BERYL KONSTANTINE**
**4th FORM - SCHOOL REPORT**

English Language: There's no doubt Carlotta has a large and varied vocabulary, but it would be preferable if she could make more use of words that aren't profanities. Nevertheless, there is no doubt Carlotta is an effective communicator as she rarely fails to keep her honest opinions to herself. Regrettably.

English Literature: If it were possible for Carlotta to do all her book reports and analysis on Anna Sewell's *Black Beauty*, she would receive an A for every assignment. What a shame she doesn't display the same enthusiasm or insight for *Twelfth Night* or the war poets. Patchy.

Maths: Carlotta most definitely has a head for numbers, as proven by her skills at forbidden bookmaking for both flat and hunt racing, and for organising sweepstakes. If only she'd apply the same dedication to algebra and trigonometry in class, she might have a future as a mathematician.

History: Trying to teach Carlotta history is a lost cause. I'm quite convinced that if any of our esteemed war heroes from history had battled her, we'd have lost every war.

Geography: Unless we're studying Greece, Italy or any city worldwide where an equestrian event is held, forget it. I've all but given up.

Science: Carlotta has no interest in traditional science, and I have no interest in trying to generate that interest. Her only talent in Chemistry is to create increasingly pungent stink bombs. Quite frankly, I'm at my wit's end with her and her last day in my laboratories cannot come soon enough.

Languages: Already being fluent in Italian and Greek, Carlotta finds it almost unfairly easy to pick up other languages, such as French, Spanish, German and even Latin. It's just her attitude towards learning them that is lacking.

Music: Knowing all the words to chart hits does not a musician make! Carlotta would do well to remember that. Absolutely tone deaf.

Drama: All I can say is, it follows Miss Konstantine wherever she goes.

Domestic Science: Carlotta's claims that she'll never need to cook because her family has help may well be true, but isn't really a good enough reason for her to refuse to apply herself. I doubt she can boil a kettle without assistance. Hardly a feat to boast about.

PE: Despite having no ambitions to be included in any of the school's teams, Carlotta is formidable at almost every sport she participates in, mainly due to her tendency towards aggression and her impressive fitness levels. She is not, however, either a team player or a gracious loser, and not for nothing is she known as Calf-whacker Konsto on the hockey pitch. In my opinion, she's a liability and a lawsuit waiting to happen.

Equitation: Carlotta is one of my very best students: talented beyond measure, driven, dedicated and intuitive. I have no doubt there's a very successful career in the field of equitation in her future and that she'll go on to make this school proud. It's a pleasure to be her instructor and mentor. Excellent work across the board, Carlotta! Keep it up. You're a vital and engaging presence in the equestrian centre.

Housemistress's Comments: Quite frankly, Carlotta is a menace from a pastoral perspective. The list of her shortcomings and misdemeanours is endless: swearing, fighting with the other boarders, absconding, disobedience, trading blackmarket and strictly forbidden contraband, such as alcohol, cigarettes, and Reese's Nutrageous bars and jars of Sunpat Crunchy (never smooth). She knows full well that tuck containing nuts is not permitted under any circumstances on campus due to those with allergies. I would be lying if I said that she'd been a pleasure to supervise. It'll be a relief when she finally leaves this boarding house at the end of the summer term.

Headmistress's Comments: There is no doubt whatsoever that Carlotta is an extremely bright, talented and highly ambitious student. However, she struggles to focus in any subject that does not interest her, hence why she hasn't received any grade higher than a D+ from any teacher other than the Equitation Master. She remains disruptive and argumentative in class, setting a very bad example for her fellow students. There have also been serious challenges on the pastoral side, as you're already aware. Unless there is a distinct improvement in Carlotta's behaviour, both in and out of the classroom, there will be unavoidable repercussions during the coming terms.

Merits: 27 - all earned in her riding lessons, so not really an accurate representation of her achievements this term.

Demerits: 87 - a school record, but sadly not one of which to be proud. Needless to say, the rest of her form is as unimpressed as the teaching staff. Unacceptable.

## ALSO BY CRESSIDA BURTON

### THE MAGPIE COTTAGE CHRONICLES

Noël: Christmas at Magpie Cottage

(10th anniversary edition)

Lindian Summer: Summer at Magpie Cottage

(10th anniversary edition)

### THE IZZY BROWN STORIES

Incapability Brown

(10th anniversary edition)

Mistletoe & Whine

(10th anniversary edition)

### FOR YOUNGER READERS

### THE RAVENSBAY SCHOOL STORIES

(Featuring Taryn from The Izzy Brown Stories)

First Term at Ravensbay

Hunter Trials at Ravensbay

Bitter Rivals at Ravensbay

White Horses at Ravensbay

Snowed In at Ravensbay

Pony Girl Problems at Ravensbay

### STAND ALONE STORIES

## WELCOME TO THE BURTONVERSE!

## CRESSIDA BURTON'S READERS' GROUP!

Keep up to date with all the news from The Burtonverse by joining my readers' group! You'll get one newsletter a month (if you're lucky, trust me, you won't be bombarded!) containing sneak peeks, cover and title reveals, competitions and giveaways, author recommendations and probably cat spam. Plus, you'll be gifted a 100% free Ravensbay School Stories ebook short story called *Paige's Summer Pony Trek Page*, which you can download direct to your ereader. All you need do is subscribe via the link on my website.

www.cressidaburton.co.uk

I'll see you there!

Cressidax

# ABOUT THE AUTHOR

Cressida Burton knew she wanted to be a writer when she was seven years old, and never gave up on that dream. She is now — finally — a full-time author.

She writes both dark humour about family life, friendships and relationships for grown-ups — dramedy, if you like — and inspiring junior fiction for pony-mad kids age eight and above. Although, most of her grown-up fiction also contains a lot of horse and animal content, which can never be a bad thing.

She started riding ponies at age six, learning on a very opinionated scruffy bay Shetland called Olaf. She still loves horses dearly despite being told as a child that ponies were 'just a phase'. She believes she has hit the deck at least 150 times in her riding career. In her most spectacular fall she demolished a triple bar in a showjumping jump-off. She knows it was her own fault as she should've had more leg on!

Whilst all her books are set in a fictional world that's been nicknamed The Burtonverse, Cressida lives in the North Yorkshire Moors National Park with her husband — the redoubtable and very shy Mr B — and their big, floofy, orange cat, Bilbo Baggins.

www.cressidaburton.co.uk

# AFTERWORD

*Any readers familiar with the wonderful world of international showjumping will notice I've referenced some real life people in this book. Namely: Raymond Brooks-Ward, Ben Maher, Nick Skelton, Ellen Whitaker and William Whitaker. I would like to state that I do not know any of these people personally.*

*Any inaccuracies are my own and are completely unintentional.*

Printed in Great Britain
by Amazon

41140387R00274